REVENGE AT RALEIGH HIGH

1

SILVER

Samuel Adrian Hawthorne
Devoted Son.
Beloved Friend.
Talented Sportsman.

A Bright Light, Taken Too Soon.

Here, we weep, but in Heaven, the Angels rejoice, for one of their own has returned home to them.

The midnight forest breathes deep around the cemetery, drawing the night into its lungs, its mournful limbs swaying on a cold breeze as I look down upon the grave of Samuel Adrian Hawthorne. The frozen ground feels like it's pulsing beneath my feet, the beat of a somber drum rising through the non-existent soles of my Chucks, but it's only my own blood protesting the fact that I've been standing here too long. It'll be time to leave soon enough, but tonight I've come here to face a demon, and I won't go until it's slain.

Behind me, I hear the muffled *shushh*ing of waves lapping at the shore of Lake Cushman. Winter's arrived in full-force, it won't be long before the lake begins to ice over, but for now the water remains free to roll pebbles and rake the sands at the beachline.

Mallory Hawthorne, Sam's mom, refused to have her son buried in the Raleigh Gardens of Rest Cemetery on the outskirts of town. No one needed to ask why, but Mallory went around Raleigh exclaiming loudly to anyone within earshot that she wouldn't have her poor murdered son fertilizing the same ground as the sick bastard who'd killed him. Three times she's brought a petition before Mayor Griffith, demanding that Leon Wickman be exhumed and cremated, so no one will ever have to set eyes on his headstone again. Three times, Mayor Griffith has dismissed her, asking her to let the matter rest, but the chances of that happening are negligible. Mrs. Hawthorne keeps on doing her rounds through Raleigh, going door-to-door with her list of signatures and addresses, and each time she shows up at the town hall, her petition has gotten longer. It'll only be a matter of time.

Some kind of night bird lets out an eerie, plaintive wail, deep within the forest, and a cold sweat breaks out across the back of my neck. I don't *want* to be here. I don't enjoy hanging out in cemeteries in the middle of the night for the fun of it. I was drawn here, though, an undeniable force pulling on my insides, tugging me through the lateness of the night as I drove the Nova up the long, winding roads that lead toward the lake, the car's headlights guiding me toward Sam.

Devoted Son.

Beloved Friend.

Talented Sportsman.

My eyes follow the sharp line and curve that forms the letters of each engraved word, knowing without the faintest glimmer of doubt that Mallory Hawthorne believes these statements to be true.

It's amazing how little parents really know about their children. They give birth to this creature, who sucks them dry physically, financially and emotionally. As the child grows, beginning to form, developing character traits and personality quirks that make it a unique cog in the machinations of society, it becomes very difficult for mothers and fathers to really see the teeth that form on that cog. Their rose-tinted view paints their children with all the beautiful gifts they *wish* to bestow on them: kindness; loyalty; honesty; intelligence. The blind love they feel for their child builds them up to be this blameless, perfect being, brimming with so much potential that their offspring might as well be the second coming of Christ.

So, when they find out that their blameless, perfect child is really a monster, it's no great surprise that they won't accept the truth. Some cogs don't fit into the places assigned to them. They make the machine skip, their teeth too sharp and too grating. They are square pegs that won't fit in round holes. That doesn't mean that the determined and the persistent won't keep on trying to jam them into place, of course. Mallory Hawthorne will believe her son was a saint until the day she fucking dies.

I suppose he *was* quite good at sports.

"Sammy just got back from surfing in Hawaii. D'you think he's hot?"

The memory rushes me like the cold water of the Cushman tide. I try not to let my mind catch on it, but the sights and sounds of that night are bright as comets when they flare across the landscape of my mind and just as unstoppable: Sam, standing shirtless in front of the bathroom mirror, face split with a grin as he stoops down to do a rail of coke. Jake standing behind me, grinding his hard dick up against my ass as he trades suggestive looks with his friends. Sam, queuing up Sublime and cranking the music loud to mute my screams. Sam, handing Jake the razor he uses to cut away my clothes. Sam, leaning his bodyweight against me, holding me down as Jake paws at my naked body. Sam taking his turn, climbing on top of me, his breath reeking of whiskey, eyes unfocused, that terrible, mindless grin still twisting his features like some circus clown maw.

And then, after all of that was over, Sam, downstairs at the party…

I blink rapidly, gouging my fingers into my palms, hoping that the pain will shock me out of the past, but it's too late.

I recognize the song blasting through Mr. Wickman's state of the art, thirty-thousand-dollar speaker system, but I'm not really hearing it. It's impossible to hear much over the high-pitched ringing in my ears. My mouth still finds the shape of the lyrics as they pump out into the living room, though. My lips work of their own accord, silently repeating the chorus of the song like a prayer. I feel nothing. Even when I trip on the last step of the stairs, twisting my ankle as I lurch forward, barely catching my footing before going sprawling across the dove-grey marble floor in the foyer, I feel absolutely nothing.

The house is packed to the rafters. There are faces here I don't recognize. Or...maybe I do know them. Everyone looks unfamiliar as I stumble toward the front door, bile boiling in my stomach, choking me, clawing its way up the back of my throat.

"Silver? Silver, Jesus, what the hell are you wearing? Is that one of Mr. Wickman's shirts?"

There's a girl standing in front of me. Fine wisps of her beautiful red hair are stuck to her forehead, curled, captured in the sheen of her sweat. She's wearing a royal blue dress that makes her eyes look as bottomless as the sea. Her pupils are blown wide open.

Halliday. Her name is Halliday.

She's one of my best friends, and she's frowning at me like she's just realized something is very, very wrong. "Silver? Oh my god, Sil, is that blood?"

Robotically, I look down at where she's pointing. I've been slumped in the bottom of the shower for...I don't know how long I sat there with the freezing cold water hammering against my skin. I thought I'd gotten it all. I thought I'd cleaned away all of the blood. The insides of my thighs are slick with it, though.

Fresh. Bright. Red.

I couldn't find any pants...

I reach out, my hand grasping at thin air as I try to hold onto something. "I'm going to throw up."

"Shit, let's get you outside. You need fresh air." Halliday wraps an arm around my shoulder, rushing me to the door. I barely make it down the front steps and to the lawn before I drop to my hands and knees and retch into the grass. Nothing really comes up. I puked at least three times in the shower before I blindly staggered down the stairs, so there's barely even a mouthful of stomach acid to bring up this time. It burns like nothing else, though. The taste is foul.

When I sink back onto my knees, Halliday has an arm wrapped around her own body and a hand covering her mouth. Her Pacific Ocean eyes are full of tears. "Silver, what the hell happened?" she whispers.

She already knows. She suspects. If she didn't, she wouldn't be looking at me the way she is. I'm so fucking tired, I could fall asleep right here on the lawn. "I need to go home, Hal. Can...can you find my purse?" The sound of my own voice surprises me. I sound normal. I sound sober. I sound like me. *I'm not me anymore, though. I'm a tragic, broken imposter, occupying a tragic, broken body that belongs to someone else. Three people, to be precise: Jacob Weaving. Samuel Hawthorne. Cillian Dupris. This mangled, uncomfortable shell of muscle, flesh, and bone belongs to them. They baptized themselves in my blood, and now I'm theirs...*

Halliday stifles a sob. "Silver." Her hand shakes as she reaches out, stroking a tangled strand of damp hair out of my face. "I think I should call your dad."

I whip around, eyes finally focusing properly on her face. "No. I don't want him here. I don't want to talk. I just wanna go home. I need my purse, Halliday."

My phone's inside that Tory Birch clutch. House keys. If I don't find my keys, I won't be able to get inside the house without waking up Mom and Dad...

"Please. Just go inside and find it so I can leave."

"Where...?" she whispers.

I swallow. My throat's so raw, it feels like I'm choking down broken glass. "Upstairs. Top floor. The bathroom at the end of the hall."

"Okay, I'll find it. I'll find Kacey, too. She'll know what to do."

I feel myself nodding.

Time passes. I start to shiver, but I don't feel the chilly night air. I'm detached from myself, unmoored, my psyche trying to float away downstream, but no matter how hard I try to kick and swim away from the misery of my own existence, I find I'm still trapped within it. I have no idea how long I wait on my knees in the grass. Eventually, I get to my feet, wobbling like a newborn deer, and I walk to a window, peering through the glass.

It's sheer luck that I immediately see Halliday. That she's even in the hallway at all. My eyes catch on her red hair. She's animated, her hands moving in the air, gesturing toward the front door. In front of her, Kacey's tapping furiously into her phone.

My best friend looks worried. Her eyes are sharp, spearing people through as she holds her phone to her ear. The light from the screen casts a blue glow across her face. Nervously, she tucks her hair behind her ear, and—

My chest pinches tight, a sharp pain spreading like the roots of a tree across my ribcage.

Sam...

Sam's joined them, and he's listening to Halliday frantically speak. She points to the front door, undoubtedly telling the story of me, wearing nothing but an oversized dress shirt with blood staining my thighs, collapsed out on the front lawn.

No. No, no, no. God, please, no.

Sam turns, eyes narrowed as he heads toward the door. Toward me. My heart almost explodes in my chest.

Run! Run, Silver. Go!

I am paralyzed. I couldn't fucking run if I tried.

The door opens, spilling warm light out into the darkness, and I pray for the sound of Halliday's voice. She hasn't followed behind Sam, though. He's come out to me alone.

The soles of his shoes crunch against the gravel pathway. He's standing right next to me. He's less than five or six inches away. It feels as though a ten-ton weight is pushing down on the back of my head, preventing me from looking up into his face.

Sam's bemused laughter is quiet, but it seems loud over the thumping bass of the music still playing inside. "Didn't you wash that dirty little cunt, Parisi?"

I flinch, making myself smaller inside my head, shying away from his voice. His hand reaches out, his fingers tracing the line of my jaw. I freeze. I don't make a sound. "Your friends are in there, rallying the troops," he says mildly. He barely sounds interested let alone fazed by this information. "Just curious. Are you on birth control? If you wind up pregnant, that'd probably be really bad, don't you think? You'd have to explain that you went whoring around with not one but three guys at a party. Your parents would probably be pretty disgusted, I reckon."

My mind is a void.

My ears ring louder than ever.

My heart thrashes, trying not to seize.

Sam hooks a finger under my chin, forcing me to meet his gaze. He looks down on me like I'm the most repellant thing he's ever had the misfortune of seeing with his own two eyes. "*I hear the morning after pill's pretty effective. Dillinger's is open twenty-four hours now, too. Seems like your best bet would be to make a stop there before you head home. Be silly to take any chances. What d'you think, babe?*"

Babe.

Babe.

Babe.

Babe.

I can't stop the word from repeating over and over in my head.

Babe.

Babe.

Babe.

I clap my hands over my ears, screwing my eyes shut, refusing to breathe. If I stop breathing, I might pass out. I might fucking die. At least if I'm dead, this madness will finally stop.

Sam's hand drops to his side. "*Are you listening?*"

I'm not. I can't. I'm not. I can't. I'm not. I can't.

"*Crazy fucking bitch.*" *His jabs a finger into my chest, sneering viciously, his false indifference vanishing in a puff of smoke.* "*I'd be really careful how I handled what comes next if I were you. You're gonna be faced with a choice. I'm gonna give you a piece of advice, Parisi. Right now, you're standing at a crossroads. To your left lies graduation. The end of school. Summer with your friends. You finish your time at Raleigh with a smile on your face and we all part as friends. The other direction?*" *He shakes his head, disappointment forming on his face.* "*To your right leads copious amounts of pain and suffering. Humiliation. Embarrassment. You won't make it to graduation if you head in that direction. Jake'll make sure of it. You shouldn't have defied him like that upstairs. You really got under his skin. You fucked up his head real bad.*"

I'm not in my right mind. The frigid, cold water from the shower must have addled my brain. If I was thinking straight, I'd make sure to stop the slightly deranged bark of laughter from exploding out of my mouth.

Sam's eyes harden like flint. He tuts under his breath, taking a step back toward the house. "*All right, babe. It's your fucking funeral. Remember that.*"

He goes inside.

I press my forehead against the glass of the window, finally dragging a shaken, terrified breath down into my burning lungs. When I look up, Sam's in front of my friends again, hands in his pockets. He's talking to Kacey, his face very calm, his shoulders relaxed. Kacey, on the other hand? Kacey's becoming visibly more and more agitated. She turns red, her icy-blue eyes filling with the kind of cold, dead fury that generally means someone, somewhere is about to be publicly eviscerated. A minute passes. Two. Sam doesn't stop talking the entire time, words spilling out of his mouth like a goddamn oil slick, and Kacey does nothing but stand there and listen. At one point, Halliday reacts to something he says, covering her mouth with both hands. Kacey's posture stiffens, so much tension pouring off her that it looks like she's about to go nuclear. Halliday tries to say something to her, but she spins on her and snaps, snarling at her through her bared teeth.

Sam finally stops talking. He shrugs, grins at the girls, and then pivots on the balls of his heels and walks away, rejoining the chaos of the party that's still surging all around them. Kacey spears Halliday through with a look that makes my blood run cold.

Still, I am a fool, though. Still, I don't see it coming.

When Kacey and Halliday emerge through the front door of the Wickman house, I expect my best friend to take me in her arms and hold me. I expect her to stroke my hair and tell me everything is going to be all right. I expect her to turn that legendary rage of hers into sharp cutting words, hone them into lethal weapons, and to send them flying at the boys who hurt me.

I have never been so wrong in all my life.

When Kacey comes to a halt before me, she doesn't meet my eyes. She tosses something at my feet, sighing tiredly. It's my purse. "What did I tell you?" she spits.

"Wh—what?"

"What did I tell you before, in the bathroom with Zen? I said he wasn't for you, didn't I? I told you not to get involved with Jake. Now look at the steaming pile of shit you've landed yourself in. I'm sick of your crap, Silver. Honestly, I am."

Halliday dips her head, crying quietly. She looks from me to Kacey and then back at me, as if what she's seeing take place cannot be stopped, but she can't look away.

Kacey finally looks up. She's always been hard. Always had trouble dealing with her feelings. Anger has always been the only emotion she's ever felt safe unleashing on the world, but even her anger is absent now as she looks me up and down. "You made your bed, Silver. I'm afraid you're gonna have to lie in it. Go home. I don't even want to look at you, and neither do the other girls. The Sirens can't be seen to be hanging around with trash like you."

It happens just like that. Quick, like tearing off a Band-Aid. Kacey leaves and she doesn't look back. She does pause on in the doorway of the house, the light throwing her into shadow as she waits with one hand resting against the doorjamb.

"Halliday! Get inside this house now, or you'll find yourself stuck out there with her forever."

She doesn't mean stuck outside the house. She means stuck on the outside, shut out from the light and warmth of her good graces, forever shivering in the loneliness of the long shadow she casts. Halliday gives me one last, torn look, before she leaves and follows Kacey inside.

The next hour is hell. Alone, I walk barefoot to the end of the driveway and wait for the Uber I order on my phone. The driver thinks I'm drunk and nearly doesn't let me in the car. He threatens me with extortionate cleaning bills if I throw up, but finally drives me across Raleigh to the pharmacy on the high street. Just as Sam said it would be, Dillinger's store front is lit up, the only business besides the gas station that's still open at three a.m. on a Friday night.

The Uber guy knows I'm not drunk now. He's actually kind of concerned for me, I think. "You want me to wait for you, kid?"

I haven't even looked at him once. I've sat on the backseat, vibrating with terror because I've managed to trap myself in such a small space, alone with a man. "No, I'll be fine. Thank you." My legs threaten to ditch me in the gutter when I climb out of the car. It takes some convincing, but I manage to talk them into keeping me upright.

The Uber driver's window buzzes down. A face appears there, but still I don't look at him. "I'd prefer to see you walk through your front door if it's all the same to you," he says. "My name's Harry. I got a daughter your age. I'd feel like a shit father if I didn't make sure you got back safely. Looks like you've had a bit of a tough night."

A tough night...

I try and think of an adequate word to describe just how tough tonight has been, but I don't think the English language harbors a word brutal enough. It is possible to walk home from town, but it'd would be a miserable hike with no shoes, feeling like my world has just ended. I could call for another Uber, but chances are high the next driver will also be a guy, and maybe next time that driver won't be so concerned about my wellbeing. Maybe he'll see me as an opportunity and take advantage. I am so, so fucking tired. "Okay. I won't be a minute."

The lights inside Dillinger's Pharmacy are too bright. A strong medical, herbal smell hits me as soon as I walk in, making my head spin. The dress shirt I stole from Mr. Wickman's laundry basket has an ink blot above the left-hand breast pocket that's shaped almost like a crescent moon. I dab at it self-consciously—ridiculous, since I'm naked underneath the shirt and the material barely hits me mid-thigh. Not to mention my face is still stained with the remnants of my mascara, I'm covered in blood, and my feet are absolutely filthy.

The woman behind the counter sees me and stops dead, a phone handset half raised to her ear. "Sweet Mary, Mother of God," she breathes. "What on earth's happened to you, child?" She's in her fifties. Blonde hair, greying at her temples. Short. A little stocky. Not a lick of makeup on her face. Her eyebrows are out of control. I can't seem to stop noticing the details of her. When I get close enough, arriving at the counter, I smell her—talcum powder and Altoids—and I almost burst into tears. I don't even know why.

"Dear, is everything all right?" She puts the phone's handset back in its cradle. "You look like you've been in the wars."

"I—" My voice breaks. I have to clear my throat. "I need...the morning after..."

The woman's face leeches of all color. Her facial muscles relax in the weirdest way, like when an actor in a film pretends to die and everything about them just sags. She braces herself against the counter, steadying herself for a second. Then she reaches out for me and takes my hand. "Why don't you take a seat by the cough medicine over there, sweetheart. I think I should probably call the police."

"No! No. I just want the get what I came in here for and go home. I—" My throat's closing up. No matter how hard I try to speak, I can't seem to get the words out. The pharmacy clerk wobbles, the edges of her distorting strangely. I think I'm going to pass out, but then I realize that I'm crying. "I just...I want to go home."

"Okay, okay. Dear Lord in Heaven, help me," the woman mutters. She lets go of me long enough to hurry down one of the narrow shelves behind her, stand on her tiptoes, and retrieve the correct box. She places it gingerly *down between us, looking ten years older than she did when I walked in here a few moments ago.*

"Can you—will you open it?" I ask stiffly. The box is sealed in thick plastic, the kind they package razor blades in. You always need a pair of scissors to get through that stuff. I have no hope of ripping into it with my teeth. The woman peers at me from beneath tightly banked brows.

"Don't you want to wait until you get home, sweethear—"

"No."

She nods, her hands moving quickly as she produces a boxcutter from the pocket of her white jacket and deftly slices through the thick plastic. She removes the box from its casing and hands it to me. I can hardly hold the damn thing still as I fumble to get it open. It takes three attempts to rip the cardboard tab up, and then another two tries to successfully tug the sealed blister pack that contains the one tiny pill free from inside.

"Here, let me get you some water."

I don't wait for water. I pop the metal foil on the back of plastic sheet, thumbing the pill free from the other side, and I throw it back as quickly as I can, swallowing hard.

I walk out of the pharmacy without another word.

It isn't until I'm home, sliding my key into the front door, creeping my way up to my bedroom, desperate not to wake Mom and Dad, that I realize I didn't even pay for the pill.

A distant siren wails, setting me on edge as I retreat from the waking nightmare. I'm back in the cemetery, back in the freezing cold, staring down at Samuel Hawthorne's grave. It's all still so fucking fresh in my mind. It feels like it happened yesterday. Sometimes, it's as though no time at all has passed and I'm still stuck inside my own paralyzed body outside that window, looking in, unable to move or turn away as I watch my friends turn against me.

"What the hell did you say to her, hmm?" I whisper at the headstone. "What the fuck did you say to Kacey to make her react that way?"

I've been asking myself that question for a very long time now. It must have been bad. Really fucking bad. I asked Kacey once, in the days after the party, and she'd spat in my face. *Literally.*

From his cold, lonely grave, Samuel Hawthorne refuses to confess his secrets.

I sigh, setting the bag down that I've been holding onto tight this entire time. Metal clanks on metal as I unzip the top of it, taking out a chisel and a hammer from inside. Dad's tools, borrowed from the garage. Most of his time's spent in front of a drafting desk these days, but back when he was in college he took a stone masonry class. He's been promising himself that he'll get back into it at some point, but so far he hasn't had the time.

I have no idea how to use the chisel and the striking tool I've taken out of the bag, but I understand the general premise. Plant the chisel. Hit the chisel. Leave a mark.

I get to work.

It's more difficult than I imagine it would be, but twenty minutes later I achieve what I set out to accomplish. My stone working skills leave a lot to be desired, but the word I've chipped deep into Sam Hawthorne's headstone is perfectly legible.

Devoted Son.
Beloved Friend.
Talented Sportsman.
RAPIST

Mallory Hawthorne's a fucking amateur. She thinks no one knows that she's the one who sneaks into the Raleigh Gardens of Rest every Tuesday night and scrawls the word *murderer* onto Leon Wickman's headstone. While red spray paint might look rather dramatic, it does come off with a stiff brush, soap, and a little elbow grease.

I, on the other hand, have thought this through long and hard. There's no way in hell anyone's washing *this* away.

TEXT MESSAGE RECEIVED:

+1(564) 987 3491: your not gonna make it to graduation, silver.
your gonna wind up wishing youd never been fucking born.

2

ALEX

I've done some pretty shady things in the past. Up until now, I've never fucking killed anyone before, though. In my hand, the gun Monty pressed into my chest as I left the Rock an hour ago feels like a ticking time bomb. It's a thing of beauty, all sleek lines and cold, unforgiving black steel, but I fucking hate the thing. I want nothing to do with it.

Some people might assume my hatred of guns comes from my recent brush with death in the Raleigh High School library. At night, when I'm alone in the trailer, I sometimes find myself pressing my fingertips into the neat, violet scar I earned myself that day, flinching, my body jolting with the memory of the burning metal hitting my chest. I still feel that same breathless, creeping cold, seeping through my veins when I close my eyes sometimes, too. However, that isn't the reason why I have to grind my teeth together, battling to keep my arm steady as I aim the gun at the back of Peter Westbrook's head tonight.

No.

I hate guns because of what happened the day I came home from school, a skinny six-year-old with both front teeth missing, and I found my mother lying in a pool of her own blood with half her fucking head blown off. Compared to that memory, the knee-jerk recall of the moment six weeks ago when Kacey Winters shot her ex-boyfriend and inadvertently hit me in the process, is a walk in the fucking park.

"Listen, man. I don't know what Monty told you, but I don't owe him shit," Westbrook grouses. He doesn't seem all that bothered by the fact that I'm pointing a gun at the back of his head. He seems a little bored. Clearly, he doesn't think I'm going to shoot him, but he did drop reluctantly down to his knees when I barked out the command ten minutes ago. "He placed an order. He got what he paid for. Five cases. I know Monty's not too shit-hot with math, but this is simple fucking kindergarten stuff, kid. *One, two, three, four, five.*" He shrugs, sighing under his breath. "Maybe the stupid bastard should stick to slinging shots and shooting porno down in that basement of his. You can tell him from me, he's not very good at—"

The butt of the gun makes a dull cracking sound as I bring it down on the back of Westbrook's head. I could have split his fucking skull open with such a heavy monster of a weapon but I've opted for mild concussion instead. "What's the point in opening your mouth, Pete, if all you do is lie? I don't have a clue what Monty ordered. All I know is that he's missing a black duffel bag. I don't know what's inside the bag, and I don't wanna know, either. I was told to come here and collect it...and I was told to make life really uncomfortable for you if you didn't hand it over."

A thin stream of blood runs down the back of Westbrook's neck, leeching into the white fabric of his collared shirt. I can't stop staring at the redness of it. The man turns his head ever so slightly, his face in profile, a knowing, smug smile pulling his mouth up at the corner. "And how the hell are you planning on doing that?" Clearly, he thinks I'm wet behind the ears. Inexperienced. So green that I'll hesitate the second things begin to get violent. Over the past month, Monty's tasked me with all kinds of fucked up assignments, though. I've been recovering from a goddamn gunshot wound, aching every time I twist without thinking, but my boss at the Rock hasn't given me much of a break. Seems like I've been getting my hands dirty every other fucking day. If I have to make Westbrook hurt so I can get the fuck out of here and back to Silver, then I won't fucking hesitate.

There isn't much I wouldn't do in order to get back to Silver.

Casually leaning back against Westbrook's desk, I consider how best to deal with the lying sack of shit. Monty's careful with his words to the point of paranoia. He's never *told* me to break anyone's bones. He's never commanded me to put someone in the hospital directly, but his intentions are always very clear. If I don't come back from Bellingham with this black duffel bag, Monty expects me to wreak havoc here tonight. He'll be sorely disappointed if I leave this guy standing.

I've resigned myself to the fact that I'm going to have to lay into Westbrook, when he disrupts my thoughts. "You're the Moretti kid, aren't you?" he says. "Jack's boy."

The fact that he's used my father's nickname doesn't really mean much. Giacomo's hardly a common name around these parts; most people were more comfortable referring to him as Jack. It doesn't mean he knew him. I still hesitate, though. My father fled Washington State so long ago that it *is* unusual to come across anyone who remembers him. Hearing him mentioned here, in this dark, seedy office, with its lacquered wood paneling and its plush cream carpet underfoot feels...just fucking...*wrong.* "Your Pop never liked Monty," Westbrook says mildly. "He'd probably spit teeth if he knew that limp-dicked bastard had laid a claim on you."

"Shut the fuck up, Pete. My father's irrelevant. Do you have the bag or not?"

Smiling, Westbrook lets his head hang loose, his chin resting against his chest. He's in his forties—a well-dressed, well-made, solid looking dude with hands the size of fucking shovels. I think he used to be a bare-knuckle boxer back in the day. He certainly made a lot of his money placing bets in rigged fights. "I'm curious. Has Monty ever explained *why* he took you in, Moretti?" he asks.

I clench my jaw, grinding my teeth together. "*The bag.* Tell me if you've got it, or I'm gonna fucking rip your arms out of joint."

"He used to do runs for Monty, y'know. Your old man. Just like you are now. Though Jack was a little more convincing when he showed up on a guy's doorstep with a mind to threaten him. It was his eyes. So fucking dark and soulless. There was something primitive about ol' Jackie boy. When you looked at *him* and he looked back at *you*, you lost all hope. You saw right away that he wasn't like other men. He operated on a level that the rest of us have evolved away from. Sex. Food. Money. Power. Those were the only things that mattered to Jack. The bare essentials required for survival. There was no appealing to his empathy. No sense of injustice. He didn't possess either. There was only the bottom line for Jack. God help you if you ended up on his shit list."

I was five when my father bailed. Old enough to have a few memories of the man stored away in the back of my mind, but young enough that the edges of those memories seem soft and blurry, like they might not even be real, or perhaps I imagined them. I remember feeling glued to the floor when the sick fuck was mad at me, though. I remember panic crawling insidiously up the back of my neck every time he raised his fist to strike me…because I knew with a concrete certainty that he was going to follow through.

Westbrook's barking up the wrong fucking tree if he thinks bringing up my father is going to endear him to me. If anything, he's making this situation much, *much* worse. "You got kids?" I ask, my voice as stiff as my posture.

Westbrook laughs. "If I say yes, are you going to spare me the torture of this bullshit interrogation?"

"Answer the question."

"Yeah, I got kids. Three. Two boys and a girl."

"Nice. You beat 'em? Abandon 'em? You raise your fist to their mother?"

He doesn't say anything now. The smile slips slowly from his face.

"Probably best if we don't talk about my father and we concentrate on the matter at hand, huh, Pete?"

The ice in my tone must chill him. He swallows thickly, adjusting his weight. "There's always bad blood between a father and his son. There's always a reason why one hates the other. Jack didn't abandon you, though, Moretti. He ran because Monty—"

I've officially had enough of this bullshit. I won't listen to another word that comes out of his mouth. I'm done. I'm used up and spent by men like Peter Westbrook—men who renege on deals, who waltz around in their thousand-dollar suits, driving their Mercs through the gates of private, guarded communities, where they're safe and protected from the outside world. Westbrook's the worst kind of stuck up asshole. A bigot, through and through. He wasn't born into a life of comfort and luxury. He was born in the gutter, just like me. He's raised himself pretty damn high over the course of his lifetime, and I respect that, but fuck me if I'm going to let the motherfucker think he's better than me because of it.

I discard the gun; the metal clunks heavily as I set the weapon aside on Westbrook's desk. The flick knife I pull from my pocket doesn't fill me with the same discomfort as the gun. I actually feel a little relieved as I turn the handles over, flipping the blade open, pivoting the knife so that the spine of the metal is pressing against the edge of my hand.

Held like this, it would be so fucking easy to slit his throat. To open up his carotid and have him bleed out. All it would take is a casual, effortless swipe of the hand.

My shoes, wet from the rain and caked with mud, leave dirty prints on the cream carpet as I slowly walk around the prone man in front of me. I come to a stop in front of him, a sick, tight feeling in my stomach when he looks up at me and I see the first flickerings of real fear in his eyes. It was easy to mock me when I was standing behind him. It was easy to forget what he was dealing with, no doubt. His mind presented him with the bare facts: I am nothing more than a seventeen-year-old high school student, employed to do Montgomery Cohen's grunt work.

Towering over him now, though, Peter sees me for what I truly am: a man, broad, strong, and unrelenting, made hard by the violence I have already borne witness to in this life. I'm no wilting boy-child, quaking in my boots, unsure of how to proceed. Peter knows this the moment I stoop down a foot in front of him, giving him the chance to take a good, long look into *my* eyes.

I raise my hand, flicking the knife open and closed.

Peter flinches.

"I—I told you," he stammers. "Monty placed the order. I gave him the order. This black bag bullshit is…it's fucking *bullshit!* The bag has nothing to do with him!" He's going red in the face now, a vein pulsing in his left temple. I doubt anyone's ever burst into his office and threatened him before. He's sure as shit never had to answer to the likes of me. "Don't you understand?" Westbrook spits, straining at the cuffs that are restraining his hands behind his back. "He's getting fucking greedy. He's fucking *manipulating* you!"

I tilt my head to one side, pouting. "So, he's telling tales, sending me out in the middle of the night to steal random bags from you. That it?"

"Yes!"

"And he'd do that because...?"

Westbrook growls, frustrated, rolling his eyes. "Come on, smartass. This is Bad Guy one-oh-one. Power means respect, and respect means fear. Fear means obedience. Obedience means more fucking power. It's an endless cycle, and Monty wants more. That bag...it means power. Whoever owns that bag becomes a very powerful man overnight. He's sent you here, knowing I'll never hand it over. He knows I'll kill you before I give it up. What's that tell you, huh? He doesn't give a shit about you. You're disposable. A means to an end. Nothing more than an amusing toy he'll get bored of, the same way he gets bored of all his other toys. You think you're the only project kid Monty's taken under his wing? I hate to break this to you, Princess, but you're not that fucking special. There were plenty before you, and there'll be plenty after you, too. You're gonna end up dead or in prison. Either way, you're fucking insane if you think Monty will give a shit. About any of it."

Time to go, Passarotto. *You have to leave. Don't be foolish,* mi amore.

When she was alive, my mother was never all there. Not really. Her thoughts were so scattered, her mind drifting from one idea to the next so rapidly that it was impossible to keep up with her sometimes. Now, when she comes to me, softly whispering her words of advice and her warnings into my ear, she's much clearer, her mind free of the fog that always clouded it over. I know *I* did this, that *I* gave this to her this clarity in death. She didn't live long enough to help me through the difficult transition from boy to man. She wasn't there to tell me what the fuck I should have done when I first met Silver. Over the years, whenever I provoked Gary into beating the living shit out of me with his belt, or before that even, when one of the other cold, bitter fuckers who 'took me in' decided to tan my hide, she wasn't there to protect me. Sometimes, she shows up like this, though, whispering quietly over my shoulder, gently nudging me toward safety.

It's my own sense of self-preservation doing the whispering. It's not really her. She was buried eleven years ago, for Christ's sake, the worms finished up their work with her a long time ago, but I choose to believe her influence over me is far from dead and gone.

I set my jaw, quickly lifting the blade of the knife up to Westbrook's throat. The edge of the steel is so sharp, I barely even show it to his skin before a thin, crimson line forms below his Adam's apple and the shining surface of the blade is stained with blood. "I don't care what his motives are. I don't care if he's lying. Monty sent me here with a purpose, and I have nothing better to do tonight than fulfill it. You know your options. I'm done fucking talking to you. If I have to stand here any longer, I'm gonna start putting this knife to good use. Y'know…they say the cuts don't even hurt at first, when the knife's so sharp. You could be missing more of your body parts than you'd like before you really start to feel it, and by then…" I shrug. "I might not be inclined to stop."

"All right, all right. Jesus Christ, kid. Ease up."

I lean into the blade a little, pressing more of weight behind it. A warning. A promise. A threat.

"Whoa, whoa, whoa! Fucking *stop!*" Westbrook snaps, trying to jerk away from the knife. He only succeeds in catching himself on the tip of the knife, though. The slice at his throat I just gave him was only a papercut; if he's not fucking careful, it's going to end up cutting his *own* carotid. "Fine! Fine! The bag's here! It's fucking here, I swear. Goddamnit, will you back the fuck up! I can't give it to you if I'm fucking dead."

I withdraw the knife, plastering a grin across my face. I can see myself reflected in Westbrook's eyes and boy oh boy do I look fucking insane. So fucking what, though? In situations like these, it helps if people think you might be a little unhinged. "On your feet, then," I say brightly, grabbing him by the elbow and tugging him up. "Show me where the bag is, hand it over, and that'll be the last you see of me."

Again, the guy laughs bitterly under his breath. He obviously doesn't believe that's true, but he's smart enough to keep his doubts to himself. His legs are shaky as he heads toward the office door, where he huffs impatiently, arching an eyebrow over his shoulder at me. "You're gonna have to open it if you want to move this thing along," he snaps.

I collect the gun I set down on his desk, returning it into the waistband of my jeans at the small of my back, and then I open the door to Westbrook's office, holding it for him obligingly. "After you. I insist."

Westbrook grumbles malevolently as he storms out into the hallway, taking a right and walking off at a fast clip. I follow after him, keeping pace, carefully eyeing every door and hallway that branches off from the main corridor, making sure I'm not about to be taken unawares. It's Monday, so Gimlet's, Westbrook's club, is closed. It's after six in the evening, so it's unlikely we're going to run into anyone, but you never know. It never pays to let your guard down.

At the end of the hallway, Westbrook hangs a left, heading toward a large, rivetted door that's been painted red. Looks like it's made out of reinforced steel. Pete juts a hip out, jerking his chin down at the left-hand pocket of his pants. "The key's in there. I'd tell you to uncuff me so I can get it out, but I'm not stupid enough to think you'd do it."

"Bully for you. Congrats on not being stupid." I stick my hand into his pocket and pull out the set of keys quickly. I'd planned on hanging at the bar this afternoon. Paul invited me for a beer, but the moment I stepped foot inside the Rock, Monty had me cornered and was handing off this shitty job to me before I could say no. This was *not* how I'd planned on enjoying one of my only days off this week…and ending up with a handful of another man's dick and balls is only going to sour my mood further.

There are five keys on the Westbrook's fob. "Which one?" I demand.

"The gold one, there. The old looking one," Westbrook mumbles. "It opens both locks."

There are, indeed, two locks on the red, reinforced steel door. I use the key he pointed out, quickly unbolting the door and then pulling it open.

Inside, a bright, cold strip-light casts a stark blue glow over the small room beyond—a liquor store, lined with shelves that span from floor to ceiling, laden with a supply of booze that would last me a goddamn lifetime.

"In there, at the back," Westbrook clips out. "On the floor, by the bottles of Jim Beam."

I give him a tired, weary look. "Pete, I'm going to be so disappointed if I find out this door automatically locks when it's slammed closed."

His weak, irritated smile confirms that he was going to try and lock me inside the liquor store. "Can't blame a guy for trying, right?"

"Just fucking move, before I decide to lock *you* in there and set this place on fucking fire. I hear death by smoke inhalation's a pretty miserable way to go."

Westbrook stumbles a little as I shove him inside the liquor store. He reluctantly makes for a bank of whiskey bottles at the far end of the room and halts, sighing.

"All right. Here you go," he says, kicking out with one of his leather shoes. "The magical, mysterious bag Monty sent you over here for. It's been nothing but fucking trouble since the moment I laid eyes on it. Untie me and get the fuck out of my sight, before I call in some friends and have them play soccer with your dismembered fucking head."

"Sounds like a good time. Real talk, though. Friends? You're fucking detestable. I can't picture you having many *friends*, Pete." I join him, snatching up the bag at his feet by one of its handles, determined not to bother trying to guess what's inside it by its weight. A hard thing to do, though. I never know what's inside any of the packages Monty sends me to drop off or collect, but this run has felt different from the get-go. There was something off about the desperate edge to Monty's voice when he told me I *had* to get this bag for him. The look on his face was nothing short of weird.

"The key?" Westbrook snaps, spinning around to give me access to the cuffs behind his back.

I'm already walking away, though.

"Hey! Hey, don't you dare, you fucking punk!" Westbrook yells after me. "There's no cell phone reception down here. No one's coming in until nine tomorrow morning."

I pause in the doorway, hand resting on the cool steel, pitted steel.

It takes me all of three seconds to weigh the pros and cons of leaving Peter locked in his own liquor cellar overnight. Pro number one: it's a fucking *liquor cellar*. The guy can have a great time if he sets his mind to it. Two: if he can't use his cell phone down here, then he can't call any of his goons to chase me down and ruin my night. Three: imagining the look on Westbrook's face when he realizes the hand cuffs he's wearing are fucking novelty cuffs and a stick insect could pop them open makes me fucking laugh.

Cons: Hmm. Well, damn. Doesn't look like there are any of those...

That settles it, then. Westbrook's spending the night locked up in his little box. I give him a halfhearted shrug as I swing the door closed. The guy charges, trying to reach the exit before it has a chance to slam shut, but he's too fucking slow.

"Hope you're not claustrophobic," I call to him through the door. From how muffled the angry shouts are on the other side, I doubt that he'll have heard me. "Have a nice night, Mr. Westbrook."

The freezing night air tries to rip right through me as I step out of the emergency exit at the back of Gimlet's. The wind's been howling for days now, tearing through the Whitson Valley, knocking down Raleigh's street signs, felling dead trees, causing chaos and blocking the roads in and out of town. It felt like the Camaro was going to fucking roll on the drive over to Bellingham. The weather's even worse here. Not only is the wind so much stronger as it comes raging in off the bay, but the threat of snow is hanging heavy and pregnant in the air, promising to make the drive back to Raleigh seriously sketchy.

If I were smart, I'd wait the weather out. Hang tight in a motel for the night. Watch some bad T.V. and gorge myself on vending machine food. I don't want to waste the money on the room, though, and this storm isn't a twenty-four-hour squall. Once this cold front takes hold, it's going to snow, and it's going to snow hard. Not just for hours, but for days, and there is no way in hell I'm getting stuck in goddamn Bellingham for that long. Not with Silver Parisi expecting me to meet her in Raleigh. The very hounds of hell couldn't keep me from making *that* appointment.

It takes a couple of minutes to jog down Culver and cross over a couple of blocks to the parking lot of the Night Stop Convenience Store where I left the car; by the time I hurl myself into the driver's seat and I slam the door closed behind me, my hair is stiff with ice and my eyes are streaming like crazy.

Somewhere in the world, the sun's shining right now. There are beaches, and coconuts, and cocktails, and people are walking around in their goddamn swimsuits, but I can't for the life of me think where such a place might be because my fucking brain is too fucking frozen and I can't form a coherent thought.

The fingers on my right hand ache and throb as I fumble with the car keys—an unpleasant reminder a day five years ago when I'd been playing my guitar a little too loud for Gary Quincy's liking. I curse angrily under my breath, annoyed that I've even allowed myself to remember the man, which is dumb really. I'm covered in scars, and plenty of my bones crunch and crack courtesy of all the injuries I've suffered at other people's hands. I should be used to this kind of thing by now. But there's something about *this* injury that makes my insides burn. Gary knew how much music meant to me. I'd wanted to play professionally. I'd wanted to pay my bills by playing the guitar, and he'd taken hold of my hand and slammed it in his door to his truck over and over again...

I can still play, thank fuck. If I stretch out my hand and use the bands I was given to strengthen the muscle and the tendons, there's no real reason why I couldn't make a living through my music, one way or another, but...

Every time I feel that fucking ache, I also see the hatred and the spite in Gary's rheumy, spiteful eyes, and deep down inside, I know that it's fucking true. That motherfucker didn't end up totally destroying my hand like he'd wanted to, but he *did* succeed in destroying my dreams for good.

TEXT MESSAGE RECEIVED:

+1(564) 987 3491: Your fucking disgusting. I don't no how u can even bear to look in the fucking mirror without puking. Im gonna cut your face up.

3

SILVER

There many different ways to love.

There's the kind of love that exists between friends. The lifetime bond of camaraderie that sometimes forms in the space of a summer afternoon, playing outside on the streets, riding bikes up and down the sidewalk and collecting bugs in jars. There's the love a person bears for their siblings or their parents. An intrinsic, deep-seated love that is always there, and always remains, through slight and disagreement, spanning decades and distance and so much silence.

And then there's romantic love. The kind of love poets have written sonnets about for hundreds of years. Romantic love, the lynchpin of all good stories. The all-consuming, burning fire in a heart that can create or destroy in the blink of an eye. The kind of love that inspires heroic acts of sacrifice, while also being the root cause of murder, jealousy and hideous acts of revenge.

Like nearly everyone else on the face of the planet, I'm well acquainted with the story of Romeo and Juliet. I've read the book. The adaptations. I've seen the movies. I've swooned over the devotion and all of the suffering held within the pages of Shakespeare's tragedy, but I've never understood it. Never really felt it before. Now, though, that fire burns in *my* chest. I feel it from the moment I wake up to the moment I go to sleep at night. Seems to me, no one else in the world has ever been this turned-around by someone before, this consumed or swallowed whole by another living, breathing, flawed human being.

This love is so overwhelming, so hot and so bright, that it has to be unique in all of creation. Because how would the world keep on spinning if everyone felt this way? How would governments not collapse, and wars not cease, and the whole of society not come to a crumbling standstill if there were other people in this world who felt for one another what I feel for Alex Moretti?

It's late. On the corner of High Street and Paulson, a figure stands in the shadows, leaning against the brick wall of *Harrison's Home Hardware and Electrical Supplies*, looking up at the sky. He doesn't seem to have a purpose as he gazes at the heavens. Doesn't seem to be waiting for anything in particular. A passerby would probably frown at his presence, casting suspicious eyes over him and making their small-town judgements of him as he does nothing more sinister than dare to stand still and scan the midnight sky for stars.

At first glance, his hair, thick with waves, is impossibly dark. Up close, it's easier to see that it isn't black but a very dark, textured brown—the darkest of browns—shot through with the odd stand of red that unexpectedly catches the light from time to time. His eyes are dark, too. I've seen such warmth and humor in them before, but that isn't what the rest of the world sees when they look into his eyes. Strangers are generally met with a cold, predatory disregard. I suppose the sterile assessment of his gaze could sometimes be described as frightening.

Vines with full-bloomed roses and studded with thorns circle his throat like a collar, the black ink peeking above the neck of his shirt, hinting at what else might lie beneath the fabric of his clothes. His jeans are ripped, his leather jacket worn, the collar popped against the biting wind and the halfhearted sleet, but there he stands, at ease, oblivious to the fact that winter has officially arrived, giving off the impression that he simply doesn't feel the cold.

He's an artist's rendering of something fictional and make-believe. A charcoal smudge against a bleached-out backdrop, drawn in swift, sure, mad lines that defy the laws of physics and confuse the eye but somehow seem all the more real because of it.

I see him, and I see all of these things about him, in the time it takes to inhale a lungful of sharp winter air and step off the curb on the main street, heading in his direction. When he looks over and sees me, our eyes lock, and I realize just how incredibly, totally, absolutely fucked I am.

Alex Moretti isn't just the kind of guy you fall in love with in high school. He isn't just the guy who steals your heart for a summer, and then fades from your affections, becoming nothing more than a rose-tinted memory in your rearview mirror. Alex Moretti is the kind of guy who sweeps into your life like a wildfire, torching anything and everything you've ever cared about before he makes himself perfectly at home, rooting himself down so deep into your soul that it becomes impossible to differentiate where you end and he begins.

A slow, wicked smile spreads across his handsome face and my heart does a triple pike backflip off a fifteen-meter high board. The world's such a big fucking place, and Raleigh is so damn small. The odds that I'd be born here, and that Alessandro Moretti would end up moving here to work at an establishment of ill-repute are so infinitely small that it all feels orchestrated. Like the universe picked out the trillions of molecules required to construct our individual bodies and arranged for them to come together at this specific time, in this specific place for some specific purpose.

Alex pushes away from the brick wall of Harrison's Home Hardware and Electrical Supplies with a leonine grace and begins to walk toward me like some sort of demi-god, freshly fallen to the earth. The flare of amusement in his dark eyes promises trouble. He meets me at the curb, slowly removing his hands from his pockets and placing them on my hips. A second later, my feet are off the ground and he's lifting me up the lip of the sidewalk and planting me down next to him.

"Hey there, *Argento*," he says, the left-hand side of his mouth tilting upward so that the faintest hint of a dimple marks his cheek. "Figured you were about five minutes away from standing me up."

A slow smile aches at my mouth. "So, if I'd shown up in five minutes, you'd have given up on me and left?"

He's so tall—an imposing, muscled, broad figure of a guy, towering over me, dark hair backlit from the sodium-yellow glow of the street light over our heads. He still looks entertained, his eyes slightly narrowed as he dips down closer to me. His warm breath chases away the cold night air as he whispers softly into my ear. "You know I wouldn't have left, *Argento*. I'm a lovesick dog. You told me to meet you here, so here I would have stayed, in the rain and the snow and the cold until you eventually came to find me and put me out of my misery."

My pulse quickens in the hollow of my throat, erratic and dizzying. He's playing. He wouldn't have waited here for me if I'd stood him up. No way. He would have come to find me. He would have tracked me down no matter what the weather was doing and stolen me away into the night, kicking and screaming. Except I wouldn't have fought my abduction. He won me fair and square. I belong to him now, the same way that he belongs to me. We're connected, sealed together, so immersed in each other that some days I'm a little intimidated by how in tune we are. Cut one of us and the other bleeds. Maybe not physically true, but emotionally...

Alex stands straight, cupping my face in his palms. It's below freezing tonight. He's been waiting outside the hardware store for god knows how long, but his hands are still warm. "Your hair's full of snow," he murmurs.

"So's yours." A fat flake lands on the tip of his eyelashes, brilliant white against the black, curved strands that rim his eyes. For a second, the very sight of him standing in front of me, his strong jawline, and his pronounced cheekbones, and his intense, penetrating gaze boring into me makes my ribs squeeze tight in a protective cage around my heart.

He's so devastatingly handsome. He's so imperfectly perfect. He's so...he's so fucking *dangerous*. I've always been so careful with my feelings, even before Jacob Weaving came along and blew up my life, but now it feels as though I've been reckless. I put on a good show for myself. Pretended I wasn't going to fall for the most inappropriate guy to ever walk through the doors of Raleigh High, but it was all an embarrassingly flimsy act. I knew I was going to hand myself over to him blindly, with a rash kind of abandon that now scares the living shit out of me.

If he wanted to, Alex could crush me in a way that would affect me for the rest of my life. He could break my heart into a trillion pieces, grind it to dust and scatter it on the frigid northerly wind and there would be no way of retrieving it. I'd have to live out the rest of my days, a heartless, broken, hollow girl with the aching memory of his lips on my mouth and there would be nothing I could do about it.

His salacious smirk fades a little as he rubs the pads of his thumbs lightly across the lines of my cheekbones. "What is it? What's wrong?"

I am amazing at hiding my thoughts and feelings. *Amazing.* Which makes it all the more intimidating that Alex can just look into my eyes, reach down into my soul, and pluck out my truths. I have no way of hiding myself from him.

Nervously, I smile, forcing out a shaky laugh. "Oh, y'know. Just pondering how terrifying you are."

His smile turns tight. Reproving, and just a tiny little bit sad. He bumps the end of my nose with his own, playful, but there's a heaviness to his voice when he speaks. "And here I was, thinking I'd found a girl who wasn't afraid of me."

"I'm not afraid of *you.* Just what'll happen if..."

He arches an eyebrow, very still, waiting for me to continue.

"If you decide to move on, crush my heart under your boot heel, and break me," I rush out, giving him another round of awkward laughter that sounds kind of pathetic, actually.

Alex's face goes blank, but his eyes burn with a fire that makes me forget we're standing out on a snowy street in the middle of November. "Break you?" he whispers. "I don't break the things I love, *Argento.* I fix them. I repair them. I treasure them. I do ridiculous, insane, very illegal things to make sure I don't lose them. I sure as hell don't *break* them. I also do not wear boots."

I'm not an insecure person. I'm not the kind of person who worries about their boyfriend leaving them all the time. At least, I hope I'm not; I have zero experience when it comes to boyfriends. The stakes just seem so high in this particular situation that a little worry seemed prudent. Looking up at Alex, all of that worry and niggling doubt disintegrates, though. He's telling the truth. He dug up a dead man through eight feet of frozen dirt to get his mother's necklace back, for fuck's sake. If he'd do that for a necklace, then what *would* he do for me?

He leans down, pressing his mouth against mine, and I fall slack against him. It happens every time—my body is so ill-equipped to deal with Alex kissing me that it always feels like I'm about to disintegrate myself. Like the molecular bonds that fuse my cells together are shaken loose by his closeness and I'm slowly, irreversibly beginning to drift into the ether. He parts my lips, guiding them open, and I moan softly into his mouth as he slips his tongue past my teeth, probing and sweeping, insistent as he tastes me. I lean into him, my back arching, my chest crushing up against him, and Alex slides a hand down to the small of my back, pulling me even closer. His breath hitches in his throat, catching, and he lets out a pained groan.

I'm so grateful that I didn't wear gloves as I reach up and wind my fingers into his hair. The thick, fullness of it feels amazing as I collect myself up off the floor long enough to kiss him back. His breath quickens, dragging in and out of his nose as he sucks my bottom lip into his mouth and roughly bites down. The sharp spear of pain makes me gasp, a startled, needy, pant of sound that seems to have a pretty wild effect on Alex. He slides his other hand away from my face, around to the back of my neck, and he grips me there, holding me in place against him as he forces my mouth open wider, tugging at my top lip.

My head spins faster than a centrifuge as he grinds his hips forward and his erection digs into my hip, demonstrating just how rock-hard the kiss is making him.

Oh, my fucking god...

If we weren't standing on the corner of the busiest street in all of Raleigh right now...

Screw it. I'm not thinking straight. I'm barely thinking at all as I slide my hand between our bodies, using the thick wool of my jacket to shield my actions, and I take hold of Alex's cock through his jeans.

He stops kissing me instantly. Pulls back. Stares down at me, pupils blown, full lips parted, cheeks flushed against the cold. "Silver—"

I squeeze, my fingers closing around the thickness of him, slowly moving up down to stroke...

Alex's eyes shutter closed. "Holy fuck. What are you doing?"

"What I've been thinking about doing since this morning," I whisper into his open mouth.

I feel him smile against my lips. "You've been turned on all day, *Dolcezza?*"

"*Yes.*"

He groans again, his fingernails digging into the back of my neck. "Fuuuck. You have no fucking idea how badly I want you right now."

"I think...I do."

"Why? Are you wet, Silver? Are you wet for me right now?"

I dip my head, letting my hair hide the fact that I'm blushing like crazy, but Alex takes hold of me by the chin, lifting my head until I have to meet his eyes. "Oh no. No way. I'm not buying the shy act when you've got your hand on my dick." His laughter is deep, gravelly, rough with desire. The sound of his need, so blatantly fucking obvious in his voice, sends a shiver of anticipation chasing down my spine. "Get your ass over here." He takes me by the hand, tugging me toward the brick wall of the hardware store where he was leaning a moment ago.

My jacket is thick enough that I don't feel the sharp texture of the brick against my back when Alex leans me against the building, but the icy cold manages to seep through just fine. It doesn't matter, though. Nothing matters, because Alex is nuzzling his face into my neck, placing searing kiss after searing kiss against the sensitive skin at the base of my throat, and I can't remember how to breathe. He's close against me, chest pressing up against chest, but there's still room for him to mirror my brazen move and slide his hand between our bodies. He doesn't touch me over my jeans. His hand quickly dips below the waistband of my jeans, and then his fingers are deftly pulling my panties aside, and—

"Ahh! *Fuck!*" I tip my head back against the brick, sucking in a sharp, agonizingly cold breath as Alex's fingers find my clit.

"*Christ, Silver.*" I look up at him and almost pass the fuck out when I see the wild expression on his face. "You're not wet," he pants. "You're fucking *soaking.*" With small, deliberate sweeps of his fingers,

Alex rolls my clit, rubbing it in a circular motion, and I have to bite back a startled cry.

"*Shhh*," Alex growls softly. "Hold it in, *Dolcezza*. My needy girl. Don't worry. I'm gonna give you what you need. I'm gonna make you come." With a swift, gently thrust, he pushes his index finger forward, slipping it inside me.

I freeze, unable to move for a second as I register what he's just done. My body's gone into shock. A hot, burning pulse of pleasure fires between my legs, and I let out a soundless whimper. Alex grins mercilessly, a raw, fascinated glint in his eyes as he watches me react to his touch.

"That feel good, *Argento?*" he whispers.

"Ye—*fuck*. Yes, it feels good."

He releases a pleased sigh. "Glad to hear it. Now what do you want? You want me to fuck you with my fingers?"

The charged words skate over my skin, inciting a very physical response from me. I tighten around Alex's fingers and he snarls, deep and low at the back of this throat. "Fuck me. Your body's giving me a resounding fuck yes." He grazes his mouth over mine, pausing to flick at my lip with the very tip of his tongue. "I'd like the words, though. I wanna hear you say it. So I know…"

Oh shit. How the fuck am I going to get *those* words out? I've come a long way since we started dating, but it's not exactly easy for me to say things like that. Alex's mouth is filthier than a sailor's, but I'm still figuring out how to voice what I want in no-nonsense terms. "I—" Fuck, it doesn't help that I'm so turned on right now, I can barely make my mouth work. "I want it, Alex. I want you to fuck me with your fingers. *Please*."

Pride shines in Alex's eyes. "Good girl. Brave girl." He peppers the side of my face with kisses as he slowly pumps his index finger inside me, and my mind goes utterly and completely blank. Fuck, that feels… that feels so fucking *good*. I struggle to keep myself upright as I wind my arms around his neck, bringing him down to kiss me.

This is really risky. It's late, and the streets are dark. There aren't many cars on the roads. I haven't seen anyone actually walking on the street since I parked the Nova, but the fact remains that Alex Moretti is fingering me in public, and I'm letting him do it. Anyone could see us. At any second, someone could walk around the corner and stumble across us, sprawled up against the wall, breathing heavily, Alex's hand working steadily between my legs. Best case scenario: embarrassment levels would be high. Worst case scenario: we'd be taken down to the sheriff's office for performing lewd acts in public.

I should put a stop to this. It'd be really fucking stupid if we got caught, but...

I can't make him stop. Fuck, I don't *want* him to stop.

Alex bites at my neck, teeth gouging into my skin, and I lean into the pain of it, relishing every second. His fingers work faster, expertly teasing wave after wave of pleasure from me, and I am a boneless marionette, entirely at his mercy as he puppets me, bringing me closer and closer to the edge.

"Oh, fuck. Fuck, Alex. *Please.*" I don't even know what I'm asking him so desperately for. For him to stop? For him to put me out of my misery and send me hurtling over the precipice of my orgasm? I can't decide. All I know is that both my body and my soul are on fire and any moment now I'm going to be lost to the flames.

"Let go," Alex rumbles into my hair. "Stop holding back. Give me everything, *Argento*. Let me have it."

God, I can't take it anymore. I can't fucking think. Moving quickly, I push him back far enough that I can rip open his leather jacket, hike up his t-shirt and unbutton his jeans.

"Whoa, Silver, sto—" His protest cuts off when I drive my hand down the front of his jeans and I take hold of him. The words come to a jarring halt on his lips. A deep, satisfying pleasure courses through my veins, racing around my body, when I see how badly my touch is affecting *him*. He wants me. He craves me just as badly as I crave him, and that knowledge makes me feel so fucking powerful. I'm quick but gentle as I reposition him, teasing his dick so that it's upright and the swollen head of his cock is protruding from the top of his jeans. Alex looks down at his erection, at my hand that's shoved down his boxers, exposing him, and a violent, urgent shudder racks his body.

"*Silver...*"

"Don't tell me not to. I want you to come, too."

"In your hand. Here, in the street?" he growls.

"*Yes.*"

"Fuck." His mouth crashes down on mine, and I surrender myself to the madness of the moment. I don't give a shit if someone walks around the corner anymore. I don't care if Sheriff Hainsworth himself rolls up in his squad car and slaps a pair of handcuffs on us. The only thing that matters is the heavy, pulsing need churning inside me. The frantic, animalistic need that grips me as Alex consumes me in his kiss. The dazed, tense look on his face when he pulls back, as I begin to work my hand up and down the length of his erection.

His free hand claws at my shirt; he fists the material, yanking it up around my neck, and the next thing I know he's pulling the cups of my bra down, exposing my breasts to the winter air, taking a painfully tight nipple into his mouth and sucking on it hard.

"Ahh! Shit! *Shit!*" I let my head fall back against the wall again, panting as he licks and bites, thrusting his fingers into me faster and faster, my pussy aching with pleasure. He's rigid in my hand, slick, pre-cum wetting his soft, silken smooth skin, making it so easy for my palm to glide up and down his shaft. Alex lets out a savage, raw snarl, angling his wrist, using his thumb to rub against my clit as he continues to drive his fingers inside me, and I can't fucking take it anymore.

"Fuck, Alex, I'm—you're gonna make me come," I pant.

"Good. Fucking do it. Do it. Come for me, Silver. Come on."

The orgasm isn't a slow, gradual build. It's instant, explosive, and takes me out at the knees. I can't keep quiet. I know my urgent, breathless cry of ecstasy echoes down Main Street, too loud, too obvious, but I can't bring myself to care. Alex has some sense about him, at least. He clamps his hand over my mouth, pressing his forehead against mine as I buck and shudder against his hand, riding out the most intense orgasm I've ever fucking experienced. I close my teeth around one of his fingers, clamping down, my eyes rolling back into my head, and Alex swears harshly under his breath.

My pulse is racing out of control. I close my hand tighter around his dick, shuttling my fist up and down his now fully exposed cock, and Alex hisses through his teeth. "God, Silver. Careful. If you don't stop—"

I'm not going to stop. My entire body is still tingling and numb from my climax, but the powerful implosion of it has subsided and it's *his* turn now. I grab hold of him with my other hand, using it to rub and squeeze the tip of his dick as I jerk him off, and Alex lets out a guttural, wordless, rasping sound. His eyes flicker between my face and the narrow gap between our bodies; he seems gripped by the sight of my hands working and teasing at him, and I realize very fucking quickly that the fascination on his face is a major turn on.

He falls forward, bracing himself against the wall with both hands over my head, baring his teeth as he stares down at what I'm doing. I quicken my pace, using my thumb to massage the fat bead of precum that's pearling against the head of his cock into his skin.

"Jesus Christ, Silver. Jesus…I'm—*fuuuuuck!*"

It's my turn to watch in fascination now, as thick ropes of come erupt from him, jetting over my hands and up the sleeve of my jacket. My shirt's still hiked up around my neck, my breasts still naked, and I gasp when another surge of the white, hot fluid lands on my bare stomach.

Alex shivers as I continue to work my hands up and down his length. I'm sticky, covered in his come, but I don't stop. Looking up, I find Alex's eyes closed, his lips parted, his head hanging between his shoulders as he tries to catch his breath. He jumps, too sensitive, hissing through his teeth when I rub my fingers over the tip of his cock again. "Jesus wept, you're trying to kill me," he huffs. "Stop, stop, I can't fucking take it."

I let him go, feeling rather proud of myself. It goes without saying that he makes me feel amazing, but knowing that I can make him this kind of crazy? Well…it's seriously fucking satisfying. Alex opens one eye, groaning when he catches sight of me. "Fuck, I'm sorry, *Argento.* I've made a fucking mess of you. No, no, don't touch anything. Stay still."

He puts himself away, fastening his pants with quick, sure movements, and then he's stooping at my feet, gathering snow in his cupped hands. I bite back a scream when he presses it against my stomach, using it to clean away his semen; Alex grins like the bastard that he is. "Sorry. Sorry, it's not funny, I swear." The way his eyes are dancing with amusement tells me that it is funny, though. The melted water runs down the front of my jeans, making me squeal, and Alex grabs the bandana hanging from his back pocket, using it to catch up the remaining wetness, drying me off with it, then slowly, veeeeery slowly he corrects my bra, straightening the fabric and guiding the cups back into place, covering my breasts. He fixes up my shirt next, and then collects more snow, reverently cleaning himself from my hands, apologizing again, softly and seriously this time, as he takes care of the mess he made of my jacket sleeve.

His dark hair falls into his face. His eyes flicker upward from under drawn brows, assessing me through his wavy, tumbled locks, and my heart summersaults. "That wasn't supposed to happen," he confesses. "I can't keep my hands off you. I have no idea how the fuck I'm supposed to restrain myself."

My fingers are wet and numb from the snow. I close them around Alex's hands, every part of me alive and singing even from this small contact between us. "Restraint is seriously overrated, Alessandro. Who needs it anyway?"

His full lips press together, holding back a smile as leans down to me, resting his cheek against my forehead. I nestle into him, winding my arms around him, beneath the thick, musty smelling leather of his jacket, and the universe and all its mysteries click into place. I don't know exactly how long the sun will burn for. I don't know how black holes work. I still don't know if there is life on other planets, but none of that's important anymore, because here, in Alessandro Moretti's arms, everything makes perfect sense anyway.

"Silver? Is that you?"

I whip my head up, pulse thumping everywhere at the sound of my name. Standing under the street light, eight feet away, Mr. Saxman from the convenience store—one of my father's high school friends— is standing stock still with a bulging brown paper bag in his arms. He's squinting into the shadows, hair dusted with snow, concern strewn across his face. I dig my fingers into Alex's back, horror coursing through me as I realize just how mortifying it really would have been if one of my father's friends *had* shown up a few minutes ago. Alex huffs out a breath of laughter into my hair, refusing to turn his head.

"Uh...hi, Mr. Saxman. How are you?"

His eyes crawl up and down Alex's back, presumably trying to figure out who I'm clinging to like a lost soul out here in the freezing cold night. He takes a step forward but then pauses, seeming to think better of it. "I'm good. Everything okay here?" His voice is sharp. Suspicious.

"Of course. Everything's perfect." Plumes of fog billow on my breath, catching in the yellowed glow thrown off by the street light. I mention nothing about the fact that I'm wrapped around a dark-haired guy in a leather jacket that Mr. Saxman has probably never seen before, and Alex still doesn't turn. He just hums into my hair—a contented, relieved sound that almost makes my brain short out.

"Okay, well...I don't mean to interrupt. It's too cold to be loitering around out here, though. Maybe you should think about heading on home?"

"Yes, Mr. Saxman. Don't worry, we were just about to leave."

"Glad to hear it." He heads off slowly down the high street, eyes still boring into the back of Alex's jacket, the fresh snow carpeting the sidewalk making stiff, creaking sounds beneath the soles of his boots.

Alex begins to laugh, his shoulders shaking as he plants a kiss against my temple. I pinch his side, making him yelp. "Jerk. You could have at least made eye contact with the guy. He would have been less suspicious if you'd smiled and introduced yourself."

Alex leans back, an eyebrow arched in disagreement. "That guy would have taken one look at me and decided I was trying to mug you or something, *Argento*. You know it. I know it. Better I left him guessing. Come on, let's get some coffee before the blood freezes in your veins."

TEXT MESSAGE RECEIVED:

+1(564) 987 3491: You're dead, bitch. I'm hack out your tongue and fuck your dirty, lying mouth.

4

SILVER

"I don't know. Maybe he's, uh…well. I mean, he's not exactly cute, is he? I s'pose you could say there was something…*charming* about him?" I am being seriously generous with my compliments right now, but my father looks mortally offended. He takes a step back in the hallway, folding his arms across his chest, frowning over the tops of his horn-rimmed hipster wannabe glasses at the subject of my concern. A small, black, furry creature stares balefully back up at him, baring its teeth, letting out a low, hostile growl.

"He's just confused is all," Dad says defensively. "He was locked up in a cage for months."

"Exactly. Which begs the question…don't you think he should be a little happier now that he's been liberated? He looks like he's gonna chew your eyes out. Don't—god, don't move. I think he's gonna lunge."

Dad gives me amused side-eye. "And here I was, thinking I'd raised a fearless, strong daughter who wasn't afraid of anything. He weighs fourteen pounds, Sil. I think I can take him."

I screw my nose up, partly to block the smell emanating from the small animal guarding the entrance to the kitchen like his very life depends on it, but also because I'm not all that sure my father *could* take him. "He's wiry, Dad. Like, *muscular*. He could probably jump from there and rip your throat out."

Dad tuts, shaking his head at me in a disappointed manner. "I'm seconds away from disowning you. That dog is the sweetest, kindest, gentlest little soul I've ever laid—*shit! Holyfuckingshit!* Did you see that? He fucking lunged! He fucking *did!*"

For one brief, brilliant moment, my father holds his hands to his throat like he really did think the dog was going to clamp its jaws around his neck and bite down. He drops his hands to his side as soon as he catches me smirking at him. "Listen. This is not my fault. You didn't see him at the pound. He was all sweet and doe-eyed, lying on his back, staring up at me from inside *his prison*," Dad stresses for effect. "I thought I was doing him a favor bringing him home with me. He didn't start displaying any of these murderous tendencies until I got him inside, out of the wind, and the front door was closed. Then it was like a switch flipped and he turned into this raging little psychopath. I can't get into my office, Silver. I'm gonna have to take him back to the pound first thing in the morning."

"Whatever you think's best," I reply, my voice light, my tone going up at the end.

"Cold, Silver. Real cold. The hell is wrong with you? There's no way he can go back to the pound. They kill dogs when people return them. Problem dogs. D'you want them to kill Nipper?"

"Nipper? You called him *Nipper*?"

"He's six years old. Someone else named him Nipper a long time ago. He's used to it now. I can't go around changing a dog's name just because it makes him sound..."

"Bitey?" I offer.

"Yeah, well. He hasn't actually bitten anyone. Yet. Not that I know of, anyway. They have to tell you that kind of stuff when you adopt a dog, right?"

I crouch down, rummaging in the bag of dog treats Dad bought for the savage little fucker, taking out a little bone-shaped morsel and gingerly holding it out to the dog. "What *is* he anyway? He looks like a miniature hippo with fur. A *lot* of fur."

"They didn't know," Dad admits. "They said they thought he was some sort of terrier. Maybe."

Nipper's quick, dark eyes dart to me, and he growls, exposing his teeth again. I toss the treat toward him and it lands at his feet. He skitters back, legs splaying in every direction as he scrambles to gain purchase against the hardwood, ears flat against his head as he turns tail and bolts, whimpering, into the kitchen. I groan, standing up straight again, dusting my hands off against my jeans. "I mean...are you sure it's even a *dog*? And why bother? We both know this is some weird attempt to lash out at Mom."

Dad rubs at the back of his neck, suddenly very focused on the light fitting above his head. "Jesus, I had no idea how dusty that thing had gotten. I think we're gonna need to get a cleaner soon, kiddo."

"Dad. I'm embarrassed for you. Your avoidance tactics need serious work. Just admit it. You got a dog because Mom's allergic to them and you want to make it as unpleasant here for her as possible."

"Your mother moved out well over a month ago, Silver. I never had a dog before because I *couldn't* have one. Now I *can* have one. I don't see anything wrong with that. I'm not trying to make it uncomfortable for her here. I'm not even thinking about her now. This isn't her home anymore. She has her own house. She can *not* have a dog there."

Fuck. I should have thought about it a little harder before bringing up Mom. After I sat down and told my parents about what happened to me at Leon's Spring Fling party, things got bad. Really, *really* bad. Mom was hysterical, and Dad... I've never seen him so furious before. He hasn't stopped being furious, either, since I still haven't told him the names of the boys who attacked and raped me in that bathroom. I wasn't ready to part with that specific piece of information then, and I'm still not ready to part with it. I just couldn't bear the thought of my father heading out into the night to find the monsters responsible for hurting me and hurting them back, because I saw that he wanted to. I saw the murderous look in his eyes, and I knew I needed to give him time to calm down before I handed over their identities.

Mom waited all of a week to sit down with Dad and confess that she'd been cheating on him with her boss for the past six fucking months. Later, after Dad had smashed the glass coffee table in the living room and mown down the neighbor's mailbox as he'd fled the house, she'd told me sadly that secrets had eaten our family alive and there was nothing left to do anymore but be honest with one another and see what could be repaired once all the smoke and the debris had cleared. She'd moved out that night and taken Max with her.

It was strange. She didn't even ask if I would go with her, as if she'd already known there wouldn't be any point in even posing the question. I was always going to stay with Dad, because Dad was my person and I was his. I don't know when my father and I formed our quirky little coalition, but now that Mom's gone and Max is only here on the weekends, I realize that it's kind of been Dad and me against the world for some time now. It's terrible to admit this, and I would never say it out loud, but...it doesn't really feel like all that much has changed.

It has for Dad, I'm sure. He woke up one morning, knowing his high school sweetheart loved him and the home they shared was a happy one. That evening, he found out his daughter had been hiding something monumentally horrible from him for months. And then, just to top it all off, his wife pulled him aside and told him she'd been fucking another guy behind his back.

That has to do something to a guy. My suffering, pain and hurt has made him feel weak and riddled with guilt, like he failed to protect and take care of me. Mom's betrayal has made him feel like half a man. He's doing a stellar fucking job of hiding it, but I know this is the lowest point in his life. If he wants to rescue a dog, even a dog as ornery and potentially rabid as Nipper, then who the hell am I to stand in his way?

I don't apologize for bringing up the subject of his cheating wife. I've learned over the past month that, when something bad happens to a community, to a person you love, it's all too easy to tiptoe through your days, cringing and apologizing as you trip over accidental references and difficult topics, and the act of constantly saying you're sorry becomes both exhausting to you and infuriating to the other person. Dad and I have driven each other to the point of madness with our apologies.

Instead, I thump him in the arm, nodding my head in the direction of the kitchen. "You think we could trap him in there if we form a pincer movement? You close the living room door, and I get the hallway?"

The color's already fading from Dad's face. "Why? Are we quarantining him in there and writing the kitchen off as a no-go zone? 'Cause I need to rescue the coffee maker if that's the case. I can survive without a lot of things but caffeine isn't one of them."

"I was actually thinking we could go to Harry's and order some tacos."

He scowls. "It's not Tuesday."

"You can eat tacos on other days of the week, Dad."

"Heresy."

"Don't be so miserable. It's time you had a shave. Time you left the house, too." I stand behind him, placing my hands against his shoulder blades, urging him toward the stairs.

"Nice try, kiddo. You'll recall that I was growing this beard *before* the apocalypse. I am not shaving."

"Damn."

He reluctantly climbs the bottom step of the stairs. "I'm not really feeling Harry's, Sil."

"Come on. It'll be fun. My treat."

"You do realize that I have more money than you. A lot more money. I can pay for my own two-dollar tacos."

"Which makes my offer to pay even more generous. God, will you stop resisting me!" I slap his shoulder, growling. "I need to get out of this house. It's starting to feel like a tomb. And, Dad, I didn't want to have to tell you this, but you're starting to smell real bad. If you insist on keeping the beard, then you've at least got to take a shower."

"I was considering becoming a hippy and wallowing in my own natural odor full time."

"Nice. That shouldn't damage your future dating prospects one little bit." My left hand is still on his back, so I feel the muscles in his shoulder tense. We haven't talked about what he wants to do next—if he's planning on giving things another shot with Mom, or if that's it, they're done, and he'll be filing for divorce. I honestly haven't been able to think about it. Sure, selfishly, things still feel pretty normal for me right now, but if my parents get a divorce, I don't know how that will color my view of the world moving forward. I don't really know who *I* would be in a world where my parents weren't the notorious *Cameron and Celeste* anymore.

At the end of the day, it doesn't really matter what I think. This is their thing. Their issue. Their life together. I'm old enough and mature enough to understand and accept that. Max, on the other hand…god, I have no idea how he's taking any of this. He must be so fucking confused. For an eleven-year-old, this whole mess must be frankly terrifying.

It's Max's twelfth birthday soon. It's always been our family tradition to take him to the aquarium over in Bellingham, but god knows what's going to happen now. Mom's definitely going to want to spend the day with him, and so is Dad. Are they going to end up fighting over him like he's some kind of pawn, to be used to hurt the other person? I really hope not. I couldn't bear to stand by and watch that happen.

If Mom and Dad do get a divorce, then at some point one of them is going to start dating again. Eventually, new people will be introduced into Max's life, people that just shouldn't be there, and he's going to have to grow up in this strange, alien childhood that I never had to endure. We are going to turn out very different people because of it, and that, to me, is the saddest thing in the world.

These thoughts all occur to me in one harrowing split second. Dad places a hand on the banister railing, turning around to face me, and when I see the look on his face, I get the feeling that the same thoughts all just occurred to him, too. If I could, I would ease the heavy burden he's carrying on his shoulders. I'd remove the frown that creases his brow every waking moment of his day. If someone could wave a magic wand and give me one shot at time travel, offering me the opportunity to go back and change just one thing, I wouldn't change what happened to me in Leon Wickman's bathroom. I would go back and find my mother the day before she first allowed herself to fall prey to her desires and sleep with her boss, and I would tell her about all of the hurt and pain she would cause if she didn't remember that she was a married woman.

"I don't think we need to worry about my future dating prospects," Dad says wearily. "Raleigh's a small town. I went to high school with most of the women here. I wouldn't date any of them even if they were single. None of them have changed since we were seniors, and they weren't particularly nice people back then. I don't suppose any of us were."

"Dad—"

"Screw it," he says loudly, slapping his hand against the banister railing. "This conversation just got really dark and depressing, didn't it? I *do* need to get out of the house. Maybe those tacos aren't such a bad idea after all. Give me twenty minutes and we'll head out." He turns and charges up the stairs before I can say anything else. Not that I wanted to continue the conversation, of course. It really did get dark and fucking depressing.

I manage to corral Nipper in the kitchen while Dad's upstairs getting ready, and I have the kitchen cordoned off, the dog safely secured inside, by the time he comes down dressed in a fresh, pressed button-down shirt and a clean pair of jeans. He looks like a brand-new person. A much happier person than the man who looked down at me on the staircase just now. He even manages a smile as he snatches up his worn red Converse from the shoe rack by the door and begins to jam them onto his feet.

"I'm not sure I'd call that appropriate footwear, Dad. The weather's not so great."

"Don't be such a baby. I've been wearing Chucks come rain or shine since the eighties. Pretty sure I'll be fine."

We're laughing together, joking around, arguing about which music was better, the eighties or the nineties, when Dad pulls the front door open and a piece of debris hurtles past the doorway.

"*Jesus!*" He bars the doorway with his arm, halting me from stepping forward.

The projectile—probably the best term for it—turns out to be one of the fence posts from the McLaren's yard next door...and it narrowly missed Dad's face. The staked end of the post is now buried in our front lawn, the post itself sticking out of the lawn at a weird angle, wobbling from the force with which it hit the ground.

There's at least four inches on fresh snow on the driveway, wet and slushy, thick as cement. In patches, the ground is visibly water-logged and muddy. When a blast of frigid, icy wind swirls around the porch, trying to find its way inside the house, Dad issues an unspoken retreat and shuffles us back so he can slam the door closed.

"Fine," he concedes. "I guess I'll find my site boots." Seconds after the words leave his lips, the lights in the hallway flicker out and die.

~

Me: Worried about you. Do you still have power? Ours is out.

Alex: Yep. Separate grid over here. In case you forgot, Salton Ash is a five-star trailer park.

Me: Dad and I are at the diner. Come meet us?
Alex: Doubt the wholesome Raleigh types would appreciate me bringing down the neighborhood. Have to work in a couple of hours anyway. Pick you up for school tomorrow?

Me:

Me: Yes, pls.

Alex: Silver?

Me: Yeah?

Alex: Ti Amo, Tesoro

Me: I know what that one means. And I love you, too.

In some small towns when the power goes out, the locals batten down the hatches and stay indoors, waiting out Mother Nature with their families, checking their storm lanterns, rifling in the kitchen drawers for batteries, borrowing scented candles from their bathrooms and making sure to open up the freezer door as infrequently as possible to avoid defrosting the food inside.

Not in Raleigh. For the most part, the people of Raleigh all band together, bringing whatever non-electrical entertainment they might have at home, from Scrabble boards, to decks of cards, to coloring books for the children, and everyone converges at Harry's. It's a community institution, and all are welcome. One year, Halliday's mom even brought a piñata she'd purchased in advance of Halliday's little brother's birthday, and the kids had had an impromptu party. They chose the songs they wanted to hear on the juke box, and danced and played until they were so tired they collapsed one by one to the diner's floor and slept, dropping like exhausted seven-year-old puppies.

As Dad and I adhere to Raleigh tradition, heading in the direction of the diner, the sky's so dark it almost looks like dusk is approaching. The horizon is a bruised, angry looking shade of purple. Even at the beginning of winter, the days are normally bright by eleven in the morning. Not today, though. Halfway to Harry's, the heavens grow even darker, and Dad has to turn on the van's fog lights as we cautiously complete the rest of the drive across town. Out of the windshield, swings in front yards rock and spin crazily, trees sway wildly, bowing too far for safety, and yet, despite the madness and all of the toppled-over trash cans, there's a stillness to the world. It feels abandoned, deserted, like the end of the world really did take place while Dad and I were holed up at the house and no one thought to tell us.

The parking lot at Harry's is full, so we have to leave the van on the next side street over. Dad links arms with me as we make our dash from the safety and warmth of the van toward the single story building blazing light out into the late morning gloom. I shriek at the cold wind that lances through my jacket and drives its way down the back of my shirt. The sound of my cry is ripped away by the wind so quickly that I don't even hear it.

"Cam! Silver! You made it!" Behind the counter, Harry's wife Kaitlyn is busy setting muffins out onto a large metal catering tray. She looks a little harried, her steel-grey hair falling loose from the normally neat and tidy bun on top of her head, but her eyes are bright and she's smiling from ear to ear. She lives for this stuff. So does Harry. It'd be easy enough for them to close up shop on a day like today. The diner invariably gets trashed by so many bodies crammed into such a small establishment, and no one pays for anything. It costs them money to host Raleigh's residents at the diner on bad weather days; any other small business owner would see that as more of an inconvenience than a blessing.

Kaitlyn and Harry are cut from a different cloth, though. Running the diner has never been about the bottom line for them. They've always kept their prices as low as possible in an effort to make sure that even the families who only have a little can afford to come and eat at their place every once in a while. And it's a point of a pride for them that people rally here. A point of pride that they've created a place where the people know they'll be safe and taken care of in times of need.

"Barely, Kate. By the skin of our teeth," my father replies to the old woman. "There's a transformer down on Ridgehurst by the looks of things. Power company's probably gonna take five hours to get to the damn thing. How's the generator holding up? You got enough gas?"

Kaitlyn winks at me, laughing. "He's a worrier, isn't he? The generator's fine. We have enough gas to keep it running for the next three days if needs be. Why don't you help yourselves to a coffee and find somewhere to sit? I'm gonna need some help in an hour or so, once Harry has lunch ready, if you'd like to pitch in."

"Of course."

The diner's busy, but it's not bursting at the seams just yet. We've arrived just in time. In an hour, there won't be any seats left at all, but for now I actually manage to score us our own booth. I slump against the padded back rest, groaning with relief as the first sip of the coffee Dad brought hits my lips and travels down my throat. Warmth spreads out across my chest, and the cold that sunk into the marrow of my bones outside finally begins to thaw.

Dad looks out of the window to his right, a soft smile suspended on his face, but his eyes seem distant. Sad. The chatter of our friends and neighbors surrounds us as they gossip and laugh together, but the contagious, lighthearted atmosphere inside the diner doesn't appear to have infected my father. My heart thumps painfully, so hard it feels like it's struggling to beat. I reach across the table and take his hand, giving it a reassuring squeeze, and he looks over at me. The smile spreads to his eyes, warming the sadness right out of his expression, but I'm no fool, and I know my father. He is not okay.

"Silver, I wanted to…I wanted to speak to you, but…I don't really know how. I'm not very good at this kind of stuff."

Ah, now this is a look I recognize, too. I let go of his hand, drawing back into my seat. A tightness spreads across my chest, fingers of panic clawing up my spine. He wants to talk about happened. He wants to ask again for the names of the boys who assaulted me. I can't —I don't think I can—

Thoughts burst inside my head like bubbles, popping before they have chance to fully form. I cannot talk to him about this. Not now. Not yet. I wish there was a way I could, but…

"Stop. I can see you shutting down already. I'm not—" He shakes his head, the muscles in his jaw popping. His frustration's plain as day. "I'm not going to ask you about *that*. I just want to know if you're happy, Silver. That's all. You seem like…" He drums his fingers against the table. "You seem like you're content enough. I hear you laugh. I see you smile. And all the while I'm thinking… fuck, I hope she's not pretending. I hope…she doesn't feel like she's dying inside, and she thinks she has to fake being happy to protect us from what happened to her. Because that...I couldn't bear that, Silver."

My instant response is to reassure him. To jump in with a promise that I'm fine, and that I'm perfectly happy these days. But he doesn't want to hear that. He wants the truth from me, and I owe him that much. I've kept so much from him for so long that imparting this small piece of honesty seems vital now. I clear my throat, leaning my temple against the window next to me; the glass is cold and spackled with condensation, but I barely even notice as I consider my father's question.

"Some mornings, I wake up...and I can feel a pair of hands closing around my throat. It's like the fear rises up inside me when I'm asleep and there's nothing I can do about it. I don't have nightmares about what happened anymore, but occasionally I think the truth of all that violence and panic catches up with me when I'm unconscious and it just...festers. And when it's like that and I wake up, I can sometimes bring it all with me into the waking world, and...it's enough to make me feel like I'm going to fucking die."

My father's head drops. His eyes are cast down into his coffee mug but I can read the devastation on him. These are things he never thought he'd hear me say, and it's killing him to hear me admit the hard truth.

"But when I wake up like that, Dad...that feeling doesn't last long. It takes less than a minute for me to remember how to breathe again, and then..." I duck down so that I'm in his field of vision, so he can see that I'm smiling and that it's genuine. "Then, I remember that it's all over and done with, and it's in the past. Yes, it's hard to be at school a lot of the time. And yes, there are moments when I'm so fucking angry that I feel like I'm going to explode. But there are far more moments, when I'm with you or I'm with Alex, when nothing affects me whatsoever. I feel invincible half the time now, and that? That feels great. I'm not saying that I'll ever be able to forget what was done to me, or that I'll just get past it and there'll come a day when I don't even think about it anymore. That'd be a lie.

"What happened to me...it *is* an injury. My body healed from it, but I think the scar of it will always remain inside me. But a scar is proof of healing. A scar is a testimony to strength. I'm not ashamed of it anymore. It's a part of me, and I'm slowly figuring out how to accept all of those different, separate parts of myself, no matter how ugly or twisted they might be, because they make me who I am, right? I am okay, Dad. I promise. When you hear me laugh, when you see me smile, it *is* real. It *is* the truth. Always. Okay?"

Dad leans back in his seat, resting the coffee cup against his chest, propping it up against his solar plexus. His hair's much darker than mine. His eyes are dark, too. It used to hurt me so fucking much that I didn't look more like him. It never seemed right to me that I ended up looking so much like Mom, with her hair color and the same blue-grey eyes, the same shaped face even, with the same slightly upturned nose. I always felt as though, if I looked more like him, then I would *belong* to him more, somehow. I don't feel that way anymore. I know I belong to him, like I know the sun is going to rise in the east and set in the west. I don't need to see his eyes staring back at me whenever I look in the mirror, because I've realized I want to be like him in other, more important ways.

He's kind, and he's strong. The man can do basically anything he sets his mind to. He's relentless when he decides he's going to accomplish something. He'd do anything to help someone if they needed him. He knows how to really listen when someone is speaking, and not just wait for his turn to speak. I wasn't born with any of these qualities coded into my genetics, but my father shows me every day that there are choices I can make that will result in me being a better fucking human being because of it.

I already know it, have already felt it for years now, but I'm proud as fuck that he's my old man. I think, from time to time, that he might be proud to have me as a daughter, too. This sneaking suspicion is confirmed when he speaks again. "You are one remarkable young woman, Silver Parisi. You know that?" he tells me.

"Of course," I reply primly, giving him a little seated bow. "I'm one in a million."

"You should never have had to deal with any of that shit on your own. I can't tell you how sorry I am that you thought you couldn't come to me. I'm seriously disgusted that neither your mom nor I noticed things had changed with you. Neither of us will be winning a 'parent of the year' award anytime soon. That was just fucking disgraceful."

"It's okay, Dad. I get it. I might tease you about being old, but I know you're still young. You want a life for yourself outside of just being someone's Dad. You're entitled to that. You were working on your book. Mom was—"

Mom was busy having an affair and fucking the shit out of her boss.

I shudder, closing my eyes. "It doesn't matter what Mom was doing. I am okay now, and that's all that matters, right?"

Dad shifts in his seat, watching me for a moment. He drains what's left of his coffee and sets his mug down on the table between us. "It's because of him, isn't it? Moretti? *He's* the reason why you're okay."

"Oh, lord."

He smirks. "What?"

"I really don't want to talk about Alex with you."

"Why not?"

"When a girl has a conversation with her father about the guy she's seeing, things inevitably jack knife and take a turn for the worse. I can't think of anything more disturbing than you trying to give me a safe sex talk right now."

He laughs—one single, solitary bark of laughter—and I realize it's the first time I've heard that sound in what seems like months. It's a relief to know he's still capable. "Silver, I was seventeen not that long ago. Feels like it was last week, for Christ's sake. I'm not going to give you the safe sex talk. I'm gonna trust that you're being smart, and we're gonna pretend like neither of us actually even said the word 'sex' out loud. I only want to know if he's made things better for you, Sil. 'Cause if he has…then I can only be grateful to the guy."

I sit very still, staring down at my hands, thinking.

Thinking about Alex Moretti.

How can I explain to my father that Alex hasn't just made things better for me? That's he's *changed* them entirely? How can I tell him that I know I've found a missing piece of my soul and I never want to be apart from him without sounding like an infatuated, simpering teenaged idiot? Do I even know the words to describe the swelling, rising, euphoric sensation in my chest whenever Alex simply *looks* at me, or the way I feel deeply, fundamentally, intrinsically *safe* whenever I find myself wrapped up in his arms?

There's just too much to say on the topic of Alex Moretti...so I keep things simple. "Yes. It is," I answer. "In a way, it's because of Alex that things are better for me. He's...*mine*," I say quietly.

"He's *yours?*"

I can't decide if Dad looks like he's about to laugh at my stupid claim, or if he's about to yell at me for being moronic enough to think the world begins and end with a boy from high school. Bracing, I wait to see which version of him I'll end up with, flinching a little, but Dad neither laughs nor ridicules. "Okay, kiddo," he says simply. "I know how that feels."

God. The poor guy. That's how he felt about Mom. I sigh, turning to watch the snowflakes streak past the diner's window, cringing at the sight of the bundled-up figures hunched against the cold, hurrying down the street toward the hardware store.

"You looking for him?" Dad asks quietly. "You think he's going to show up?"

Slowly, kind of sadly, I shake my head. "He doesn't know Raleigh well enough. And Raleigh doesn't know him well enough, either. Not everyone's as badass as you, Dad. People are judgmental assholes sometimes. I don't think he feels welcome."

"You should invite him," Dad says over the top of his coffee mug.

"Oh, I already have." I smile ruefully. "I think it would take five personal invitations from five other members of Raleigh to convince my boyfriend he was wanted here. And even then he *still* probably wouldn't come."

5

ALEX

Me: I miss you.

Me: I need you.

Me: I fucking want you.

It's seven in the morning, still dark outside, and I've typed the same message to Silver at least fifteen times, asking her to come over. She'll still be asleep, curled up in her nice warm bed, but if I could have my way, I'd disturb her slumber and ask her to come all the way across town just to see me. Pretty fucking selfish, I know. Which is why I deleted the messages I typed out, grumbling under my breath each time, groaning at the fact that I can't get the thought of her out of my head and I keep picturing her in the little shorts she wears to bed. I'm basically about to explode.

It's fucking freezing in the trailer, like sub-zero arctic fucking temperatures, which would usually be enough to make my dick forget how to function and have my balls retract up inside my goddamn stomach, but not this morning. Nope, this morning my raging boner is impervious to the cold. It's demanding some hard-core attention and there's absolutely nothing I can do about it.

I'm done jerking off. I haven't touched myself since before I went and found Silver up at the cabin. All right, well…I may have been feeling a little sorry for myself in the hospital after having major surgery to remove the bullet that was lodged in my chest. I might have jerked off then, just the once, but I figure that didn't count since I'd nearly just fucking died and all. Fucking sue me. Apart from *that*, I haven't made myself come.

I've been saving all of my pent-up sexual energy for Silver, and holy fuck has it been worth it. At this point, I'm a professional at delaying my own orgasm; I can hold off forever if needs be, and I take great pleasure in doing just that. I've waited for her. Cultivated the patience of a fucking saint. I've kept my hands to myself and I've played it cool. It hasn't been fucking easy holding back, but there's something truly bitter sweet about denying myself and making sure it's Silver who comes to me for attention.

That way, the release is so much fucking greater when it comes, but I'm also never second guessing myself. If we have sex, it's because she's wanted it. There's never been any doubt. She's made the first move. She's crawled for it on her hands and her knees because she's wanted it so fucking bad, and I know without a shadow of a doubt I haven't coerced her into anything simply because *I'm* fucking horny.

Fog plumes on my breath, clouding above my head as I lie in bed, staring up at the bedroom ceiling. I contemplate getting up so I can turn on the heating *and* get a fire going in the wood burner, but the prospect of throwing back the covers is just too much to fucking handle right now, so I remain bundled up, trying to convince myself that I'm a good guy and I should *not* text Silver.

My phone buzzes against my chest underneath the blankets less than a second later, and the salacious, hungry part of me crows with delight: it's from Silver. Who else would be messaging me at this time in the morning? And if she's awake…then would it really be so bad if I suggested she drive her fine ass over here immediately?

I bite my bottom lip, riddled with anticipation as I check the screen of my cell phone…and then I see the name at the top of the text and curse like a fucking sailor. It isn't from her after all.

Monty: You still got the bag?

I'd barely made it home the other night. The roads were hazardous, and the driving snow ended up blowing directly into the Camaro's windshield, making it almost impossible to see where the fuck I was going. It came down so thick and fast, I couldn't even see the road after a while. It's a miracle I didn't wind up wrapped around a street lamp, but the St. Christopher around my neck must have been working overtime or something because I made it back to meet Silver in one piece. Monty called just as I'd arrived home later, wanting me to wait to hand off the bag, so I'd been spared the need to go out into the cold for a second time in the early hours of the morning and I'd gone straight to bed. I didn't see him at the Rock during my shift last night, so I've been sitting on the thing ever since.

Me: Yeah, it's in the trunk of my car.

Monty: I'll send someone over for it this afternoon.

Me: Copy that.

He was sweating the night he'd told me I had to go out to Bellingham. The bag had seemed vitally important. Now he's not planning on retrieving it until this afternoon? Doesn't make much sense, but whatever. Not my business. I'm just glad he didn't say he needs me to drive it over there right now.

It's almost time to throw my ass in the shower and get ready for school. I'm going to have to get up in a minute anyway, but for now the warm cocoon of my bed is demanding that I sta—

My thoughts grind to a halt at the sound—a clicking, scraping sound, off to the right, in the living room. A metallic grating noise that doesn't belong in the silence of the early winter morning inside of my trailer. It's a quiet sound at first but grows increasingly louder as I slowly get up out of bed and pick up the handle of the woodcutter's axe I keep beside the bed.

My chest and my feet are bare, but there's no time to find socks and a shirt. Someone's trying to bust the lock on the trailer door, and I'm about to give them an epic fucking headache. Poor, stupid son of a bitch. Should have done a little research before deciding to pick *my* trailer to break into. The blinds at the windows in the living room are drawn; outside, dawn is breaking over Raleigh, but the weak morning light is barely enough to lighten the gloom, and I almost crack my shin on the corner of the coffee table as I tiptoe around it.

Pausing, I wait by the door, axe held high over my head, waiting…

The brass handle slowly turns…

I rip the door open, already swinging, teeth bared, anger firing in my veins. But when I see who's standing there on my front doorstep, eyes wide in horror, it takes every ounce of strength I possess to angle the axe's blade to the side, driving the honed metal into the door frame.

Silver's father opens his mouth, eyes locked on the axe now buried in the door jamb next to his head. He inhales a long, seemingly endless breath. When he's let it out, he turns to look at me and arches an eyebrow. "And a good morning to you, too, Moretti."

Oh…fucking *shit*.

I wrench at the axe handle, ripping it from the doorframe, not knowing if my weak ass smile should be nervous, awkward, sheepish, or all three. "Mr. Parisi. Morning."

He folds his arms across his chest, huffing down his nose. "Is this how you greet everyone who pays you a visit, or just the fathers of the girls you're sleeping with?"

Okaaay. Not too sure how to respond to *that* one. "It's how I greet people who appear to be breaking into my place?" I offer, my voice trailing up at the end into a question. Much safer to just avoid the comment about me fucking his daughter. Acknowledging *that* comment can only lead to disaster.

Now it's Daddy Parisi's turn to look a little awkward. "Yeah, well, I knocked but there was no answer, so…"

"No, you didn't."

"I'm sorry?"

"If I heard you shuffling around out here, screwing around with the lock, you don't think I'd have heard you actually trying to get my attention?"

He stares at me, dark eyes boring into mine. A moment later, he shrugs, shoving his gloved hands into the pockets of his thick down jacket. "Okay. Fine. You're right. I didn't knock. I was trying to break in. I just figured…"

I'm paying attention. Like, *really* paying attention. I've met Mr. Parisi a number of times since the night I sat down next to Silver and she told her parents that she was raped. I've been polite, respectful and I've made damn sure I never let things get too far with Silver under his roof. It would have been pretty fucking shitty to have had him walk in when I was balls deep in his pride and joy. All in all, I've been a model boyfriend, and he's been…well, he's been Mr. Parisi. Quick with the self-effacing jokes. Smart. Quiet, as a rule. Observant —I know when I'm being watched.

I haven't really been able to get a solid read on the guy, to figure out who he really is, but never in a million years did I suspect he was the type of guy to break and enter. This is a new, highly interesting version of Mr. Parisi that I'm keen on meeting face-to-face.

He grimaces, kicking the toe of his rubber boot against the concrete step. "I wanted to see for myself what kind of shit you've got going on, Moretti. Silver…she's serious about you. And I know how things are for a guy like you. I wanted to see if there was a stripper in your bed. I wanted to see if there were needles sitting on your counter tops. I didn't want to give you any time to hide anything that might be damning."

Okay. Fair enough. So, I might not appreciate the judgement, or the mistrust, or the invasion of my fucking privacy, but I respect his motives. He's here looking out for Silver. He's doing his job as a father. Letting my head drop back, I narrow my eyes, studying the guy. He's nothing like any of the bastards I've found myself stuck with in the past. I don't get alarm bells with Mr. Parisi. If anything, I think he's pretty cool, which is weird since I decided a long time ago that parenthood, with immediate effect, turns people into raging assholes.

Taking a step back, I hold the door open, jerking my head inside. "Come on, then. Take a look. I'll make sure to keep my hands where you can see 'em."

He looks unsure, slightly annoyed and tired. Poor fucker probably hasn't been sleeping much. I guess insomnia's a reasonable side effect of infidelity and rape. "You think I won't call your bluff?" he asks flatly.

"I'm not bluffing. Come in. I'm three seconds away from dying of hypothermia." It's fucking true, too. I don't have a clue what the official word on the weather is, but it's still snowing—at least another fifteen inches must have come down overnight and from the grey, ominous, brooding morning that's breaking now, it doesn't look like it's gonna stop snowing any time soon, either. Definitely not the kind of temperatures you want to stand around in, not wearing a shirt.

Mr. Parisi grunts as he climbs up the step and enters the trailer. I grab the t-shirt I was wearing last night from the back of the couch, quickly throwing it on, pretty pleased that I've been able to cover and tidy up a little at the same time. The trailer's by no means spotless, but I keep if fairly clean and in order. Gary, fucking psycho that he was, would try and knock out a couple of teeth if he found my corner of the basement in disarray. When I first moved in here, into my own space, where I could do whatever the fuck I wanted without conse- quence, I trashed the place on purpose. It felt like I'd won some sort of war every time I walked in through the door and had to step over mountains of dirty clothes and empty beer bottles in order to reach the couch. Wasn't long before I was back in the habit of tidying up after myself, though. As it turned out, living in filth and chaos is pretty miserable.

Mr. Parisi casts a dark look around, taking everything in. His expression is blank, concealing his thoughts as he walks around the perimeter of the living room, scanning the book shelves, the side table where I keep the record player, the coffee table, and the little end tables by the couch that I snagged from a yard sale last summer.

"No ashtrays. You don't smoke?" Mr. Parisi asks.

I prop myself up against the wall, raising my eyebrows. "Occasionally. Only when I've had a beer or two. Never around Silver."

"So, you drink, then."

I give him a wry look. "I'm seventeen. I work at a bar. Yes, I drink."

He flares his nostrils. "Around Silver?"

"Yes. But never in excess. Never so I can't take care of her properly."

"Does *she* drink?"

I laugh softly under my breath. "I think I'm holding up pretty well under this impromptu inspection, but I'm not going to narc on your daughter. You know Silver. You know who she is, right?"

He glares at me, jaw working. "Of course I do. She's a good girl. I trust her."

"Then you don't need to be asking me questions like that. You know she drinks, but you also know she's smart. She doesn't get herself into dangerous situations or do shit you need to worry about. Not after what happened…"

An anguished flicker of pain flares in the man's eyes. I see my own feelings reflected in his face as he pivots to face me; it's all there, the fury, the anger, the fiery need for vengeance. "She still won't tell me who hurt her, y'know. She won't give me their names," he says quietly.

"Yeah. I—I guess she's just handling it the only way she feels she can."

"But *you* know who did it, don't you?"

"Mr. Parisi…"

"Why would she tell *you* and not *me*?"

I open my mouth, relying on the fact that I usually know what to say in most situations, but this time I don't. I grasp for an answer to give to him, one that makes sense and might even make him feel better, but that answer just isn't there. "I honestly don't know. Maybe...she's just worried about you. Your family's been through a lot of shit lately, right?"

He blows out a hard breath, grinding his teeth together. "That doesn't matter. It shouldn't matter what's going on in our lives. She should know that she can count on me to be there for her no matter what."

I have zero experience dealing with parents who actually care about their kids. Honestly, seeing the raw emotion on Mr. Parisi's face is freaking me the fuck out; I have no idea how to react to it. I doubt he'd be stoked if I waltzed up to him and gave him a hug, so I do the only thing I can think of and pretend I haven't noticed the way his eyes are shining a little too brightly. "She knows you care about her. She knows you're there for her. She came to you in the end, when she was ready. She'll give you the missing pieces of the story, too. You just need to be patient with her."

Mr. Parisi seems to think on this. I'm stunned when the guy sighs heavily and collapses down onto my sofa. I've been waiting for him to charge through the rest of the trailer, continuing on his mission to track down all of my illusive hookers and blow, but it appears that mission has been abandoned for the time being.

"You love her," he says. A statement.

I set my jaw, lifting my chin. "Yes."

Mr. Parisi glances at me out of the corner of his eye and laughs bitterly under his breath. "No need for the posturing, Moretti. I'm not here to tell you to stay away from her. I do want to know one thing, though."

"All right. Ask."

"If you love her, then..." His voice cracks. He has to take a second before he can finish his sentence. "What did *you* do to those motherfuckers when you found out what they'd done to her?"

Fuck.

It feels like he's just landed a right hook right to my gut.

I growl, banging the back of my head against the wall behind me. "Nothing. I didn't do a single thing."

"*What?*" Silver's father looks like he's about to leap up from the sofa and fasten his hands around my throat. I wouldn't blame him, either. "She trusted you with that information…and you did *nothing*? How the hell can you say you love her if—"

"She made me promise."

"I don't give a shit! If you care about someone—"

"If you care about someone and you make them a promise, you keep it no matter what. How many promises have *you* made to Silver? And how many of them have you broken? Because I've only made the one so far, and I don't intend on breaking it. Not Ever. She made me swear to her that I wouldn't use violence against them or break the law. She tied my fucking hands. Right now, all I can do is bide my time. There *will* be justice for the people who hurt her, believe me. I'm not going to just let them get away with it. But I've earned your daughter's trust. It's the most valuable fucking thing in the world to me, and there's no way in hell I'm breaking it."

The poor fucker's taken his gloves off, and his hands are balled into fists on the tops of his knees. I can see it written all over him: this man needs to hit something. Or someone. He's been through hell and back recently and he's had no fucking release from any of it. If he doesn't hit me right here and now, then it'll only be a matter of time. At some point, he's going to snap, he's going to hit *something*, and when he does there are going to be some real fucking fireworks.

He's a tall guy, the same height as me. I doubt he's really worked out in a long time, but he's fit. In relatively good shape. I'm sure I'd be able to take him in a fight, but it's a really bad fucking idea. I can't let things get that far. Silver would be devastated if I ended up trading blows with her old man, but more than that, I bear him no ill will. Fighting with him wouldn't do anyone any real favors, even if it did help him temporarily blow off some steam.

Time to enter peacemaker mode, then.

I sigh, pushing away from the wall and crossing the living room to join him on the couch. He flinches when I sink down next to him, as if I've suddenly jarred him from a waking nightmare that had taken him over and clouded his mind. His fists unclench reflexively.

"When I was ten, I was staying at this group home for boys. It was bad there," I tell him. "We slept in dorms. I can't really remember how many kids were in my dorm but there was a pretty big group of us.

Must have been between fifteen and twenty kids or something. I can't remember when it started, but there was this guy who used to come into the dorm at night and take one of the kids away with him. The boy had been dropped off at the home when he was six. Hadn't even known his own name, so one of the nicer female attendants decided to call him George. This one guy, Mr. Clayton? He took a shine to George. At one in the morning, nearly every morning, George would take Mr. Clayton's hand as he pulled him out of his bed, and he would pad barefoot with him in silence out of the dorm—"

"I don't think I want to hear this story, Alex."

Unblinking, I stare at the clock by the television, waiting for the bright, glowing number five on the end of the digital display to change to a six. "You're right. I don't need to go into details," I mutter. "We both know what was happening to George. I knew back then, too. I convinced myself I didn't. Told myself George was being shown special treatment. That Mr. Clayton preferred George to all of us other boys, and he was sneaking him out in the middle of the night to give him candy and let him watch T.V. in his private apartment instead of in the drafty, damp home room where the rest of us were sometimes allowed to hang out. I've felt guilty about that for years. That I didn't stand up and say something that might have stopped Mr. Clayton creeping into our dorm like some sinister fucking shadow after midnight."

"You were a child, Alex."

"I was *afraid* is what I was. I'm not afraid anymore, though. I'm not hiding under my bedsheets, pretending to be asleep now, okay? I swear to *you* that I'm not gonna let those pieces of shit get away with what they did to your girl. The wheels are already turning. It might take a little while, but a day of reckoning is coming, I can promise you that."

The man stares at the clock on the wall, too. He seems to simmer on what I've just said for a very long time. Eventually, he says, "I suppose I'm just going to have to be satisfied with that then, aren't I?"

"For the time being, yes."

He sucks in a long, slow breath, closing his eyes, and it's as though a wave of relief has just washed over him. "Fine. But I'm her father,

Alex. I should be the one carving up those sick little fuckers. It's my *right*."

I don't respond to that. He needs to sit in it for a second, to ruminate on what he's just said without me adding anything to it. Eventually, he grimaces, shaking his head. "That was a stupid thing to say. I have no right to anything. It didn't happen to *me*. I know that. I'm sorry."

"Hey. No need to be sorry, man. You're fucked up. You're fucked up because of what went down. I'm fucking up because of it, too. Ironic, really, that Silver's the only person with any real *right* to anything, and yet she's the least fucked up out of all of us."

He smiles sadly, his eyes roaming around the room again, taking everything in for a second time. He's not pretending to look for drugs now. He's just…seeing the place. "She's always been like that," he says absently. "Really well put together. Mentally. Even when she was a kid, she handled every upset, big and small, with this weird kind of understanding and…just this resilience that always blew us away. She's so damn strong. I think that's why her mother and I kind of forgot we were her parents for a second there. Before all of this, it hadn't occurred to me that Silver might actually *need* anything from me in a very long time. She's just so unshakeable."

She's broken down in front of me before. Just that once, outside the cabin. I understand what he means when he says that she's unshakeable. I know how people tick. I can see when they're about to snap, and I never thought Silver might break down the way she did. I went up to that cabin in the middle of the night, and it didn't occur to me for one second that it might be a bad idea, because she'd been vulnerable and hurt before. Because she hadn't known I was coming, and she might have been scared by an unexpected vehicle pulling up out of the dark, down that long, winding driveway. I'd just assumed it would be fine, because she seemed…*so well put together*, as her father just said.

A soft, rushing sound disturbs the silence as an avalanche of snow slides from the pitched eve above the window behind us and lands with a *whoompf* outside. "They tell us all kinds of stories when we're kids, about us being stronger than them," I say quietly. "Women. Truth is, we're the weak ones. We need to think we're protecting them to protect *our* egos. Meanwhile, they're the ones keeping us together half the time."

Mr. Parisi nods slowly, bathed in the watery, insubstantial light of the morning that's snuck its way through a crack in the blinds and is hitting him square in the face. "You are righter than you know. We're forever underestimating them, aren't we?"

We sit in silence for a while, both deeply lost in our thoughts. When the clock by the television reaches seven forty, I sit up, rubbing awkwardly at the back of my neck. I've never had to kick my girlfriend's father out of my place before. "I'm gonna have to get ready for school, Mr. Parisi."

He blinks rapidly, looking a little stunned. "Jesus, I'm sorry. I was a million miles away. I forgot... No school today. Half of the faculty are snowed in. The storm's going to get worse this afternoon. They're saying tomorrow's officially going to reach blizzard status. Coldest temperatures recorded in the last twenty years."

"Shit."

"Yeah. *Shit*. Get some things together. Enough for a couple of days. If we head back now, we might be able to grab some supplies at the store before everything shuts down."

"I'm sorry. Get some things together?"

Mr. Parisi groans halfheartedly, getting to his feet. "Well, I promised myself, didn't I. I swore, if I didn't find you over here in bed with some other girl and there was no hypodermic hanging out of your arm, I'd take you back home with me. Only until the storm passes, that is," he adds quickly.

"I don't...I still don't get it. *Why?*"

"Well," he says slowly. "Silver said something yesterday about you that made me think. And I know just how fucking miserable living in a trailer can be if they're not weatherproofed."

He means well, I know he does, but I can't help but be a little offended. Heat rises up the back up of my neck, burning the way embarrassment and shame are wont to do. "I've taken care of this place. See for yourself. Watertight. No drafts. It'll be blazing hot in here once I've—"

"Alex, Alex, whoa, whoa, whoa. I didn't mean anything by it. I know you're capable. I can see with my own two eyes that you're managing perfectly fine here by yourself. What I should have said...*fuck*." He huffs. "I'm sorry. What I should have said is that it sounds like most of us are getting snowed in for the next few days. And I know how much it would suck to be snowed in by yourself. And I know how happy it would make my daughter if you were snowed in with *her*. So...Christ. There's no need to make this harder than it already is, okay?"

The heat, along with my anger subsided the second he told me he knew that I was capable. Now, I'm just a little entertained by this whole series of events. He's inviting me, in a stilted, roundabout way, to go hang out at their place so I won't be alone. Part of me wants to laugh at the absurdity of it—I've been alone most of my fucking life. What's a couple more days, shut off from the outside world?—but the rest of me is kind of fucking numb. No one's ever come for me before. Shown up to take me away, so I'll be safe, and warm, and around other people. I don't really know what to do with that.

I get up, wondering if I even have a bag big enough to gather three days' worth of clothes inside. "Uh, thank you, Sir. That's very kind..."

Silver's father rolls his eyes, exasperated. "For the love of god, don't call me Sir, Moretti. That sounds absolutely fucking ridiculous. Just call me Cam, for Christ's sake."

6

————————————————

SILVER

The house is silent as the grave when I wake up. It's strange to lie beneath the covers with my eyes closed, hearing absolutely nothing. Not too long ago, I'd have been burying my head under my pillows, trying to block out the chatter of the television in the living room, and Max's tuneless, obnoxiously loud singing in the bathroom down the hall, while Mom and Dad hurled a volley of shouted questions back and forth at one another downstairs.

I remain still, eyes closed, trying to gauge what time it is without checking the Mickey Mouse watch resting on my nightstand, and a heavy, regretful burn settles over me, taking root in my chest. I used to be frustrated as hell by all the early morning noise and commotion, especially on the weekends when I was supposed to be able to sleep in, but now the silence that hovers in the empty rooms of this house feels almost deafening.

How did this even happen? Were there signs that things were falling apart, right before they disintegrated, and no one fucking noticed? Could my parents have done more to love one another? Could *I* have done more to keep us all together?

These questions plague me more and more; it hasn't escaped me that Mom began her illicit affair with her boss one month after I was attacked at Leon's party. I was sullen during that month. Quiet, withdrawn and scared. My fear hadn't manifested itself in the way it might have in other teenagers. I got really, *really* angry. I lashed out. I refused to listen to or obey simple requests. I fought with my Mom over every single little thing, roaring at her whenever she opened her mouth to say something, and in turn she snapped and sniped at me, grounding me day after day for my insolence. It was a *bad* month. If I hadn't been so difficult, would she have gone looking for comfort in the arms of another man? Would she and Dad have emerged through the other side of whatever rough patch they were going through and been fine if I hadn't been so unmanageable?

These 'ifs' serve no real purpose, I know. Life's one big spiderweb of decisions, actions, cause and effect, one domino after another toppling, knocking the next one down, then the next, then the next. Trying to unravel what would have happened if one small thing in the Parisi household had been different is not only impossible but futile; the past is set in stone and there's no changing it now, no matter how badly I might want to go back.

I throw my duvet over my head, fully aware that it's still snowing outside. I can *feel* the weight of the sky bearing down on the house. It's probably been dumping all night, which isn't the best. Getting to school is a hair-raising experience on heavy snow days, and—

DING!

Shit. My cellphone buzzes on the night stand next to my bed, disrupting the silence. I start, nearly jumping out of my damn skin, but then a slow, secret smile spreads across my face. I have no clue what the official time is, but I do know it's early. There's only person who'd be texting me at this time in the morning, and a message from Alex is definitely worth opening my eyes for.

Blearily, I prop myself up on one elbow, blinking rapidly, giving myself a second to accustom myself to the grey, weak morning light before I reach over and pick up my cell. I'm disappointed when I see the message isn't from Alex after all, though. The number on the screen isn't even saved in my contacts. I rub at my eyes as I click on the blue text box, opening up the message.

+1(564) 987 3491: Stupid lying bitch. Why don't u just fucking kill urself.

Oh.

That was stupid of me. There *is* one other person who'd text me at this time in the morning. Not Jake. Jake wouldn't be so stupid. He'd never leave hard evidence of his hatred, that could possibly be traced back to him. But for the past six weeks, *someone* has been sending these messages to me, making my phone chime more and more frequently. And I haven't said a word about them. I've ignored them, or tried my best to anyway, but they're becoming increasingly more hateful.

Stupid...lying...bitch....

Why don't u just fucking kill urself.

I cover my mouth, not blinking, staring at the screen, and for a long second I think I might be about to burst into tears and let out a furious scream at the same time—the conflicting emotions feel like they're going to rip me in two.

I was such a fucking fool. After the shooting, I allowed myself to forget. Raleigh was, and still is gripped in a fog of grief. My fellow classmates have been walking around in a daze, trying to remember how to be carefree teenagers again when there are still bullet holes in the plastered walls, and reminders of violence lurk down every corridor and hallway. People were too distracted to make life hard for me, and I became complacent, daring to lift my head and look around. I allowed myself to believe I was no longer a target for hatred and cruelty, and it was stupidest fucking thing I could have done.

And then I got the first text message.

People don't forget. People don't move on. People aren't intrinsically good, no matter how badly I want them to be. High school is a

Battle Royale, a fight for survival, and no one stays their hands for long. In order to make it through the experience unscathed, people will hurt and cut and bite and kick at anyone who appears weaker than them in order to get ahead. And to the students of Raleigh High, I am the easiest fucking target there is.

I tuck my knees up under my chin, a wave of sadness rippling over me as I stare at the phone lying there on the mattress two feet away. Sadness, quickly morphing to anger. So many people died when Leon walked into Raleigh and opened fire. We were taught a hard, painful lesson...but it seems some people still haven't learned. People fight back. When you corner an injured animal, eventually it kicks and bites back even harder, and tragic things happen.

I'm done ignoring these messages. I don't plan on participating in this vicious cycle of cruelty and short-sightedness. I just fucking *won't*. I'm done bowing my head and pretending I don't notice them staring. Pretending I don't hear the awful, sickening things they whisper about me as I walk to class. I am done *taking* this. I'm not going to hide from it anymore, or let them get away with it. I'm going to face whatever abuse is hurled at me head-on, and I'm not going to back down. Because...fuck them. Life itself is a fragile, tenuous thing. It can be taken away or snuffed out at any moment. If I have another twenty-three thousand days left on Earth or only another one hundred, I'm not going to allow a small-minded, hateful group of idiots to make me scared for a single one of them.

My hand is surprisingly steady as I pick up my phone. I'm relieved as I tap out a reply to the message. *Relieved*. God...how have I not realized before now? All of this time spent being afraid of my classmates at Raleigh? It's been exhausting. Living on the edge of panic, twenty-four hours a day, seven days a week, permanently existing in this maelstrom of fight or flight...it's been quietly grueling in a way that I haven't realized until this very moment. And now that I've made this decision—that I won't be an active participant in their abuse—it feels like I've severed the taut cord that's been dragging me underwater, trying to fucking drown me.

I hit send, and then study the one-word reply I've sent, the buzzing in the back of my head fading to nothing but static.

Me: COWARD

It's appropriate. It says it all. That one word was all I needed to send. Somewhere in Raleigh, a student who goes to my high school is also studying my response, and it's shaking them to their core…because they know it's the truth. For some reason, whatever that might be, they're scared too. And with that one word, I have reached down their throats, closed my hand around their heart, and I've *squeezed*.

"SILVER! OUT OF YOUR PIT, KIDDO! WE'VE GOT COMPANY!"

Downstairs, the front door slams closed, echoing throughout the empty house. The sound of my father's voice floats up the stairs, quieter than the drill sergeant-level holler he just blasted up at me, and I realize that he's laughing. Boots being kicked off; bags being dumped on the kitchen counter; cabinet doors slamming shut. From the racket, there are eight people in the lower level of the house and they're as clumsy and heavy-footed as a herd of elephants.

"Silver! If you're not down here in five minutes, I'm going to tell Alex about the time you shit yourself at Seattle Zoo."

What?

Ooooh no.

Uh-uh.

No fucking way.

Alex isn't here. He can't be. It's too early. He's not supposed to pick me up for another…wait. What time is it? I snatch Mickey up from the bedside table, gripped with horror when I see that it's nearly time to leave for school and Alex probably *is* here.

"Fuck, fuck, fuck!" My foot catches in the bedsheets and I nearly eat dirt when I launch myself out of bed. The Seattle Zoo shit story is not a good one. If my father breathes one word of what happened that day, I'm going to fucking kill him.

This is the problem with parents. They spend years cleaning up your vomit, teaching you how to use a bathroom, how not to shove peas/coins/marbles up your nose, dealing with you screaming and basically being a little bastard, and all the while, they're biding their time, waiting for the day to arrive when they can tell someone you deeply care about that when you were seven years old, you sneezed so hard in front of the giraffe enclosure at Seattle Zoo that you soiled your underwear.

In my bathroom, I throw water at my face, jam my toothbrush into my mouth and try to tame my hair all at the same time. I bounce on the balls of my feet, willing myself to go faster, and I end up scraping my gum with the plastic head of the toothbrush. Hurts like a bitch, but there's no time for pain right now.

I kick my way into some jeans, wriggle my way into a clean Billy Joel t-shirt, and fly out of my bedroom, taking the stairs three at a time.

"Dad? Dad! I swear to god—"

I screech to a halt in the doorway of the kitchen, astonished by what I'm seeing. Dad's leaning against the counter by the sink with his arms folded across his chest, looking a little bemused as Alex crouches down next to the kitchen island, scratching Nipper's belly. The dog's mouth is open, his tongue lolling all over the place as my boyfriend rubs his fingers into his wispy fur; it looks like the damned dog is smiling.

"Huh. Well, that's just typical."

Alex looks up, the vine tattoo wrapped around the base of his throat clearly displayed above the collar of his plain black vee-neck t-shirt, and he winks at me. "Morning, *Dolcezza.*" His voice is so deep. It resonates around the kitchen, reflecting off the tiled floor so that I feel the rasp of it through the soles of my bare feet. His thick, wavy hair is in his face again, falling into his eyes. It's absolutely fucking criminal that he can make me feel so flustered, pinned to the spot, with nothing more than a second's eye contact. And in front of my father no less.

Perfect.

I look up at Dad and nearly keel over from embarrassment when he arches a cool eyebrow at me. He knows me better than anyone. I'm sure he can tell what I'm feeling right now, and that thought is fucking mortifying. "*Dolcezza?*" he asks lightly. "My Italian's a little rusty. What does that mean?"

Alex quickly lowers his head, hiding a smirk. He's pretending to be absorbed in petting Nipper, but I know the truth. I can only see the crown of his head and muscles pulling tight against the back of his t-shirt but Alessandro Moretti's a little embarrassed, too. "Ahhh, it's just a term of endearment," he tells my father.

Dad's bemusement deepens. "I have the Google Translate app on my phone and I know how to use it, Moretti. If you're planning on using a foreign language to secretly seduce my daughter, think again. *I will know.*"

Oh, fucking hell. Come on. *Really?* I screw my eyes closed, groaning as I turn my face to rest my forehead against the door jamb. "Dad, just…no, okay? *No.*"

Alex stands, shoving his hands into his pockets. He's the picture of composure as he faces my father and gravely says, "I wouldn't worry. Your daughter doesn't know a lick of Italian, either. I couldn't seduce her with it if I tried."

I need to go back to bed. I need to go for a run. I need to get the hell out of this house. Basically, I need to be anywhere but here right now. This cannot be happening. There's no way my father and the guy I most definitely am having sex with are discussing my seduction.

"Specifically, *Dolcezza* means sweetness," Alex continues, smirking. "You really don't have anything to worry about."

"Sweetness?"

"Sweetness," Alex confirms. He says the word lightly, like it's nothing. Like it's a saccharine way of showing the affection he feels for me. My father doesn't know that this is the word Alex growls while his head is between my legs and his tongue is working my clit. That it's the word Alex grinds out as he licks his fingers clean of me after he's just fucked me with them and made me come.

"Sounds innocent enough," Dad announces brightly, shoving away from the sink. I'm pretty sure I've turned crimson my face is burning so fiercely. "English for the next three days, though. Probably a good idea, don't you think?" He slaps Alex on the shoulder, giving him his trademark *that's-an-order-not-a-request* tight-lipped smile.

I'm too distracted by what my father just said to enjoy Alex's poorly veiled awkwardness. "Uh, what do you mean, the next three days?"

Dad swipes his phone up from the counter, making his way

toward his office. "Haven't you checked the Raleigh portal? You're off," he says absently. "Too much snow. We're gonna be trapped here. I'm gonna work on the book, and you two," he says, eyes flitting from me to Alex and back again, "are going to keep your hands to yourselves. I'm seriously too young to be a grandfather. I don't want to have to murder anyone, either, Alex. My face is just too pretty for jail."

7

ALEX

BEN: I don't like the thunder.

Me: Don't worry, bud. It'll be over soon. Did you make the fort?

Ben: Yeah, but it's not very good. The ones you make are better.

Me: I bet it's awesome. Why don't you take your flashlight in there and read one of the Spiderman comics I got you? By the time you've finished, the storm will be over.

Sitting on the couch at Silver's place, watching T.V. alone with her, is seriously fucking surreal. If I were Cam, I'd have left my ass to rot in that trailer and been glad of the fact that my daughter's loser boyfriend couldn't get to her for three whole days, but instead I'm full of the Philly cheesesteak he prepared for dinner and I'm curled up with Silver, wondering how the fuck I'm going to do the decent thing and not fuck the shit out of her the moment he goes to bed. I'm not used to all this trust. It's weird. It's making me *feel* weird.

I've been mistrusted and disbelieved my entire life. If something ever went missing at a foster home, I was prime suspect number one. If there was ever the slightest reason for fireworks, it was always my fault, regardless of the fact that it actually *wasn't* my fault. Made things pretty simple, really. If people expected the worst, there was no real pressure to do better. Under Cameron Parisi's roof, however, I've been gifted with the highest of expectations, and it's fucking killing me. This is the first real opportunity I've had to *not* let someone down. Silver's father's a smart man. Smarter than most. I'm sure he knows exactly what he's done, the sly bastard.

Ben: I can't find my comics. I wish you were here.

I tighten my grip on my phone, huffing under my breath. The beautiful girl sitting next to me brushes the tips of her fingers lightly against the back of my neck, humming softly. She must feel the stress radiating off me. "Everything okay?" she asks. "This is the season finale. Don't you wanna know who dies?"

"Sorry. Can't concentrate. Ben's freaking out. The snow hasn't hit Bellingham properly yet. It's raining like crazy over there. Thunder and lightning. Ben hates thunder. Always has."

Silver sighs softly, leaning her head against my shoulder. "You're feeling bad that you can't get to him?"

I take a second to reply, trying to figure out what's troubling me the most. "I'm angry at Jackie. Ben's a super sensitive kid. Afraid of the dark. Hates being trapped in small spaces. Thunder scares the shit out of him. She knows all of this, but she doesn't do anything about it. She makes him ride out shit like this on his own. She makes him take the elevator up to his therapy appointments every week, even though the doctor's office is only on the third floor, and it makes Ben cry every single fucking time. It's like she enjoys scaring him, and…" I work my jaw, attempting to come up with a way to express myself that doesn't involve murder.

"And it makes you want to kill her," Silver finishes for me.

"Yeah, it makes me want to fucking kill her."

Silver's quiet for a while. A huge battle scene plays out on the television, too dark to really see which of the show's main characters are surviving and which of them are being cut down by the enemy. After a particularly brutal and bloody beheading, Silver whispers softly, "You'll be eighteen in five and a half months."

"Yeah."

"And then Ben will probably be able to come live with you, right?" She sounds hesitant, unsure, and my palms break out into a nervous sweat. I've been thinking about this a lot recently. Ben coming to live with me. I'll never leave him with Jackie, it's not an option, but it was just me before. I didn't have anyone else in my life to consider. Things are going to change if I'm the sole caretaker of an eleven-year-old. I'll essentially be playing the role of a father to him and that's bound to have an effect on my relationship with Silver. It's a lot to take on, dating a guy who has to look out for a child twenty-four hours a day, seven days a week.

I fidget, repeatedly winding a loose thread from the seam of my jeans around the tip of my index finger and then unravelling it again. "I get it, y'know. If it's too much. It's not exactly every teenager's dream come true, being landed with a dependent. It's not…it's not *cool*," I rush out. "If it's too much to deal with…me taking him on… then I understand. I'm not gonna hate you if you don't think you can hack it."

Slowly, she turns away from the television, her posture stiff, her expression unreadable. "Would you walk away if things were different for me? If something happened to my parents and I wanted to take care of Max?"

I don't even hesitate. "I'd *never* walk away. I couldn't. No matter what was going on, I'd always be there for you."

"So what makes you think I'm any more capable of abandoning *you*, Alessandro Moretti? I've already been through hell and back and *you* were the one who helped pull me out. I love Ben. He's the sweetest kid. Helping you take care of him won't be a burden, it'll be a pleasure, but that's beside the point. Whatever happens, no matter how difficult, I'm never going to bail on you just because things get hard." She smiles softly, placing a light kiss against my mouth...and I just sit there, rigid as a post.

Goddamnit, Moretti, what the fuck is wrong *with you? Get your shit together.*

I eventually remember to kiss her back, but I probably do a piss-poor job of it. My head's reeling, see. From what I've learned of people over the past seventeen years, people do not stick around when the going gets tough. They disappear in a puff of smoke, so quick you can't see them for dust. My father left. The boys' home turfed me out at the first signs I might be a '*troubled kid.*' After that, it was a slew of foster families closing their doors on me and Ben, one after the other. Even my mother bailed on us. Yeah, she was sick, and looking back now it had been a long time coming, but she made a decision when she put that gun in her mouth. She decided that ending her own life was preferable to hanging around and taking care of her sons. Only one person remained constant for more than a six-month period after my mother died, and that was Gary Quincy. Horrifying, really, since Gary put a roof over my head for one reason and one reason alone: so he could fucking break me.

And now, here's Silver—an impossible girl, who shouldn't even exist. Too strong. Too fierce. Too beautiful. Too perfect. And somehow, against all sense of reason, logic and justice, she's fucking *mine*. She just looked into my eyes and told me she'd stay by my side, no matter what, and I damn well believed her. None of it...fuck, none of it makes sense.

Silver rests her head against my chest, snuggling into my side, and I'm overcome with a paralyzing sense of falling—a dizzying, unbalanced, nauseating sensation that has panic rising up the back of my throat in hot waves. This feels *so* good, being here with her. It feels like life is finally taking a turn for the better, and that's fucking terrifying. Because real life doesn't just do a one-eighty and suddenly everything just fucking works out. It just fucking doesn't. Something terrible always happens. Something brutal and soul destroying, and all the good feels like it's being sucked right out of the world.

I've been too bad to deserve anything this good. The universe has forgotten about the shit-kicking it decided was my birth right and appears to have gone on vacation, but it won't be long before it remembers what a worthless piece of shit I am and sets the natural order of things back in motion.

In the meantime, I have no real choice. I'm going to choose to believe that Silver will stand by me when I get custody of Ben. I'm gonna make sure I enjoy every single goddamn second I get to spend with her. I'm going to try not to think about it, to overanalyze every passing moment. I'm going to *hope*. And that, perhaps, is the most dangerous thing of all.

The guest bedroom Cameron assigns to me is on the ground floor. There are two other guest rooms upstairs, but Silver's dad is obviously keen on putting as much space between me and his daughter as possible. I get it. It makes perfect sense, and I'm happy to play by his rules. Well, maybe not happy, per se. Let's call it grudgingly willing. It's fucking torturous, though, knowing that Silver is in bed upstairs, less than fifty feet away, and I'm forbidden from falling asleep with her naked in my arms. That's the crux of it—the whole forbidden thing. Fruit's overrated, but the second someone makes it forbidden, I suddenly have a taste for that sweet sugar.

The guest room's masculine, the walls painted slate grey with a deep maroon feature wall. The sheets on the king bed are grey to match the walls, patterned with a neat black pinstripe. Heavy brass instruments sit on top of the chest of drawers and are being used as book ends on the shelves—they look like they were designed for calibration and taking measurements. Architectural knick-knacks, most likely. On the wall above the bed, a huge gilt frame mirror dominates the room, reflecting back the space, making it appear even larger than

REVENGE AT RALEIGH HIGH | 81

it already is.

The Parisis aren't just well-off, I realize, as I shrug out of my shirt, hanging it over the back of the leather armchair by the window. They're fucking *rich*. The well-heeled, quiet kind of rich that makes me think there's old money involved. New money speaks much louder than the understated luxury of Silver's place. It screams. There's nothing showy or over-the-top here. If it weren't for the sheer size of the place, the colonial columns, the ostentatious length of the driveway, and the solid quality of all the furniture, you'd easily think you were in a very normal, middle-class American home.

It's late, almost one in the morning, and Cameron's still in his office two rooms over, hammering away at his keyboard. I climb into bed, trying not to sigh out loud like a fucking loser when I feel the sheets against my bare skin. I have no idea what makes them so different to the sheets on the bed back at the trailer, but they're cool and crisp and make me shudder with pleasure.

I've never been great about falling asleep quickly in new places. I'm ready to spend the next hour tossing and turning, my mind speeding at a hundred and twenty miles an hour, worrying about Ben, but then...

...I'm out fucking cold.

~

"*Alex?*"

I stir, turning over onto my back.

"*Alex?*"

Skimming the surface of consciousness, thoughts begin to form in my sleep-clouded head.

"Alex! Wake up, for fuck's sake. I'm freezing my ass off here!"

My eyes snap open, and for a suspended moment I'm confused as fuck. Where the hell am I? And who the hell is grumbling at me in the dark? It takes a swift pinch to my side to jump start my brain, and I remember Cameron coming to get me at the trailer.

Silver's standing beside the bed, framed in the moonlight that's pouring in through the window behind her. Arms and legs bare, she's wearing a silk camisole and tiny little red silk shorts—nothing more than scraps of fabric that leave very little the imagination. Her nipples are erect, peaked beneath the lacy detailing on the camisole, and my dick stirs, quicker to rouse than the rest of me. Her hair's loose, hanging down past her shoulders in thick waves. Her features are cast into shadow, but I can just about make out the shape of a frustrated smile as she prods my chest through the bedsheet.

"Move over. I'm gonna catch hypothermia in a second."

My first thought is to throw back the covers, grab hold of her by her hips, and pull her down on top of me. I'm barely awake, and my body is craving her desperately. But...

I groan, scrubbing at my face with one hand. "Silver. Fuck. Your dad'll freak out if he knows you slept in here."

"Who said anything about sleeping?" she whispers. "I'll be tucked up, back in my own bed in an hour. He'll never know."

Oh, come on. My dick's well past stirring now. I'm hard as fuck. All I can think about is driving myself deep into the back of Silver's throat. "*Argento.* You're *killing* me. I'm trying to be the good guy here."

"*Oh.* Hmm." She hums softly, as if she's a little disappointed. "And here I was, looking for the bad boy I fell in love with. I didn't realize he'd left in the night without saying goodbye."

Well. Fuck. Me. Running. I shift in the bed, pulling myself up to lean my back against the mahogany headboard. My eyes have adjusted to the dark and I can see even more of her now. She knew what she was doing when she came down here in those night clothes. The clingy fabric hugs the curve and swell of the underside of her tits, accentuating their shape and fullness, and I have to bite the inside of my cheek to stop myself from groaning out loud.

"Are you trying to provoke me, *Argento?*" I rumble. "*Because it's probably not a good idea.*"

She turns her head, and the moonlight paints her features silver. She grins recklessly, arching an eyebrow. "Why not? Don't you want me?"

"That's not the point."

"Because *I* want *you.* I was lying there in bed, and I couldn't stop thinking about you. I wanted your hands on my skin. I wanted my nipples in your mouth. I couldn't stop thinking about your cock between my legs, the tip pushing slowly inside me. I got so wet I couldn't take it anymore. I started touching myself. I couldn't stop. And then that wasn't enough. I had to come down here and have *you* touch me..."

Fuck.

Cruel. So fucking cruel.

I've bitten the inside of my cheek so hard my mouth is flooded with the tang of copper. "I'll never be able to fuck you again if your father castrates me, *Argento*. Is that what you want?"

"*No*," she says a little petulantly. "But that isn't going to happen. I heard him snoring a minute ago. He sleeps like the dead. And we'll be quiet."

"Silver—"

She cuts me off, silencing my next objection before I can even say it out loud; with sure, purposeful movements, she reaches up, taking the delicate, thin straps of her camisole and sliding them over her shoulders. The entire garment slides down her torso. Moonlight bathes the porcelain perfection of her skin, bleaching it white, and it's all I can do not to launch myself out of the bed, snatch her up in my arms, pin her to the wall and sink my raging hard-on inside her.

Looks like all bets are off. My abysmal attempts at restraint have all been for nothing. "You really shouldn't have done that," I growl.

Silver tilts her head, lips parted, her eyes a little wild. Her hair falls over her shoulder, another curtain of silk, momentarily obscuring her left breast. Slowly, she reaches up, trailing her fingertips over the round swell of her flesh, brushing the hair out of the way again, revealing her nipple, and it's almost too fucking much to bear. "Why?" she whispers. "Do you like my body, Alex? Are you hard? Do you like looking at me naked?"

Fuck. I haven't been able to keep my hands off Silver since we started seeing each other, and she hasn't been able to keep hers off me either, but she's never been like this, so forward and demanding, crystal clear about what she wants and determined to get it. It's turning me on so much, there really is no way I'll be able to rein myself in anymore.

"Run," I snarl, slowly sitting upright. "If you don't want me to hold you down and fuck the shit out of you right now, I suggest you'd better *run*." My hands work of their own accord, taking hold of the sheets, pulling them back, and I see the shadow of hesitation in Silver's eyes. Is she second guessing her actions now that she's got me on the hook? Maybe she can tell that she's about to get a little more than she bargained for.

She swallows hard but remains standing beside the bed. "I'm not going anywhere."

Brave, silly Argento. She came in here with a fire burning inside her, not realizing that her body was a tinder box. She had no idea what kind of inferno she'd start when she slipped out of that camisole. She had no idea how quickly she was going to get swallowed in the blaze. The floorboards are cold beneath my feet as I get out of the bed and stand in front of her.

She's as delicate and fragile as a china doll. Her features are so finely shaped and graceful that they contradict her true nature. It doesn't matter how strong she is now, though. Unless she tells me to stop, that she doesn't want me to touch her, then I'm going to devour her and to hell with the fucking consequences.

Silver retreats a step, head craning back to look at me properly. The muscles in her throat work as she swallows again. "Take those shorts off. Now," I command. "If you want to come in here and tease me, Silver, you'd better fucking commit." I'm only wearing a pair of sweatpants, no underwear, and my cock protrudes out in front of me like an iron staff, tenting the soft material. I'm not embarrassed by how turned on I am. Far from it. When Silver's eyes dart down to the situation between my legs, I grab hold of my dick through the sweats, squeezing until I make myself curse.

"If you're not naked in three seconds, *Argento*, I can't be held accountable for what comes next." I'm being pulled down into the madness of my own lust, but beneath it all I'm still thinking perfectly clearly. The moment I see hesitation flickering in her eyes, the moment I sense her heart skip a beat out of anxiety and not desire, then this all stops. I would never hurt her. I'd never ask her to do something she didn't want to. I'd definitely never make her do something against her will and Silver knows that.

She proves that when she takes hold of her shorts by the waistband and slowly pushes them down over her hips and then her thighs. I watch, fascinated, as she steps out of the puddle of red silk at her feet, my heartrate ramping up, the muscle kicking like an angry mule against the inside of my ribcage. She's more than I could ever have dreamed of. How could I have possibly dreamed of a girl like her, when even the beautiful things I've experienced in this lifetime have all been ugly in comparison?

My palms are burning, itching for me to reach and touch her, but I'm not ready yet. I want to take her in some more. I need to savor her. Taking a step forward, I'm pleased, and hard, and aching all over when she mirrors my action, stepping back, away from me. I gave her a chance to run and that time has passed. Silver knows this well enough, but it still looks like she's planning on dancing with me a little all the same.

Another step forward and Silver skates back, her bare ass nearly hitting the wall behind her. Her gaze flickers toward the bedroom door, and I relent a little, angling myself instinctively, making it clear to her that she *can* get to the exit if she decides she wants to bolt.

Her nostrils flare as she looks back at me. Her back straightens, shoulders pulling away from her ears, and she shakes her head. "I don't want you to do that," she says. "Don't give me an out. If I want one, I'll ask for it."

I pause, hovering a foot away from her, pulling in slow, long, deep breaths in an attempt to calm the roaring in my head. "You're in control of your fear?" My voice is muted in the heavy quiet of the room.

Silver looks up at me, her jaw jutting out in defiance. "Yes. I can handle anything you throw at me."

She is so, *so* wrong. God, I've never met anyone so fucking wrong before in my entire life. I'm hardly going to give her a demonstration to prove that point, but still. *Wrong.* Reaching out for her, I take a lock of her hair and twist it slowly around my fingers. "You don't know what you're talking about..."

"You think I don't know myself? I'll prove it to you." Her tone is steady, confidence pouring off her strong enough that I'm almost convinced by her statement. "Kiss me," she commands.

Kiss her? I smirk, my cock pulsing painfully in beneath my sweats, begging to be unleashed. If she thinks me *kissing* her is going to prove anything, then she's got another thing coming. I don't think she's thought this through properly, but still…I'm hardly going to deny her a fucking kiss.

Prowling forward one last step, Silver tenses up when she realizes she's run out of space and there's nowhere for her to retreat to now. Her hands remain slack by her sides as I bend over slightly, lowering my mouth to hers. The kiss is like a searing brand, hot and dizzying. Her lips are so soft and pliable. The moment I make contact with her, my imagination riots over what could be done with such a soft, sweet, fuckable mouth. I've had my hands in Silver's hair, guiding her head down as she takes my cock as deep as she can, but I've never made her gag on it before. I've never asked her to go beyond her capabilities. I've never asked her to give up oxygen in order to take another inch of me.

A slideshow of deviant, filthy images present themselves to me as I slip my tongue inside her mouth. Things I would never dream of really doing with her, because of everything she went through with Jacob, Cillian and Sam on that bathroom floor. It isn't just that, though. She's good. She's sweet. She doesn't need to be warped by my every vile perversion.

She whimpers as I kiss her deeper, burying my hands into her hair, crushing my body up against her chest. Squirming, she seems to want to get even closer. Her breath is frantic as she takes hold of me by the wrist and guides my hand from her hair down…I think she's encouraging me to touch her breasts, but she halts my hand by her neck, guiding me to the column of her pale throat.

I suddenly realize what she wants from me, and a surge of need fires around my body like a bullet exploding from a gun. She wants me to choke her. My fingers tighten reflexively around her throat, just for a second, a deep chasm of satisfaction yawning open in my chest, but then I'm ripping my hand away, clenching it into a painful fist. "No. No fucking way. I'm not doing that," I pant.

Silver grabs my hand, holding it to her throat again. "You are. I want you to."

This time I move my whole body away from her, not trusting myself to stick to my decision. "No fucking way. We aren't getting caught up in that kind of power play bullshit, Silver. Trust me. You don't want it."

A stunned look of confusion passes over her face. "Trust *me. I do.*"

"Silver—"

"Haven't you done it before?"

"Of course I've done it before."

"Aren't you into stuff? Doesn't it turn you on?"

"It doesn't matter if it turns me on. It's not…it's not right. Not for us, anyway."

The confusion on her face disappears in a heartbeat, swiftly replaced by hurt. "So…you've fucked other girls before and been rough with them. You've liked it, it's turned you on, but you won't do it with me because…what, I'm too *broken?*"

"No, Silver. You're not fucking broken. I know that more than anyone."

"Then what? Why won't you do it, even if I'm asking you to?"

Fuck, I hate the way she's looking at me. Like I swore I could give something to her, something that's important to her, and now I'm going back on my word. Sighing heavily, I return to her, taking her face in my hands and I kiss her again. Relief floods through me when the stiffness in her muscles eases and she relaxes against me. I don't want to disappoint her. I don't want to let her down. I also don't want to do something she thinks she's ready for, only to scare the shit out of her and send her spiraling headfirst into some kind of dark fucking PTSD nightmare that she never re-emerges from either.

My logic must be kind of obvious, must make *some* kind of sense to her, because Silver pulls away, resting her forehead against my chest, and says, "I'm not stupid, Alex. I don't need handling with kid gloves. I know what I want."

I smooth my hand over her hair, resting my chin on the top of her head. This is fucking brutal. My blood is molten lava in my veins. My erection's now so hard and painful that I want to pick her up and take her right here where we stand. "Okay, then why do you want *that?*" I ask. I have to know. If she can't give me a reasonable answer, then there's no fucking way I'll ever consider doing something like that with her.

At first, I think I've got her stumped; she doesn't say anything for a long time. But then her even voice breaks the silence. "I don't want to feel breakable. I want to feel like I'm in control of my own body. It excites me to think of handing myself over to you, knowing that you could do absolutely anything to me, because I trust you and I know you'll never hurt me, but the risk of it…the risk of it excites me, Alex. Is that what you need to hear to be okay with it?"

"Don't tell me anything because you think I *need* to hear it."

She takes my hand again, but this time she doesn't try and wrap it around her throat. She firmly thrusts it between our bodies, down in between her legs. I react the same way any hot-blooded male would react. I stroke my fingers through the folds of her pussy, finding her clit, and her point is instantly proven. She's not just wet; the insides of her thighs are slick with her need.

"Fuck," I hiss between my teeth. "Holy shit, Silver."

"I was thinking about you on top of me when I was touching myself upstairs. I was thinking about you holding me down. I was thinking about your hand around my neck, cutting off my air supply while you fucked me so hard I saw stars. And now you won't give it to me."

If I had to complete a sobriety test, I'd fucking fail. I'm drunk on Silver. Wasted on her. The way she's talking, the way she's pulling my strings, the things she's asking of me…I hate that it's all affecting me so badly, but I can't fucking deny any it. I want to dominate her. I want to own her body. I want to possess her in a way that feels new and a little frightening even to me, for fuck's sake, and if I start…

Jesus, forgive me, there won't be any stopping.

"Alex, I—I need it," she whispers. "*Please.*"

I have limits. There are lines even I won't cross, but when Silver begs me for something with this kind of despair in her voice, I can't fucking say no to her. When she shoves her hand down the front of my sweats and grabs hold of my dick, whimpering as she closes her fingers around me, I know I'm going to give in to her. I shouldn't fucking do it. It's so fucking dangerous, and it could jeopardize every-thing we have, but I'm fucking lost to her.

I rub my thumb over her lip, snarling like a savage dog as I push it into her mouth, past her teeth, and I press her tongue down, feeling her shake against me. "Say the word, Silver. Say the word when you've had enough, because I—I don't think I'll know when to stop."

My hand is around her throat a second later. The base of her skull is flush against the bedroom wall, and my fingers are driving into her pussy, thrusting up inside her. Her eyes are wide as I tighten my hold around her neck, and she lets out a strained desperate moan as I lean my weight against her, making it hard for her to breath.

My dick's so hard and so fucking swollen that it feels like it's going to explode as she pumps her hand up and down my shaft. She isn't holding back. She's jerking me off so hard that it actually hurts, but the pain only urges me on, making me react in kind, fucking her with my fingers until her back is bowed and her eyes are tightly shut, her face turning a worrying shade of crimson, visible even in the dark of the room.

"I want you, Alex. Fuck. Please. I need you inside me right now. I can't take it. I need to come."

It's a relief that she can actually still speak. It's a relief that I'll be able to hear her if she tells me to quit. My heart's racing as I pick her up, bodily lifting her from the floor, my fingers gouging into her skin as I carry her over to the bed and I throw her down on the mattress. My sweats are down my legs and gone in an instant. She claws at my back in a frenzy, and I snap out a rough, tight string of curse words as I shove her legs open and fall on top of her. There's no hesitation. No moment of caution while I check to see if she's okay. God help me, I push myself inside her so forcefully that her whole body tenses, locking up, her back curving away from the bed.

"Alex! Fuck, Alex! Oh my god!"

I draw back, and then slam myself into her, my synapses firing, every part of me out of control—but no, there it is. I feel it: one tiny, tenuous strand of restraint, pulled taut in the back of my head, warning me not to go too far. So long as that single strand exists, I know I'll be able to keep myself in check. We're balancing on a knife's edge, though. I don't want to mark her. I don't want to bruise her...

But then Silver's hand is winding its way into my hair, pulling hard, and she's issuing an order through her bared teeth. "Bite me, Alex. Fuck, bite me. I want your teeth on me. Make me scream."

I do it. I bite down on the tender skin of her shoulder close to her collar bone, and Silver lets out breathless, wordless scream that catches me off guard. I clamp my hand over her mouth grinding my teeth together as I growl into her skin, knowing it's already too late.

Too late for everything. Her father probably heard her. I'm too close to coming now to stop, and so is she. We cling to each other, hands digging into each other's flesh, both of us possessed, rapt, maddened by the sensation of our bodies moving against one another in time, seconds away from diving headfirst into a black, dizzying decent.

The shockwave hits me like a hammer to the back of my head. It's pleasure, but not like any other kind of pleasure I've experienced before. This is almost panicked, chaotic pleasure, cutting the tendons in the backs of my legs and my arms, rendering me useless as I thrust into her one final time. Silver's thighs tighten around my waist, squeezing hard enough to make me see fucking stars, her head thrown back, her face a rictus of oblivion.

"Oh my god. Oh my god. Oh my god." She chants the words over and over, her cheeks flushed with blood, crimson from the exertion and the savagery with which we took one another.

I hold onto her, muttering sweet things into her damp hair, a sated weight lying heavy in the center of my chest, knowing full well that this is what that it must feel like to lose your mind.

Our breathing eventually slows, and when I pull back, looking down at Silver, she looks up at me with dazed eyes, pupils swallowing her irises, contentment etched into the features of her face. It's only when I allow myself to look down and I see the smear of dark red against the paleness of her skin that I understand what I just did.

I bit her so hard that I drew blood.

"Fuck!" I shove myself up, reeling away from the evidence of my own stupidity. "God, I'm sorry, *Argento*. I didn't mean to…"

She frowns, looking down at herself, straining to see why I'm so horrified. She touches her fingers to her shoulder, her brows knotting together when they come away red. *"Oh."*

If the pleasure I felt a moment ago when I was still inside her was great, then the guilt that follows is inconceivable. I can't wrap my head around it. "Where's…fuck, where's your first aid kit. Let me find something to—"

Quickly, Silver sits up, placing her hands against my bare chest. "No! No, Alex, stop. Don't freak out. It's okay. It's okay."

"NO! IT'S—" I stop myself, trapping the words behind my teeth. Shouting's the worst possible thing I can do right now; it'll only make

things worse. Taking a deep breath, and then another, I sit back onto my heels, covering my face with one hand. "It's *not* okay," I force out. "I shouldn't have done that."

Her hands brush over my shoulders—soothing, placating circles that should make me feel better but don't. "Alex, *please*. Don't do that. Really, I'm fine. I asked you to do it. I *told* you to. It turned me on, for fuck's sake. I just wanted you so badly. I needed it to hurt."

I needed it to hurt.

Christ.

I let her pull my hand away from my face, even though I'm still stumbling over the fact that I made her fucking bleed.

"Alex, look at me, okay. *I love you.* It's what I wanted. You're being silly. It's a tiny little graze. There's barely even a mark. Now, please... will you just hold me? I wanna lie on your chest for a second before I have to go back upstairs."

I do look at her. I look deep into her eyes, trying to find some sort of hurt or disturbance there, but there's nothing. She seems totally... normal. The knot of distress that's cinched tight around my heart loosens a little, but it doesn't disappear altogether.

I'm vibrating, full of nervous energy as I lie back down on the bed beside her and she wriggles her way into my side, resting her head over my heart. My erratic pulse doesn't slow until I feel her fall slack against me and she passes out.

I wait until I'm sure she's well and truly out for the count before I carefully pick her up from the bed and carry her up the stairs to her own room.

8

SILVER

The wind howls and moans all day Saturday, rattling at the windows, and great curtains of snow sweep across the Walker Forest, shrouding the Sitka, larch, and the mountain hemlock in shawls of white. Dad manages to speak to Mom and Max in the morning, making sure they're safe, and when the power goes out again around three in the afternoon, he descends into the basement to turn on the new generator he purchased from Home Depot with a gravely smug look on his face.

If my father heard any of the noise I made last night when I paid a visit to Alex's room, then he doesn't say anything about it. Honestly, I doubt he knows I snuck out of my room and tiptoed down the hallway, past his room, and down the stairs. When Kacey and I were still thick as thieves, I used to sneak out of the house every other night and I never got caught once. I know precisely where every creaky floorboard is in this house. I also know just how deep my father sleeps.

Alex spends an inordinate amount of time doing push-ups and sit-ups without his shirt on. I sit and peer at him over the top of the book

I'm pretending to read, enjoying the view, but also slightly worried. He's tense. Agitated. Pulled taut as a bowstring, ready to snap any second, and I know why. I pushed him into doing something he was uncomfortable with, and now he just can't seem to make peace with himself. He paces in front of the bay window in the living room with his hands on his hips, huffing and blowing like a horse that's been ridden too hard. It's painfully clear that he wants out of the house. He's trapped, and it hurts like hell that he wants to get away so badly. I do understand, though.

I barely recognized myself last night. I have no idea what possessed me to ask him to be so rough with me. I'd been laying there in bed, every single, messed up text I've received over the past few weeks repeating themselves in my mind, and I'd wanted to feel like I was in control for just one second. I knew what I needed to make myself feel better, and I was right. It made me feel electric, alive, and I don't regret it for a second—even if I did wake up with a very obvious bite mark just below my collar bone. I'm not planning on showing it off, of course. The round-necked sweater I pulled out of the back of my closet hides it well enough without looking too obvious. Alex isn't stupid, though. He took one look at me in the sweater when he stumbled into this kitchen earlier, hair all over the place, and a deeply unhappy scowl darkened his handsome face.

Things are slightly better on Sunday. The storm subsides and the sun even makes an appearance. I spend the afternoon sporadically checking on the Raleigh High Portal, waiting to see the dreaded blue box at the top of the screen, announcing that school will be back in session tomorrow. It's nearly dusk by the time the site's updated and the box appears, confirming that life will be continuing on as normal in the morning. When I see it, I'm struck by a nauseating wave of nerves. I haven't received another text message since the one that came in on Friday morning, but walking through the doors of Raleigh High is still going to be stressful. I'm going to be walking down through the halls, staring into the other student's faces, wondering which one of them told me to fucking kill myself.

I still haven't told Alex about that, or any of the other messages. I *am* going to. I know it isn't smart to keep something like this from him, but…I just need a moment. He's going to flip the fuck out when I show him the texts, and I want to pretend for just one more day that things *can* be normal for us.

Sunday night, I pluck up enough courage to creep into the guest room again, but this time I don't strip naked and demand to be choked. Alex is asleep. He doesn't even stir when I lift back the covers and climb into the bed next to him. He only wakes up when I slide my hand over his chest, fitting myself into his side. His face is in profile, all shadows and highlights. When he turns to look at me, I see that the storm he's been weathering has broken, too.

"*Dolcezza,*" he whispers. "*Sei la mia vita.*" The sheets rustle as he raises his hand and uses the tip of his index finger to stroke a line down the bridge of my nose and over my lips. I lean into him, and he places a gentle, soft kiss on my mouth, achingly sweet, but that snap of fire still exists between us, ready and waiting to ignite and burn the whole world to the ground at a moment's notice.

"What did that mean?" I whisper, when he pulls back.

Alex dons a small, crooked smile. "It means...that I'd do anything for you. It means that I'm *weak* for you."

My heart is either swelling or breaking, I can't tell which. I'm not the only one who's had a difficult past. Alex has had more than his fair share of unhappiness and hardship to contend with, and the experiences he's had to endure have made him unbelievably strong. Being strong has kept him alive, kept him in one piece...so to hear him tell me that I've made him weak? Well...I really don't know how to feel about that.

TEXT MESSAGE RECEIVED:

+1(564) 987 3491: Bitch. U think you're better than us? Your worthless. Keep your head down, or your gonna die screaming.

9

SILVER

The struggle for power in high school could be compared to the political strife of many South American countries. For years, a dictatorship state exists. The lower classes are ruled over by one singular tyrannical oppressor, hell bent on keeping the people in their places. The next second, the people have risen up, overthrown the despot, and everything is in complete chaos.

Different factions vie for supremacy, opposing parties battling to rise above the others. Anarchy reigns supreme. The people are finally free, but suddenly there are no rules and no consequences for poorly-thought-out actions. The people begin to whisper behind their hands that maybe things were better under the tyrant after all. At least then, they knew which way was up.

Without Kacey stalking the halls, striking fear into the hearts of her fellow students, Raleigh High is basically upside down. All of the different cliques are trying to fill the power vacuum and it looks as though things are going to get ugly soon. When Alex and I arrive on Monday morning, a huge crowd has gathered in the waterlogged parking lot and it looks like World War Three is breaking out. I'm still jittery from the shitty text I received this morning, the one that I barely managed to hide from Alex as he handed me my phone, and so my nerves are already jangling when a high-pitched scream cuts above the shouting and jeering.

"What the *fuck?*" Alex hisses under his breath. He won the rock-paper-scissors contest we held to see who would drive, so he kills the Nova's engine and hands over the keys to me, getting out of the car to see what the hell is going on.

A lot of the snow that fell in the storm has already melted, and I have to hop from one patch of concrete to another to avoid stepping into any ankle deep, ice cold puddles as I follow behind Alex; even though he's wearing his white Stan Smiths, Alex doesn't seem to notice the fact that he's wading through four inches of water.

"Dirty fucking slut! I'm gonna knock your fucking teeth out!"

A cheer goes up from the crowd of gathered students. They're forming a ring, four people deep, around what sounds like a raging cat fight. One of the guys from the football team, Bronson Wright, whips around wearing an angry sneer on his face when Alex tries to push through the crowd. The second Bronson sees who jostled him, he backs down, the whites of his eyes showing.

"Sorry, man. I thought..." Bronson doesn't finish. He just moves out of the way so Alex can get by.

It's been like this ever since school started up again after the shooting. In every way that counted, Alex used to be an outcast like me. People were intrigued by him. They were intimidated by him, but even with Zen's relentless pursuit of him they didn't accept him. Now, things have changed. People still look at him with suspicion and fear, but their expressions are also tinged with begrudging respect.

Alex Moretti took on Leon Wickman and got shot for his troubles. Alex Moretti nearly died taking down a murderer. Alex Moretti is now a demi-god to our fellow classmates—a demi-god they both love and hate in equal measure.

Bronson falls into the *'We hate Moretti camp'* since he's on the football team, but he's also not stupid. He knows he'll get his ass kicked if he starts any trouble. Alex takes my hand, guiding me along beside him through the crowd. Bronson glares down at me as I shuffle past him, piercing me through with daggers sharp enough to cut. Obviously just because I'm with Alex doesn't mean anything to him. I'm still the girl who caused trouble for the King of Raleigh High. Three guys from the football team might have died when Leon walked into school and opened fire, Sam Hawthorne amongst them, but Jacob Weaving is sadly still alive and kicking and he hasn't changed one bit. He still wants to punish me for humiliating him as he raped me. And that means that his dumb ass cronies are all still charged with the task of making my life as miserable as possible.

I wonder what they'd say if they knew how terrified their glorious leader was in that music booth. Would they still follow him so blindly if they knew what a cowardly piece of shit he is?

Normally, I'd duck my head and avoid Bronson's spiteful glare, but not today. I made myself a promise and I intend on keeping it. I'm not going to be cowed by these assholes anymore. I won't be intimidated or beaten down by them. Drawing in a deep breath, I beam up at Bronson, treating him to a dazzling smile that contains the barest hint of condescension. He's not expecting this, obviously. His scowl disappears, shock and surprise widening his eyes instead.

"Lying little bitch," he hisses after me. I might have pretended not to hear him in the past, but this morning I cast a look back over my shoulder, arching a bored eyebrow at him, and the gesture has the desired effect—it looks like he has steam coming out of his ears, he's so angry.

"Arrghh! Get...the...fuck...off me!"

Alex breaks through the crowd, and there, in the middle of the circle of bodies, is Zen, doubled over, caught in a headlock by Rosa Jimenez. When Kacey was around, Rosa was second tier Raleigh Royalty. She's been dating Laughlin Woods for the past three years, but during that time Zen must have made well over fifty plays for her boyfriend. Zen always found it entertaining to flirt with him, constantly trying to fuck him even though she knew it would hurt Rosa, because it didn't matter back then. She was untouchable. One of Kacey Winter's coveted Sirens. So long as she had Kacey watching her back, then Zen got away with murder. With Kacey nearly a hundred miles away in Seattle now, however, it looks like Zen's discovering what payback feels like and she's not enjoying it all that much.

Rosa locks her arm around Zen's throat, jerking her down to her knees, and the girl screams as the dirty parking lot snow drenches her jeans. "Come on, cunt. What are you gonna do? *What are you gonna do?*" Rosa snarls. The crowd hollers, some of them chanting for Zen to get up, but most of them are siding with Rosa.

"Fuck her up!"

"Hurt her, Rosa!"

"Kill the bitch!"

I watch, horrified, as Rosa pulls a glinting piece of silver from her back pocket and suddenly she has a cruel-looking serrated hunting knife in her hand.

"Shit!" The kid standing next to me, a nerdy type from computer club, catches sight of the weapon and turns, bolting toward the school building. Half of the other the spectators do the same, backing away from the scene with their hands in the air and fear in their eyes. The other half are frozen, their feet rooted into the ground, unblinking.

Alex's hand tightens around mine. I can already see him jumping into this melee, putting himself in another dangerous situation that might cost him his life, and horror blooms like an ugly flower in my chest. *Not this time, Moretti.* Not *going to happen.* I close my other hand around the top of his arm, digging my fingers into the leather of his jacket. He immediately looks back at me, tension in the lines of his face, and I shake my head.

"Don't. God, please don't. Not this time."

Rosa holds the knife in front of Zen's face, showing her the wicked blade. "How you gonna fuck with other people's guys with your face all cut up, bitch?" Rosa spits. "You still think it's funny, huh? Still think it's your god given right to try and take what doesn't belong to you?"

I loved Zen once. She was one of only four other people in the entire world who really, truly knew who I was. I would have done anything to protect her. A little over a year ago, I would have charged at Rosa myself, desperate to get her the hell away from my friend, but now a cold and indifferent shield goes up around my heart. This is really fucking bad, but there is such a thing as justice, there *has* to be, and too many people have gotten away with far too much at Raleigh High. Maybe it's time that people started paying for their sins.

Zen screams, a high pitched, reedy, pathetic sound, and my stone-cold resolve falters. Rosa grimaces, jabbing at Zen's face with the knife, and I see the determination in her eyes. She's not just here to scare Zen this morning; she's here to *hurt* her. Witnessing the intent on Rosa's face is seriously fucking disturbing.

When did we become this? At what point did rape, murder and assault become acceptable to the students of this school? Was there a defining moment that made one of us snap? Did the actions of that one person then make it okay for three other people to discard common decency and take whatever *they* wanted? Has this all been a domino effect of pain and suffering, because of one small, defining moment that might have seemed insignificant at the time but is now responsible for eighteen lives?

Rosa slashes with the knife, but she doesn't follow through on her threat and cut Zen's face. She grabs a handful of Zen's hair instead, hacking and sawing at her wild, bouncy curls, and then letting clumps of it flutter away on the breeze.

"No! No, no, no, not my hair. *Pleeease!*" Zen sobs. Her hair has been a part of her identity for as long as I've known her. Zen's one of the vainest people I've ever come across, so this? Hacking off her hair? It'll feel almost the same as scarring up her face to Zen. At least this isn't permanent.

"WHAT IN GOD'S NAME IS GOING ON HERE?!"

Principle Darhower's roar of anger splits the air in two, deafening even over the shouting of the crowd. He charges into the knot of people, his navy-blue tie flapping in the wind over his shoulder. His suit pants are soaked well past the ankle. Rosa looks up at him, hesitating for second, but she doesn't let go of Zen or the knife.

"Ms. Jimenez. What the *fuck* are you doing?" I've never heard Darhower curse. Not even after the shooting. His face is so purple, he looks like his head is about to burst open from all the pressure building up inside of it. "Haven't we had enough of *this* to last a lifetime?" he demands. "What the hell are you trying to accomplish here? What do you think's going to happen now?"

"I don't know," Rosa admits. "I don't really care what comes next. This little slut just needed to pay—"

"Drop the knife, Rosa," Darhower grinds out. His hands are on his hips, his head bowed, shoulders heaving. "I swear to you now, if you drop the knife, we'll work together to figure this out. If you don't, the situation will be beyond my influence."

Zen whimpers, tears coursing down her cheek. Our eyes meet for a split second, and for the first time in over a year, I'm not met with disgust and contempt. I'm met only with fear.

"What do you mean?" Rosa demands. "Beyond your influence?"

"What do you think I mean? Sheriff Hainsworth's on his way. Ms. Gilcrest's calling your parents as we speak. If the Sheriff pulls into this parking lot and finds you holding another girl at knife point, things are going to be very bad for you. *Very* bad."

Rosa swallows, turning the knife over in her hand. She stares the principal down, searching his face, perhaps looking for some sort of sign that he's lying. Her shoulders relax, her body loosening, and for a second I think she's going to let Zen go. But then she rips Zen's head back, grabbing another giant handful of her hair, and she saws through it crazily, slashing out with the razor-sharp knife, cutting more and more of Zen's hair away.

"*ROSA!*"

Next to me, Alex shakes his head, eyes hard, jaw clenched. "Holy fuck," he mutters under his breath. "It's like fucking Lord of the Flies up in here. I thought Raleigh was supposed to be one of the *good* schools."

Zen sobs as Rosa finishes up her insane task, throwing the last puff of Zen's hair right into her face. Her hair is shorn so close to her scalp in places that Rosa's blade must have nicked the skin; a thin trail of blood runs down the side of her head, following the curve of her skull, coursing around the back of her ear and down the side of her neck.

In the distance, the high-pitched wail and throb of a police siren echoes over the trees that surround Raleigh High.

Rosa Jimenez drops the knife.

Alex has been fixed on the girls the entire time.

He hasn't noticed the grim presences of Jacob Weaving, standing apart from the crowd, shooting knives at *me*, like he's plotting my very slow and painful death.

ALEX

Monty: Couldn't get the bag. Bring it here by four? I have news on the Weaving situation.

It's a running joke that Mrs. Webber, our AP math teacher, is so short-sighted that she wouldn't be able to make out a bus before it hit her. The woman's near-blindness works in my favor as I openly reply to Monty's text from my seat at the back of the classroom.

Me: Sure. See you then.

I ask no questions. I say nothing about the Weaving situation, or the fact that he promised to help bring down the entire family. It's better if I don't even type their name in a message. According to Montgomery, everything still going according to plan. As per Silver's request, whatever trick the old man has tucked up his sleeve is legal and won't cause any physical harm to Jacob, but I'm increasingly less and less enamored by the promise I made.

I want to break the law.

I want to hurt Jacob.

I want to fucking kill him.

Thankfully, Silver doesn't have any classes with the piece of shit. They might not have believed her when she went to Darhower and told him what had happened, but they sure as hell made sure they weren't on the same class schedule afterward. At Mr. Weaving's request, I seem to remember hearing. He didn't want a lying, vindictive, spiteful little bitch anywhere near his son. Such a fucking joke. Jacob's ass should have been beaten black and blue and then thrown in fucking jail. Instead, Silver was treated like garbage and she was moved from her classes as punishment for telling tales. How is any of that right?

Bellingham was rough. The shit that went down there would give most people nightmares, but even there the administration ran things by the book. If someone was discovered to be bullying or harassing the other students, they were gone. And sexual assault claim? Fuck, the cops would have been there before you could even *breathe* the word rape.

Raleigh likes to present a well-to-do façade to the outside world. A lot of rich motherfuckers send their kids here in light of the fact that the closest private school is all the way over in Seattle and they want to keep their children close. The building itself is beautiful, and the facilities are all brand spanking new…but at its core, Raleigh is a rotten fucking apple. Take a bite and you won't struggle to come across something foul that will leave a bad taste in your mouth.

This year, it's the Weaving family pulling the strings, with their obnoxiously large donations to the football team and Mr. Weaving's unwelcome presence on the school board, but Jacob will be aging out of Raleigh in a year's time and Mr. Weaving's interest in the school will graduate right along with his son. There isn't a shadow of a doubt in my mind that there'll be another meddling parent with deep pockets who'll happily step into the breach once Caleb Weaving's made his exit and taken his check book with him. It's just the way these things go.

Regardless of how it happened, I'm glad Silver doesn't have to sit in a classroom with Jacob. I, on the other hand, am not that lucky. We're in History together, as well as Spanish, English and Graphic Design; I find myself sitting next to the sick bastard at least once a day, and it takes everything in me not to pile drive my fist into the sick fuck's face.

Thirty minutes after I reply to Monty's text, the bell rings and I make a fast escape. Silver's on the other side of the building, so chances that I'll see her between classes are slim, but for once she isn't the reason I'm bolting from Math. There's someone I plan on paying a visit, and I don't want Silver knowing about it.

I find Cillian Dupris close to the boy's locker rooms, talking to the Neanderthal who thought about starting a fight with me this morning for knocking into him. Cillian sees me charging down the hallway toward him, makes eye contact, and practically shits himself. Before the shooting, he might have tried to bail before I could reach him, but that's not quite as easy anymore, given that he's wheelchair bound.

He scrambles, trying to navigate his way around Bronson, but there are too many people bustling by, choking the corridor, and he isn't able to bully a path through the crowd. His buddy doesn't even give him a hand and get out of his way.

My hackles are up when I finally reach Cillian, a red-hot heat burning down my back. I ball my hands into fists, imagining how satisfying it would be to grind my knuckles into his face. "We're going to have a chat, you and me," I inform him.

Cillian works his jaw, eyes unsure as he looks up at me. He was a tall guy before one of Leon's bullets hit him in the back and shattered three of his vertebrae. He used to use his size and his build to intimidate everybody around him. He used the fact that he was so much bigger than Silver to *hurt* her. It must be a real blow to him that he now has to look up to meet the eyes of every single student at Raleigh. "Go fuck yourself, asshole. I don't have anything to say to you," he spits.

Maybe he's hoping that there's still some sort of residual respect for him floating around the school. Maybe there actually is, and the people he trampled all over on a daily basis before he lost the use of his legs are still frightened of him, one way or another.

I, on the other hand, have never been afraid of him. If he thinks he can cow me with a bit of attitude, he's going to be sorely fucking disappointed. "That's okay. I don't really need you to say anything. You only really need to listen."

Quickly, I take hold of the handles at the back of his wheelchair, pushing him away from the locker rooms. "Hey! Hey, get the fuck off me, Moretti. You are making a big mistake. Jake's gonna flip his shit when he hears about this!"

Hah. Poor bastard. I lean down a little as I push him toward the set of double doors by the technology block, heading for the exit. Only he can hear me speak above the chatter and the gossip of our fellow classmates. "You think Jake gives a fuck about you now, Cillian? You think you're any use to him whatsoever *now*? You're off the football team. You'd be useless in a fight if Jake got himself in trouble. The only purpose you serve to Jacob Weaving these days is that of a distraction. He'd push you into oncoming traffic if he thought it would benefit him somehow. Other than that...I'm willing to put money on the fact that he doesn't even want to fucking *know* you anymore."

Being paralyzed from the waist down would be an awful outcome for anybody. A small part of me wouldn't wish this fate upon my worst enemy, but you know what? Fuck that small part of me. This is exactly what Cillian Dupris deserves.

Plenty of people watch as I wheel Cillian out of the school building, but no one does a thing to stop me. That piece of shit Bronson probably is running like the little bitch that he is to go and find Jacob, but that doesn't matter. What I have to say to Cillian won't take long, and even if it did, I am *not* afraid of Jacob fucking Weaving. Let him fucking come, if he can be bothered.

The sky is clear, so pale it's almost white as I push Cillian down the ramp toward the stand of trees behind the tech block. Along a small pathway, beyond the line of the trees, there's a steep siding that leads to a small gully if you have the stones to scramble down to it. Some of the students like to smoke pot in the little hidden gully, but with so much snowfall over the past few days, it's impossible to even see where the drop off is, let alone a route to climb down to it.

The tires of Cillian's wheelchair are rugged, with a deep tread that bites into the snow with ease. "Nice rig you've got here, Cillian. Folks really hooked you up, huh? This thing must have cost a pretty penny."

"Fuck you, man. Where the hell are you taking me?" Cillian's doing his best to maintain an outward display of dignity, but I can hear the frustration and the embarrassment in his tone, muddled in with a healthy dash of fear. It's smart of him to be afraid. I'd be fucking terrified if I was in his position, and the boyfriend of the girl I'd raped was pushing me into a dim, eerie forest, where my body might not be found until spring.

I don't supply him with an answer to his question. This isn't my first time at the rodeo, after all. I know that fear is an entirely psychological beast. It festers and grows fat on the back of what *might* be far more than it feeds on what *is*. The longer Cillian's left worrying about what I'm going to do to him, the better.

I only have to travel another fifty feet down the small snow-covered pathway that cuts through the trees before we're out of sight from the main building, but I take him an extra fifty just for good measure. And the whole time I'm pushing him, Cillian is babbling like a lunatic.

"You don't want to do this, man, I promise you. You're gonna regret this, big time. My father's gonna have you shipped off to fucking Stafford Creek for this. You ever been inside a supermax prison before, Moretti? They're gonna eat you a-fucking-live. Alex? Alex! Fuck, come on, man. There's no need to get this crazy over a fucking girl. They're all insane, am I right? You know how they get. They drink too much, hook up, don't wanna look like a slut, so they start slinging mud. You know what they're like, man! Look, stop! Stop, stop, okay, okay! Jesus fucking Christ! All right. It wasn't my idea. It was all Jake's idea. Me and Sam, we didn't even know what he was planning until he brought her up there. Neither of us touched her. Silver Parisi isn't my type anyway. I—fuck! I like redheads! I didn't touch her!"

I come to a halt, grinding my teeth together so hard it feels like they're about to shatter under the strain. Slowly, I walk around Cillian's chair, and the snow beneath my sneakers creaks.

There's real terror in Cillian's eyes. He tries to push himself away from me, back the way we came, but the wheels of his chair only sink into the looser snow that I've parked him in. Purposefully slow, my face purposefully blank, I crouch down in front of Cillian so that I'm at his level. The guy who hurt my Silver snivels, wiping at his nose with the back of his hand.

Still, I don't say anything.

"All right, man. All right. Fine. I *did* do it. I *did* touch her. I *did* fuck her. But you don't understand what it's like, man. Jake's a fucking psychopath. You go against him and it's like signing your own death warrant. This place is no walk in the park. You've got to try and get ahead, to be better than everyone else, or—or you end up being walked all over. Without Jake, I'd have been left behind."

"So. That's it, then. Your reasoning? You forced your fingers up inside a girl...you brutally raped her because of *social standing?*"

"No! No, you're not listening to m—wait, wh—what the hell? Where are you going?"

I'm guessing there are about a hundred and forty feet, total, between here and the entrance back into Raleigh. It won't be impossible for Cillian to make it back inside, but it sure as hell won't be fun. His chair's pretty much useless to him now. He won't be able to wheel himself back along the path without assistance, and I sure as fuck am not going to be giving it to him. I've already started to make my way back toward the building. I pause briefly, turning back to face him.

"You raped a girl, and yet here you are, getting left behind anyway. And, from what I hear, you're *fully* paralyzed from the waist down, huh, Dupris. I'm no doctor, but even I know that means your dick'll never work again. I'd say that's pretty fucking poetic, wouldn't you?"

"C'mon, man, please! If you leave me here, I'm gonna fucking freeze to death!"

"Ahhh, don't be such a defeatist, Cillian. What's the point in giving up before you've even tried? There's every chance you'll make it inside before you freeze to death. You're right, though. It *is* pretty cold. If I were you, I'd get crawling."

ALEX

My conscience is like an underdeveloped muscle. It rarely gets used, so it's atrophied over the years. It still kicks and twinges every once in a while, though, when I'm pondering something really terrible from my past...or when I'm plotting something truly fucking vile for the future. I feel absolutely nothing as I stalk back into Raleigh today, though, relishing the warmth as I head for statistics. The idea of Cillian sitting out in the cold, waiting for someone to come and find him, to rescue him and wheel him inside, so he doesn't have to flop to the ground on his belly and worm his way back into school like the fucking snake that he is? I'm crowing with delight over *that* one. The temperatures are sub-zero outside. The students of Raleigh High aren't stupid enough to go traipsing around out there for the hell of it in this kind of weather, which means the chances of someone stumbling across him are dismally low. He's going to have to weigh his pride against his will to live, and eventually he'll make the decision. He'll crawl, and he'll know for a second what it feels like to be vulnerable, degraded and humiliated.

What I've just done is definitely bending the rules Silver set out. I haven't officially broken them, per se. At least I don't think I have. I, personally, didn't lay a finger on Cillian, so I can't really be blamed for hurting him. Declining to assist someone if they find themselves in a tricky situation? Hmm. That one's a bit of a grey area. There are two sides to that issue—a heads and a tails on a coin of morality that could potentially fall either way. I don't give a fuck, though. I have zero fucking regrets.

It could be argued that the universe has already meted out justice to Cillian, taking his ability to walk, preventing him from ever having sex again, but I don't believe in karma or the divine judgement of the universe. My mother believed in God and all the saints of the Catholic church. She chose to see the hand of divinity in her everyday life, attributing even the smallest coincidences and mishaps as the pleasure or disapproval of her almighty maker.

I don't know if God exists. What I do know is this: if we were created by some higher power, and there *is* some sort of balance to be answered to for our actions, we sure as fuck aren't asked to answer for our sins in this life. Good people die horrific deaths, while the evilest creatures imaginable walk around with the sun on their faces, fortune favoring them at every turn.

This life is chaos. Every path, action, decision, and consequence is a crap shoot, and there's no one watching over us, stacking the deck, tweaking our outcomes, guiding the course of our lives one way or another. Call me callous. Call me wretched. Call me whatever the fuck you want to call me. It doesn't matter. I won't be relying on omnipotent deities, faeries, divine spirits, yin, yang or the ever-expanding universe to teach the bastards who hurt Silver that there will be consequences for what they did to Silver. No, one way or another I'm gonna take care of this one personally.

Statistics passes in a blur. The bell for lunch buzzes, and everyone charges for the cafeteria. I'm about to make my own way to the library —Ha! Me, in a fucking library!—where Silver and I have been meeting up for lunch every day, when my phone buzzes in my pocket.

SILVER: Music room. Five minutes?

Huh. Looks like she's after a change of scenery today. A strange choice of location, though. I change course, going against the flow of bodies that are all heading in the same direction toward the cafeteria, a salmon swimming against the current. It isn't difficult to push my way through. The crowd parts for me like the red sea, students hugging the walls, tripping over each other to get out of my way as I beeline for the stairway that leads up to the music rooms.

When I was first sentenced to finish out my high school career here in Raleigh, the other kids looked at me like I was a curiosity. A mystery box wrapped up in leather an ink, and they weren't entirely sure what was inside. A couple of people poked and prodded at the box, shaking it to see if they could guess at what it contained, but all of that changed after the shooting. Now, people seemed to have decided that I am, in actual fact, *Pandora's* box, and I should be left well alone at all costs lest I bring about the end of the fucking world.

Again.

Hah. Fucking. Hah.

I take the stairs three at a time. Having long legs is a blessing. Inside the music room, Silver sits by the window with a guitar on her lap, playing a slow, melancholy tune as she stares out of the glass at the white world beyond. I look at her and every single thought that was rushing around my head a second ago fades to black.

She's bathed in cold winter sun, the profile of her face outlined in brilliant white. From this angle, the light's refracted through the lens of her eye, picking out and illuminating only the faintest hint of blue. Stands of her hair catch at the light, glowing like fine filaments of gold around her head. The sight of her like that, playing so absently, fingers moving up and down the neck of the guitar, telling their sad story, the collar of her plain grey t-shirt hanging loose, exposing her shoulder… god, it makes my chest ache. I'm still getting used to feeling like this about another person. Love has been a stranger to me since I was six-years-old, and now it's swept into my world like a goddamn hurricane, blowing the doors off my sanity and upending everything I thought I ever knew.

"You planning on just standing there, or are you gonna come play with me?" Silver asks softly. So much for her not realizing I'd arrived. I master a stern expression as I enter the music room properly, coming to a halt in front of the instruments, making a show of picking out the perfect one. Silver laughs quietly under her breath, her fingers still plucking at the strings of the guitar she chose for herself; she left her own at home today.

With a flourish, I take the oldest, most battered looking guitar from the wall, brandishing it like a trophy as I pull up a stool opposite Silver.

"Interesting choice," she observes.

I test the strings, correcting their tuning one at a time. When I'm happy that it's ready, I allow myself a tiny smile. "Old guitars are the best. The wood's warm. It's done all its shifting and warping. Old guitars like this have absorbed a lot of music. They always carry the sweetest notes."

It sounds stupid, but Silver doesn't laugh. She cants her head to one side, her eyes narrowed, like she's seeing the instrument for the first time. "Show me," she says.

My turn to laugh. "Yes, ma'am. Your wish is my command."

∾

SILVER

They say music runs in families, in your blood, but I don't know if that's particularly true. I'm the only musical person in my family. Dad waxes lyrical about playing the drums in a band with his friends in high school, but I've seen the man tap out a rhythm against his desk and trust me…I think *he* might have been the reason the band broke up their senior year.

Mr. Scott, the music teacher who originally taught me to play when I was a kid, gave me the mechanics of playing a guitar. The bare facts. Hold your fingers *here* to create this sound. Pluck *here* to make this sound. Now strum like *this* to create rhythm. What he didn't give me was the longing in my veins whenever I heard something beautiful being played. That was already inside me. Over the years, I've relied on YouTube to find talented guitarists who made me feel that way when they played. I watched and I studied them, pausing, replaying, my fingers stumbling over the strings, until I finally figured out how they made their instruments sing and then I made mine sing along.

I have never seen someone make a guitar weep in person, the way Alex makes the scuffed, ancient old guitar in *his* hands weep, though, and the sight is breathtaking.

His posture is terrible, back badly bent over the guitar, head turned to one side as he listens intently to the music pouring from his fingertips. Mr. Scott always used to chide me if my back wasn't ramrod straight, my head up, eyes forward instead of down on the strings. It's clear that Alex isn't watching what his hands are doing to ensure he hits the right strings. His finger picking and his fretwork are flawless. He's watching his hands, as if he's following along with them on a journey and the music is painting a picture that he wants to witness as it comes into being.

And the music itself...

God.

Dark. Rough. Complex and quiet in places, brash and furious in others. The ebb and flow of the melody isn't what I'd call beautiful to the ear. It's more than that. Better. It pulls at me, sinking its claws down deep into my bones, possessing me in a way that only happens once or twice in a lifetime if you're lucky.

I forget to breathe as I watch him create his masterpiece. It dawns on me as he closes his eyes, straightening up, tilting his head back, the flow of the music darkening, lowering down into a frenzy of dark, bassy, frenetic notes, that this music *is* Alex. It describes every part of him so perfectly that I realize he isn't just playing a song for me. He's showing me who he is, sharing himself with me in the most intimate, moving, personal way he knows how.

I set my guitar down, propping it up against the wall by the window, planning on closing my eyes so I can focus on nothing but the music. I can't do it, though. Alex has to be *seen* like this. The tattoos on the backs of his hands shift as his fingers fly up and down the strings—a rose and a wolf, performing in concert, one asking a question and the other answering without skipping a single beat. His dark hair has fallen into his face once again, obscuring his features, but I catch the charcoal outline of his eyelashes against his cheeks, the tiny frown line between his brows, the white flash of his front teeth gouging into his bottom lip, and each individual feature makes my heart surge.

He's easily the hottest guy I have ever laid eyes on. No question of that. But like this, with a guitar in his hands, playing like he's been possessed, he is more than just a man. He's a force of nature, a storm trapped inside a glass bottle, raging and desperate to get out, and I can't fucking look away.

The music rises, rises, rises, more frantic with every second. Just like the other night in the guest bedroom, he has me by the throat and it feels like he's *squeezing*. I press my legs together, my nipples throbbing painfully, unable to sit still. I'm so turned on by what I'm seeing, what I'm hearing, that I don't actually think I can stand it for another second—

The music ends abruptly, cutting off on a discordant, jangling note.

I gasp out loud.

It feels as though I've just misstepped, distracted, and I've just walked off the edge of a cliff. I have to firmly press my palms against the tops of my thighs to stop myself from wobbling on the stool. Alex opens his eyes, brushes his hair back with a casual sweep of his hand, and then arches a sardonic, amused eyebrow at me, smiling like the very devil himself. "What? No standing ovation?" he murmurs. Fuck, his voice is like gravel, rough and raw, just like the music he just severed from his body. My ears are fucking ringing.

"So damn arrogant, Alessandro Moretti," I rebuke, but I'm breathless, my voice uneven and feverish. He can hear the effect he's had on me. He bites back a smile, turning the guitar over in his hands, looking down at it for a second appreciatively before he sets it to one side, leaning it against mine. Next second, he's on his feet and closing the already narrow gap between us. I shiver as he cups my face in his hands, tilting my head back so that I have to look at him.

He's a towering masterpiece in a Kings of Leon t-shirt and holy fuck do I want to climb him. He breathes deeply and then sighs, angling his own head to one side as he studies my features. "Well?

What do you think? Was it okay?" He sounds curious now. Intrigued. Genuinely interested to hear what I thought. What a ridiculous thing to ask; his question is akin to Mozart asking Justin Bieber if he thinks 'Rondo Alla Turca' is any fucking good. I'm basically nowhere near qualified to answer.

"Ahh. Y'know. It was all right."

Alex grins like a fiend. "All right?"

"Yeah. All right."

He nods, still smiling broadly, running his tongue over his teeth. "You're a harsh critic, Argento. I'll have to do better next time."

If he does any better, he's going to set the fucking world alight. I can't find the words to tell him this, though. His smile fades from his face, a serious look taking the place of his amusement. "Why are we here, Argento? You haven't been up here since..."

Since the shooting. Since Alex hurried me inside the sound booth and told me to lock the door behind me. He's right. I haven't been up here since that day. I was scared out of my mind when Jacob, Cillian and Sam held me down and forced themselves on me, but that fear didn't even come close to the fear I felt in that sound booth. I wasn't just afraid for myself, then. I was terrified for Alex, so petrified something would happen to him that it felt like I was going to have a nervous breakdown behind that insulated, reinforced door.

Measuring my words, weighing each one, I explain why I wanted him to meet me here, in a place that now feels haunted by dark memories. "I figured it was time to reclaim the space. After everything that happened with Jacob, I used to come and play here during my free periods. It was a sanctuary. I want it to feel that way again. Plus, I'm going to have to start teaching after school again soon, and I won't be able to do a good job if I'm on the brink of a panic attack every time I step foot through the door now, will I?"

Alex nudges my knee with his leg. "You can take your time, though. No need to rush everything all at once. If you're not comfortable here..."

I look around, taking in the sheet music tacked to the cork board, the scales chalked onto the board, the brass music stands in a regimented line against the opposite wall, and I'm surprised when I reach an unexpected conclusion. "Hmm. Really. I'm okay. Being here hasn't affected me the way I thought it would. I thought we could eat lunch here, since it's too cold for the bleachers. You hungry?"

The concern on Alex's face transforms into something altogether different. Something mischievous and Machiavellian. "Oh, Silver. You have *no* idea how hungry I am."

It doesn't take a genius to figure out that's he's not hungry for the pastrami sandwich I made for him this morning and packed in my bag. A hot blush creeps up my neck, a shiver of anticipation chasing down my spine. It's criminal that he can make me feel this way with nothing more than ten little words. In fairness, I was already turned on by the sight and sound of him coaxing that tempest out of the guitar, but still...

"Huh. Sounds to me like someone's mind's in the gutter. I'm surprised," I say airily.

Alex fastens his bottom lip between his teeth again, pinning his flesh there for a second. He's biting down hard enough that his lip has turned white. In one casual, possessive move, he reaches out and palms one of my breasts through my t-shirt, growling at the back of his throat. "And why is that?" he muses. "Let me think for a second. Could it be that you wanted me to hurt you the other night, and I haven't touched you since?" I suck in a sharp breath when he jerks my shirt down over my shoulder—the shoulder that bears the bruised wound where his teeth broke my skin. His eyes are hard, appraising and unreadable as he considers the half-healed mark. I let out another surprised gasp when he yanks my bra strap down, shoving the lacy cup of my bra out of the way, and he frees my breast altogether. My skin burns under his ravenous gaze more than it does against the cold air of the room.

"Yes," I admit. "I thought you were mad at me."

His dark eyes seem bottomless as they bore into me. "And why would I be angry with you?"

He pinches and rolls my nipple, squeezing sharply, and a spear of pain jolts between my breasts, firing on a direct path to my clit at the apex of my thighs. "Ahh! *Because!*"

"Because? Tell me, *Dolcezza.*"

"I—I don't know. Fuck, Alex. Someone could come in."

He pointedly ignores me. It only takes a second for him to pull down my shirt even further, removing the other strap from my shoulder and tugging my bra down all the way, so that both my tits spring free. He fills his hands with me, angrily kneading the swell of my breasts. It hurts, but in the best kind of way. A way I've been craving for a long time now.

"The truth, or you're gonna get punished," Alex warns. "Tell me the truth, and I'll eat your pussy right here and now. I'll make you come so hard you'll need me to fucking carry you out of here." A low, deep rumble emanates from somewhere deep in his chest. "If you don't, I'll use your mouth to make *myself* come. And I won't be gentle. I'll be rough. You won't be able to breathe. I'll fuck your mouth so hard your gag reflex will hate me until we both turn thirty." His voice is soft, almost apologetic. Electricity relays up and down my torso, snapping and firing at the nape of my neck, crackling in the pit of my stomach. The thought of it, the prospect of his hands in my hair, holding me in place as he thrusts himself deep down the back of my throat—it makes me so damn nervous but so fucking turned on at the same time that I almost whimper out loud.

As if he knows precisely what I'm thinking, Alex places a rough palm against the slope of my neck, sliding it around until he's firmly holding the back of my neck, his fingers pressing firmly, deliciously into my skin. "Are we going to continue with the charade, Silver? Or are you going to admit it? You want me to use your body for my own pleasure, however I see fit, don't you? Especially if it's just that little bit degrading. Especially if it *hurts*."

"I—Alex—" I'm breathing so fast, I'm beginning to feel a little dizzy. Shame flowers on both my cheeks, bright crimson blooms of embarrassment that make me want to hide my face from him. He has hold of me, his grip like steel, preventing me from turning away.

"No. No, own it. Face it," he commands softly. "And when you've done that, tell me *why* you want that."

Panic snakes its way around my insides, some kind of wall forming a partition in my mind. "I don't know why. It's just—it's normal, okay? Some people just *like* it. I wouldn't have thought you'd be narrow minded about—"

"Don't deflect. I'll give you anything you want, Silver, always...so long as it's for the right reasons. I'll hurt you until you're screaming and you can't fucking take it anymore, if that's what you really want. My pleasure's rooted in yours. If you're turned on by something, it will drive me fucking crazy too, because it's what you need. But you need to face the why of it, *Dolcezza*. You want to be hurt. You want to be hurt *sexually*, and there's a reason for that."

I have no idea what he's talking about. I try to figure out what he could possibly mean, but all I'm met with is that endless, impossibly high, featureless wall inside my head that cannot be scaled. Alex is the one with vine tattoos up his arms and around his throat, but it feels as though there are spiked thorns beneath *my* skin right now, scratching against one another uncomfortably. "Alex, stop. Please. Whatever point you're trying to prove, it isn't making any sense. I just—I just fucking want you. Isn't that enough?"

We lock eyes, and I see the conflict in him. He wants to press this, to keep digging at it, worrying at the subject like a broken tooth until I give him the answer he wants to hear. I can't, though. It's impossible for me to give him what *he* wants. My eyes are pricking so strangely, it's bewildering. "Please, Alex."

I watch his resolve crumble. "Okay. Fine. It's okay. I'll stop." His hold on the back of my neck loosens. I feel like I'm floating up off the stool, toward the ceiling, when he lets me go.

Both my shirt and my bra have slipped down around my waist now. Alex slowly sinks to his knees, his black t-shirt pulling taut across his chest as he rocks back onto his heels, taking hold of me by the thighs. His fingers find the button of my jeans, popping it open, and he carefully unzips them, tugging the denim down over my hips.

"I thought I was going to be punished?" I try to sound joking, but there's a hint of disappointment in my words that must be obvious to Alex. God, what the hell is wrong with me?

"I'm afraid we're gonna have to meet somewhere in the middle on this one," he tells me. "I'm all for games, Silver, but they're only fun when both parties are aware that they're playing."

"What does that mean?"

"It means lift your ass right now, so I can get these pants off you. I need your pussy on my tongue before I officially lose my shit." His tone brooks no argument.

I obey him without question.

As soon as he's ripped my pants and my underwear from my body, he falls between my legs with a fury that makes my head spin. His mouth is so hot, it feels as though he's painting my clit with fire. "Oh my god! Alex! Alex, that's...that feels so fucking good." It's a miracle I can even get the words out. My synapses are short circuiting, sending my thoughts scattering in every possible direction.

I have to bite back a scream when he forcefully pushes his fingers inside me, nipping at the inside of my thigh with his front teeth.

"Quiet," he orders. "Make a sound and I'll stop. Is that what you want?"

I almost make the mistake of answering him. He narrows his eyes, giving me a warning glance up the length of my body, and a manage to stop myself just in time. "Well?" he asks. I see that his lips are wet from the slick heat between my legs and I have to try doubly hard not to cry out. Instead, I nod, letting him know that I'll obey his rules, even if it kills me.

"*Good.*" He drives his tongue back between the folds of my pussy, flicking and laving, grinding the flat of his tongue into me so hard that I find myself bucking and rocking against his mouth. Just as he did with the guitar, he uses his hands to conduct a symphony, except this time my body is his instrument. Using both his index and his middle finger, he fucks my pussy, pumping them quickly inside me, harder than he has before, and my body feels as though it's coming alive.

I'm balancing so precariously on the stool that I'm probably going to fall off any second. I have to cling to the smooth wooden seat beneath my ass to prevent myself from tumbling to the floor.

"Fuck, your tits look amazing when they bounce like that," Alex snarls. He takes my left breast in his free hand, clasping hold of my nipple between his thumb and his index finger, and he rolls the swollen knot of flesh so hard that I can't help it.

"AHHH! Alex!"

The cry is out before I can pull it back. Alex growls, baring his teeth, withdrawing his fingers from inside me. "*Disobedient,*" he accuses.

"Please. Please. God, Alex, I need to come. *Please.*"

"You're making it worse."

I bite down on the inside of my lip. I will not speak. I will not moan. I will not make a sound. Alex waits a second, his eyes running me through, stretching out the moment, torturing me just a second longer…but then he flicks at my clitoris with the tip of his tongue, thrusting his fingers back inside me, and my head lights up with fireworks. This time when he pinches my nipple, savage enough to make me want to pull away from the burning agony of the pain, I don't make a single fucking sound.

Alex sucks at my pussy, massaging my clit with his tongue at the same time, and my head rips back, hanging loose between my shoulders.

For all intents and purposes, I'm naked. My tits are bare, my legs are spread as wide as they can go, my pussy exposed to anyone who might walk into the music room, but I don't care. All that matters are Alex's teeth applying a dizzying pressure to my clit, promising more pain, and his fingers, which are now slamming into me so hard that I can hardly breathe around the sensation.

I chant to myself, the words searing the back of my throat. *Fuck-fuckfuck. Please…let me come. Alex, let me come.* Down to the last muscle, my body tenses; I'm a quivering wreck as I hover on the brink of annihilation, waiting for it to claim me. The crushing sensation builds and builds, ready to crash over me any second. Alex reads my body as easily as an open book. He rumbles, curling his fingers inside me, beckoning me toward my climax, and that one small movement sends me hurtling over the edge.

My body takes over, my thighs clamping hard around Alex's head. His teeth find the sweet, sensitive spot just to the inside of my thigh again, and I can't take it anymore. I let the tumbling, falling madness take me, riding it out blindly, my eyes rolling back into my skull.

"That's it. Good girl. Show me. Show me how much you need it," Alex hisses.

I convulse against him, everything suddenly much too much, too sensitive, the feeling of his fingers inside me, his thumb against my clit, enough to make me squirm off of the damn stool. "Shit, stop, stop, stop. I can't…I can't…"

Can't handle how good it feels one second longer.

You see, Alex knows this as well as I do: Pain and pleasure are interchangeable. What should cause us to cry out in agony sometimes evokes ecstasy. And the afterburn of an orgasm can sometimes feel so intense that tolerating it for one moment longer becomes physically impossible.

Alex laughs darkly as he withdraws his fingers, enjoying the way I shake and shiver just a little too much. "It's like watching a star explode when you come, *Argento*."

I'm too slack-limbed and dazed to ask him whether that's a good or a bad thing. Getting to his feet, he draws me to him, letting my head rest against his stomach for a second while I catch my breath. I feel like a cat, deliriously content and satisfied as he gently pets me, running his hands over my hair, whispering things to me in Italian.

"*Shhh, respire cuore mio. Rilassare. Tutto a posto. Sono qui, mi prenderò cura di te.*"

I persuade myself not to ask him what he's saying. His voice is hushed, little more than a whisper. I get the feeling the soft susurrus of his words are for himself and himself alone. The silence is shattered a split second later by the blaring shriek of the bell. Both of us nearly jump out of our skin. "Fuck." Alex snatches up my jeans and thrusts them at me in a hurry. "Quick, *Argento*. We need to get the fuck out of here. Immediately."

I'm laughing, my heart beating out of my chest as I pull my clothes back on, hands fumbling over my bra straps, my heels getting caught inside legs of my pants. A clamor of voices and footsteps echo up to us through the open door to the music room, signaling that not one but a number of people are racing up the stairs towards us. I've just jammed my right foot back into my Converse when Sophie Maines comes flying through the doorway, her eyes as big as saucers. Three other freshman bustle in behind her, all young girls I don't know.

"What the fuck are you doing in here? Haven't you guys heard?" Sophie pants, slapping her palm against her chest. "There's all kinds of crazy shit going on outside Darhower's office. Cillian Dupris was found half frozen down by the gully. They think he's been out there for hours."

Cillian Dupris' name is like a slap to the face. I recoil from it, physically taking a step back, the stool behind me tipping...until Alex catches it up and sets it back on its feet.

A low, mournful siren wails in the distance, growing louder and louder; all six of us stand in front of the bank of windows in the music room, watching the small white block-shaped vehicle racing up the winding hill toward Raleigh.

An ambulance.

"Poor Cillian," Sophie says. "First he gets shot by that lunatic and ends up in a wheelchair. Then he winds up falling out of it in the snow and suffering from exposure. It just doesn't seem right."

"Seems perfectly right to me," Alex counters under his breath.

I dart a sideways look at him, ears burning, feeling...what the hell am I feeling? "*Alex?*" I hiss through my teeth.

He doesn't answer me. Doesn't even look away from the window. The line of his jaw is hard, a muscle ticking in his neck. "Come on. We'd better get to class," he says stiffly.

The ambulance finally pulls into the parking lot. Karen Gilcrest, Principle Darhower's assistant, totters out across the slushy snow in her high heels, hands fluttering everywhere as she gesticulates wildly back inside the school, calling out to the EMTs. Alex gives the scene below one last bored, uninterested glance, then takes me by the hand and pulls me away from the window.

The halls are empty as we head toward physics, and our footfall echoes off the walls. I'm too disturbed by the mental image of Cillian being lifted onto a gurney to even really notice the sound. The beautiful boy with the black hair and the intricate ink, leading me down the hall, away from the fray at the entrance of the school, begins to hum a jaunty, bawdy kind of song that makes you want to tap your foot. Sounds like an old pirate reel.

I pull at his hand. "Alex? Alessandro Moretti, tell me you had nothing to do with this."

He looks down at me over his shoulder, a wry smile tugging up one side of his mouth. Utterly remorseless. "As a proud citizen of this fine country, *Dolcezza*, in this particular instance it is my right and privilege to exercise the fifth."

ALEX

The Rock is wall-to-wall bodies when I walk through the front door. The walls are running with condensation from all the body heat, sweat, and evaporating snow the crowd have trekked in on their winter boots. It's always like this after bad weather. Trapped inside for days, the locals go a little stir crazy holed up in their own houses, so the moment the roads clear and the snow ploughs have finished their work, people converge on the bar *en masse*. I would have entered in through the back of the building, but the parking lot was a fucking nightmare and I couldn't even get to the entrance.

"Alex! Hey, baby boy! Come to join the party?" Stella, one of Monty's favorite dancers, shouts at me from the stage. She's completely naked, but I'm a fucking pro at this game. I perfected the art of maintaining eye contact with the girls a long, long time ago. "Come on, baby. Pull up a pew. I'll give you a dance, my treat." She gives me a wriggle of her shoulders, making her tits bounce for me, and the group of punters seated at her feet all groan and grouse—they've probably been sitting there for the last fifteen minutes, dropping dollar bills at her stilettoed feet, and now she's offering a free dance to some punk kid who just showed up out of the cold? Yeah, that's enough to make any man gripe.

"Next time, Stell. Gotta find the boss man," I shout back at her. There won't be a next time, of course. I've never fucked with the girls here. Why? First and foremost, I'm not fucking stupid. If I caused drama within the walls of the Rock, Monty would have my fucking hide. Secondly, fake tits gross me out. However, both of those points are academic now because I'm with Silver, and all other women are dead to me.

Stella's really sweet. She's one of the younger dancers, a freshman in college; my old friends at Bellingham would have gnawed off their own right arms for a chance at fucking her, but my skin feels like it's crawling as I shove my way through the heaving press of bodies on the bar floor, heading for the door by the bathrooms that reads *'Employees Only.'*

Paulie, the bartender, is rushed off his feet, hands flying every-where, pouring numerous drinks at once, knocking a flowing beer tap off with his elbow. He notices me and shouts a hello as I disappear through the door.

Takes a moment for my eyes to adjust to the darkness in the hall-way. I step over stacks of empty boxes and narrowly miss kicking over a row of empty Jack Daniels bottles as I negotiate my way down the corridor toward Monty's office. When I turn the corner, weirdly pumped, adrenalin surging through my veins, I catch the old man standing outside the doorway to his private sanctuary, pinning a guy up against the wall by his fucking throat. The guy—some piece of shit in a leather jacket with a buzzcut—pats down his pockets, searching for something. A gun? A knife?

Monty doesn't seem perturbed by the potential that he might be about to get shot or shanked. He stabs a finger into the guy's face, flecks of spittle flying as he snarls. "I didn't ask you to tell me where he *isn't.* I told you to *bring him here.* Instead, you're sitting at the bar, drinking off my promo tab, trying to get your dick sucked? Did I not tell you this was urgent?"

The punk gurgles. I can't tell if he's trying to say something or simply trying to breathe. Finally managing to stick his hand into his pocket, he goes to pull something out and I decide I've seen enough.

I drop the duffel bag I've been carrying to the floor and charge down the hallway, a threatening growl on my lips. Monty never gets angry. For him to be this openly pissed off, this Neo-Nazi looking asshole must have really fucked up, and I'm not about to let my boss get stabbed by him.

My fist's raised, body prepped for a fight, when two things happen: the punk pulls out a tattered, worn piece of paper from his pocket, and Monty sees my barreling approach. He holds up a hand, calling me off before I even reach them.

"Calm, Son. No need for any of that. Jonas was just explaining something to me, weren't you, Jo? Go on in and make yourself comfortable, Alex. I'll be with you in a second."

I'd argue, offer to stay, but then I make eye contact with Jonas and see that the guy's absolutely shitting himself. He might look like a hardened thug, but he won't be causing any trouble for Monty, that's for sure.

I go and grab the bag I just dropped, giving the old man a tight smile as I head into his office. Monty boots the door closed behind me, but I can still hear his furious words.

"An *address*? What the *fuck* is wrong with you?"

"I thought you'd want to pay him a visit yourself, boss!"

"For fuck's sake. There's a reason why you're not on Q's payroll yet, Jonas. You can't follow simple directions. I didn't ask you to *think*. I made it real fucking simple for you. 'Bring him here' means exactly that, motherfucker. Why the fuck would I want to drive all the way to Vancouver and drag the piece of shit across borderlines myself?"

"I'm—I'm sorry, man. I'll go now. I—I I can be back here with him by morning."

Monty curses colorfully. "You fuck this up and Q's gonna relegate you to prospect quicker than you can say shit-kicker. Get the fuck out of my sight, boy, before I demote you myself."

Ahh. Club business, then, not bar business. I forget Monty's even affiliated with an M.C. most days. He's diligent about keeping those two parts of his life separate. Church and State, he calls it, church being his club, state being the Rock. He's always preferred the two organizations never cross over unless it's for pleasure, but seems as though there was no helping it today.

When he barges into the office, slamming the door closed behind him, the old man's so angry he looks like he's going to burst a blood vessel. "Fucking moron. I swear that son of a bitch was dropped on his head repeatedly when he was a child." He collapses into his chair with an *umpfff*, setting his hands down on the black bag that I've placed on his desk for him.

"I needed this three nights ago. *Badly*," he tells me.

"Sorry, man. You asked me to keep hold of it. Then the snow—"

"I know, I know. You're not to blame. I just…" He pinches at the bridge of his nose, sighing heavily. "Just been one of those weeks. Don't suppose you took a peek inside?" His voice is weary, but he's added a dash of playfulness to his tone.

Unlike Jonas, *I* am not a dumb motherfucker. "Nope. The contents of that bag are none of my business."

Monty nods, smiling from ear to ear. "Good. Glad to hear it." And then he unzips the bag, opening it up right in front of me. My eyes hit the ceiling. My midnight runs for Monty have been a science experiment of sorts. Paradoxical. A demonstration of the legitimacy of the Copenhagen interpretation of quantum mechanics. Schrödinger explained the experiment best with his cat analogy, but in this circumstance, there is no box and there is no cat. There have been bags, and there have been theoretical drugs. Without looking inside any of the bags I've been running for Monty, the drugs have both existed and not existed at the same time.

Once I look inside, the contents of the bags will manifest themselves into being and there will be no denying their existence one way or another. What I'm trying to say, in a round-about way, is that ignorance is fucking bliss. If I see bricks of coke in that bag right now, I become complicit in something that, up until this very moment, I would be able to deny…

"Ahh, quit being such a little bitch," Monty mutters under his breath. "Here. Hold this." He offers something out to me. I look down…and it's too late. I've just been handed a fucking gun. A mean-looking silver thing, big enough to blow someone's fucking head off. I've never held a gun this big before.

"Desert Eagle," Monty informs me, leaning forward across his desk, steepling his fingers. He's frowning at the weapon like it's a rearing cobra and it's about to strike at him any second. "Heavy, huh? Hard to come by, Desert Eagles. Not really the kind of gun you wanna be carrying around stuffed in the back of your waistband. Too ostentatious. Conspicuous, you could say."

I lay the gun down on his desk, muzzle pointing away, toward the door. "Guns aren't really my thing."

"Me either," Monty agrees. "A necessary evil sometimes, though. You disposed of the one I gave you the other night like I asked? Wait, never mind. That doesn't matter right now. This bag belongs to an enforcer in Seattle. Some hotshot who likes to carry the tools of his trade around with him wherever he goes. I hear he's pretty good at torturing people. Jesus Christ, would you look at this?" Monty's eyebrows nearly hit his hairline, which is impressive given the fact that he's receding. In his hand: a weird metal contraption with handles that looks like a caliper or some sort of vice. The ends of it are sharp. Wickedly sharp. The kind of damage you could inflict upon a person with something like that...

At least it's not fucking drugs. There are other items and implements visible through the opening of the bag. Handcuffs. Scalpels. Brass knuckles. Small boxes containing god knows what. A huge hunting knife in a sheath. Aside from the gun, none of it is *illegal* though.

I can't help myself. "And this shit's so important to you because...?"

Monty smirks, zipping up the bag and dumping it on the floor at his feet. "Collateral. There are people chasing this guy all over Seattle right now. Something in this bag is worth *big* money, and they want it bad. The bag's mine now, which means whatever they want inside it is mine, too. I'll be presiding over a bidding war on Black Net by the end of the day."

You need to be into some dark shit to even score an account on Black Net. Not just drugs, or guns. Gangs and criminal entities trade in flesh on that site every day of the week. I've heard you only need fifteen grand in your back pocket if you're looking to hire someone to commit murder on your behalf. Monty's always been hungry for power and money, just like Westbrook said, but fucking around on a site like the Black Net? That's kind of surprising, even for him.

It's not my place to judge. Definitely not my place to get involved. I'm giving this one a wide fucking birth. "Hope you get what you want for it," I offer. "In the meantime, you said you had news about Weaving?" Up until now, Monty's been closed-lipped about his ideas for the Weaving family. He asked me to give him until Christmas, and Thanksgiving is next week. I'm running out of patience.

Monty waggles his eyebrows, rocking back in his chair. It's rare to see him looking *this* pleased with himself. "Caleb Weaving's been running all kinds of shit through his warehouses for years. Anything he can turn a profit on. The Dreadnaughts used to make runs for him sometimes, but Caleb's a fucking snob. He never wanted to deal with Q in person, so he had me act as go-between. Some shit went down last year, and the cops caught wind that Caleb had his hand in a particular pot that he should have been leaving well alone. They pulled him in for questioning. The bastard was squeaky clean, of course. He threw Q and the boys under the bus, though. Said they were smuggling in counterfeit goods through the port in Seattle. Cops raided the Dreadnaughts' shop and found all kinds of stolen Chinese tech. Goods worth well over three million to the right buyers. All Caleb's stuff. That motherfucker walked away without a speck of dirt on him, and three of Q's boys ended up with seven years apiece because of it."

This is all news to me. The Weaving family are disgustingly rich, but as far anyone in Raleigh is concerned, Caleb Weaving built his burgeoning empire off the back of stalks of wheat. Nearly every single farm you drive past in Grays Harbor County is owned by the Weaving family, and the ones that aren't are all paying a premium to grow Weaving's genetically modified seeds. They have no choice in the matter. The farmers who refused to sell to Weaving in the nineties soon found themselves slapped with lawsuits because they were found to be illegally cultivating a crop containing seeds patented by Caleb and his board of cronies. The seeds were either blown onto their land and grew there naturally, mingling in with the pre-existing wheat crops, or Weaving hired someone to sneak onto their fields at night and plant them there by hand. Either way, the result wound up being the same: the farmers had to either sell to Weaving, pay him a ridiculous annual premium for his seeds, or face ruin, bankruptcy and eventual foreclosure at the expert hands of Caleb's legal team. It's hardly surprising that a man who would stoop to those levels would also be dealing in smuggled goods along with god only knows what else.

"Q's been keeping tabs on that fucker ever since then. He's been compiling a dossier of Weaving's illegal activity, and he's ready to sell the bastard out. Anonymously, of course. If any of our other connections found out the Dreadnaughts were willing to hand over information like that, there'd be serious fucking consequences. No one would do business with them ever again. More likely, one of the other gangs would gun anyone wearing a Dreadnaught patch down in the street. You know how these things go. Snitches get fucked, even if they were the ones who got fucked first."

I crack my thumb knuckles, taking a moment to wrap my head around everything he's telling me. "Getting Caleb Weaving sent down would be pretty fucking sweet, Monty. It'd tarnish their family name for life."

"But?"

"But my problem isn't with Caleb. It's with his son. Jacob's the one who hurt Silver. He's the one who needs to pay."

Monty grins, flashing me a wall of teeth. "Patience is a virtue, kid. I'm not done yet." He takes his time pulling open the drawer to his desk. I'm practically squirming in my seat as he takes out a plain manila envelope, sets it down and slides it across the desk toward me. "Take a look." He pulls a smoke out of a pack by his laptop, places the filter between his lips and lights the end. "I think you're gonna like what you see."

The envelope's thin. Whatever's inside isn't that substantial. When I open it up and take out the contents, I find a small stack of enlarged photos in my hand. They're dark and a little grainy, but it's still easy to make out what's going on in the images. There's a figure in the center of the frame, and he's holding a woman by the roots of her hair—a young girl, wearing a Raleigh High cheerleader's uniform. Her face is contorted into a mask of pain, her hands grappling at the figure's wrist, trying to free herself of the guy's vicious grip. I flip through the pictures one at a time, my stomach knotting tighter and tighter as the scene between the two people becomes progressively more violent. The end photo is difficult to look at. There are four people in this image. The girl's on her back, two guys at her head, holding her down on the ground by a swimming pool. She's been stripped down to her underwear, the Raleigh Roughnecks shirt now floating on the surface of the pool. Her bra has been pulled down her body, exposing her tits, and the guy who was dragging her by her hair in the first image is positioned between her legs, his pants shoved down around his thighs.

It's a horrifying scene. The girl's clearly trying to fight her way free, her hands clenched, her mouth open in a silent scream, tears streaking mascara down her cheeks. The guys forcing her to the ground are all wearing the same, frenzied, lurid expressions. I take one look at it and the gas station burrito I ate on the way over here churns in my stomach, trying to rise up the back of my throat.

My imagination has painted a fairly graphic scene of what went down with Silver, and that's been bad enough. This is so, so much worse. This is what it would have been like for her. This is how scared she would have been.

I slide the photos back inside the envelope, unable to look at them anymore.

My head's fucking pounding. I clear my throat, trying to ignore the fact that, more than anything, I want to fucking throw up right now. My mouth is sweating like crazy.

"Seems as though the apple doesn't fall far from the tree," Monty says delightedly. "Young Jake has been helping his father on a number of his runs recently. We have plenty of shots of him attending meetings with his father. Handling very *large* amounts of heroin. And now Q's added this little tell-all to his dossier of evidence. Jake'll go down for his involvement in his father's illegal dealings anyway, but this... this is the kind of shit you really wanted him to go down for, right?"

Oh yeah. Monty *is* right. Because the figure in the photos, the person committing the most heinous crime of all in that final shot, is none other than Jacob Weaving himself. Both Sam and Cillian are proven guilty in that picture too, but with Sam already long dead and rotting in the ground courtesy of Leon Wickman, only Cillian can be held accountable alongside the captain of Raleigh's football team.

"Q's planning on handing everything he's collected over to the DEA at the end of the week. I didn't wanna say anything until I knew it was definitely happening. Plan was green lit this morning, though. Figured it was high time I filled you in. Your girl won't need to testify if she can't hack a court room. What he did to this girl alone will be enough to convict Jacob of rape. It'll be just one in a long list of charges. I knew seeing that would make you fucking happy."

Happy isn't exactly the word I'd use to describe how I'm feeling right now, but he's correct. Those photos will be enough to convict Jacob and Cillian.

"Jacob has a penchant for Raleigh High cheerleaders, huh?" Monty observes, pulling on his cigarette. "You know that one, kid?"

"Yeah." The word comes out hard, stiff and unhappy. I did recognize the girl Jacob was man-handling the moment I laid eyes on her. "Her name is Zen Macready."

"She friends with that pretty girlfriend of yours?"

"Used to be."

Monty's mouth turns down at the corners as he nods, filing this information away. "Since the DEA'll be dragging your boy Weaving off in cuffs at the end of the week, that gives you five days, man. Five days to plot, and plan, and exact revenge however you see fit. What have you got in mind?"

I stare at the manila envelope now neatly tucked underneath the edge of Monty's laptop, and, surprised, end up muttering words I never thought I'd hear myself say. "Nothing. I'm not gonna do anything. He's gonna be arrested at last. The sick motherfucker's gonna go to jail for a very long time, and he's gonna pay for what he's done. I don't need to do a damn thing."

Monty's eyes sharpen, his bushy, thick eyebrows tugging together to meet in the middle. "Are you fucking kidding me right now?"

I shake my head. "Silver's all I care about, man. If Jake gets what's coming to him and I don't even need to get involved, then fuck yeah. That's a fucking win. Justice is done, and I don't have to risk serious jail time that'll take me away from my girl."

Monty laughs softly, shaking his head. He stubs out his smoke and fishes in his pack for another one, barely taking a breath in between.

"God almighty, I never thought it'd happen to *you*, kid. You went and got yourself some high-grade pussy, and it's made you fucking soft."

He can laugh at me all he wants. He's going to mock me over this until the end of time, but I don't fucking care. I'm not gonna act like a dumb, arrogant prick and get my hands dirty just to prove I'm a man, when there's a chance I could lose everything because of it.

Monty heaves a sigh when I don't defend myself. A thoughtful look forms on his face. Looking down at the bag on the table, he hums under his breath, then slowly zips the bag back up, pushing it across his desk toward me.

"You'll change your mind, son. And when you do, I'm sure this'll come in handy. Use whatever tool tickles your imagination. Probably not safe to keep it here anyway. I've laid eyes on it. I know it'll be safe with you. Just don't let anyone else touch it, you hear? 'Specially not Q, or any of the other Dreadnaughts."

I'm pushing the bag of torture implements back toward him, shaking my own head, when Monty slumps back into his chair, clenching his jaw.

"Thanks, kiddo. Sorry for all the to-ing and fro-ing with that thing. You know, you're actually doing me a really big favor."

And that's it. Just like that, with a few simple words, he's made it impossible for me to say no.

+1(564) 987 3491: The entire team's gonna get a ride next time. When u gonna let us feed that greedy cunt, Parisi? We're gonna make you fucking bleed.

SILVER

"Oh, my goodness! *Silver?* This *is* a surprise."

Mrs. Richmond looks genuinely shocked to see me when she opens up the front door to her house. I'm shocked I'm here, too. I would have texted my brother to let him know I was outside and he could have just come out to meet me; that would have been the easiest way to manage this uncomfortable situation, but Max still hasn't got a cell phone, so I was shit out of luck in that department.

When Mom messaged and asked me if I could pick my brother up from the Richmond's, I immediately typed out a message, telling her absolutely, categorically no freaking way. I haven't been over here in a really long time, after all. I used to visit at least once a week with the other girls. We'd rotate between houses, which generally meant the Sirens spent time at each other's places regularly. Since everything went down with Jake, however, I've made sure to avoid even driving down this street at all costs.

Mom hasn't asked me for anything since she moved out, though. Not a single request or favor. As a point of principle, she's been trying to show me that she doesn't need to lean on me the way she did during the months leading up to her separation from Dad, and honestly, it's been kind of amazing. I love Max. I never minded the cooking or cleaning, or running errands for her, but it also does feels like I just got my life back. Mom's been working as a freelance CPA for the Mayor's office, though. Started out as a temporary position, but they spoke with her last week and told her that it could become permanent if she was willing to put the work in. She needs this job to afford the rent on her new place, so when she told me their month-end budget meeting ran long and she couldn't get away today, I made the decision to swallow down my anger at her and show her a little support.

Kacey's been gone for well over a month. Melody, Halliday and Zen are still stuck together like glue, but they haven't been on the attack where I've been concerned, so I figured standing on the Richmond's doorstep for five seconds while Max got his shoes wouldn't be that big an ordeal.

I was wrong, though. It feels so normal, being here. Like I should just waltz right on and make myself at home. On Thursdays, I used to teach guitar to a kid around the corner from here and occasionally I'd stop by and pick up Halliday when I was done. We'd go grab a milk-shake at the diner or go swimming at Lake Samish in the summer-time. The front door of the house was never locked. I'd let myself in and park myself on a stool by the breakfast counter, grazing on what-ever fruit was in the bowl there by the key tray while she got ready for us to leave. So much has changed since then. Being here *isn't* normal anymore. I'd never dream of letting myself in and making myself at home these days.

Mrs. Richmond opens her mouth, then closes it again. She doesn't seem to know what to say. Her hair's longer than I remember, but it looks a little lank and her roots are showing. She always used to be so well put together, but today, in her sweatpants and her oversized *Raleigh High Class of 1990* t-shirt, I barely even recognize her.

"Would you like to come in?" she asks, blinking rapidly. Her voice is three octaves higher than usual. Strained. "The boys are still in the back room. I told Max your Mom would be by to get him soon, but they were in the middle of a campaign apparently and didn't want to stop. Shouldn't take them long to get finished up, though."

Fuuuuck.

Goddamn boys and their video games. I do *not* want to step foot inside this house. I definitely don't want to hang around while Max finishes up a campaign on whatever new game he and Jamie have become addicted to. If he knows I've come to collect him instead of Mom, he'll use it to his advantage and take forever to leave.

I shift from one foot to the other, glancing back at the Nova over my shoulder. "*Uhh...*" God, how the fuck am I supposed to say no without coming off like a jerk? I should have left the car's engine running or something. "Sure, Mrs. Richmond. Thank you. I—that would be lovely."

I'm not sure what reasoning Halliday gave her mom when I stopped coming around here, but from the way Mrs. Richmond keeps looking at me out of the corner of her eye, her daughter didn't paint me in a very good light.

Inside, I toe my shoes off and slide them under the mail stand, out of the way. Force of habit. Mrs. Richmond loiters in the hallway for a second, and then nervously rubs her hands together. "All right, then. Well, you know your way to the back room, don't you. Why don't you go and light a fire under your brother? I need to check on the oven. I'm making lasagna and everything seems to be burning recently."

Relieved that she doesn't want to stand around and chat, I let her go without complaint. She hurries off toward the kitchen, her head bowed, feet moving double time, and I head in the opposite direction, toward the conservatory at the rear of the house known as the back room, where the Richmond children have always been relegated to keep them out of sight.

Neither of the boys look away from the television screen when I enter the room. They both know I'm there, though.

"It's not seven yet, Silver," Max says firmly. "I've got five more minutes."

"It's ten minutes *past* seven, actually," I say, looking down at Mickey. "And I have somewhere to be, so you need to get your butt up out of that chair and drag it to the car."

"Hey, Silver."

"Hey, Jamie."

"Don't be *nice* to her," Max tells his friend. "She's gonna mess up the game."

Jamie's always been sweet. Kind. Polite. Usually the complete opposite to Max. His hair is even redder than his sister's—more of an orange than an auburn, and his face is a constellation of freckles. He's a sensitive kid. The kind that needs a little more affection than your average eleven-year-old. I dread what's going to happen to him when he reaches high school.

"Don't be a butthead, Max. Save the game. You can pick up where you left off next time."

My brother hammers at the buttons on the game controller in his hands and a strafe of gunfire shoots across the T.V. screen. The loud rattle of sound is unexpected and makes me jump. That's what I tell myself. My heartrate isn't through the roof, and my palms aren't sweating out of nowhere because the sound mentally dragged me, kicking and screaming back to the halls of Raleigh High, the day Leon killed eighteen of my fellow students.

"Mom doesn't mind waiting for me when she comes. Just chill out," Max snaps. "I'll have to wait a whole week to finish otherwise. I'm not stopping just 'cause you wanna go hang out with your stupid boyfriend."

Whoa. Max has never had an attitude like this with me before. When the fuck did he get so mouthy? "I have a lesson to teach. I'm not trying to rush off with Alex. He's working tonight, so you can stow that crap right now. Get your shoes. Get your bag. We're leaving."

He ignores me.

I am not in the mood for this bullshit. I'm not hanging around the Richmond's place a second longer than I need to, either. I can't just pull the plug on the game console like I would at home, though. That wouldn't be fair to Jamie. It's not his fault my little brother is being a little asshole. Poor Jamie slowly lowers his controller, biting his lip anxiously as he looks back at me.

"It doesn't matter if we have to wait," he tells Max. "I won't play without you, I promise."

On the screen, a gruesome looking monster with jagged teeth

leaps out, thrashing with horrifying claws. The scene in the game flashes red, the controllers rumbling in the boys' hands.

"Shoot, shoot, shoot!" Max hollers. "It's killing you!"

Jamie looks torn. He frowns at the game, then hangs his head, choosing not to play. The screen goes bright red, and then a scrawled tag appears in white lettering. The words *'Game Over'* pulse on the screen, and Max lets out a furious yell. "Jesus, Silver! Look what you've done. Why the hell do you have to ruin *everything?*"

He jumps to his feet, throwing down his controller. The handset bounces off the chair he was sitting on, the plastic making a cracking sound, the batteries flying out of it. Jamie's mouth falls open, forming a perfectly round O. He doesn't make a sound, despite the fact that my shit of a little brother has probably just broken one of his controllers.

"Right. That's it." I lunge for Max, grabbing him by the scruff of his neck. "You'd better hope that still works or you're gonna be paying for a new one. Move, before I pick you up like a baby and carry you out of here."

Max rips himself out of my grasp, spinning on me, his face beet red. "God, Silver. You're such a fucking *bitch!*"

I've been called the darkest, harshest, cruelest things over the past year, by people I thought were my closest friends. None of that hurt as much as this, though. I feel like I've been slapped. Max hurtles past me out of the back room, his footsteps ringing out down the hallway. The front door slams closed a second later, but I can't seem to make my legs function in order to after him.

What...the...*fuck?*

My eyes are stinging like I just rubbed soap into them.

"Sorry, Silver," Jamie mumbles quietly. "It was my fault. I wanted to start another campaign."

"No. Don't worry. It's not your fault at all. Max is...he's..." I don't know what Max is. He isn't acting like my little brother, that's for sure. "Tell your mom I said thank you for having him over, Jamie. I'm sure he'll see you at school tomorrow. Unless I murder him in his sleep tonight, that is."

I grind my teeth together so hard as I head for the door that a tension headache begins to pulse behind my right eye. That little fucking piece of—

The thought is cut short when I turn a corner in the hallway, and collide with—

Fuck.

With *Halliday*.

Her bag crashes to the floor, and her phone goes skidding across the mahogany floorboards. Tubes of makeup roll out of her bag, pens and her diary tumbling out onto the ground. For a second, she just stands there, staring at me, eyes wide, surprise all over her face. I try to marshal my own horrified expression, but then I look down, at where her thick winter coat has fallen open and I see what she's wearing.

A skimpy bikini top, barely more than two triangles of navy-blue material attached to a few pieces of string, and a pair of kick shorts so small they barely cover the top inch of her bare thighs. Again, for the second time in less than a minute, I find myself thinking the same thought.

What...the actual...fuck.

She sees me frowning at her outfit and quickly covers herself, wrapping her knee-length down jacket around her body, cinching it at the waist. Before either of us can say anything, Mrs. Richmond emerges from the living room. "Oh, Silver, I'm sorry. I thought you'd left." She looks from me to her daughter, a tentative smile spreading across her face. "Oh, it is nice to see you two side-by-side again. I—I know things have been difficult amongst you girls lately, but honestly, my heart has been breaking that you had such a falling out. Looking at the two of you now, gosh…I have to say I hope you're on your way to working things out."

Halliday doesn't breathe a word. She quickly looks down at her feet, breathing deeply. I don't really know *where* to look.

"You're off to work, sweetheart?" Mrs. Richmond asks.

"Yeah. I'll be late if I don't leave now," she says sullenly.

"It's so nice of them over at The Rockwell to make an exception for Halliday. They don't normally let people waitress until they're eighteen. They must have known how good she'd be. And they're generous with their wages, too. When I was waitressing fulltime, I barely brought home a couple of hundred bucks a week. Halliday's earning three times that, aren't you, Sweetheart?"

Um...Waitressing? I've been to the Rock, and I know full-well there are no waitresses. If you're brave or hungry enough to order food from the kitchen, you have to do it at the bar and collect your food from the service hatch when they call your number.

"Yeah, I guess I was lucky," Halliday mumbles. She scoots down and collects her things back into her bag while I stare down at her, too many cogs whirring in my head to provide any assistance. "I've really gotta get going." Without a backward glance, she bolts for the door, leaving it yawning open after her.

And I realize, more than a little numbed by what I've just seen, that one of my ex-best friends has been stripping behind her mother's back.

ALEX

The bar's sorely understaffed, so Monty offers me triple pay to stick around and bus. I agree, but not for the money, per se. My mind's racing a mile a minute, and with Silver teaching lessons for the rest of the night, the prospect of heading back to the trailer and waiting out the silence alone doesn't sound very appealing. People continue to pour in through the door as the night progresses, and the next six hours whip by in a blur of spilled beer, smashed glass, rowdy arguments, and a few thrown punches.

Halliday shows up and takes to the stage. I don't acknowledge her presence, and in turn she pretends I don't exist—an unspoken arrangement that I wholeheartedly support. By midnight, the place has cleared out. The snowstorm might have passed but the roads are still hazardous, especially after the dark, and the cops are always out in force after a busy night at the Rock. No one wants to wind up in a ditch, or worse, having to try and pass a sobriety test when they've had more to drink than they should have.

Paulie cuts me loose at twelve thirty. I head out front, the same way I came in, bracing against the cold, pocketing my wages for the night, and I'm about to climb into the Camaro when a hand lands on my shoulder, roughly spinning me around.

When you grow up in foster care, or at least in the kind of foster homes *I* grew up in, you develop some pretty sharp reflexes; my fist is swinging even before I register who's trying to manhandle me. In my world, hesitation will only get you killed.

The fucker behind me is nothing more than a black streak as they duck, darting back, beyond my reach.

"Tut tut, Moretti. Holy shit. Getting a little slow in your old age?" a voice says teasingly. I take a step forward, homing in on the piece of shit who's trying to jump me, but then my ears catch up with my brain and I realize that I know the voice. I know it really well.

The secondary uppercut I was about to send flying halts in midair. There, in front of me, wearing a leather jacket that looks a little *too* new and a pair of ridiculously tight stonewashed jeans, stands a guy I never thought I'd see again.

Well, fuck me sideways.

"Zander Hawkins. As I live and breathe." I don't sound all that happy to see him. Understandable since the last time I laid eyes on the fucker, he was paying a fucking tank of a kid named Jorge fifty bucks to start a fight with me in the cafeteria of a shitty juvenile detention center. I was pretty sure Zander was going to wind up killing someone before he was released from juvie and wind up having his ass transferred to a legit prison, and yet here he fucking stands. And it's the *here* of it that's bothering me. "What the *fuck* are you doing in Raleigh?"

Zander shrugs one shoulder. "Had some business with your man in there. Got called down from Bellingham. I heard you were working here, so I stuck around. Thought a catch-up was in order. Old time's sake, y'know?"

Zander's almost as tall as me, with the same angry spark in his eyes. In juvie, he spent most of his time with a pair of weights in his hands or at the squat rack, working out like a fiend. I chose to pass my time getting ripped, too…which is how we became friends.

"Old time's sake?" I have no fingernails to speak of, what with playing the guitar religiously every day; if I did, I'd be digging them into my palms, trying to distract myself with the pain while I decide what the hell I should do here. For eleven months, Zander was at my side, looking out for me, ready to brutalize anyone who looked fucking sideways at me. I made a couple of other friends during my incarceration, but Zander was more than that. He was like a brother. And to then have a brother betray me the way he did, so grievously, the day before I was released? Yeah, that fucking sucked.

Javier grins at me in that *devil may care but I sure don't* way of his. He hasn't worried for one second about how he'll be received. He's just shown up, shoulders thrown back, middle finger held up at the rest of the world and expected me to be pleased to see him. Well, the fucker's got another thing coming. He was ready for the first fist I sent his way. I stopped the second. The third comes out of nowhere and takes us both by surprise. My fist connects with his jaw, landing heavy and hard, right where *he* showed me to hit, once upon a time.

Pain roars up my arm like a column of fire, settling into my shoulder joint and spearing up the nerve endings in my neck. Hurting someone else always ends up hurting us, too, one way or another. It's the natural order of things. Action and consequence. I relish the throbbing pulse of pain in my hand, welcoming it gladly, happy to accept the trade off as Zander Hawkin's eyes roll back into his head and he hits the fucking deck.

I rarely smoke. Every once in a while, when I'm particularly vexed, I'll light up and savor a single cigarette while I contemplate dark thoughts, allowing myself the length of said cigarette to rage and fume. To break bones in my head and set the world to rights. When I hit the filter and stub it out, though, that's it. I shrug my way out of the darkness, putting away the anger, and I wash my hands of whatever violence I allowed to steep in my veins. I'm usually a lot calmer by the time I've completed the ritual, but tonight that calm is nowhere to be fucking seen.

I'm on cigarette number five and I still can't seem to stop my knee from bouncing like a jackhammer. *What the fuck is he doing here? What the fuck does he want? And why the hell did he hang around to see* me? The

Rock's parking lot is nearly empty by the time Zander stirs. He groans on the back seat, swatting at his face with the back of his hand like he's trying to shoo away a swarm of flies.

"*Nuuugghhh.* What the *fuck*, Moretti?"

I exhale a lungful of smoke and flick the butt of the cigarette out of the window. It sizzles out when it hits the snow. "Quit the shit. It's late, and I'm tired. You know exactly why I popped you."

He grabs hold of the chair's headrest in front of him, using it as leverage to pull himself upright. I'm pretty fucking pleased with myself when I note the dark shadow of a bruise that's already forming along his jaw. "If you're still mad about Jorge, then you're being a dumbass," he complains, rubbing the back of his head. "It was an Irish goodbye."

I glare at him in the rearview. "I don't think that means what you think it means."

"Ehh, whatever." He waves me off with one hand. "It was *like* an Irish goodbye. It was juvie. I couldn't leave before you to avoid a miserable goodbye, so…y'know."

"So you paid someone to try and stab me. You're a fucking psychopath."

Zander grins like a madman. A madman with a very sore head. "You didn't miss me, though, didn't you? I was doing you a favor. Can I get one of those smokes?"

"How about you go fuck yourself."

"Awww, I never had you pegged as the kind of guy to get all butthurt over a little shanking between friends. C'mon. *Give.*" He holds out a hand, gesturing for the pack. Reluctantly, I slap it into his hand. He chuckles darkly under his breath as he takes a cigarette out and lights it. "Be real, Moretti. If you'd walked out of Denney as my best freakin' pal, what would you have done next?"

"I'd have visited—"

"Exactly. And pardon me for saying so, but *fuck that very much.* Last thing anyone wants to do after they get out of a place like that is go back to fucking visit. And if I'd had to watch you stroll in and out of that place, footloose and fancy free, it would have made my last few months feel ten fucking times longer."

"You do realize you could have just told me not to come back."

Zander picks a flake of tobacco from the end of his tongue, frowning at it before he flicks it away. "We all have our own way of doing shit, don't we? I don't know why you're getting so bent out of shape, anyway. Jorge didn't even get close. You put that sack of shit in the infirmary for three weeks."

"And if someone had ratted me out? Said it was me who broke his damn ribs? I'd still be fucking stuck there!"

"All right, all right. In hindsight, it was probably a stupid idea. But my intentions were good." He clutches at his chest with one hand, dramatically fisting his leather jacket. "I just couldn't bear to part as friends."

For fuck's sake. "Just get out of the car, Hawk."

"Don't you want to ask me what business I had with Montgomery?"

"*No.*"

"Well, you should. You should *really* want to know."

"I've been running my ass for the past six hours and I'm too beat to be playing stupid cat and mouse games with you, okay? I only threw your ass back there so you wouldn't catch hypothermia. You're awake now, though. Isn't it time you were dragging your ass back to Bellingham?"

Hawk's laughter is too loud for someone who just had a few of their front teeth loosened. "I'm not going back to Bellingham. I'm gonna be sticking around for a while. I've heard the school system here in Raleigh is pretty fucking impressive."

Oh no. Oh *hell* fucking no. I cut a murderous look at him over my shoulder, the muscles in my shoulders tightening to the point of discomfort. "Not fucking happening, Hawk. Raleigh's nothing like Bellingham. This is a nice town. You can't just stir up shit here and expect there to be no consequences."

The guy who watched my back for me at Denney slumps back into his seat, wearing an affronted expression. "Me? Stir up shit? *Dude.* I've had enough of the Washington State judicial system to last a lifetime. I'm on the straight and narrow. I plan on graduating with flying colors and making something of myself. You'll get no trouble from me, Scout's honor. Now…you feel like giving me a ride? I've managed to score myself a pretty fucking sweet crash pad."

My blood feels like it's about ready to boil over. "Get out of this fucking car right now, Zander Hawkins, or I swear I'll put you in the fucking ground."

His cocky, shit-eating grin doesn't falter as he clambers out of the car. I can still see it plastered across his face in the rearview as I burn off into the night, leaving him standing alone in the dark.

SILVER

"Hey! You said Halliday was working at the Rock. You didn't say she was *stripping!*" Tuesday morning rolls around and I've had all night to stew on what I saw at the Richmond's place. Before, when I was still a Siren and still friends with the girls, we wore some pretty questionable outfits when we hit up a party. I've been wracking my brain, trying to come up with some sort of alternative explanation for Halliday's attire last night.

Maybe she was going to hang out at her ex's place or something. Guy and Halliday aren't together anymore, haven't been for a long time from what I gather, but they still seem to be close. Guy's on the swim team, and unlike Leon, who took his spot very seriously, refusing alcohol like it was literal poison that would claim his life with one small sip, Guy and his twin brother Davis throw more ragers than any other teenager in the history of Raleigh High. I checked Instagram, though, and there were no parties last night. People would have been posting about it if there was, and there was nothing. Tumbleweed. Which leaves me with only one logical response, being that Halliday is wrapping herself around a pole.

Alex looks tired behind the wheel of the Camaro. There are shadows under his eyes the color of the angry winter morning. He sighs heavily under his breath. "She made me promise," he says stiffly.

"I'm your girlfriend. You're supposed to tell me everything," I counter.

He does look a little remorseful. He still stands by his silence, though. "My promises are watertight. Not just sometimes, for some people. *Always*. The only reason I'd ever break confidence with someone else is if it might hurt *you* in some way. Otherwise, I don't get to pick and choose. That's not the kind of man I want to be. Sorry, *Dolcezza*."

God, I hate that he's right. I hate that I can't be mad at him for not telling me this. Halliday and I aren't friends anymore, and it's really none of my business what she does with her free time anymore. Still, this feels big. Important. It feels like something I should have known, because *Halliday* should have told me.

And then I realize that I'm an extra shitty person because I'm keeping secrets from him, too. My *own* secrets, for fuck's sake. I haven't told him about any of the text message I've been receiving, I've been deleting them just as quickly as they've been coming in, and it feels as though the weight of that single undisclosed piece of information is choking me to death. Even thinking about the texts makes me feel uncomfortable in my own body, like my skin's crawling with fire ants. I quickly put all thought of them away, tossing the knowledge into a deep, dark, bottomless box in my mind, where hopefully it won't be able to bother me again for some time. My ugly thoughts and memories have a way of crawling their way back out of my mental prisons, though.

I feel the heat of Alex's gaze on the side of my face, and I glance at him out of the corner of my eye. God, I've been so distracted with the Halliday thing that I've barely said hello to him. He's dressed in a rare white t-shirt with a Dead Kennedy's logo on the chest. His familiar leather jacket is nowhere to be seen, replaced with a red and black flannel, the sleeves shoved up to his elbows. It's below freezing outside this morning, but Alex obviously cranked the heat in the

Camaro up to eleven before coming to meet me; he doesn't seem at all bothered or prepared for the fact that he's probably going to freeze once we reach school. Not as bad as Cillian Dupris must have frozen down by the dell, but still.

I still haven't even unpacked how I feel about the knowledge that Cillian's in the hospital right now, courtesy of Alex. I can't decide if he broke my rules, but it's obvious that *he* doesn't believe he has. He didn't beat Cillian with a tire iron. He didn't raise his fists to him. But he did put him in a situation that could have cost him his life, but…I find I'm not angry at him. I feel *relieved*, in a way.

I can't stop staring at the tattoos on the backs of Alex's hands—the fearsome wolf and the beautiful rose. The rose represents Alex's mother, but I've come to realize that it also represents his kindness, his loyalty, and his integrity. The wolf's meaning is obvious; it's never hidden what it was from me. It's a bannerman for Alex' strength, his courage, his determination and ability to overcome. Now, it's also a fierce sigil that represents his unfaltering ruthlessness.

The tendons in Alex's forearm pull taut, the roses and vines that creep on up his arm shifting as he flexes out his hand. "See anything new?" he asks, his voice low and amused. Oh shit. I've been staring, and none-too-subtly.

"Sorry. I just…got lost in my own head for a second there." It's a piss-poor excuse, but it *is* the truth. "My dad…he told me to tell you this morning that you're expected for Thanksgiving. No excuses."

Swift topic change there, Silver. Smooth. Well done.

God, inner monologue me can be such a sarcastic little bitch sometimes.

Alex sucks his bottom lip into his mouth, frowning as he stares ahead out of the windshield. I do love being wrapped around him on the back of the bike. I love how free and wild it feels. I even love the cold knifing through my clothes and the wind threatening to pluck me off the back and send me flying, but this morning I'm not sad that Alex has had to put his motorcycle away until the snow and ice calms down. This morning, I'm quietly, unreasonably giddy that I get to stare at him while he drives and think about sucking that bottom lip of his into *my* mouth.

He's more than just a seventeen-year-old high school student with a penchant for trouble. He's the fucking devil incarnate, come to tempt in the most distracting ways possible, and I'm not complaining about it one little bit.

The bridge of his nose wrinkles in a surprisingly endearing way that doesn't really look right on his usually extra-serious face. I'm fascinated by the sight of it. I'd pull out my phone and take a picture of it, but I'm not quick enough. As soon as it's formed, then it disappears again. "I'm not really a Thanksgiving kind of person," Alex says under his breath. "I usually try and avoid the holiday at all costs."

I swivel in my seat, arching an eyebrow at him. "You have something against turkey, Alessandro Moretti?"

"Just pumpkins, actually. So orange. And...*bumpy*."

"Bumpy?"

He nods.

"All right, well, I'll make Dad promise to ease back this year. He usually decorates every room in the house with them, but for you..."

"For me, he'll hang them from the rafters and fill the living room with them from floor to ceiling," he jokes.

"Maybe. But only because he likes you."

Alex's mouth twists a little. "He *likes* me." He seems entertained by the concept.

"Yes. And you're the only person the dog likes, so you basically have to come. Mom's taking Max to see my aunt in Toronto, so the house will be too empty otherwise."

"What about you, *Argento*?"

"Hmm?"

"Do *you* like me?" I can tell a wicked smirk is itching at the corners of his mouth. He's trying his best to suppress it. If I didn't know him so well now, I wouldn't even be able to tell he was trying so hard to hold it back—his features look like they're carved out of stone—but I can see it in his eyes.

I lean back in my seat, studying my nails, affecting boredom. "Oh, I don't know. I guess you're tolerable."

Unexpectedly, the car swings to the left and the engine cuts off. Out of the fogged-up wind shield, I notice the looming, grey shape of Raleigh High School and a number of blurry smears of color hurrying toward the main entrance, trying to get out of the cold. Alex unclips his seatbelt and quickly leans over, planting a hand against the window next to me to brace himself. He's so fucking close. The smell of him floods my head. He's the only person in the whole world who can make me feel dizzy and drugged with just the slightest trace of their pheromones. Case in point: I can't form a single coherent thought right now, as I stare up into his dark eyes and slowly, slowly, drown in him…

I can't fucking breathe.

He lowers himself an inch, his mouth over mine. He's so close to kissing me. His lips are two tiny millimeters away from touching mine…

My heart's wedged itself in the bottom of my throat.

I feel like I'm slipping, falling, disintegrating….

"We arrived in the nick of time," Alex whispers. "I was going to pull over and find out just how much of me you could *tolerate*. But…" He pulls away, sinking back into his seat while he twists, reaching onto the back seat for his bag. I'm reeling, still waiting for the pressure of his mouth on mine, drunk on the smell of him. "Looks like we're going to be late. We'll have to find out some other time." The smirk he was reining in before has been unleashed in full force now. The crooked quirk of his mouth is far more potent that an all-out grin. Alex Moretti's little smirks are like gift wrapped secrets, hinting at what they might hide but giving nothing away. He says plenty when he puts them into effect, and right now he's saying, '*I know you fucking want me, Argento. You're mine to play with. Mine to tease. Mine to drive crazy with the simplest suggestion of a kiss.*'

And he's so fucking right. Even if he didn't tell me about Halliday.

"I heard she's been transferred to some sort of mental facility. Margo, my neighbor? Her mom told *my* mom that she tried to drown herself in their pool last night. I mean, who does that?"

"Who still hasn't drained their *pool*."

"It's an indoor pool, dummy."

I know exactly who the girls next to me are gossiping about, as I make my way into the locker rooms. Laurie Gulliver and Jade Prescott

—both members of the Raleigh Sirens, girls Kacey used to haze back in the day, when she found it funny to terrorize the other cheerleaders to the point of nervous breakdown. It's funny, but I don't think I've ever heard them say so much in one go before. In the past, it was always, "Yes, Kacey." "No, Kacey." "Sorry, Kacey." There was only one thing Kacey enjoyed more than giving those poor girls hell, and that was when she had one us do it instead. Me, Halliday, Zen, Melody: all of us are guilty of making these girls cry at one point in time or another.

They sound delighted that one of their previous tormentors might have been carted off to the loony bin, and I can't say I blame them, really. We were fucking terrible to them. Zen's the only one of us with an indoor pool, and all of Raleigh is still buzzing about her cat fight with Rosa Jimenez. Doesn't take a detective to figure out that Laurie and Jade must be gossiping about her.

"She's gonna have to shave her head, y'know. No way she'll be able to pull that off. Her skull's a weird shape," Jade titters.

Laurie rolls her eyes. "Her head looked perfectly normal to me. Rosa left her with an inch of hair in a few places remember. I'm telling you, she's going to show up at school today with a head full of the most expensive, amazing looking extensions and it'll be like nothing ever happened. This kind of shit doesn't stick to the Kacey Winters' crew."

"It stuck to *Silver*," Jade counters.

It's then that they notice me behind them, pulling my Raleigh sweater and sweatpants out of my gym bag. The girls fall ominously silent. I'm used to overhearing all kinds of shit about myself, so I'm not going to be losing sleep over Jade's off-the-cuff remark. At the end of the day, she's right—the shit really did stick to me. I don't think the girls have ever been caught so blatantly talking about me, or Zen, or anyone else for that matter, though, and they don't seem to know what to do with themselves.

I pull off my shirt, quickly replacing it with a Raleigh High School Sirens tee, wanting to get dressed as quickly as possible. Technically, I shouldn't be wearing the Siren's shirt—I haven't been on the squad for a long time now—but it doesn't matter. A second later and my Raleigh sweater is hiding the article of clothing from sight anyway.

Laurie and Jade still haven't started talking again; the silence in our little corner of the locker room is growing more awkward by the second. Eventually I can't take it anymore and I turn around to face them. "Zen won't get extensions. She's too proud to cover up what happened. She'll shave her head," I tell them. "And she'd never try and drown herself. It's not her style. If Zen was going to kill herself, she'd be a little more theatrical." I think about it for a second. "She'd probably hang herself. Somewhere public. She'd get a kick out of the fact that someone would have to find her swinging from a light fitting."

The color drains from the girls' faces. They look like they've seen a ghost. Both of them stare at me, eyes wide and unblinking as I continue to get ready, shimmying out of my jeans and donning my grey sweatpants. It isn't until I'm doing up my sneaker laces that they dare breathe a word in my direction.

"With both Kacey and Zen out of school..." Jade begins. She has to look to Laurie to supply the rest of her sentence.

Laurie doesn't seem all that happy to help out. "With both of *them* gone now, we were wondering...are you planning on trying out for the squad again?"

My head snaps up so fast I almost give myself whiplash. "*I'm sorry?*"

"The squad," Jade says weakly. "There are two spots open now, and the girls on Kacey's backup list, well...they kind of died in the...shooting...so..."

What the hell are they suggesting?

I shake my head a little, trying to understand. "I—Are you—" *Nope. Still not making any sense.* "Are *you* asking me if I'll rejoin the Sirens?"

Jade and Laurie trade a wary look. Laurie's the one who speaks. "I mean, we have all college acceptance letters based on our athletics records. If the squad doesn't do well this year at the NCC, we can basically kiss our hopes of getting into a decent school goodbye. And you...well, you were never captain material..."

"Gee. *Thanks.*"

"Nothing personal," Laurie adds quickly. "We're not captain material either. But you were a great flyer and you always showed up for everything, made sure you gave it one hundred percent, and that's what we need right now. Someone reliable who'll do a good job."

Jesus Christ, don't bowl me over with flattery or anything. I've never received such a glowing recommendation before. "I don't think so. I've got a lot going on right now. I don't really have the time. What with guitar lessons, and, um, having to help out at home and all that." I don't even really know what excuse I'm giving them, only that I'm totally stunned they'd even ask me. Not long ago, they wouldn't have acknowledged I was a living, breathing entity. Amazing how quickly things change. With Kacey gone, the head of this particular snake has been cut off, and the body no longer knows what to do with itself.

"Okay, well, if you change your mind…" Jade mumbles. "Also…" She casts her eyes down at her feet, picking nervously at one of her fingernails. "If you remember, could you please tell your boyfriend, um, thank you for…" She trails off, unable to finish.

"We were in the library that day," Laurie says. Her voice is harsh. A little sharp. I recognize the anger in her tone for what it truly is—the only way she can talk about what happened without falling to pieces. "I saw the look on Leon's face. He would have shot every single one of us if he'd had the chance. We'd all be dead now if Alex hadn't tackled him."

I nod, eyes flitting from one of the girls to the other, unsure how to proceed here. "Okay, well…if you want to thank him, maybe it would be better coming from you," I suggest.

Jade snatches up her gym shoes, clutching them to her chest. She shakes her head violently from side to side. "I can't. He's terrifying."

She pads away quickly in her socks, ponytail swinging wildly as she heads for the gym.

I've managed to sort through most of what happened with Jade and Laurie by the time I've showered and gotten dressed after volleyball. It was the shock of another student addressing me on purpose that did it. It's been forever since I've spoken to any of my classmates in a normal, everyday way, that I couldn't stop wondering when the hammer was going to drop. When they were going to laugh in my face. When they were going to start whispering behind their hands, giving me vicious sidelong looks caustic enough to strip paint.

The moment never arrived, though, and all through gym class, all I could think to myself was, 'You cannot *rejoin the Sirens. You cannot rejoin the Sirens. You cannot rejoin the Sirens.'*

Trouble is, I've missed it. I've missed being on the squad more than anything else I lost during my great downfall. The Billy Joel-loving, Chuck Taylor-wearing, guitar-playing, badass version of me is kicking against the very idea that I might want to become a cheerleader again. It's telling me that I'm better than that, and only vapid monsters place any stock in a cheerleader's uniform. Another large part of me (that doesn't listen to Billy Joel) knows that isn't the case, though. There are plenty of girls on the cheer squad who aren't brainless, vain dimwits who just want to flirt with boys. Some of the girls on the squad joined because they are actual athletes, and they love taking part in such a fun sport. I always envied those girls. I was never allowed to say it, of course, but they were the true stars of show.

I take my time brushing my hair, waiting for the hallways to clear before I leave the locker room. I have a free period next and a date with some text books in the library since Alex has History, so there's no need to brave the rush of people all trying to make it to their next class on time.

You cannot rejoin the Sirens. You cannot rejoin the Sirens. You cannot rejoin the Sirens.

I'm repeating the mantra on repeat when I do finally make my exit. My phone buzzes in my back pocket, and I'm reaching to take it out when I see the door to the boy's locker room swing open and someone emerges.

My blood is instantly ice-cold.

Jacob Weaving.

His bag is thrown over his shoulder, just the one strap, effortlessly cool-looking. Naturally, he's wearing his letterman jacket. His blond hair is swept back in that douchey way that makes him look like he just came from an Abercrombie and Fitch photo shoot. I recognize that he's handsome, the same way you look at the sky and register that it's blue, but I'm also so repulsed by the sight of him at the same time that I almost double over and puke onto the hallway floor.

His blue eyes harden to steel when he sees me. "Well, if it isn't Boudicca herself." The venom in his voice is shocking; this isn't the playful, slightly arrogant Jake he presents to the rest of the world, when there are other people around to see. This is the hate-filled, spiteful, evil piece of shit who had his friends pin me down while he tried to sink his increasingly flaccid dick inside me on a bathroom floor. I think, perhaps, I'm one of very few people who have ever met the *real* Jacob. I can't decide if I feel sorry for him, having to hide how hideous he is as a person all the time, or if I'm grateful that he has the decency to do it.

I roll my shoulders back, setting my jaw, meeting his gaze with indifference; I know just how crazy it makes him when I don't respond to him with fear. I learned that the hard way, with that cold bathroom tile digging into my back and Sam Hawthorne kneeling his bodyweight onto my wrists, so heavy it felt as though the bones would break at any moment. "I'm shocked," I say coolly. "I had no idea you knew who Boudicca was."

His warped sneer is ugly and makes his face barely recognizable. "Oh, I know exactly who she was. She interfered, stood up to the wrong people, and got herself killed for it."

Hah. Makes sense that he would skip the part where the Romans invaded her city, killed her family, and she led the charge against them, rallying her people, and proceeded to make life a living nightmare for them, almost pushing the Romans out of London altogether before they finally caught and killed her. She was brave. A warrior. She was courageous and sought justice in the face of unbelievable odds, even though she knew she would ultimately die. If Jake wants to pick a figurehead for stupidity as a warning, then really, he picked the wrong woman. It's an *honor* that he would compare me to Boudicca.

I shouldn't have waited for everyone to get to class before leaving the locker rooms, because now the hallways are deserted. Jake smiles like the snake that he is when he realizes this. I have nowhere to go as he crosses the hallway to stand in front of me. "Jade Prescott's boyfriend just told me she asked you to rejoin the Sirens," he says. I hate myself for flinching when he reaches out and takes a piece of my hair, wrapping it thoughtfully around his fingers. I can't help it, though. I am wired to recoil from him. I should have been wired that way from the beginning. It should have been obvious to anyone who looked close enough that Jake was a vile, cruel, despicable human being, but I didn't know any better back then. I was too blinded by his looks to see him for what he was.

"Back away, Jake," I snap, knocking his hand away. "After your performance in that music booth, quaking in your boots and pissing yourself at the smallest sound, I'd have thought you'd be more than willing to steer clear of me."

His eyes are narrowed into murderous slits as he considers my face. His lips are parted and wet—a sight that would once have made me daydream about kissing him. It only reminds me of his mouth fastened around my nipple now, his teeth viciously grinding against the bud of my flesh. "What, you think I'm worried about you telling people I embarrassed myself? Pssshhh, come on, Silver. Don't be ridiculous. We both know no one'll believe you. They didn't believe you the last time you opened that whore mouth of yours and tried to tattle on me, did they?"

I'm too hot. Too cold. My skin's clammy, a nervous sweat breaking out down my back. It's true. No one believed me when I went sobbing into Principle Darhower's office. I wouldn't let them call my parents. I wouldn't let them call the police. The Raleigh High administration saw my unwillingness to report the 'alleged' crime to the authorities as a sign that I was making it all up. Never mind the bruises on my face...*and* the ones between my legs.

I draw in a shaky breath, aware that Jake is moving closer, but my mind is shuttering, my thoughts a whirlwind of panic. He's quick, grabbing me by the back of my neck with a strong hand, and the next thing I know he's jerking me forward, planting his mouth down on mine.

It only lasts a fraction of a second. A disgusting, terrifying moment when he's kissing me, trying to force my mouth open, and I can't pull myself free from his grasp. My reactions finally kick in, urging strength into my arms, and I shove against his chest, making him trip backward over his own feet, sending him stumbling into the middle of the hallway. "God, you really are stupid, aren't you," he hisses.

"You're the one with the fucking death wish. What do you think Alex is going to do when I—"

He drops his bag. The sound of it clattering to the floor echoes down the corridor, but there's no one around to hear it. I barely have time to take a step back before he's charging me, his hand closing around my jaw, fingers digging into my cheeks, and he's slamming the back of my head against the wall behind me. "I'm not worried about that dumb motherfucker, Silver. I'm not even *slightly* worried. Wanna know why?" He spits the words out so hard that a fleck of his saliva hits my top lip. "Moretti isn't a concern to me, because you're not going to breathe a word of this to him, or anyone else. I've been doing some research on your boyfriend, and he's walking a very fine line. One wrong step and he's gonna find himself behind bars for a very long time."

"He hasn't done anything wrong," I grind out.

Jake's breath reeks of stale coffee; my stomach turns when it hits my face. "Really? You sure about that? Has he told you about his boss's affiliation with those Dreadnaught losers who run drugs down to Seattle? Hmm?" He cracks my head against the wall again and my vision splinters, shards of light dancing in front of my eyes. "Has he told you about the little midnight runs he goes on for Montgomery Cohen? Has he mentioned anything about *that*?" He laughs under his breath, the sound manic and unhinged. "Jesus, under normal circumstances, I'd have my father pin something on the bastard. Something that couldn't be swept under the rug in a court of law, but I don't even fucking need to this time. There's plenty of legit ammunition to hand. So you, Silver Parisi, you are gonna keep you dirty little mouth shut, and I am gonna do whatever the hell I like. Understand?"

The pain in the back of my head is breathtaking.

"Do. You. Understand?" Jake spits. Maybe I nod. I don't think I do. Perhaps it's my dumb silence that Jake accepts as my agreement. He smiles broadly, flashing his perfectly straight, white teeth, and ice flows through my veins. "Good. Now that we've got that ironed out, why don't you and I find somewhere a little more private to talk, hmm? Wouldn't want someone stumbling across us and coming to the wrong conclusion now, would we?"

He fists my hair, using all his strength to pull me forward and then he smashes my head back against the wall one last time. A scream builds in the back of my throat, but I'm so dazed, so stunned by the fireworks exploding in my skull that I can't force it out. My legs barely keep me upright as Jake, still holding onto a fist full of my hair, begins to drag me toward the door of the boy's locker rooms.

"N—no!" Even through the panic and the pain, I know Jake can't be allowed to drag me through that door. If he does, he'll be able to take his time with me, do whatever he pleases, and no one will find us for hours. An electric current jolts me, bringing me back to my senses. All of the nights I've lain awake in my bed, wondering if I could have fought back harder in Leon's bathroom, if I could have screamed louder, if I could done anything different to prevent what came next— all of those long hours come crashing down on me now, and I decide. There won't be any room for doubt this time. I'll kick, and scream, and gouge and bite. There's no loud party to mask the noise I make today. I will use every last scrap and ounce of strength in my body before I allow him to humiliate and violate me again. I will fucking *die* before I let him touch me.

The roar builds deep down in my chest. I'm operating on sheer survival instinct as I drive my foot forward, using it to hook around Jake's ankle, and then I'm pushing him forward, ramming him with every bit of momentum I can muster. He staggers, unbalanced, but he's still standing, still holding onto me by my hair.

"Oh, Silver. *Silver, Silver, Silver.* Is that *seriously* the best you can do?" The mockery in his voice sends a wave of fury screaming through me, and something strange happens. I seem to step out of myself, distancing myself from what's happening. I see him wrenching on my hair. I see the malice in his eyes, and the look of cold detachment in mine, and I witness as I pull my fist back and I drive it up into his perfect Abercrombie and Fitch fucking face.

His head rocks back, blood spraying from his nose, and his hand goes slack, releasing his hold on me. I seize the opportunity and throw another punch. This time, the blow lands on his jaw, and pain fires up my arm, burning in my wrist. My form might not have been the best but I had surprise on my side. Jake topples sideways, still very conscious but visibly a little stupefied by what I've done.

Good.

The smart thing to do would be to run, but I'm not thinking clearly. I clamber up on top him, straddling his chest, and I bring my fists down on his head, putting everything I've got behind the punches. The skin across my knuckles splits. Pain and sheer insanity cycle around my body, pushing me on, encouraging me to keep on hitting him. Jake tries to grab hold of my wrists. He manages to grab one of them—my left—but I still have my right free. I clench my fist extra tight and drive it down one last time. Jake lets out a strangled shout, and then I'm flying backward away from him, skidding across the other side of the hallway. He's kicked me off him. I sit up quickly, ready to launch myself at him, but he's not even looking at me. He's propping himself up on one hand, blotting at his nose with the back of his hand. His letterman jacket is covered in blood, as is the front of his white t-shirt.

For a second, he stares down at the back of his hand, at the blood slick on his skin, wearing an expression of abject confusion. How many times has Jacob Weaving been punched in the face before? I'm betting not very many. Nowhere near *enough* times, that's for sure. Well, I just upped his tally by a good twenty times or so.

I'm bracing for the explosion. It's coming any second. Jake's going to jump to his feet and fly at me. He's going to fucking kill me when he gets his hands on me. But then...

Down the hallway, a door opens and Mr. French peers down the hall, squinting at us. "Hey! What the hell are you two *doing*? Stay right there!"

Jake and I stare at one another. A message of mutual hatred passes between us, so thick and foul that it chokes the life out of me. Jake breaks the exchange first, baring his blood-coated teeth at me as he scrambles to his feet and bolts in the opposite direction. I'm unsurprised; there's no way he'd want to get hauled to Darhower's office for fighting, given who he was fighting, and the fact that he definitely looks like he came off worse.

I don't give a shit if I get hauled over the coals in front of Darhower. It's hardly going to damage my reputation any, but Jake's pride won't allow such a thing to happen. His footsteps ring out down the hall as he runs toward the science block, and a dead weight settles in my stomach.

This thing between me and Jake, it just escalated up to an eleven. No way he's going to let it lie now. No way in hell. He'll be after *my* blood soon enough. Revenge to a wronged member of the Weaving family is a prerequisite of the highest order.

I'm not as weak as I once was. Maybe I'm fired up from actually getting the better of him just now but fuck it. If Jacob wants to retaliate, then I say so be it. And the sooner the better.

I look up, and Mr. French is standing over me with his hands on his hips. He's disapproval radiates off him like heat from a fire. "I think you and I had better have a talk."

ALEX

Ben: I don't wanna see Louie's Great Adventure on Friday. I want to watch Dread Station II. Can we?

It's my night to pick up Ben and take him out for dinner. Thankfully the roads through to Bellingham have been cleared properly, otherwise I'd missed my night, and I doubt Jackie would let me take another one to make up for it. She's too fucking spiteful to be that understanding.

Me: I thought you liked those animated movies? Dread Station's a horror flick. And it's the second part in the story, dude. You won't know what's going on.

Ben: I've already seen the first movie. It was awesome. Blood and guts everywhere. All of my other friends have already seen the new one. Please!

I'm so focused on my phone that I almost walk into one of the guys from the football team. He growls, begging me to make the wrong move so he can start something. I'd love the opportunity of a punch-up—there's some kind of fire zipping around inside me today that's hard to ignore—but I'm on my way to meet Silver by reception and she sounded like she needed me to hurry.

Me: All right. Fine. But we're gonna have to sneak you in. If anyone asks, you're fifteen and you have a growth defect. And you can't tell Jackie. If you have nightmares, I don't want her calling me at three in the morning to scream at me. Deal?

Ben: You're the best!

I'm already regretting giving in to him. Last summer, less than six months ago, for fuck's sake, the kid was content to go and watch whatever Disney or Pixar movie had just come out. We'd split a bucket of popcorn and smash ice cream into our faces, and he'd gurgle like a drain he'd laugh so hard.

Now, he's shot up three inches out of nowhere, wants to watch people flay each other's skin off and perv on half-naked chicks. What the hell was I like at eleven? I was tougher than Ben, that's for sure, but I wasn't really interested in watching movies. I was only interested in surviving, and having to defend yourself at every turn, physically and mentally, will make a kid grow up faster than usual.

I put my phone back into my jacket pocket just as I turn left into the small corridor where Karen's administration office is located. As gatekeeper to Principal Darhower's domain, Karen is strict about who she allows to walk past her desk. The balding fuck in the office at the end of the hall doesn't take kindly to people banging on his door without checking in with her first, so she watches everyone and everything like a hawk.

"H...A...W...K..."

"Yes, yes, I know how to spell Hawkins. Just...sign there on the bottom of the...yes, that's right. Now, you'll need to take these papers home for your parents or your legal guardian to sign."

Oh, come the fuck on.

You have got to be kidding me.

I didn't give Zander a ride last night. I thought he was just trying to cause shit and get my back up. I left him there in the Rock's parking lot, and by the time I got home, I'd forced myself to put him out of my head. Zander always was good at riling people up. He's never been afraid of stretching the truth a little in order to get a rise out of them, which is why it's such a shock to see him standing at Karen's window now, leafing through a bunch of papers with a studious frown on his face. I didn't think he was serious about enrolling at Raleigh.

I do a double-take when I see what he's wearing: a white polo shirt, pressed beige khakis with a fucking line down the front, and a red down body warmer. A fucking *body warmer*? I must look incredulous. I *am* incredulous. What kind of bullshit stunt is he trying to pull here? Last night, he was wearing a Dreadnaughts cut, rippled up jeans and a band shirt. He looks like Prep School 101 right now. His hair is neatly brushed to one side—fuck, it looks like he actually washed it—he's clean-shaven, and every single one of his tattoos is covered. To look at him, you'd think he was group leader of a church fucking summer camp.

I walk right up, leaning on the ledge of the counter outside Karen's office, and I arch a sardonic eyebrow at him. "What the *fuck*, Hawkins?"

"Excuse me, Mr. Moretti. Language! If Principal Darhower hears you cursing like that, he'll have you in detention for a month."

Zander wrestles an amused smirk from his face; I know why he's so entertained. Threatening people like Zander and me with detention is so inane and pointless that it's pretty fucking funny. *Detention?* At Denney, we were locked away, kicked, starved, spit on, cursed at, had freezing water turned on us through a high-pressure fire hose…I mean, that's not even the half of it. Having to sit in a room and complete some random thousand-word assignment on why swearing is really bad doesn't pose much of a deterrent to our ilk.

Poor Karen. She's quite conflicted. On the one hand, from her perspective, I've just rocked up and gotten into this new kid's face, and New Kid looks like he comes from decent, respectable stock. I *should* be reprimanded for my behavior. On the other hand, I'm also the kid who found her, frantic and afraid, the day a gunman waltzed into Raleigh and started shooting people. I helped her, calmed her, told her to find somewhere safe to hide until I could come back for her. And then I'd nearly died trying to save the entire fucking school.

I can see the conundrum play out over her face. It's quite the show.

She'd probably feel less sympathetic toward me if she knew the truth. I wasn't trying to save the entire school that day. Did I want anyone else to get hurt and die? Of course not. But I only jumped Leon in that library to protect *one* person. Silver was all that mattered…

"I'm sorry? Do I know you?" Zander asks, crinkling his brow in my direction. Well, hot damn. He must have signed up for some amateur acting classes after I left Denney, because that shit was almost believable. "I can't say I recognize you, friend. *Maybe you're confused.*"

There's a very clear message in his words. *Back off, man. You're gonna fuck this up for me, and it's important.* He wants me to disappear, but I don't know if I feel like playing along with this ridiculous charade. If Zander's arrival at Raleigh had anything to do with his meeting with Monty last night, Monty would have told me. He knows I'm a student here. No way in hell he would have charged Zander with some sort of task here without at least giving me a head's up first. Which means he's likely here on Dreadnaught business, and guess what? I don't give a flying fuck about the Dreadnaughts.

I tap my lips with my index finger, frowning at him. "Yeah. We know each other all right. I believe we spent some *time* together over in Bellingham. You and your buddy Jorge made life difficult for me, if I remember correctly."

I know what it sounds like when Zander laughs. He has a brash, raucous, uncontrollable belly laugh. People used to throw shit at him to make him shut up, because once he started it was impossible to make him stop. The stiff, reserved little titter that comes out of him now does not belong to Zander. He must have stolen it from some preppy piece of shit on T.V.

I tilt my head to one side, nodding as I pull my mouth down at either side—the expression of someone who is more than a little impressed. "You been practicing that?"

"Time to move on, Mr. Moretti. We only allow one student at the window at a time, so…I'm…you need to move along," Karen stammers out. I'm proud of her, really. Apart from stumbling all over her words, she sounded very firm. That probably took balls.

"Okay, Karen. You win." I shoot her a wink. Looking back at Zander, I gift him with something far rarer: *a smile.* "Well. Looks like we'll have to catch up another time, Zander. Soon, I hope. It's always nice to get to know new people. I haven't been registered at Raleigh very long, either, so we have something in common."

"Thanks," he says, plastering a broad, fake-ass smile on his face that perfectly matches all of the other fake things about him. "I'll look forward to that. It's real nice of you to reach out and wanna make friends. I appreciate it."

God, I'm going to knock him the fuck out again if I have to stand here one more second. I give Karen a tight-lipped smile as I push away from her window. *How's Silver going to react when she finds out one of my ex-buddies from juvie has enrolled here at Raleigh, and he looks like he's up to no good? Speaking of which, where is—*

As soon as the thought begins to form in my head, the door at the end of the hallway begins to open. Darhower's door. And there, emerging out of the principal's office, is the girl in question.

Long, wavy brown-blonde hair. The same grey and white baseball tee she was wearing this morning when I drove her to school. Same faded blue jeans and Chuck Taylors. The bruises are new, though. The broken skin across the backs of her knuckles. The flecks of blood all down the front of her shirt, and the dark red, almost black blotted mark on her right thigh. She walks toward me down the hall, weaving slightly, like she can't quite seem to get her gait right or something, and I nearly combust right where I mother-fucking stand.

What...the...fuck...happened...

Her head snaps up, as if I said the words out loud instead of roaring them inside my head. She looks confused. Kind of dazed. Over her shoulder, Principal Darhower follows behind...behind *Cam?* Oh, fuck. They called in *Cam?* This is really fucking bad. I don't say a word when Silver reaches me. I take her into my arms, hugging her to me, knowing that the contact is probably what she needs most of all. I make eye contact with Cam, and I can't tell if the guy's glaring at me, through me, or just into fucking space. He's visibly shaking. I haven't known him for very long or spent a great deal of time with the guy, but I would never have pictured him like this—too angry to function.

"Mr. Moretti, that behavior isn't appropriate in a school hallway," Principal Darhower clips out.

Fuck me. If he thinks he's going to prevent me from comforting Silver, then he must be smoking crack. "I'm *hugging* my girlfriend, not trying to strip her naked. I think my fellow students will survive the impropriety."

"Don't push your luck, Moretti. Your stay here at Raleigh could easily be cut shor—"

He rambles on, reminding me of how tenuous my place here is, and how quickly I could find myself behind bars, etc., etc., etc., by the grace of god, blah, blah, blah, but I'm not listening. I'm stooping down, searching Silver's face, trying to read what happened there without having to ask her to put it into words. I don't have a fucking clue what's gone on, but I do know Silver. It's unlikely she told Darhower anything. She might have told Cam, but I can't know for sure.

"Are you okay?" I whisper.

Her eyes are wet and shining. She's stiff, her emotions kept well hidden from her face. It's as though she's wearing some kind of mask. Her features are all where they're supposed to be, it's *her*, but there's something different about her. She's thrown up a ten-meter-high wall and she's not letting anything through. I'm relieved when she blinks, giving me a hint of a weak smile, and a flash of her normal self breaks through that wall.

For me.

She lowered it for a second *for me.*

"Long story," she says quietly. "I'll tell you later."

She's either keeping her mouth shut because she doesn't want Darhower and her father to hear, or because she wants to explain things to me somewhere else, away from Raleigh...which means it must be really bad. If she thinks I'm going to lose my shit, then something seriously fucked up has happened.

Darhower clears his throat. "Mr. Parisi, I think it's best if you take Silver to the hospital now and get her checked over—"

"*Hospital?*" Oh, fuck no, he did not just say hospital.

Silver reaches up and takes my hand from her face, squeezing it. She kisses the inside of my wrist, sighing under her breath. "It's okay. Just a bump on the head, Alex. I'm fine. Principal Darhower thinks it'd be best to go get it looked at. The school needs to avoid any liability if I end up with concussion or something."

"Liability?" I pierce Darhower down with a shotgun stare. "That's what you're worried about? *Liability?*"

Darhower rolls his eyes. "You're a seventeen-year-old student with a pretty poor track record, Alessandro. You know nothing about running an education facility of this size and importance to the community. Please do not interfere in matters you do not understand."

Oh. Oh, *really?* I am going to fucking kill this bastard the first opportunity I get. Despite his atrocious attempt at comb over, the overhead strip light bounces off Darhower's bald spot as he turns to Cam.

"Were you aware of Silver's association with Alex, Mr. Parisi? Seems as though it would be something they would try to hide, given Alex's past run-ins with the law."

Cam's still glowering like a madman. He turns his dark eyes on Darhower, the muscle popping in his jaw. "Yes, I know they're dating."

Darhower shoves his hands into his pockets, rocking back on his heels. "Really? Well, I have to say I'm surprised that you'd allow Silver to—"

"Alex has been through hell and back. His actions in the past might not be commendable, but I would have behaved and acted out far worse than he did if I'd found myself in his shoes."

"Cameron, he dug up a *parole officer* and urinated on his cadaver. That's not just an infringement upon the law. It's mentally—"

"He also defended this school against a very dangerous, very real threat recently, too. Have you forgotten that? And the *parole officer* Alex dug up had beaten him black and blue for years. He was a sick piece of shit that got off on hurting young boys. I'm glad Alex dug him up. If I'd have been there, I probably would have dropped my pants and taken a shit on the bastard right next to him."

Principal Darhower recoils, his mouth falling open.

"You're a fifty-year-old bachelor with no kids of your own, Jim. You think sitting in your office back there, day in and day out, somehow makes you an authority on what it's like to raise kids but you have absolutely no fucking idea. So how 'bout *you* don't interfere in matters *you* don't understand. Come on, Silver. Let's get you out of here."

I've never wanted to high five anyone so badly. No adult has ever stood up for me like that before. Cameron Parisi is a fucking *badass*. He shoots me a dry, sidelong look as he takes hold of Silver's hand and begins leading her toward the exit. "Come by the house when you're let out," he tells me quietly. "It's pizza night."

"You got it."

Silver pulls away from him quickly, turning back to me. She falls into my arms, hugging me tightly and pressing her mouth to my ear. "I love you. Just...don't freak out, okay?"

It's only when she and Cam have exited through the double doors that lead out to Raleigh High's parking lot that I realize I'm standing in the hallway, not only Principal Darhower, but also with Zander Hawkin's prep boy alter ego. Darhower seems to snap out of his troubled reverie at the same time. He bares his teeth at me, grimacing, like I'm nothing more than a bad taste in his mouth. The feeling is fucking mutual.

He spins on the balls of his feet like some sort of Nazi general and quick-steps back down the hall toward his office, leaving me alone with Zander.

"I'm guessing that was our supreme leader," he says mildly. "Can't say I liked *him* very much. Let me know if you wanna break into his house and fuck him up while he's sleeping. I am *so* here for that."

ALEX

I was already planning on trying to kidnap Silver for a date tonight, but Cam's invitation/order to come over for pizza has made things much easier. He answers the door, still wearing that dark fury on his face—a fury I recognize all too well. It's the kind of pervasive anger that soaks down into the roots of your soul. It's the kind of anger that will set everything to rot if you leave it unattended. "In the kitchen," he says stiffly, turning away from the door and disappearing into the house. "Silver's asleep. I don't want to wake her up just yet."

I point my thumb over my shoulder. "Should I come back later?"

"No. I wanna talk to you."

Uh oh. *I wanna talk to you.* That doesn't sound good. Was I too quick to assume Cam was defending me back at Raleigh? He could have just wanted to stick one to Darhower. I might be about to get the I-don't-want-you-hanging-around-my-daughter-anymore talk. That would be a little out of the blue considering how cool he's been with me, but I wouldn't be surprised. Darhower's snide remarks might have made him think twice about how liberal he's being where I'm concerned.

The kitchen smells like melting cheese and pepperoni. My stomach growls, reminding me that I haven't eaten all day. I assume Cam must be keeping some take-out pizza warm in the oven, but then I see the flour on the marble kitchen island and the small dishes of toppings in bowls set to one side, and I realize that he's actually *making* the pizza.

"Don't look so surprised. I've been pretty slack about immersing Silver in her Italian roots, I know. And my mother might not have taught me the language, but she did teach me the food. Come on. Come and make yourself something."

I hesitate.

The last time I made pizza, I was a child. I was with my mother. She was still alive, and my father was gone, but everything was still *normal*. Everything was still as it was supposed to be. Most of my happiest childhood memories revolve around standing on a stool in the kitchen with my mother, when she was in one of her calmer phases and she wanted to bake and cook.

"Don't you like pizza?" Cam asks bluntly.

"Yeah, of course."

Good job, Passerotto. *Now knead the dough. Like this. Dig your knuckles in. Yes, that's it. Now stretch it out. Ben fatto, amore mio!*

Since the shooting, I haven't heard my mother's voice very often. It's like a swift kick to the gut now, remembering her laughter as I tried to tease and shape my own pizza base in our small kitchen when I was a kid. I walk over to the sink behind Cam and wash my hands, then roll my shirt sleeves up to my elbows, taking up a spot at the island opposite Silver's dad. He jerks his chin toward a covered ceramic bowl as he sprinkles cheese liberally over the pizza he was nearly finished making before I knocked at the front door. Inside the bowl: a large wad of dough. The smell of proving yeast hits the back of my nose as I rip off a handful and slap it down onto the marble, beginning to knead it with my hands. Turns out this rote motion is something you don't forget.

For a minute, Cam and I work in silence. Eventually he's happy with his pie, and he goes to place it in the oven with one that's already cooking. When he returns, he cracks open a bottle of beer and plants it down in front of me. "I'm going to hurt someone," he says firmly. "And I need you to tell me *who* I need to hurt."

Oh shit.

This is a test.

The beer *and* the statement.

Fuck it.

I pick up the beer and take a deep swig, trying to buy myself some time. The bottle's half drained by the time I lower it from my lips. "What happened with Silver today?" I ask quietly. "If you're talking crazy about wanting to hurt someone, then I need to know."

Cam's jaw works while he considers this. He pushes his glasses up the bridge of his nose. "The night Silver was born, I was about to get on a plane to DC. Some company offered me an internship on the east coast, and I thought fuck it. I'm too young for a kid. Celeste'll be fine if I go. She's so damn strong, and her family are all here to help her. What good am I gonna be to her anyway? I was freaking the fuck out. I'd never been so scared in my entire fucking life. I'd already arrived at the airport when I got the voicemail from Celeste's mom that she'd gone into labor. I sat there and told myself that going back would be the worst thing I could possibly do. I'd make more money in D.C. I'd be able to support them better financially if I was in a bigger city instead of trying to carve out a meagre existence here in Raleigh. I'd be able to make a life and a name for myself on the other side of the country that I'd never be able to do in this Podunk town, and one day...one day my kid would be able to really think about what I did and why I did it, and they'd actually be *proud* of me for making the tough call. Can you imagine that? I was actually trying to convince myself in that airport that I was doing Celeste and the baby a favor." He laughs bitterly.

"I sat there with all these texts flooding in because I wouldn't answer my ancient Nokia fucking cellphone, and I made up my mind. I was gonna go. I was gonna go. I was gonna go. They opened up boarding for my flight and I sat there, watching everyone else show their tickets and get onto the plane, and I told myself that over and over again. Cameron Parisi, you are getting on that goddamn plane to D.C. and you are not looking back. Don't you dare fucking look back.

They called my name over the loud speakers. Said I had five minutes to get my ass to the gate or the plane was gonna leave without me. They had no idea that the guy they were waiting on, holding up the whole flight, was the guy with the backpack at his feet, sitting on the chairs in front of the check-in desk, staring at that walkway down to the plane like it was of the gates of hell itself.

"With a minute to spare, I got up, grabbed my bag, and I gave the woman my ticket. She ushered me through, told me I'd barely made it...but my feet wouldn't fucking carry me forward down that walkway. Celeste and I hadn't found out if we were having a girl or a boy. Early in the pregnancy, it was easier to be less scared. I'd even been a little excited. The idea of that kind of surprise appealed to me. But standing in that airport, about to leave forever, I realized that I hadn't even seen my child's face. I didn't know who it was I leaving behind. And that...that hit me right here," he says, thumping the center of his chest with his fist. "If I left then, I'd *never* know. Celeste would tell me if it was a boy or a girl. She'd let me know what she'd called it. She might even send me pictures after a while, when she was less angry and less hurt, but I would never get to truly know that child. And I couldn't bear that thought. It fucking crushed me.

"I went twenty over the speed limit the entire way back to Raleigh. I arrived at the hospital just in time for the birth. Celeste never even knew how close I came to abandoning her. I never told her. She was just so grateful that I was there when the time came that...I don't know. It seemed cruel to tell her that I'd almost left. Then...Silver. She came into the world with this strange little frown on her face, like she was so damn confused by what had just happened to her. She screamed when she realized that she wasn't in her safe, warm little cocoon anymore, and I mean *screamed*. The nurses couldn't get her to stop. She didn't even stop when they put her on Celeste's chest. She howled and screeched the entire time, until the nurse took her from her mom and handed her to *me*.

"I'd never held anything so tiny, so fragile before. My heart was beating out of my fucking chest when I looked down at her little face. She opened her eyes. She saw me, and I saw her, and it felt like the world was snapping into focus for the first time in my life. *Really* into focus, like I could finally see what was important, and it was the tiny little girl looking up at me like I'd hung the goddamn moon. She stopped crying immediately, and we just stared at each other for the longest time, wondering who the hell the other person was. One of the midwives took a look at her, all bundled up in her blankets, and said, 'There you go. She just needed her daddy is all.' And that...that fucking *killed* me. This child, this helpless infant that I already adored and worshipped more than life itself? I'd almost walked away from her, and she'd *needed* me. I made a vow right there and then that I'd never leave her. I'd *never* not be there if she needed me in the future. I'd always protect and care for her, and I feel like I've done a pretty fucking good job at that, Alex. Up until this year, I've been everything I swore I'd be to her. Her protector. Her champion. Her provider. The one person she can turn to when she's hurt or sad. But something happened, and now everything is seriously, *royally* fucked up, and I didn't take care of my daughter when she needed me, Alex. I can't begin to tell you what that does to a guy when he has that realization. So please know that I will fucking *destroy* you if you don't tell me who hurt my daughter, and I will do it gladly with a smile on my face because I am *done* not being there for Silver when she needs me."

Holy fucking shit. Cameron's lost his ever-loving mind. He's threatening me to get what he wants, which isn't typically a great plan where I'm concerned. Usually, I rebel against threats on principle alone, but Cam—

"Dad? Who are you talking to?"

I nearly jump out of my skin when I hear Silver's voice in the hallway. Cam leans back, plastering a smile on his face that definitely wasn't there a moment ago. When Silver enters the kitchen, hair a little mussed, cheek red from her pillow, her father looks like he hasn't got a care in the motherfucking world. Silver's eyes light up when she sees me, and a sharp, painful knot tightens in my chest. I'm never going to get used to another human being looking at me like that. Like I deserve all the love and adoration in the world. I'm not worth three seconds of this girl's time, and yet somehow she's permitted me to fall head over heels in love with her, and it's just...it's fucking unbelievable.

"We're out of those little pimento olives you like," Cam says, kissing his daughter on the top of her head. "I'm gonna run over to the store and pick some up. If you guys think of anything else you'd like, shoot me a text and let me know. I won't be long."

He scoops up a set of keys from a dish by the backdoor and lets himself out without another word.

"*So* smooth," Silver says, with a heavy dose of sarcasm. "He's making himself scarce so we can talk."

I spin my half-drunk bottle of beer around, eyes boring into the side of her face. There are more bruises developing under her skin, leaving purple-black shadows that weren't there before when I saw her outside Darhower's office. My anger is a steel glove, tightening its grip around me. A living, breathing thing, just under the surface of *my* skin that wants me to lose my cool and start smashing things out of frustration. I can't though. I need...I need to stay fucking calm, or this is going to be a disaster.

"That was nice of him," I say. "We *do* need to talk." I take a beat to even out my breathing. Only when I think I've got my shit locked down do I permit myself to open my mouth again. "Do you have any idea how difficult it is to go through an entire afternoon and half an evening not knowing what happened to someone you care about? To see them hurt and obviously upset, and have no idea why, what happened, or who did it to them?"

She looks down at the kitchen island, hair forming curtains around her face, hiding her remorse. "I'm sorry, Alex. If I'd told you about what happened in a text or a call, you'd have gone and done something stupid, and I can't have you doing that. If you beat someone, or broke something, the consequences would be much more dire for you than they would for anyone else."

"Because I'm trailer trash?"

She looks up at me with sad, steady eyes. "Because you've already been in trouble before, and some people in this town would love nothing more than to see you sent away, where you'll no longer be a thorn in their sides."

I let my head fall back, stifling a growl. "Let's stop pretending, Silver. We both know who did this to you, don't we? This has Jacob Weaving written all over it. Please just tell me what happened. Tell me you're all right. Tell me what you need. I'm going fucking crazy."

"Okay. But you have to promise—"

"No. No more fucking promises!" I'd already made my mind up about that one before I left Raleigh this afternoon. It's been murder trying to find a way to bring Weaving to justice with the constraints Silver set in place blocking me at every turn. I'm not going to tangle myself up in any more restrictions. The time for that has long passed.

"Then I can't tell you," Silver says reluctantly. "I'm going to deal with the situation myself. I—"

"NO!" Pain lashes around my wrist, shooting up my arm as I bring my hand crashing down onto the marble top. I don't want to shout at her. I don't want to be that guy that gets mad when he doesn't get what he wants, but this is just too much. Silver's eyes round out, surprise and shock warring for real estate on her face. "You aren't in this alone anymore! This is no longer a secret story of abuse that you have to carry around like poison in your heart, pretending like it's not fucking killing you on the inside. Squirreling this shit away, it's fucking toxic. I am fucking *here*. I fucking *love you*. I promised you that you would *never* have to deal with this shit alone, and you're making it impossible for me to keep that promise. What is it, Silver? Do you feel like you're supposed to be able to bear the weight of this all by your-self? Do you think you'll look weak if someone else picks up a weapon and helps you fight a couple of these battles? Because that's not how this kind of thing works anymore."

Silver looks like she's walking a fine line between misery and rage. She's shaking, her eyes filling with tears. "Anymore? What's changed, Alex? Nothing. Those bastards at Raleigh are always going to—"

"*You've* changed! *I've* changed! *Everything* has fucking changed! When someone hurts you, I have to fucking bear it, too, because I love you more than I've ever loved anything in my entire, miserable fucking life. You're my fucking heart and my soul, and I will defend those two things with my own goddamn life. I can't bear for anything to happen to you. I can't see you hurt and not feel it. I can't see you suffer and not have something wither and die inside me. I can't see you wounded and not feel like I'm fucking failing you. If you're asking me not to react to this, you're asking me not to care about you anymore. You're asking me to cut the damn wires to my fucking heart, and I cannot...*will not* do that."

She isn't breathing. She's frozen in place, trembling, her eyes brimming over as she stares at the center of my chest, like her gaze can pierce through the material of my shirt, through my skin, through bone and muscle until she's looking upon the very organ I just mentioned. I hope she can see it. I hope she can see how fucking broken and worn it is, that it's held together with string and fucking duct tape. I hope that she can see how much it's fucking hurting right now.

"It's hard admitting that I need help," she whispers under her breath. "I've never had to do it before. Maybe I'm too proud. But how am I supposed to tell you difficult things like this when I have no assurances that you aren't going to do something that will inevitably end up in you being taken away from me?"

"You *trust* me. That's how. I just found you, *Argento*. I'm hot tempered and reactive, but I'm also really fucking smart. I'll never jeopardize us. Nothing is more important to me."

A single tear streaks down her cheek, and pain knifes into my chest. I can't fucking bear to see her cry. It's harrowing. "You're right. You do already know who did this," she says, gesturing to the bruising at her throat and her cheek. She seems so dejected. "I'm not going to say his name out loud."

I blow out a breath down my nose. It may be freezing outside, but there's a desert wind howling around inside my head right now, growing hotter and hotter as the seconds pass, scorching everything in its path to cinders and ash. "Was he alone?" I grind out. "Or did he have someone with him?"

"Alone," Silver mutters. "We were alone."

My stomach revolts, nausea climbing up the back of my throat, making my mouth sweat. "Why did he do it?"

"I don't know. I made him angry. Why does Jake do anything? He tried to kiss me. He kept smashing the back of my head against the wall—"

Oh. Fucking. No. He. Did. Not.

"—then he tried to drag me into the boy's locker rooms, and I...I just snapped. I punched him. I kept on punching him until he let me go. Next thing I knew, he was on the ground and I was on top of him, and my hands were bleeding. I couldn't stop hitting him. I think I broke his nose."

I root myself through the kitchen floor, mentally sending out anchors down into the basement, down through the house's foundations, deep into the frozen earth below us. I fix myself in place so that I can barely move a muscle, and it takes every ounce of strength that I possess.

I'm going to fucking kill him. I'm going to fucking skin the bastard alive. He's going to die screaming, and I'm going to relish every last second of it.

I exhale out a shaky breath, pressing down the dark thoughts that rear up inside my mind, filing them away to be dealt with later, when I don't need to prove to the girl I love just how reasonable and calm I can be.

I ask the only important questions that matter in this moment. "Are you okay, *Argento*? What can I do?"

Silver lifts her chin, steel forming in her eyes. With a swipe of her hands, she bats her tears away. She's a complex creature, this one, but I know how the gears and cogs turn inside of her. She and I are very much alike. She's hurting and she's afraid, but I can't treat her that way. I can't walk around the kitchen island and hug her. Not right now. Maybe in an hour or so, I'll be able to take her into my arms and press her to me. I'll be able to make her feel safe. If I so much as think about coddling her now, her hurt and her fear will take a turn for the worse. She'll lash out in a destructive way, and that won't help. Against my own better judgement, I stand fast and let her breathe.

"I'm okay. A little sore but I'll live. If you want to help, then maybe we could all just act normal. Just have a nice night and make some food. I don't want to think about it anymore. Is that okay?"

Not thinking about it anymore is tantamount to burying your head in the sand, but things are tenuous right now and Silver needs time to process things. After a long moment, staring into her face, I give her what she wants. "Fine. But if I find out you're one of those monsters who put pineapple on their pizza, I'm gonna have to reassess this entire relationship. Some things just can't be overlooked.'"

She smiles, and it's like the storm brewing inside the kitchen has just broken without ever reaching its climax. I'm relieved. I'm able to pretend, to joke and to laugh. To not look at the bruises she's wearing and go to

DEFCON 1. I'm able to do all of this because I got really fucking good at hiding my feelings back when I lived with Gary fucking Quincy, and I can stow my emotions when I really have to. But inside, I'm a fucking mess.

Cam returns, and the evening continues like nothing at all is out of the ordinary. The three of us laugh and shoot subtle digs at one another as we construct our food. As we eat, we talk about light things. Unimportant things. I ask Silver if she wants to come and see Dread Station II with me and Ben on Friday. It's almost as if tonight is a normal night, the same as any other, and we're all having a great time. The underlying, niggling current of tension in the Parisi household, however, is studiously ignored but felt by all.

This is not okay. This is not okay. This is not okay.

At just after ten, Silver pushes her plate away, groaning, and looks at her dad. "Alex is staying the night?" She poses it as a statement, but really it's a question.

Cam opens his mouth, looking down at his own empty plate, but I speak before he has a chance. "I actually have to get back to Salton Ash. There are a couple of things I have to take care of back at the trailer."

Yeah. I have to Google a few new interesting torture methods and sharpen my fucking throwing knives.

Silver looks disappointed, but I think she's still exhausted from the nightmare of a day she's had. Cam leaves us alone while I say goodnight to her at the bottom of the stairs. "If you need me, text me and I'll come running," I whisper into her hair. Now's the time for that hug. I pull her into the circle of my arms, and the righteous vengeance I've been tamping down all evening roars in my ears, deafeningly loud. She feels so fragile pressed up against my chest. So small. There's barely anything to her. The thought of Jacob Weaving laying his hands on her, when she seems so vulnerable with her head nestled into me, below the crook of my chin, makes me want to raze all of Raleigh to the ground.

"I have a meeting with the social worker first thing tomorrow morning, but I'll see you at school?"

Silver tips her head back and I kiss her deeply, stroking my thumbs over her cheeks. It takes more will power than I possess to let her go.

It's insanely hard not to follow up the stairs behind her, but somehow I find the strength to do it.

I don't leave immediately. I wait at the foot of the stairs until I hear the door to her bedroom click closed. Then I head straight for Cameron's office; I enter without knocking. The guy's standing in front of his imposing desk, leaning against the polished oak, his hands driven deep into his pockets.

Obviously, he was expecting me. "Well?" he asks.

I set my jaw, flaring my nostrils. This is a bad idea. It's a really bad fucking idea, but I don't really care anymore. It has to be done. "The guy's name is Jacob Weaving. And don't worry. You aren't gonna be the only one doing the hurting. We have until Friday night to make him suffer, and there's a bag of tricks in the trunk of my car that'll make the job easy."

ALEX

"Everything seems to be in order. I'm impressed that the place is so clean and tidy."

Maeve Bishop, my official social worker, stalks around the trailer like she's inspecting a prison cell and she's pleasantly surprised by the conditions. I grunt from where I'm slumped in my seat on the couch, waiting for her to sign off on her never-ending paperwork so I can get the hell out of here. "I'm not an idiot, Maeve. I do know how to wash dishes and tidy up after myself."

She gives me a reproving look over the top of her clipboard. The infernal fucking clipboard. I'm sick to death of the sight of them. For years I've had them brandished at me like they give the person holding them some sort of power over me.

"No need to get pissy," Maeve rebukes. "Just doing my job. You know you should have told us you weren't living with Montgomery anymore. You should be thankful they're signing off on your new living arrangements at all. It's highly irregular that they'd let a teenager, still in school, live alone, let alone someone with your track record for…"

"Anarchy?"

"Issues with authority."

I smirk at that. I s'pose she's right. She wanders through to the kitchen again, checking for the third fucking time that the stove actually ignites, and hot water comes out of the tap when she turns it on. "Not long now, anyway," Maeve calls to me. "It'll be your birthday soon, and I won't have to pay you anymore of these visits."

"Yeah. Right." Don't I fucking know it. My birthday *is* coming up soon. Five months and change. April twenty-seventh. That piece of shit, Gary Quincy, always used to tell me that they must have gotten my date of birth wrong by a month. He loved to sneer that I was the biggest April fool's joke of all.

"I visited Ben last week," she says, walking back into the living room. "He told me Jackie was taking him on vacation to Hawaii after Thanksgiving. That'll be nice for him, don't you think? She's going to home-school him there until after Christmas. Can't remember the last time I managed to get away."

I just stare at her blankly. Jackie and I are hardly on great terms, but we do communicate from time to time about Ben's well-being. She hasn't mentioned that she's planning on taking him to Hawaii. She sure as shit hasn't told me she was taking him away for six fucking weeks. It's supposed to be my year to take Ben on Christmas Day. Something sour and cold pinches in my chest.

"No fucking way."

Maeve perches herself on the edge of the coffee table, sighing deeply. She was bright and sunny a second ago, telling me how great it is that Ben's being taken away for the holidays, but now her mask has slipped, revealing the truth beneath it: she knew I was going to react badly to this news.

"Come on, Alex. You don't need to cause a stink. Think of Ben. Six weeks in the sun, getting to play on the beach every day? Jackie said she's signed him up for surfing lessons. Regular kids with regular families aren't lucky enough to get a vacation like that these days. For a kid in foster care, it's basically unheard of. Can you imagine any of your old foster-carers shelling out to treat you like that?"

"No," I answer stiffly. "They were all too busy trying to burn me with their cigarettes."

Maeve's a good coordinator and she's great at filing her paperwork. She's not very good at the emotional side of her job, though. She gets uncomfortable when people like me tell her the raw, unadulterated, bare facts of life. If she could have it her way, she'd spend her days believing that kids placed in the care system are fussed and adored over like cute little puppies and nothing bad ever happens to them.

Idealists should never be placed in roles where society will probably let them down; eventually, Maeve will be so jaded by the things she sees and hears in this job of hers that she'll probably end up moving to a cabin in the woods and she'll forsake humanity altogether. Or it'll all get to her so badly, she'll end up snapping and killing someone.

She pulls on a tiny thread that's worked free from the hem of her pencil skirt. "Look. Okay. Jackie asked me to tell you about Hawaii. I told her I thought it would be better if it came from her, but she was worried about you causing a scene when you take him out on Friday. She said in exchange for Christmas, you can have Ben for Easter."

"I'll already be Ben's legal guardian by Easter. And fuck Easter, anyway. Why would she try and trade Christmas for *Easter*? Some bullshit religious holiday—"

"*Christmas* is a religious holiday."

I give her an arctic look. "Don't pull that shit. Christmas is about presents, candy and food to kids these days. It's special. Easter's just a week off in the middle of the fucking semester."

Maeve splays her hands. She looks remorseful, but she isn't going to do anything about the shitty situation. I already know what she's going to tell me. I stare up at the popcorned ceiling while she spews out the usual bullshit lines. "Alex, you can accept this gracefully, or you can create problems. At the end of the day, it doesn't really matter how you take it. You *are* entitled to spend time with your brother, but when is entirely up to Jackie. She's Ben's legal guardian, and if she wants to take him on vacation for six weeks then there's absolutely nothing you can do to stop her. My recommendation?"

"Let me guess. Lie down like a little bitch and take it? Let Jackie walk all over me?"

Maeve is not impressed. "If you're still dead set on trying to get custody of your brother, then let Jackie have this one. If you act like a mature adult instead of throwing a temper tantrum, then that can only reflect well on you when the time comes to present your case before the family law court."

I glare at the side of her head. "Why do you people keep on saying shit like that?"

"Like what?"

"*If* I'm still determined on taking Ben. There is no '*if*' here. It's happening."

Maeve takes a deep breath. She opens her mouth, about to say something, but then she stops herself short. Her words seem to have upped and left her. Her gaze dips, her eyes settling on the record player on the other side of the room. "All right, Alex. This is probably the dumbest thing I will ever do in my entire career, but you've convinced me. I'll help you get your application together for custody of Ben. I'll do whatever I can to make sure this works out for you. *If* you don't lose your mind over this Hawaii thing."

I study her, searching for the lie. She's not supposed to get involved with things like that. She's certainly not supposed to *help* me. I can't find the deception in her eyes, though. As far as I can see, she's telling the truth. I may not like Maeve very much. I may not think she's right for her job, but that doesn't mean I don't *respect* her. Like I said, she's a great coordinator, and she can file a fucking form like no one else. She was the one who kept me out of prison after the whole Gary Quincy exhumation and subsequent desecration incident. If she says she'll help me put together my case, then my chances of being awarded custody of Ben just went from thirty-five percent to a solid seventy. That's a significant improvement in odds.

"Why? Why would you do that for me?"

Maeve shrugs halfheartedly, a weary look on her face. "Well. You *are* turning eighteen soon. Once that birthday rolls around, everything changes, doesn't it? You'll be an adult. And I get the feeling you're going to need the responsibility of looking after Ben to keep you on the straight and narrow."

Even though she doesn't say it, I hear what she's really implying. She thinks the responsibility of looking after Ben will be the only thing that keeps me out of fucking prison.

I haven't said shit to Maeve about Silver. A girlfriend might complicate things where CPS are concerned. But it isn't just the prospect of taking care of Ben that's keeping me on the straight and narrow now. I have *her* to think about, too.

"I need to get moving," Maeve says, picking up her purse from where she dumped it on the end of the couch when she arrived. She gets up slowly, heading for the door. "I'm supposed to file this paper-work by the end of the week." She holds her clipboard, loaded with her secret forms, aloft in the air. "You know what would look really good on this form, though, Alex?"

"What?"

"A better address. With a separate bedroom for a little boy to sleep in every once in a while."

She wants me to get a new place? I laugh quietly at the impossi-bility of such a suggestion. "D'you know how hard it is to find a reasonably priced two-bedroom apartment in Raleigh, Maeve? They don't exist. You're either looking at a five bedroomed mansion, or a rat-infested studio apartment overlooking a dumpster lined alleyway behind a bar."

She stands in the doorway with the door cracked; a rush of freezing cold air blasts the side of the trailer and comes charging in like an uninvited guest. Maeve's teeth are chattering together when she says, "Really? 'Cause I seem to recall seeing a pretty perfect spot advertised in the window of the hardware store this morning when I dropped by. The apartment *above* the actual hardware store, I believe. And the rent was pretty reasonable. Only nine hundred, including utilities."

She's got to know about my little sideline with Monty. She'd hardly be saying nine hundred bucks a month is reasonable amount of money to spend on rent to a teenager with a part time job if she wasn't. "If you've got some money set aside, I'd recommend calling in there and putting a deposit down on the place as soon as possible. I doubt it'll be available for long."

"And why the hell would they rent the place to me in the first place?" I grumble.

"Because Harry was a friend of my father's?" Maeve says lightly. "And he's doing me a favor?" She steps through the doorway and out of the trailer, but she pauses there on the step. "You've got one chance at this, Alessandro. Just one. Please don't fuck it up, or I'm gonna look like a complete moron, okay?"

Begrudgingly, I give her a military salute.

"Oh, god. This really *is* a bad idea, isn't it? Just get your ass to school, Alex. And don't let me down." The trailer almost seems to shrink when Maeve slams the door closed behind her.

SILVER

Raleigh's one of the few schools in the entire state that breaks for a full week over Thanksgiving. There are still three days left before that break begins, though. Dad tells me over breakfast on Wednesday morning that I can stay home if I'm not feeling well, but I decline his invitation to play hooky, determined not to be chased out of school by that evil little limp-dicked prick.

Dad holds a hand to my forehead, miming out the act of taking my temperature. "I don't know, kiddo. Your head feels weird."

"I don't have a temperature, Dad."

"I didn't say it felt hot. I said *weird*. If you stay home today at least, we can do a drive-by on your mom's new pad and egg the place. Sounds like fun, no?"

"*Dad.*"

"What? It's supposed to rain later on this afternoon. The mess will probably wash away before she even comes home and notices it."

I give him a wry look as I shove my notepad into my backpack. "Then what would even be the point?"

"Because *you* would know that we'd done it. And *I* would know that we'd done it. And it would make me feel good."

"Didn't have you pegged as the petty type, Father," I say teasingly. He hasn't mentioned Mom much at all lately. He hasn't seemed angry, either. Not about her, anyway. It's a little saddening to hear him joke about stuff like this, though. He *is* joking, I can hear it in his voice and see it in his eyes, but there's always an element of truth to this kind of thing. He's still hurting, which it totally understandable. They were together for twenty-three years, for crying out loud. That's a long time to get used to someone always being there, no matter what. A hole the size of the one Mom ripped open in Dad's life is going to be noticeable, regardless of how mad at her he might be.

With my backpack now hanging from my shoulder, my feet shoved into my shoes, and the keys to the Nova in my hand, I'm just about ready to leave for school. I pause for a beat in the kitchen though, leaning my elbows against the breakfast bar, standing next to Dad as he skims over the morning news on his laptop. "This isn't a break, is it? Between you and Mom. It's final. You guys aren't planning on getting back together, are you?"

Dad slowly closes the laptop, spinning his bar stool around to face me. "I don't know. I don't know anything anymore. I used to think I had everything figured out, but then this happens, and I don't even know the answers to the simplest questions. I don't even know what I *want* to happen, kiddo. The only thing I know is that this house feels much bigger than it used to now. And sometimes, I want to drive by your mother's new pad and egg the place. Beyond that, everything's far too complicated to even think about."

So, so depressing.

I leave, wishing I could make everything easier for him. Not just the Mom stuff, but my shit, too. He'd seethed inside Darhower's office yesterday, when I lied and claimed I'd fallen and hit my head. Fucking *seethed*. He'd also been hurt, and I hate that I did that to him. Most of all, I'm sick to death of worrying him all the time.

At school, everyone's buzzing about me being frog marched to Darhower's office yesterday, and it quickly becomes clear why: I'm being expelled. I'm being transferred to a military school for girls. I'm sick, and Darhower didn't want the other students to see me collapsing in the halls; someone caught me laying into the notice board outside the gym with my fists, having some sort of psychotic break. The gossip is rife. No one knows the truth, though.

How would they ever suspect that I would have fought back against Jacob Weaving and actually left a mark? It's such an unlikely scenario that I don't blame anyone for overlooking it.

With Alex's early meeting with his social worker, he couldn't give me a ride this morning. I'm sorting through the books in my locker, trying to track down my English Lit text book, when I sense the presence on the other side of my locker door. Alex promised to come find me as soon as he arrived at school, so I assume it's him. Who else would it be? I glance down, prepared to see his white Adidas sneakers on his feet, his ankles casually crossed as he leans against the wall of lockers beside me, waiting for me to close the door and finally look at him. But…the shoes I see there aren't Alex's. No way, no how. He might have had a meeting with a social worker this morning, but I know my boyfriend well. He wouldn't be caught dead wearing a pair of brown polished leather shoes. *Sensible* shoes. And khakis? Absolutely, categorically, no fucking way.

I slam the locked door closed, my hackles up. If someone wants to fuck with me this morning, then they're really going to wish they hadn't. However, standing there, waiting politely for me to notice him, is an unfamiliar face. A guy with dark hair, cropped close and swept back in a very clean, almost military cut. He's wearing a white button-down shirt so well ironed that there isn't a single wrinkle in sight. The record bag over his shoulder is brown leather to match his shoes. Everything about him looks clean and wholesome. I'm almost surprised there isn't a little black name tag over his left breast pocket, informing me that he's a member of the Church of Jesus Christ of Latter-Day Saints, and would I like to take a moment about of my busy day to talk about our lord and savior?

The guy breaks out into an unnaturally wide smile. *"Silver."* He says my name like it's the answer to a question, though what the question might have been I have no idea. I find out almost immediately, though. "The girl who tamed Alessandro Moretti," the guy says, tipping his head to one side. "Is Silver your real name, or a nickname?"

I clutch my books tight to my chest. "I'm sorry. You are...? I didn't realize we had another new student."

His broad smile transforms, adopting a more sinister edge, at odds with his missionary attire. "If only Raleigh High knew how lucky it was," he muses. "Alex and myself in the same year? I'm sure things around here are about to get much, *much* more interesting. I've already heard Alex got himself shot taking down a gunman in the library. He's always been a bit of a do-gooder but that really is taking the piss."

Do-gooder? What person in their right minds would call Alex a *do-gooder?* "*You* know Alex?"

This guy doesn't look like the kind of person Alex would hang around with outside of school, either. The hair, the clothes. The guy's stiff, rigid posture makes him look like he's got a stick shoved three feet up his ass.

He rolls his eyes, pretending to remember his manners. "Apologies. I don't know where my head's at today. I'm Zander. Zander Hawkins. Alex and I go way back. It was a real nice surprise to find out he was a student here when I registered. Always nice to see at least one familiar face when you find yourself in strange new surroundings."

There's *definitely* something off about this guy. It's not the clothes, or his crew cut, or the stiff, off-kilter way he speaks. It's all of it, combined together, that just feels wrong. Like an act. With so many months spent on the peripheries of the school, absolutely no one daring or stupid enough to talk to me, I spent a lot of time watching people. Wasn't like I had anything better to do. After a while, I got really good at understanding how people worked, what made them tick. How their body language was often a precursor to their actions, giving away what they were going to do next.

This Zander Hawkins guy doesn't seem to *have* any body language. He's reined in so tight, I get the feeling he's counting out each time he blinks inside a minute to make sure it's not out of the ordinary. What-ever this is, this bizarre charade he's acting out, he's faking it.

"You went to Bellingham, then?" I squint at him, trying to place him there. The Roughnecks have played against the Braves more times than I can count. As a member of the Sirens, I visited the Bellingham school campus whenever we had an away game, and I never knew what to make of the place. The building itself is way older than Raleigh—stone-built, solid, with creeping vines and ivy snaking up the walls. Stained-glass windows everywhere, throwing bolts of color up the walls of the high-ceilinged hallways. The place looks like something out of a gothic nightmare.

Half the students in attendance at Bellingham are from rich, well to-do families and have their noses permanently stuck up in the air. The other half…let's just say they're from a lower socio-economic tax bracket and *their* noses are usually firmly glued to a coke mirror. Despite how he's dressed right now, I'm guessing Zander hales from the later demographic.

"Actually, no," Zander says. His eyes are burning into my skin in a really weird way. He's studying me so intensely that his scrutiny is almost unbearable. "Alex and I know each other from a different…*institution*."

I don't understand. A different institu—oh. *Oh!* He knows Alex from juvenile detention! Zander grins mischievously when he sees the realization dawn on my face. "Yeah. Nice vacation spot," he says airily. "Me and your boy had some good times. He isn't beatin' on you, is he?"

"*I'm sorry?*"

Zander points to his face, gesturing to his jaw and neck. "Quite the bruise collection you've got going on there. Looks pretty gnarly. I never thought Moretti'd raise a fist to a girl, but I guess you never know."

I cover my jaw self-consciously, arranging the collar of the thick, cable knit sweater I picked out of my closet this morning higher around my neck. "Jesus, *no*. Alex would never hurt me."

Zander seems to think about this. He seems to think a lot before he opens his mouth. I get the feeling that a word doesn't make it past Zander Hawkins' lips without having been thoroughly vetted and designed for a specific purpose first. "Then there's someone in Raleigh who probably ought to be walking around with an armed detail right now," he observes. "Alex is pretty mellow most of the time. Until he *really* isn't."

"Alex knows I'm handling it," I tell him. My voice drips with ice. I don't know why, but I don't think I like this guy.

A thick silence falls over the hallway. Takes a moment for me to notice it over the beating of my blood in my ears. Zander's little disguise slips for a second, amusement burning off him like warmth from a flame as he looks at something over my shoulder, his eyes tracking something as it approaches. I'm unable to resist; I turn and look.

The crowded hallway splits apart, everyone making room for Jacob as he makes his way toward his locker. His head is held high, defiance and anger roiling in his eyes, daring anyone to mention the fact that he's got a split lip, a black eye, a deep cut above his right cheekbone, and a broken fucking nose.

"Holy shit," Zander mutters under his breath. "Someone must have taken a tire iron to that poor fucker's face."

"No." I try not to smile, but my smug-levels are almost off the charts. "I'm pretty sure it was just their fists."

"THE FUCK ARE YOU ALL STARING AT?" Jacob's roar echoes down the hall, startling Abigail Whitley, who just so happens to be standing closest to him. "I got tackled in football practice. Big fucking deal. Let's all just mind our own fucking business and get on with the day."

No one questions him. No one asks how he took so much damage to his face with one bad tackle. No one dares to refute his story. The king has spoken.

Jake always makes a point of leaning against his locker each morning, leering at me and making lewd, disgusting comments about me to his dumbass football buddies, but not this morning. He doesn't even glance in my direction as he rummages in his locker, head down, then snatches his backpack up from the ground and scurries off to class.

"Well, well. I'm pretty good at math, but I just tried to multiply five foot six against six foot three and the numbers just won't seem to add up. Seeing is believing, though, right?"

When I spin back and face Zander, the sardonic look on his face says it all. The bruises on my neck, jaw and hands, coupled with the mess that was once Jacob Weaving's perfect fucking face tells a tall tale. One that's not so easy to wrap your head around. Zander's figured it out in no time at all, though. "You really *did* handle it, didn't you?" he says, laughing.

"Yeah. I guess I did. And I'll keep on handling it for as long as I need to. Alex doesn't have to worry about me. Now, if you'll excuse me, I have to get to class."

Zander Hawkins grins devilishly, stepping to one side so I can get past him. "Of course. Heaven forbid I make you late."

I forget all about Zander Hawkins the moment I lay eyes on Alex in AP Physics. He very rarely smiles inside the walls of Raleigh, choosing to maintain his blank, indifferent exterior in front of the other students, but he treats me to the smallest hint of one as he weaves his way between the desks and slumps himself down into the chair beside me on the back row.

He smells like winter. Like fresh pine needles, and the cold, and the color green. As always, my insides do strange things when he locks eyes with me, and I feel myself come alive.

His dark, wavy hair is tumbled from the wind, and his cheeks are flushed, telling me that he just came in from the cold. When he takes his leather jacket off and slings it over the back of his chair, I can't tear my eyes away from his bare arms, covered in ink, strong and corded with muscle. I flush when I remember what it feels like to grab hold of those shoulders of his and cling onto him while he fucks me.

He looks at me, well, catches me openly staring at him, actually, and his small smile widens just a little. His eyes dip to my neck, hidden beneath my sweater, but he doesn't say a word about what happened yesterday. I could kiss him for avoiding the topic. I don't want to talk about it. From here on out, I don't want a thing Jacob Weaving does to ever mar the time I get to spend with Alex. His dark eyebrow forms a crooked arch. "What's got you looking so red in the face?" he whispers. Like raw silk, his voice is that perfect combination of rough and smooth that makes my skin break out in goosebumps.

"My red face has absolutely nothing to do with *you*." My response is mild, seemingly uninterested, but Alex chuckles ominously under his breath. He doesn't believe me for one goddamn second. "You seem like you're in a good mood," I tell him. "Your meeting went well?"

"It did. Jesus, you're squirming in your seat like you need a good fucking, *Argento*. If I'm not responsible for all the fidgeting, then I'm gonna have to find the guy who got under your skin this morning and murder the fuck out him."

Well, shit. The classroom's full of other students, all within earshot, and Alex hasn't muted his volume any. Did anyone else just hear him say that? I can't tell. If they did, then no one's stupid enough to turn around and gawp at him. They all know better. My face is *really* on fire now, though. "Oh my god, Alex. Keep it down!"

He's utterly deadpan. "My voice? Or my dick?"

"Your *voice!*" Lord, I must be a frightening shade of purple...

I knew he'd *try* to be cool about the fact that Jake pinned me by my throat against a wall. I told him that was what I needed, and I'm so glad he listened. But I also assumed he was going to be moody and surly today. This version of Alex...it almost seems carefree. Happy, as if he's just decided to stop worrying about all of it. Honestly, I'm too relieved to be offended that he doesn't seem all that bothered by what happened. Maybe this won't end up being a big deal after all.

"Good," he whispers. At least he's trying to be quieter. "'Cause there's no way my dick's gonna behave itself. That thing is well beyond my control. I'm lightheaded twenty-four seven these days. Most of my blood now lives in my cock because of you."

Fuck me, he's in a *really* good mood. He looks at me intently, stripping me down, focusing on my mouth, and I realize that I want him. Right here, right now, so bad that it almost hurts. And from the pleased smirk on his face, apparently he knows it.

"All right, reprobates," a voice calls from the front of the class. Mr. French has arrived while I was staring hungrily at Alex. He stands at the front of the class in front of a television that he must have wheeled into the classroom with him. "You'll be glad to know I am massively behind on all of my paperwork, so I have a treat for you today. You're going to be watching a documentary about rocketry, kindly made by the mathematicians at NASA, while I sit in the teacher's lounge and finish up on some admin. It's very dry and potentially boring, but I'd encourage you to pay close attention. You're going to be writing a thousand-word essay on the finer details of this documentary's contents, and I'm expecting some mind-blowing work from you all. Be warned, my friends. This *is* rocket science."

A chorus of deep groans go up around the class, but Mr. French pointedly ignores every last one of us. All of us except me, that is. He gives me a coolly appraising glance as his eyes sweep over his student's faces. "I expect you all to behave yourselves. That means no talking, no note passing. And absolutely no *fighting*."

Hah.

Does he think I'll leap up out of my chair the moment he leaves and start throwing punches? If he had any sense he would know I only lash out at others when they're threatening to penetrate me against my will. We all wait in grim silence as he cues up the documentary on the television screen. A long time ago, I would have been excited by the prospect of an hour in the dark, watching a movie about how rockets are built. Now, I'm more interested in an hour in the dark next to Alessandro Moretti.

Mr. French sets a baby monitor down on his desk, casting a warning glare over his shoulder. "I'd love to think I could trust you all not to act like a bunch of demented, hormone-riddled baboons, but sadly I know better. This thing is the Rolls Royce of baby monitors. I can hear my son fart from fifty paces with this thing, so don't even think about screwing around. I'll be back to check on you in half an hour. In the meantime, sit back and enjoy the majesty of physics. *Take notes.*" He hits play, then turns out the lights as he exits the classroom.

One of the Apollo mission rockets appears on the screen, and Alex's hand closes around the leg of my desk, pulling it closer to his own. I have to quickly shift my legs in order to shunt my chair over with the desk as the same time.

"What are you playing at, Moretti?" I hiss between my teeth.

"Just getting comfortable."

He's sitting at the desk I always claimed for myself, back before he showed up here and stole it. The same desk I dumped my bag on top of the day I met and spoke to him properly for the first time. We're tucked away in the back corner of the class, where no one can see what we're up to in the dark. Sure, there are another two people sitting to my left, and there a full row of students in front of us, too, but no one bothered to turn around to see what we were up to as my chair legs scraped the floor just now.

We are, for all intents and purposes, invisible. "Put this over your legs," Alex commands. He hands me his leather jacket underneath my desk.

"Why?" I take it, doing as he instructed, a little nonplused. It's freezing outside, but Darhower doesn't skimp on the energy bill inside the school. The classroom's perhaps a little *too* warm right now.

"No questions," Alex replies.

A moment later, I feel his hand sliding up my thigh beneath his jacket and all becomes clear. "Oh my god. Alex, what the hell?"

He drapes his arm around my shoulders, drawing me close to him. "Shhh, *Argento*. Sit back and enjoy the majesty of physics."

His fingers work quickly at the button on my jeans. The Apollo rocket on the screen begins its take-off sequences, its boosters roaring loudly out of the television speakers, masking the sound of my fly being unzipped.

He cannot be serious right now. He cannot be about to do what I think he's going to do. He—

My mind goes blank as his hand slips down below my waistband, inside the thin material of my panties. Oh...oh, holy fucking *shit*. I catch my bottom lip between my teeth, holding back a startled breath as Alex's fingers deftly work their way down between my legs, searching out and finding my clit.

I look over at the guy sitting next to my left: Gareth Foster is staring intently at the screen, tapping a pen against his notepad, completely oblivious to the fact that the girl sitting next to him is getting her pussy stroked.

Alex rests his chin on my shoulder, angling himself so that he's facing me in his seat. "Relax, *Argento*. No one cares what we're up to."

"Alex, this is... this is..." God, he sweeps his fingers up, flicking them over my clit, and I forget how to fucking speak. It's one thing fooling around pawing at each other like sex crazed animals up against a brick wall outside Harrison's Home Hardware, but the streets were deserted then. There hadn't been a soul in sight. There was no one in the music room, either. Sure, we ran the risk of getting caught, but it was a small risk. There are twenty other people in this room right now. The risk of getting caught is massive.

"*Alex...*"

Either he doesn't hear the pleading note in my whispered voice, or just doesn't heed it. He presses forward, sliding his hand further down inside my jeans, and groans breathlessly when he discovers how wet I am. He presses his lips up against the shell of my ear and mouths a string of words that nearly make me come on the spot.

"I want your pussy on my tongue, *Dolcezza.*"

I know perfectly well that he'd drop down onto his knees underneath our desks and get to work if I'd let him. I wriggle against his hand, unable to escape the pressure building between my legs. Alex knows exactly how to touch me. The small, tight circles he rubs against my pussy are designed to make me squirm, and they're doing their job perfectly. I feel like I'm floating up out of my chair and being driven down into it at the same time. This is too much. Too, too much...

Mr. French won't just escort us in to see Darhower if we get caught. This kind of public indecency is usually dealt with by law enforcement. I can't bring myself to really care, though, as Alex dips his fingers inside of me for the first time and I slide down in my chair, my hips angling themselves forward of their own accord, giving Alex more space to move his hand.

I can feel him grinning against my cheek. "Dirty Silver," he whispers. "You're staring at that television screen very hard. Are you finding this an educational experience?"

Jesus...fucking...

I grab hold of the edge of my desk, bracing myself and holding myself in place at the same time. With Alex's black jacket covering everything that he's doing, no one can see what's going on beneath the leather, but if I start flailing my legs all over the place then people are going to be able to guess. "You should stop," I say softly. "If you make me come..."

"Hmm?" His question is a low growl in my ear.

"Someone will notice. They'll—" I cut myself off, blocking off my throat entirely as Alex angles his fingers upward, stroking them against a spot inside me that makes flashes of color burst in my vision. He isn't fucking around. It doesn't matter how hard I protest, or how frantically I tell him he should stop. He means to make me come at the back of this classroom, and nothing I say is going to deter him.

If I really, really want him to stop, I'm going to have to grab his hand and physically drag it out of my pants. I close my hand around his wrist, preparing to do just that, but then I falter. Fuck, it feels...so fucking good. Alex fastens his teeth onto my shoulder, biting down playfully through my t-shirt, nowhere near as hard as I made him bite me in the guest room at home, but the effect that small spike of pain has on me is instant and dizzying. My head rocks back, my mouth falling open.

"God, you're so fucking beautiful, *Argento*." His low, rasping voice is hypnotic. I lose myself altogether as he continues to speak to me, barely loud enough to be heard. "I want my dick inside you so fucking bad right now. Shhh, don't make a sound. Don't move. You need this, don't you? You're hungry. Don't worry, I got you. Let me fuck this out of you with my fingers. Let me make you feel good."

White flares of light chase across my eyes as he pumps his hand quicker between my legs. I'm so wet, I can actually *smell* myself on him as he moves faster, circling the pad of his thumb over the slick, tight knot of my clit. Combined with his fingers pulsing and surging inside me, it feels as though he's lit an eternal fire in the very center of my core and it will never fucking go out.

"You're getting tighter, *Argento*. Jesus Christ," Alex murmurs. "Stay with me. Won't be long now, I promise. I've got you. Hold your breath. Hold it. Don't make a fucking sound. Let it come. Let it come."

I want to scream. I want to buck against his hand and grind myself into his palm. I can't, though. I can't move an inch. If I even allow myself to breathe, I'm going to make some sort of desperate, mindless sound that will let everyone know that I'm teetering on the edge of an orgasm.

"Soak my hand, *Dolcezza*. Come on. Do it. I want you all over my fingers. Come for me. Come. *Come*."

This is an order I cannot disobey. It's too late. There's no clawing my way back up this cliff face toward sanity. I'm already stumbling, tripping, tumbling headfirst into nothingness.

'For millions on Earth, the Christmas Eve television broadcast is the *defining moment of Apollo Eight. But for the engineers...and especially the astronauts...there's a critical maneuver just ahead that overshadows every-thing else...'*

I hear the words blaring out of the television, but it I don't register a single one of them. I can't focus on anything but the numbed-out bliss Alex coaxes from me with each pump of his fingers.

"Good girl. Good girl. That's it. Ride it. Ride it out."

My fingernails gouging into the wooden desk in front of me, I lock up, trembling, leaning into him as I come. The well of pleasure I descend into feels bottomless, but eventually I reach its end.

I'm too afraid to breathe for a second. I don't want to gulp at the air like I'm starving, but before long I have no choice. I pull a thin trickle of air in through my nose, my body slowly falling slack against Alex's chest, and he purrs into my hair like a satisfied cat.

"Damn, *Argento*. That was the hottest thing I have fucking seen." He nuzzles into my hair, pressing a kiss against the damp skin of my neck, and I shudder one last time as he slides his fingers out of me. Everyone else in the room is silent, watching the television screen with boredom strewn across their faces. Not me, though. I'm too busy staring at Alessandro Moretti, as he licks my come clean from each one of his glistening fingers.

2 0

ALEX

"Come on, old man. You're embarrassing yourself. Harder. Come on, *harder!*"

Under any other circumstances, I would never dream of speaking to Cam like this, but desperate times call for desperate measures. He wants to be a part of the Jacob Weaving take-down crew, but I know for a fact he hasn't had to raise a fist to anyone his entire life. That much became painfully clear the first time he swung at the heavy bag hanging in his garage…and he nearly fucking missed.

Silver had three guitar lessons queued up with her regular students after school today, so I grabbed the opportunity with both hands, putting her father through his paces during her absence. And let's just say, it has *not* been pretty.

Cameron gives me an irritated scowl as he lunges forward, jabbing at the bag like I showed him to. At least he's connecting properly with the damn thing now. That's something, I suppose. I doubt a hit from Cameron could put a man down on his ass, though. It's not as if the guy's unfit or anything. He's young, all things considered, and broad-shouldered. There should be nothing stopping him from sending the heavy bag suspended from his garage roof swinging for the rafters, but it isn't happening. There appears to be a problem, namely the fact that whenever Cameron Parisi pulls back his fist and sends it hurtling forward toward the bag…he doesn't fucking *mean* it.

It's understandable. He hasn't seen the way Jake looks at Silver. He hasn't seen the smug, self-satisfied smile on the motherfucker's face as he traipses through the hallways of Raleigh like he fucking owns the place. If he'd caught one glimpse of Jacob's eyes crawling over Silver's skin, the way *I've* caught them crawling, then he wouldn't be having this problem right now. I nearly gave myself a fucking aneurism pretending that everything was okay at school today. I wanted nothing more than to hunt down that motherfucker and tear him limb from limb, but I didn't for Silver's sake. She must have thought I was fucking crazy, skipping into physics like I didn't have a care in the world. And then making her come under her fucking desk? Yeah, I must have come across like a goddamn psychopath, but it was all I could do to distract myself from the chain of bruises that I knew were worsening under the high neck of her sweater.

"I have an old skiing injury, y'know," Cam grumbles as he jabs at the bag. "I dislocated my shoulder when Silver was six. It comes out of joint if I'm not careful."

The garage door's closed. There are three little element heaters pointed at us from Cam's barely used workbench, and the space has gotten surprisingly hot. We both shed our shirts about half an hour ago, and I've been trying not to stare at Cam's extraordinarily pale chest ever since. Not one tattoo on the guy. Not a fucking one. Weird.

I brace the heavy bag against my side, rolling my eyes. "D'you know how ultra-privileged and ridiculous that sounds? *Oh, no, my old skiing injury. I can't possibly hit something hard, or all of my money'll go flying out of my pockets.*"

Cameron pauses, straightening up a little, a warning look on his face. Antagonizing him probably isn't the best way to plant myself firmly into his good graces. He arches his eyebrows at me, and I arch mine back. I am the king of the sardonic eyebrow arch. Cam's gonna have to practice some more if he wants to compete for the title.

"What? You want me to apologize? Will that make your old skiing injury hurt less?"

"Jesus Christ, you're an *asshole*, you know that?" he mutters darkly. "What Silver sees in you, I have no idea."

There we go. Salty, salty Cameron. When he hits the heavy bag again, he puts a little effort into it. Enough that I can actually feel the hit through the bag. Not enough to make me stagger back a step, but it's something.

"If I'm such an asshole, then why are you okay with me dating Silver in the first place?"

Cameron bares his teeth as he throws another punch at the bag. "Silver's not like most kids her age. She's smart. She knows what she wants. She's also stubborn as hell. If I forbid her from dating you, in a year's time she'd be shacked up with you somewhere fifty miles away with a newborn keeping her up all damn night and I'd probably never see her again."

I'll admit, the mental image he paints throws me for a second. "She'd never do that," I say. "She *is* too smart for that. We'd never just take off and leave. We'd never wind up with a kid like that, either."

"Why not?" Cam asks sharply. "You don't want children with her?"

I choke on a number of different responses to that question. The words are all bunched up at the back of my throat, stumbling into one another. If this is another test, like handing me a beer to see if I'll drink it in front of him, then I don't know what kind of warped, fucked up game this guy is playing, but I want out. Nothing I say here will ever be the right answer. "It's getting real hot in here," I say through my teeth. "Silver said you used to go to a Mauy Thai gym on the other side of town. Why'd you stop?"

Cameron's eyes glitter as he drives a right hook toward the middle of the bag. "Shame you were so enthusiastic with all the ink. You could have been a politician later in life, the way you side step questions, Moretti. Quite the talent you've got there."

"What do you want me to say? Yeah, I wanna knock up your daughter and fill an entire house with our kids? I'm seventeen. So's Silver. Neither of us are thinking about that right now."

"You're just thinking about getting your dick touched as often as possible, consequences be damned, right?" I feel his hit this time. I'm pretty sure Cam imagined the bag was my head on that last one. A spike of anger licks up the back of my neck but I ignore it, shrugging it off. I'm used to people saying things to try and kindle my temper. Gary used to do it all the time. During the last few months under Quincy's roof, I probably would have unleashed on him and gotten in a few good hits if he'd said something like that to me. This time, with Cam, I'm not going to do that. He's so fucking worried about Silver. I'm betting he doesn't even know what he's saying half the time.

"I'm not gonna talk to you about my dick, Mr. Parisi," I tell him.

"Ahh." He stands up, straightening out of his fighting stance again, wiping sweat from his brow with the back of his forearm. "Back to Mr. Parisi, huh?"

"Until we settle on another topic of conversation that doesn't ꓵake me think you might kill me, I think it's probably for the best."

He huffs out a breath of air that I think is supposed to be laughter. "Okay, okay. I'm sorry. I'm being an asshole, too. You must be rubbing off on me, Moretti. Come on. Let's switch out."

We both wrapped our hands before we started, so I'm ready to change up with him. Cam skirts around the bag, assuming the position I was just in. I lift my hands to my face, loosely fisted, raising my guard, and Cam laughs. "Oh boy. I can see we've got some work to do here, haven't we? You need a bit of a wider..." he begins to say.

He stops trying to correct my stance with his half-baked Muay Thai knowledge when I unleash my first punch, pivoting at the ankle, knee, then hip, rotating, twisting, drawing power up through the floor, up through my body, and sending it snapping down the length of my arm as it impacts with the bag.

Cam staggers back not one step but two. He nearly crashes into the work bench behind him. "*Uffffuck,*" he groans, his surprised exclamation transitioning into a surprised curse word. "I wasn't expecting that."

"Kind of the point, right? Take people by surprise, when it matters." My loose, almost drunken style of fighting has shocked the hell out of more people than I can count. To this day, I've never lost a fight. I don't intend on losing any in the future, either.

Cam nods, panting a little as he goes back to hold onto the bag. "Point well made," he says under his breath. He's not smiling anymore.

Not angry either. His emotions seem to have fallen out of him altogether. "You know this might be the end for you guys, don't you?" he says quietly. "If we do this, she might not forgive you for not listening to her."

I chew on the inside of my lip for a second, turning that thought over in my head. I've already realized this. There's every chance Silver will never speak to me again once my plans with Cam have come to fruition. "I know it," I say after a while. "I've made my peace with it. I'll never be okay without her, but she'll be okay without me. She's stronger than I am. *She'd* be okay...and this needs to be done." I say nothing about Silver's murmured nightmares. I say nothing of all the other ways Jacob's assault is still affecting Silver...*sexually*...even if she won't admit it. Cameron just nods, as if he's noticed his own list of changes in his daughter and he doesn't want to talk about those either.

"What about you?" I ask. "She's going to hate you too after we're done."

Cam just shrugs, jerking his chin toward the heavy bag, indicating for me to hit it again. "I'm different," he says. "I'm her father. She can hate me all she wants. A daughter's supposed to hate her father sometimes. Eventually, she'll forgive me, though. She won't have a choice. I'm her blood."

21

SILVER

A ribbon of light spans from one end of Raleigh High Street to the other, small yellow fairy lights twinkling everywhere, wrapped around the trunks of the trees, individually wrapped around their branches. The storefronts have all been decorated, too. The edges of the windows in cafes, restaurants, and the boutique jewelry places alike have been frosted over with fake snow, and paper snowflakes have been taped and strung to the insides of the glass.

I remember making those snowflakes as a child in elementary school, folding the paper into little triangles and carefully using the tips of my scissors to snick out little pieces along the edge, creating a pattern when the paper was unfolded. We'd make hundreds of them at Raleigh Elementary, writing our names carefully in the middle of our snowflakes in looping pencil. One of the teachers would then go around Raleigh and distribute the decorations to the local store owners, and the children of the town would be taken up and down the high street by their parents to peer into all the windows. We'd all squeal, delighted, when we finally found one of our own snowflakes in a window, displayed proudly, our names pressed up against the cold glass.

Thomas Beekman, Aged 7.

Carlie Harrison, Aged 7.

Leoni Ali, Aged 6.

Jason Press, Aged 5 ½.

In the windows at Henry's, a little girl called Wendy Michaels has been honored six times, her small, delicate little snowflakes arranged in a circle right in the middle of the window.

Alex takes in the winter magic of the high street, the sides of his Stan Smiths caked with the fresh snow that fell earlier this evening, and I find myself staring at him once again. His hands are driven deep into the pockets of his leather jacket. Every time he takes a breath, a billow of fog clouds the air, quickly rising up through the starry trees and disappearing into the night sky. The small bursts of golden light, like little fireflies, reflect in the darkness of his sharp, alert eyes and in the waves of his almost black, swept back hair.

He looks around, studying the scene laid out before him, like he was just kidnapped by aliens and unceremoniously dropped onto the surface of another strange, unfamiliar planet.

It startles me sometimes—how madly, desperately I am in love with this person. The knowledge, the sheer depth and beauty of that love, makes me smile to myself, basking in the warmth that's kindled in the hollow of my chest because of it. "You lived in Raleigh last winter, didn't you?" I ask. "Why didn't you come down here to see the lights then?" This is obviously the first time he's seeing them.

His mouth works, lifting up at one side. "I rode through a couple of times on the bike. There was less snow last year. I didn't stop, though." Watching the people of our little town wandering up and down the street in front of us, arm-in-arm, bundled up in scarves, hats and gloves, their cheeks reddened by the cold, he looks like he's trying to understand what's going on around him but none of it quite makes sense. I suddenly realize what's going on in his head. He still feels so *apart* from all of this. He still doesn't think there's a corner of Raleigh's High Street where he might fit in.

I loop my arm through his, leaning my head against his shoulder as we make our way past Hardaker's Grocery Store and the Dillinger's

Pharmacy, nestling into him snugly, showing him that we're just like any of the other couples out to look at the lights.

We reach the Regency Theater at six-fifteen, a little early to meet Ben, but Alex didn't want to risk being late. We sit on the wall out front, taking everything in as we wait for Jackie's silver SUV to pull up.

"Looks like the inside of a snow globe," Alex muses.

"You're so far away from the rest of town over in Salton Ash. This must seem really quaint and weird in comparison to the trailer park."

"It does." He frowns, lines forming between his brows. He seems lost in his thoughts. So lost that he doesn't even notice when Jackie's SUV arrives, rolling up along the curb outside the movie theater.

I've met Jackie only once, when she picked up Ben from my house. I didn't even see her when she dropped Ben off at the hospital to visit Alex after he was shot, which has always seemed weird. I observe her as she gets out of the SUV and opens the rear passenger door for Ben, trying to see what I can figure out about the woman. No makeup whatsoever. Her mousy blonde hair is scraped back into a sloppy ponytail, and the long cardigan sweater she's wearing that goes down to her knees—seriously not warm enough in this weather—looks like it's coming apart at the seams. She's wearing Mom-jeans, and there are Uggs on her feet, a dark tideline rising up to her ankles where they've gotten wet. She looks harried and wary as she ushers Ben toward us, wrapping the cardigan sweater tightly around her slightly puffy frame, as if she's trying to use the cardigan as some sort of shield against us.

She's left the SUV's engine running, which says a lot; she isn't planning on sticking around.

By her side, Ben looks extra handsome in a black jacket with a pressed blue shirt underneath it.

Alex grins when he sees Ben. "Nice jacket, man," he says, brushing some imaginary lint from his brother's shoulder. "Looking sharp."

Ben beams. His brother's approval clearly means a lot to him. "Thanks. There was this really cool leather one at the store, well, it wasn't real leather, but it looked just like yours. I would have preferred that one, but Mom said this one would be better."

Next to me, Alex tenses like he's just been electrocuted. His eyes whip up, boring into Jackie's face like twin lasers. He doesn't need to explain his reaction to me, or to her. She's already avoiding making eye contact with him as she fusses over Ben's collar.

"All right, Buster. I'll be back to get you at nine thirty. I want you out front here, ready and waiting, okay? We've got an early morning tomorrow, and it takes an hour to get home, so…"

"I would have picked him up and brought him back," Alex rumbles.

Jackie sighs. She sighs like she's dog-tired and sick of Alex's shit. I instantly hate her. I hate her *for* him. "That Camaro's a piece of junk, Alex. It would have broken down halfway back to Bellingham. I'm not having my boy waiting out on the side of the road when the weather's like this, while you wait for one of your loser friends to come and give you a—"

Alex's jaw cracks loudly. "He's *not* your boy."

Jackie looks everywhere but at Alex. She accidentally makes eye contact with *me* and immediately shrinks away from it, disengaging. She fixes her attention on her watch. "All right. Three hours, Ben. I'll see you soon." She kisses the top of his head, turns and leaves, getting back in the SUV and then driving off down the high street.

Alex is a perfect storm, masterfully controlled, as he purchases the tickets to the movie. We head inside to buy snacks from the concession stand. Ben goes to the bathroom, and that's when Alex loses his fucking mind. He doesn't rage or shout, though. He's so, *so* quiet, which is far more worrying.

"She is *not* his fucking mother," he whispers, waiting outside the restrooms. "He is *not* her fucking son. How dare she tell him to call her that."

There's no way for me to comfort him here without drawing attention to the fact that he's fuming mad. Ben comes out of the restroom, and Alex plasters a broad smile on his face, jostling his brother, rough-housing as we make our way to the correct screen and find our seats inside. It's impressive, how he can pretend like nothing's bothering him like that. It's all for Ben's benefit. Alex gets so little time with him that he doesn't want to ruin our evening, but I know how much he's hurting right now. I can still see it in his eyes, and it fucking kills me.

The movie's terrible. It's blood and guts from the moment the opening credits scream across the screen. The violence doesn't stop until the movie ends on a brutal note, the last man standing finally losing his head as the psycho serial killer of the piece leaps out of the dark and takes a chainsaw to his neck. Ben is delighted. He pretends to chop and saw at the air the whole way out of the movie theater and all the way down the street to the diner. There's enough time for a milkshake and some fries before Jackie comes back to get Ben, so we sit in a booth and joke around.

Alex teaches Ben how to dip his fries into his chocolate milkshake, and it's like a lightbulb going on right over the kid's head. They include me in their little jokes, and Ben asks a lot of questions, but for the most part I just let them do their thing, let them be brothers, and it makes my heart hurt in my chest. Alex shouldn't have to hand Ben off to Jackie like a loaner sibling he gets to borrow for a couple of hours. He's going to be a great role model to his brother once he finally gets custody. It's just such a shame that he has to go through the nightmare of family court first. Things get nasty inside those court rooms. *Really* nasty. And now things are even more complicated, because Ben's suddenly calling Jackie Mom, and she's whisking him off to Hawaii? Jackie's smart. Alex might have secured the help of his social worker in order to build his case for when the times comes next year, but Jackie's laying her own groundwork.

He thinks of me as his mother, Your Honor. I've been able to take Ben traveling, to show him the world. I've been able to enrich his life and give him experiences he'd never have otherwise, Your Honor. What can Alex do for Ben? Really? His life is unstable and unpredictable. I am the safer bet.

I hate that this sort of game is being played. Alex has no choice, though. He either participates or he gives up any hope he has of ever being granted custody. He's going to have to be just as conniving and manipulative as Jackie if he wants to beat her at her own game. And how does Ben come through the other side of that kind of warfare unscathed?

"I have something for you," Ben says shyly, reaching into the pocket of his jacket.

Alex stares down at the small, haphazardly wrapped gift that Ben places down onto the table and slides toward him. The paper's Christmassy, covered in dancing elves. "What's this for, Bud?" Alex asks.

"I was going to wait to give it to you at Christmas, but we won't be here now. So…Mom said I should give it to you now."

Alex reacts sharply to that word again, the muscles in his throat straining, his face bleaching of color, but he doesn't correct his brother. He doesn't say a thing. He manages to smile at Ben—a sick, unhappy, miserable smile that makes me want to burst into tears—as he picks up the gift, inspecting it, turning it over in his hands. "That's really cool of you, man," he says. "Early Christmas presents are the best kind. I'll give you your gift on Wednesday, before you go away, okay?"

Ben's head dips a little. He picks at the bottom of his milkshake glass with his fingernail. "Mom said I won't be able to come next Wednesday. She said there won't be time. I can get it when I come back, though, right? That'll be like an extra Christmas, after the real one's over."

Fuck. I can't bear the void look on Alex's face.

He clears his throat. "Yeah. Yeah, man, that sounds great. I'm still going to talk to Jackie about you coming next week, though, all right? But if it doesn't work out, then that's what we'll do. In the meantime, I'm not going to open this just yet. I'm gonna wait until we have *our* Christmas, okay?"

We walk back to the movie theater, and Ben chatters away happily, telling us about the girl who likes him at school and keeps following him around; Alex is there for all of it. He interacts and he makes jokes, and Ben's none the wiser. My boyfriend is simmering with rage, though, dangerously close to boiling over.

Jackie doesn't get out of the car. She honks the horn, shouting at Ben to hurry up and get in out of the passenger window, and that's it. Ben goes, and Alex is finally able to drop his happy façade.

It's snowing again as he takes me by the hand and charges up High Street toward the Camaro. "Alex. Alex, wait. Just slow down. Where are we going?"

"The Rock," he snarls over his shoulder. "Fair warning, *Argento*. I'm about to get seriously fucking drunk, and it ain't gonna be pretty."

22

SILVER

The music thumps up through the soles of my feet, pounding and raucous. The Rock is jam-packed with half-drunk patrons, the make-shift dancefloor writhing with bodies. The tequila shots we threw back when we got here haven't seemed to make anything better. The only thing that's changed is Alex is now sullen, frustrated, and a little buzzed.

"Of course she never lets me pick him up and drop him off. If she did that, I'd get two extra hours with him, even if it is in the car. And she couldn't fucking have that, could she? Anything she can do prove to me that she's the one in control, she does it. She's trying to fucking take him away from me for good. She's gonna try and adopt him, I just know it."

"You don't know that." Playing devil's advocate seems like the only way to stop him from diving off the deep end. He's right, though. It does look like Jackie's planning on keeping Ben on a permanent, more official basis. She wouldn't be letting him call her Mom if she wasn't.

Ben was so small when their real mother died. He can't

remember a single thing about her, but Alex does. Alex remembers plenty. And to hear Ben call Jackie by the name must cut him down to the quick.

"Another round for ya, asshole!" Paul, the bartender yells at Alex over the racket. "And another shot for you, too, Angel." He's much more pleasant to me when he sets my tequila down on the bar in front of me. Alex touches his glass to mine and downs the amber liquid, drinking it straight, without the salt or the lime.

"Jesus. You really are blowing off steam tonight," Paul says.

Alex presses his knuckles into the edge of the bar, so hard it looks like it must hurt. "You have no fucking idea."

I wish I could do something to help him. Fuck, I wish I could take away this hurt. That's all I seem to wish for these days—the magical ability to stop the people I love around me from suffering. Paul only sees Alex's anger. He doesn't see his pain. He reaches a hand into the front of his bar apron's pocket and pulls something out, slapping it down onto the bar in front of Alex. "There you are. Go downstairs and give your beautiful girlfriend an orgasm or two. That'll make you both feel better in a quick fucking minute."

Downstairs.

Downstairs?

Takes me a minute to remember what takes place below the Rock, in the bowels of Montgomery Cohen's establishment. This isn't just a bar, after all. There's something far more scandalous in the basement....

The Rock's very own sex club.

Alex curves an eyebrow at the two tickets Paul has just shoved at him, his eyes turned almost all-black in our dimly lit corner. "I don't think that's the way to solve this particular problem," he says, his tone unamused. "And besides. I don't think we'd need tickets." He slides them back across the bar to Paul. "I've never needed a *ticket* to an event being held at this place."

"Tonight's different." Paul pulls a face. "There's a burlesque act down there. Monty sold spots, there was so much interest. The bouncers aren't letting anyone down unless they have one of these." He waves one of the tickets in Alex's face. "The silhouette of a naked woman has been embossed in gold on the front of the black, flocked card. At the bottom of the ticket are stamped the words, *'Admit One Only.'*

Alex doesn't seem to care about the tickets in the slightest, or what's going on downstairs. "If you really wanna make me feel better, have another shot of tequila lined up and waiting for me by the time I get back." He turns to me and plants a swift kiss on my temple. "I'm just gonna run to the bathroom, *Argento*. Stay here and keep our spot?"

"Sure."

Paul forcefully plants the tickets in my hand as soon as Alex has disappeared, swallowed up by the crowd. "If you've never been down, then you never know," he says. "Could be fun, right? Don't you wanna be a little freak, just for one night?"

Go down into the club? With Alex? The thought's never occurred to me.

Okay, that's a flat-out lie. I've thought about it all right. I've imagined what it would be like with him, to descend the stairs and see what kind of *Dante's Inferno* type madness takes place down there. The images I've conjured in my head have riled me up for sure, but the twinge of excitement I feel as I look down at the tickets in my hand are fueled by curiosity and nothing more. I don't want to go down there to put myself on display with Alex. I'm not that desperate to see a bunch of other people naked and writhing on top of one another either. I just have no frame of reference. What the hell goes on in a sex club, for fuck's sake? It's the not knowing that making my cheeks feel warm.

"I'm gonna go serve a that guy at the end of the bar. If the tickets are on the bar when I come back, I'll put them away and we'll say nothing more about it. If they're gone…well, then, I s'pose I might run into the two of you down there later." He winks, and for the first time I wonder if Paul might be attracted to Alex. I don't think he's gay, per se, but the way his eyes are shining right now…his excitement doesn't seem geared toward me in any way. Is he picturing my boyfriend sweating over me, grinding himself between my legs? Is his dick hard thinking about Alex fucking me? God, that's such a weird—

"*Hey!*" Fingers dig playfully into my sides. Alex's voice is hot in my ear. He's standing behind me, his chest suddenly pressing up against my back. I nearly hit the roof, surprised that he snuck up on me. Why does it feel like I just got caught doing something wrong, I wonder? Alex sees the tickets still on the bar and his brow furrows. "Paul could probably make good money on those things. A drunk guy in the bathroom said he paid a hundred and fifty a pop for him and his wife to bag their passes. He says it's nuts down there."

"Ahhh, he's just trying to cheer you up," I say. "Who knows. Maybe he's right. Maybe a little debauchery would make you feel better. I've never seen a burlesque show before."

Alex throws back another shot of tequila. He doesn't swallow, though. He holds the alcohol in his mouth, looking at me out of the corner of his eye. I do a shot of my own, pretending that I don't notice him staring at me. Alex eventually swallows, looking me up and down in a very odd way.

"What?" I laugh, because I can feel a flush creeping up my neck, and the way he's studying me is making me feel a little self-conscious.

"You want to go fuck down there," he says, blunt as ever.

"No! Oh my god! *No.* I just meant the burlesque—"

He steps into me, ducking down, bending his tall frame around me, taking me into his arms. His lips brush against my ear as he speaks. "I can see it on your face, *Argento*. You want to fuck down there, don't you? You want to be naked. You want all those eyes on you while I make you feel good. You want hands on you, too?"

I try to wriggle free. "No. No, no, no, Jesus, just *stop*. You're such a perv. I don't ever want anyone to touch me but you."

"Good. Because I won't be held responsible for what would happen if another man tries to touch your bare skin. I'd break every single one of his fingers. Probably both arms, too."

God, it's so hot in here. My face feels like it's on fire. I'm burning up. "Hah. But you're okay with the idea of a bunch of people *looking* at my naked body, though, right?"

"I wouldn't go that far. I'd probably glass anyone who looked at you, too. Fuck, I don't know. I guess there is something hot about the idea. People looking at you. At me. Watching us fucking, getting off on it. *Wanting* us."

"But *not* having us," I reaffirm.

"No. Definitely not. No fucking way." Alex picks up the second shot Paul set out for him while he was in the bathroom. He holds the glass to his bottom lip, pausing there, waiting for me to pick up a shooter of my own. His gaze is heavy on my skin, loaded with curiosity. He looks like he can't quite fathom what's going on in my head and it's driving him crazy.

The tequila burns like a motherfucker as it slides down my throat. Each shot I drink seems to burn less and less, though. It feels like my whole body is burning already, and the alcohol is barely making a difference.

"You want to go," Alex says. Reaching out for me, he takes hold of my loose hair and slowly winds it around his fist. "Naughty little *Argento*. If you want to go down there, just say so. Be brave and open your mouth."

"I'm—I'm—"

He arches an eyebrow at me wickedly. "Stuttering all over the place and freaking out?"

Damn it, he's so infuriating. Admitting something like this to him…fuck, first I'll have to admit to myself. Yes, I want to go down there. I want to look. I want to see. I want to experience something new and crazy. Is that so bad? Alex's tongue flicks out, wetting the swell of his lower lip, a lean, hungry look about him, and a curl of want weaves its way up my spine. "Fine. Have it your way." I slap my hand down on the tickets, drawing them toward me across the bar. They go straight into the back pocket of my jeans. "*I want to go.*"

All of Alex's pent up anger and frustration shifts on the turn of a dime. I witness it take place right before my very eyes. One second, his dark, bottomless eyes are still sparking with the powerful desire to burn down half of Raleigh. The next, they're filled with excitement and intrigue, and for better or worse, his piercing attention is sharply focused on me.

He maneuvers himself so that I'm trapped between his body and the bar, the sticky, booze-soaked wood digging into my lower back; he braces himself, hands planted firmly on top of the bar, me captured securely within the circle of his arms. A nervous thrill of energy ripples from the top of my skull, down the back of my neck, dipping over my spine, making the skin on my thighs break out in goosebumps. Fuck, the way he's looking at me right now… He wants to devour me. Consume every piece of me until there's nothing left. The things he's thinking about right now are already making me blush, and I have no idea what's going on in that handsome, beautifully tormented head of his.

Leaning close, he whispers into my hair. "It's a viper's pit down there, *Argento*. We look. We don't touch. We are not touched. Anyone tries to take liberties, I will fucking break them. If it looks like you're getting overwhelmed or stressed, I pull the plug and we walk right back up those stairs. Lastly, anything I say goes. Those are the rules. Now finish your last shot. We're leaving."

ALEX

I can count on one hand how many times I've been down here over the past eighteen months; this will make for my fourth excursion down these stairs while the Rock's 'Wages of Sin' court is in session. The first time, I had to feed the beast. I had to know what the fuck was going on down here. I was just as curious as Silver seems to be now, so I sat in one of the dark booths alone, absorbing everything that went on around me, cataloguing and filing away the writhing, naked, red-lit flesh to be assessed at a later date, when I was back in the trailer. I stayed for little over an hour, draining half a bottle of Jack in the process, but I was approached at least eight times during those sixty minutes. To my discomfort, it was mostly by guys—huge, jacked, ex-con type dudes who looked like they could eat me for fucking breakfast—asking if I would fuck their wives.

Suffice it to say, I politely declined their generous invitations. Their wives might have been hot, but even back then I wasn't stupid enough to participate in an activity that was likely to get me fucking killed.

The second and third time I came down here, I was running cases of beer down to the club because the punters had drunk the bar dry. I can't decide if coming down here with Silver tonight is the dumbest thing I've ever done in the history of my life, or if it will be just another strange thing we can say we've experienced together, but I'll admit there is a sense of anticipation relaying around my body like a train on a track, growing faster and faster as it careers down the lines.

I walk ahead of her, casting my eyes in every dark corner of the club's main bar area—a habit I picked up in juvie, as well as every foster home I ever stepped foot inside. Once I've established that there's nothing to be wary of, I look around again, forcing myself to see the place as Silver must be seeing it right now, for the very first time. The place is packed with half, and in some cases, *fully* naked bodies. From the looks on people's faces, there's absolutely nothing untoward about this. Groups gather around high-top tables, sipping cocktails, laughing and joking with one another.

Naturally, there are no windows. The bar that runs along the left-hand side of the room is lit with subtle yellow lamps and candles dotted along the shelves, in between the polished bottles of liquor. The rest of the club is bathed in red light, casting sensual shadows across exposed flesh.

At the far end of the bar: the stage is double its normal size, and three extra stripper poles have been brought down from upstairs. People—couples, and occasionally a three or foursome—lounge in the booths angled toward the stage, watching as a raven-haired woman wearing little devil horns on her head dances seductively on the stage. In her hands, she uses two large crimson feather fans to hide her body, strategically turning them over and spinning them, letting one fall only to preserve her modesty with the other at the last second. Or *nearly* preserve her modesty. She's naked, pale skin practically glowing up on the stage, the fans covering anything that might make her blush. Except, every few seconds or so, a fan will slip or be coquettishly lowered, and the curve of her breast will be visible. A flash of nipple. The apex of her thighs. And the dancer is *not* blushing.

I give Silver a sidelong glance. She's seen worse than this upstairs in the regular bar. The strippers up there get fully naked if enough dollar bills are dropped at their feet. It's different down here, though. There's a heightened sexual tension in the air. The men and women at the high-tops, sprawled out in the booths and leaning up against the bar haven't just come to enjoy the show. They've come to find some excitement of their own. To make some sort of clandestine, taboo connection with someone, even if that connection is only made when they meet a stranger's eyes and an unspoken message is passed between them.

I am nothing more than my desires.

I am here to be used.

I am here to be plucked.

I am here to command.

I am vulernablepowerfulweakbrokenhurtstrong.

"This is absolutely insane," Silver says. I watch as her eyes skate over the scene before her. She pauses on a couple in a shadowy booth close to the burlesque dancer. They're in their late twenties by the looks of things. Sleek and toned—the kind of couple who have a joint fitness account on Instagram and wear t-shirts that say *'Swole Mate'* on them. The woman is completely naked, her legs parted, and the guy sitting beside her is stroking her clit, teasing her, whispering into her ear as she stares, glazed-eyed at the dancer.

My dick stirs in my pants, already getting hard. Not because of the woman being teased by her man. But by the brief burst of dark fascination that flares in Silver's eyes. She reins it in quickly; I could believe I'd imagined it, but her breathing is a little too deep. A little regulated. She's a fool if she thinks she can hide the fact that she's turned on from *me*. I've spent far too long studying her now. I know every slight, subtle change in her mood and where it will take her.

She turns to me, smiling conspiratorially. I think she's a little embarrassed. "This isn't so bad. I was picturing some crazy mass orgy or something. Lots of people all having sex on some giant, gross bed."

I smirk, gesturing to the open, insignificant looking doorway off to one side by the stage. "Walk through there and that's exactly what you'll find."

Her eyes double in size. "Jesus."

"Along with sex swings, and racks, and little private rooms, and... well. Just don't walk through that door unless you're prepared to see some shit."

She swallows thickly. Kind of adorable, really. Kinky little *Dolcezza* doesn't even realize she's kinky yet. She's like the bud of a flower, petals all wrapped up and swaddled tight around herself, waiting to bloom. "I think I need another drink," she tells me, grabbing hold of my hand.

Behind the bar, Jasmine and Delilah are running the show tonight. They're dressed in next to nothing, little kick-shorts barely covering their expertly fake-tanned ass cheeks, tits threatening to spill out of their bikini tops any second. They won't spill out, though. They're fake and barely even fucking bounce as the girls hurry up and down the bar, serving guest after guest.

Delilah sees me standing at the end of the bar and breaks out into ˄ mile-wide grin. She gestures that she'll be with me next.

"Blondie sure has a big smile for you. I'm assuming she wants to fuck you?" Silver says teasingly. She leans up against the bar next to me, arching an eyebrow suggestively.

"She does," I say coolly.

Silver looks both horrified and amused. "Awesome. Now I'm up against porn star wannabes with perfect teeth and giant tits? I suppose I'd better make the most of my time with you if *that's* my competition."

"She isn't."

"A porn star wannabe?"

"Your competition," I clarify. "You don't have any." I angle my body, leaning into her, enjoying the scent of gardenia that hits the back of my nose when I breathe her in. "There isn't a woman in this building you need to worry about, *Argento*," I rumble. "There isn't a single woman in the world you should think about that way."

"Oh, come on." She laughs. "Guys always want their hall passes. They usually set it aside for Jessica Alba."

"Fuck that." I tangle my fingers into her hair, enjoying the thickness of it. She looks up, pale blue irises fixing on mine, and the future stretches out in front of me. It's happening more and more often. The questions that used to plague me every hour of the day, ricocheting around the inside of my head like stray bullets demanding answers, all crumble to ash. See, they're no longer necessary. The uncertainties, the decisions that will need making, the choices I will have to make... they have all been taken care of with the arrival of just one person in my life: *Silver*.

Whatever happens now, whatever I wind up doing, Silver is the only thing in my life that really, truly matters. "You've taken root now.

I'm *done*. You're all there is for me from here on out." Every word is true.

She *feels* the weight of the truth in my confession, I can see it on her face, but she chooses to continue with her line of joking self-deprecation anyway. "I'm sure you wouldn't be saying that if Jessica Alba was up on that stage, making eyes at you."

"We can stop talking about Jessica Alba now. I have no clue who she is, but she doesn't fucking matter. You are the *sun*, Silver. You're gravity. You're the air in my fucking lungs. I'm a satellite, trapped in your orbit, and I'll remain here until the end of time. My face and my dumb, wretched heart, will always be turned to you."

I'm not a romantic person by nature. I don't say these things to try and flatter her with pretty words. This is simply the confession of a helpless man resigned to a beautiful fate.

We stare at each other like we're both tumbling forward into the void of eternity, and neither one of us can stop ourselves from falling.

"Christ Almighty, that shit is far too intense for this crowd," a laughing voice says.

Female. Bright. High-pitched. Alabama accent.

Delilah.

The connection between Silver and I snaps. Suddenly, we're standing back at a bar, in a sex club of all fucking places, and there's a blonde woman leaning over the lacquered wood, sliding a manicured hand up my bare forearm. "Alex Moretti, I have begged you to come hang out with me down here and you have shut me down every time. Who is this gorgeous young thing you're eye-fucking, and more importantly...are you planning on sharing her?"

Delilah's probably not bisexual. The girls here will flirt with one another all the time if they think it'll make a customer hard. I'm not a customer, and Silver isn't just some other stripper, but Delilah's a resourceful girl. She's been doggedly trying to bed me for at least six months. I think it's become a game to her now, purely because I keep saying no. More than likely, making eyes at Silver is just another crap shoot on her part, throwing something at the wall to see if it sticks.

I withdraw my arm, finding Silver's hand and lacing my fingers through hers. "Sorry, Lilah. We're doing research for a school project. Do all strippers have Daddy issues? Care to comment?"

I'm joking. I'm never cruel to the girls. She needs to know *this* isn't happening, though. She drops the act, rising out of her, popped-hip-check-out-my-delicious-curves lean—the same lean that pays her fucking rent—and throws back her head, laughing loudly. "Such a shit, Moretti. And wow. How do I keep forgetting you're still in high school? Thanks for the unpleasant wake-up call. I probably need therapy, but I can't quit the chase with you, Jailbait."

"Age of consent is sixteen in the glorious State of Washington," I remind her. "I'm legal. Just not interested. This is my girlfriend, Silver."

"Huh. Yeah, the intense staring contest gave away the fact that you two weren't just fucking. Girlfriend, though? Bold move, Alex. I am im*pressed*. Monty tried to fuck you yet, sweetheart?" she asks Silver. "If he tries anything, don't bother trying to talk him down. Go straight for the balls. He barely feels it anymore, but it's the only version of *no* he understands."

Silver blinks. Her face has gone completely blank. Takes longer than it should for it to click: any joke about a guy trying to force himself onto Silver is going to go down like a lead fucking balloon. I squeeze her hand, shaking my head. "She's fucking with you. Monty doesn't even hit on the girls. He's all business."

Delilah pretends to pout, sighing dramatically. "Honestly, I think he's a eunuch. I'd suspect he was gay, but the guys who dance here sometimes have all taken a run at him, too, and..."—a quick shrug of her shoulders—"...*nothing.*"

Silver doesn't really know how to act. This is a strange situation, an exchange that commenced with a sexual proposition. Her awkwardness is plain in the way she tucks her hair back behind her ear, and then repeats the motion less than a second later. Trouble is, Delilah's a pain in the ass. She's as blatant as a hammer to the side of the head. But she's also super bubbly and genuinely likeable. Silver's probably having a hell of a time deciding if she's supposed to hate the woman on sight or want to go gossip about boys with her in the bathroom.

"Since you two high schoolers are only here to research a school project, I obviously can't serve you alcohol," she says formally. "But can I interest you in some soda?" The bottle of Patron Silver Delilah holds up in her hands looks nothing like soda to me. I bite back a smirk as she pours two healthy measures into a pair of rocks glasses in front of us. When I try pay, she rolls her eyes like I'm the most tiresome creature she's ever come across. "What do you think this place is? We don't charge staff members for *soda*. Get the hell out of here before you really offend me."

I plant a twenty down on the bar for her as a tip instead, we collect our drinks, and I lead the way toward the stage. The place is packed so the booths are all taken. Luckily, there's a table free right in the middle of the madness, though. Silver sits, eyes fixed on the dark-haired dancer, twin spots of color burning high on her cheekbones.

"I don't wanna be *that* person, but I can't help it. I have to ask," she hisses. "How many girls have you slept with here?"

"Inside the actual building? Or who work here, you mean?"

Silver does a terrible job of containing her horror. It's difficult not to laugh. "Who work here, I suppose," she answers.

"In that case, none."

She looks like she doesn't believe me. "All right. I'll bite. How many woman have you fucked inside the actual building, then?"

Damn, my cheeks are killing me. I want to laugh so fucking bad, it hurts. I take my time, pretending to count out my conquests on both hands. Twice. Eventually, I nod, face her, and say, "None."

"*What?*"

"I'm not gonna lie. There have been plenty of opportunities on both accounts. Monty doesn't like drama, though. He'd kill me if I brought it to his doorstep. I'm not stupid enough to dip my pen in company ink. This is hardly the kind of place you'd bring a date to get laid, either." A glaring lie, apparently, since that's exactly what the rest of the people sitting in front of this stage have done this evening.

The burlesque dancer stalks on her high heels down the steps from the stage, into the crowd in front of us, and the people around us draw in a collective breath. Her fans are still in her hands, covering her breasts, but she's being more daring with them now, letting her hands drop for a second or two longer when she teases them across her body.

Silver sips from her drink, hiding her face in her glass, but her curiosity pours off like smoke from a raging forest fire. I watch as she peers at the dancer over the top of her tequila. Her breath quickens when the woman with the black hair, smooth and straight as a ruler, selects a guy from the audience and straddles his lap, winding her arms and legs around him. She grinds herself into his lap for a second, painted lips parted, her fans dropping, pinned between their bodies, and she leans down, a millimeter away from kissing him…

…but then she quickly turns to the woman sitting beside the guy, obviously his wife from the tortured look of disbelief on her face, and grabs her by the neck, pulling her into a deep kiss.

"Holy shit," Silver hisses under her breath.

I take a sip, hiding my face in his glass. I'm trying not to smirk.

Silver elbows me in the ribs. "Don't laugh. This is all new to me," she complains.

"You're adorably innocent for someone who loves fucking so much, *Argento*." A flush of color climbs up her neck. She doesn't know what to say to that. She knows I'm right. She's acting like a little school girl who's never been touched before.

"I guess you'll have to rid me of my last scraps of innocence then, won't you, Alessandro Moretti."

Oh, Silver. Silver, Silver, Silver. Sounds like she's feeling brave. She has no clue what it would be like for me to do what she's asking of me, though. "How about we just stay here and ride this thing out. See how comfortable you are first."

She keeps her mouth shut. The show continues, growing more and more risqué as the night progresses. Delilah sends over two more drinks for us, and we both drain our glasses, both of us watching as the burlesque dancer abandons her feathers and all sense of modesty along with them. Before long, she's on her knees, three tables over, with a guy's hard cock in her mouth, blowing him while his wife strokes and fingers her naked pussy.

The tequila's gone to my head *and* to my dick. I've never struggled to maintain an erection when I'm drunk. Tonight, I'm harder than a length of fucking steel rebar, and it isn't because of what the burlesque dancer's doing. It's because Silver's tits are straining against the flimsy material of her shirt, and her breathing's a little too uneven. She's enjoying what's going on around us, fascinated by the sight of so much naked flesh. After all, it isn't just the couple with the dancer who have thrown caution to the wind. Nearly *all* the couples around us are either making out now, groping at each other's bodies, or they're out and out fucking.

She turns into me, burying her face into my neck, hiding. *"Alex…"* Her voice is thick with hunger—the sound sends a body-wide shiver racing down my spine. My arm's already around her waist. I slip my hand up underneath her shirt, tracing my fingers over her skin, drawing small circles against her side.

"Mmm? What is it, *Argento*. Are you a little…hot and bothered?"

"No." She denies it immediately, even though she lets out a small, breathless gasp right after her denial. "I'm just—"

"You want to be naked. You want me inside you. You want my hands all over your skin."

She pants again, a frustrated breath rushing past my ear. "Yes. I think—I think so."

I move my hand upward, my fingertips burning a trail over her ribcage until I reach the lacy cup of her bra. She squirms against me, and I chuckle under my breath. "You think…or you *know*, Silver? I can't do anything with uncertainties."

"I—I *know*." I am officially impressed. I never thought she'd be this brave, or this kinky for that matter. I get to my feet, holding out my hand to her, and she looks up at me with confusion in her eyes. "What? Are we leaving?"

"No, dolcezza. I'm going to give you what you've been needing since we came down here. Come on. Come with me."

She doesn't ask questions. Not even when I lead her through the mass of writhing bodies in front of the stage and pull us in the direction of the door that leads to the back rooms. God knows what kind of thoughts are racing through her head. She follows close at my back, wide-eyed as I guide her down a long hallway, passing numerous open doors, and into a large, open space that has been arranged with at least ten king sized beds.

The stage crowd is tame compared to what's happening back here. On one of the beds, three couples have all joined forces, stroking and touching each other's naked bodies. A woman with heavy, swinging, natural tits bounces up and down on top of a guy I'm guessing she didn't arrive here with tonight, while another guy lying on his back watches them fiercely, stroking his hand up and down his cock. Two of the woman make out, tongues laving and licking at each other's mouth and necks, while another woman pants and moans against a handrail bolted to the wall, being fucked from behind by a third guy.

Atop every bed, a similar debauched adventure is taking place, people grinding, and licking, sucking and fucking.

Silver casts a stunned look around the room, her mouth falling open, the tip of her perfect, pink little tongue darting out to wet her lips as she takes in our new, highly deviant surroundings.

I stroke her hair back over her shoulder, leaning into her so I can growl roughly into her ear. "How about this? Is this what you want, *Argento*? Or should we turn around now and head on back upstairs?"

The black light cast off from the bulbs overhead make her teeth and the whites of her eyes glow green and as she meets my gaze. "I want to try. I wanna see what it feels like to…to be watched."

The growl intensifies in the back of my throat. She looks so damned innocent. So fucking delicious and unprepared. I hate that I'm not a better man. I should take her away from here and whisk her away from here immediately, but that's not what I'm going to do. Her pale eyes are full of determination, which means she wants this. She's going to be pissed if I deny her. And, damn me to hell, I'm not strong enough to err on the side of sanity tonight. I've already imagined her straddling me, riding the shit out of me on top of the bed to our right, and I want it more than I want to be good.

I draw her into me, bringing my mouth down onto hers, and the softness of her pliant lips against mine coaxes a strained groan out of me. This can't be fucking real. How can it be? I'm experienced in many things. I've fucked girls before. I've fucked grown women, who have asked me to do some pretty kinky shit, but I have never done *this* with anyone. I'm blown away that I'm getting to do it with a girl I have fallen so fucking hard for, even if it might not be the best idea in the world.

I'm going to take it slow. I'm going to make sure she's comfortable every step of the way. If she's unsure even a sec—

The thought cuts off when Silver pulls back, pausing the kiss, and she rips her shirt off over her head.

Fuck. Okay. It doesn't look like she wants to take things slowly.

I stand back, half amused, half out of my mind with lust as Silver unbuttons her jeans and wriggles them down her hips. She only stops what she's doing when she's in her underwear, reaching around behind herself to unfasten her bra. "What's the matter?" she asks, staring up into my face defiantly. "You coming over all shy, Alessandro Moretti?"

I feel my lip pull back. I feel myself snarl. I don't recognize myself right now, and I sure as hell don't recognize Silver. "You're fucking magnificent," I rumble. My hands twitch, desperate to feel the soft, smooth silk of her skin beneath them. God, I wanna make her shiver and quake. I want to hear her panting cries for more over every other girl's in this room. My leather jacket comes off slow. I drop it at my feet, not giving a shit if it gets lost or stolen. My t-shirt goes next, then my pants. Silver laughs softly as she attempts to remove her bra again, but I grab her savagely by the wrists, shaking my head.

"Don't touch yourself. It's my right to strip you naked, *Argento*."

Her head tips back, and I fall on her like a winter storm. I tear the lace on her bra when I tear it from her. She gasps, fingers digging into my back as I fall to my knees and drag her panties down her body, exposing her to the world, for all to see. She's off the ground, and I'm carrying her, throwing her down on the empty bed behind us two seconds later.

There are eyes on us, watching us, feasting on our young, perfect flesh, and it seems to be driving Silver fucking crazy. She arches her back off the bed, rolling her head to one side, watching the couple on the bed closest to us fucking.

"Alex…Alex…" My name comes out of her like a whispered prayer. "God, Alex, please."

She obeys me when I push her legs apart; my brave little *Argento*, spreading her legs for me, unashamed, opening herself to me in front of thirty other people. She's fucking beautiful, like a night orchid in full bloom. I palm my dick, positioning myself between her legs, feeling the heat and weight of strangers' eyes on my back.

I rub the tip of my cock into Silver's pussy, applying pressure to her clit, and she angles her hips up toward me, frantically shaking her head.

"No. No. Just...just fuck me, Alex. Please. God, I need you so fucking bad. Please!"

I fucking love foreplay. I love it more than the actual sex most of the time, but we are so beyond any of that now.

I grit my teeth as I push myself inside her, supplying what she needs. She's so tight around me, hotter and wetter than she's ever been. I don't stop thrusting myself into her until I'm balls-deep, and even then she grinds up, rolling her hips, asking me for more. Falling on her, I rock myself forward, hissing when she reaches up and grabs hold of my hair, pulling hard.

"Harder, Alex. Please. Harder!"

I oblige her, since she's begging so nicely.

Her nails drive deep into my back, making me curse loudly, and my mind goes blank. I'm no longer aware of what drives me, but I answer its call anyway, driving myself into her over again over again, so hard that I can feel her body rock with each impact.

I love this girl. I love her more than I can comprehend, which is why I bite her when she pleads for me to sink my teeth into her skin. I close my hand around her throat when she pulls on my hands. I do whatever she urges me to, regardless of the fact that it's too much. Too rough. Too wild. Too raw, and crazy.

When she comes beneath me, frenzied, slick with our sweat, I don't care that I've broken her skin with my love, and again I've made her bleed. It doesn't matter, because Silver Parisi is slack and dazed from her pleasure and my body is numb from my own.

It's not until we're dressed and leaving the basement of the club that we both notice Jacob Weaving leaning against the wall by the exit, wearing an ugly sneer on his face.

SILVER

Thanksgiving comes and goes. Dad invites Alex to stay again for the first time since the storm, and I try and pretend not to notice the fact that Max and Mom aren't here. As a family, we have so many dorky holiday traditions that are all pointless without Mom and Max. My mother would never have allowed Alex to sleep in the house, even in the guest room, and my brother was a perfect little monster the last time I saw him, though, so I make the best of the situation.

Jackie refuses to let Alex see Ben before they take off for Hawaii. He doesn't mention it, but I know it plays on his mind as the three of us rattle around the big old house, concocting a surprisingly edible thanksgiving dinner between us. Dad cracks truly horrible jokes that make us groan. Nipper gorges himself on turkey, and even lets us pet his distended tummy while he digests his Thanksgiving dinner. He falls asleep on Alex at seven thirty promptly each night.

In the mornings that follow, Dad and Alex do something really strange. They start running together. Even weirder, they spend an hour after their run locked in the garage together, hitting a punching bag Dad hasn't used since…well, never. This gives me plenty of time to write music and get ahead on all of my school work, but I don't get to hang out with Alex until the afternoon, when he's finally changed out of his sweat-soaked clothes and showered.

When I first met Alex, I was naturally very worried about how my father was going to take a heavily tattooed, motorcycle-riding bad boy invading my life and claiming every waking moment of my day. Turns out, I should have been more worried about Dad *stealing* Alex from me. They even seem to have their own secrets and private jokes, all be them heavy disguised as underhanded digs.

The Wednesday after Thanksgiving, Alex surprises me by sneaking into the shower in my en suite…while I'm in it. He fucks me hard up against the tiles, his hand firm and demanding, mouth hot and wet against my skin, and when he comes, he roars so loud that Dad slam's the front door and leaves the house.

Reluctantly, Alex says he has to go back to the trailer after that. He has shifts at the Rock he needs to show up for, and there are other mysterious things he has to take care of over the next couple of days that are going to monopolize most of his time. He won't tell me what he's up to, but he seems excited. Energized. It feels like the world's ending when I kiss him on the doorstep of the house, sulking because I won't be able to see him again for three more days.

He laughs at my pouting mouth and over-the-top complaining, but he's the one who struggles to let go of my hand as he walks away down the driveway.

Dad does me a solid and doesn't mention the fact that he *definitely* heard us having sex when he comes home. He doesn't mention anything about the fact that Alex is gone either. Two days later, on Friday evening, he stands in my bedroom doorway with a heavy-looking black bag in his hand, face a little grim.

"Gotta go out for a bit, kiddo," he says, leaning against the door jamb. "I ordered in some Chinese food for you. Extra Orange Chicken. Should be here in about half an hour. I'm not gonna be back 'til late, probably. No need to wait up for me."

I stick a piece of paper inside the book I was reading, marking my place, and then I set it down, eyeing him suspiciously. Black jeans. Black t-shirt. Black jacket. "God, Dad," I groan. "*Please* tell me you're not gonna start dressing like Alex now. It's great you guys are bonding and all, but this is a little ridiculous, don't you think?"

Dad's eyes widen, his head tipping to one side. "I can't believe my own child would be so *hurtful*," he says theatrically. "The very last thing I'd ever do is mimic your brooding, grumpy boyfriend. Black is a classic look, Silver. You can never go wrong with black. Especially if there are clandestine meetings afoot."

"No! Dad! Are you going on a *date?*"

"No, no. *God* no. Never mind. I probably shouldn't have said that. I have to get going or I'm gonna be late. Don't forget to listen out for the doorbell, okay?"

"Dad?"

He was turning to leave, throwing his words over his shoulder at me as he walked back out onto the landing, but the second I say his name, he stops. "Mmm?"

"What's with the bag?"

"Huh?"

"The bag. The black one you're holding in your hand. What's in it?"

Dad falters, looking down at the offending article that he indeed *is* still holding in his hand. "Uhhh, just…books! Just some old architectural books I'm returning to a friend."

I narrow my eyes. "Are you lying to me, Father?"

He nods without hesitation. "Yep. Not proud of it. Hoping we can move on without this being a thing. I have a bag, and it contains a few items that I'm choosing not to tell you about. I'm afraid that's gonna have to be good enough, kiddo."

"They're not sex toys, are they? Urgh, Dad, you *are* going on a date!"

"No! No w—hey, wait. What would be so bad about me going on a date?"

I pick up my book and open it. "Well, you look like you're about to break and enter somewhere for starters. And then there's the matter of the weird facial hair you're still cultivating. If you are planning on trying to romance any new prospects soon, you should probably let me take you shopping—"

I look up from my book; the doorway to my bedroom is empty. The mere mention of shopping has always had my father sprinting in the opposite direction as fast as he can humanly manage. I think all of that running with Alex this week is paying off, though. The old man's exits have become infinitely faster.

24

ALEX

"She said I looked like I was about to go break and enter, for fuck's sake."

I clench my jaw, pulling up my hood against the cold. We've been planning for days, making contingencies in case something comes up, organizing meeting points in case we're separated, and it seemed like we had our bases covered. Cameron hasn't stopped freaking out since he arrived fifteen minutes ago, though, and I'm already trying to come up with a way to make him stay in the fucking car. The last thing we need is him losing his shit in the middle of this and blowing our cover.

"Just because she said that's what you looked like doesn't mean she *knew* that's what you were gonna do. Everything's fine. Look, if you want to go home—"

"No way. Not happening. Just pass me the flashlight. I'm not going anywhere. Jesus, at least if I'm here and we do get caught, we'll have *some* credibility. Who's going to believe that you were just passing through the neighborhood and accidentally found yourself inside Caleb Weaving's pool house?"

"I fail to see how your presence gives us credibility," I argue. "What brilliant excuse would *you* have for us being inside Caleb Weaving's pool house?"

He grumbles under his breath. "I'm a respected member of the community. I designed the mayor's house, for fuck's sake. I'm on the town planning committee. I'm sure whatever I came up with would be more plausible than, 'I got lost and the door was open.'"

"All right, Poindexter. Why don't you work on that in your head while I figure out how we're going to get around the side of the house without setting off those perimeter lights?"

The Weaving residence is a monstrosity—a disgusting show of wealth and power presented in the gaudiest manner imaginable. Cam pretended to throw up in his mouth when I killed the engine of the Impala Monty loaned me. "Who tries to combine baroque facias with art deco window casements anyway?" he'd mumbled. I was more offended that the place was painted a pale bubblegum pink color and sticks out amongst the gathered trees like a thumb that isn't just sore but has also had a hammer taken to it. The ugliest, most expensive home I have ever fucking seen. Leon Wickman's place was probably almost as costly, but that building was designed with finesse, married with an understanding and appreciation for nature. The sprawling Weaving manor is just a fucking *mess*.

"There'll be a mains box somewhere near that tree over there," Cam says, pointing. "There's an electrical box just underneath that window, too. See it? We don't want to cut any of the wiring. That'll scream foul play if someone comes across it. We can just—"

I get out of the car, making sure the door doesn't slam closed behind me. I can't sit and listen. I can't just fucking *sit* anymore. I've waited long enough. When Monty said I had five days to come and cleave my pound of flesh from Jacob Weaving's body before the cops came and carted him away, I did what I thought was right. I dismissed the suggestion out of hand. If justice was finally going to be served, then me showing up in the middle of the night to hurt the fucker would be pure, unadulterated, selfish vengeance. That decision stuck in my throat. Staying my hand felt like a missed opportunity to wreak chaos in the bastard's life, but it had also felt, I don't know, like I was growing up. Becoming a better man or some shit. And then he went and tried to drag her into the boy's locker rooms, like he thought he could still do whatever the fuck he felt like and get away with it, regardless of the fact that I'm in Silver's life now, and *that*? That altered my perspective. That brazen, fucked up act changed my mind so quickly, it nearly gave me fucking whiplash. No way was I was going to be able to stay my hand when I laid eyes on those bruises around her throat. I no longer had a choice.

Juvie's bad. Prison is worse. A strange code of honor exists between most inmates inside penitentiaries. Armed robbery; assault; theft; even fucking murder: there's a vast litany of crimes that can land you behind the bars of a cell, and your indiscretion usually won't matter to the guy you end up bunking with. But rape? Pedophilia? Those are two sins that'll usually land you in the prison infirmary for a very, very long time. Repeatedly.

Jake's not going to enjoy his time at Monroe or Cedar Creek. Whichever prison they send him to, it doesn't matter. It's going to be a living hell on earth for him. But it's not enough, damn it. The moment he laid his hands on Silver again, I knew no punishment was going to suffice unless I administered it fucking personally. I've been fighting the urge to wait until tonight to come over here. Every night, it's been tempting as fuck to sneak over here without Cam and leave a mark or two of my own on Jacob, but I've held back shown restraint.

The time for restrain is over. Now that we're here and Jacob's asleep in his bed less than a hundred meters away, I am officially antsy as fuck. Whatever Cameron has to say can wait.

I head toward the house.

Cam gets out of the Impala, hissing under his breath as he ducks down, hurrying after me along the perimeter of the gravel driveway. "What the fuck are you doing?" I hiss.

"Don't *walk*. If you're deadset on doing this, then the least you can do is *fucking run*."

He sets off, sprinting like his life depends on it, Monty's black bag, which I asked him to bring with him tonight, bouncing against his back as he darts over a small section of lawn, hitting the boundary line of the property, sticking to the shadows cast off by the forest. If someone just so happens to be looking out of a window right now, then fair enough. It'll probably be really fucking difficult to see him. He's just made his route around the side of the house three times longer, though. I duck and run straight for the ugly pink pile of bricks and wood, snarling with every step that brings me closer to Jacob.

I've considered every way this thing could possibly play out. There's a very real chance we're going to get caught, and if that happens then I am definitely, one hundred percent, absolutely fucked. I'll make sure that son of bitch gets what's coming to him before I'm carted off in handcuffs, though. I'm gonna make that motherfucker bleed.

Predictably, the security lights come on when I'm halfway around the house. Columns of brilliant white light explode into the night, cutting through the darkness like the search lights depicted in about a thousand prison break movies.

Sshhhunk. Sshhhunk. Sshhhunk.

I pause, back pressed to the wall, heart hammering in my ears, while I wait for the sound of a door or a window opening. No sound comes. Across the way, Cam's stabbing a finger in the direction of the pool house, mouthing something furiously at me. It's too dark over there in the shadows to see shit let alone read his fucking lips.

Goddamn it, Cameron.

I take off, shoving away from the wall, sprinting along the perimeter of the house, hoping like hell that no one catches sight of the dark blur racing over the grass.

Once I'm around the rear of the property, I duck down behind the poolside Tiki bar—*fucking poolside Tiki bar, FUCK these assholes*—and I wait for Silver's dad. He's seconds behind me. Cam's blowing hard as he sinks down into a crouch, leaning his head back against the bamboo framework of the bar, closing his eyes. The guy has no common sense. He looks relieved, which means he hasn't given any thought to the next part of our plan; the part where we bust into the pool house and beat Jacob Weaving's teeth right out of his head with a couple of wrenches.

"That was close," he pants.

He was so amped up the night we made pizza. So full of fire and brimstone. The steel in his eyes had impressed the shit out of me; I'd thought he would be able to handle this. Now, I'm not so sure. I don't want him getting caught. I don't want to this to go south, and for *him* to wind up in prison. "Seriously, man. Go back to the car. Plausible deniability's a thing. If you don't get seen here—"

"Fuck you," he growls. "We've been through this already. We do *not* have time to relive the *I-nearly-abandoned-Silver-on-the-day-she-was-born* story. So shut...the fuck...up."

I respect Cam. I respect the shit out of him because he gave Silver life, and I owe him a lifetime's happiness because of that. However, with every passing second, I'm beginning to see him as less of an authority figure and more of an annoying friend I want to throat punch. I don't like being told to shut the fuck up by him, that's for sure. I growl unhappily, suppressing the urge to curl my lip and show teeth.

Has he ever found himself thrown into a holding cell that reeks of piss? Does he know what it's like to be trapped in a tiny ten-by-ten windowless room with three other men, wondering who's going to hit you first? I doubt it. He's not going to accept the out I'm offering to him, though. I can see it in his eyes. He's determined to follow this plan through, irrespective of whatever it might cost him; he loves Silver just as much as I do.

"All right. Fine. Have it your way. Just don't say I didn't warn you." I get to my feet, hurrying across the patio to the rear of the house, skirting around the pool. From there, it's a straight shot to the large single-story pool house to the left-hand side of yard. The building is twice the size of my trailer, bigger than most standard sized homes. The huge bay windows are darkened, curtains drawn within. The lights are off inside, too, no warm glow escaping through cracks in the heavy fabric.

When we reach the door of the pool house, Cam sticks a hand into Monty's mysterious black bag and pulls out a wrench; he raises the tool and pulls it back, fingers closed around it in a fist, like he's about to use it to punch a hole through the double-glazed glass.

"Whoa, whoa, whoa! What the fuck are you doing?" I hiss. "You'll wake up the entire neighborhood!"

Cam looks disappointed. The guy's been ramping himself up for the past seventy-two hours. He probably hasn't been able to sleep for thinking about the lengths he might have to go to tonight. He's played out the moment when we confront Jake in his head a thousand times. He's become accustomed to the idea that he's going to have to break, smash, cut, and hurt tonight in order to accomplish his goal, and now here I am, preventing him from following through and he doesn't like it one bit.

"Try the door first," I tell him, jerking my chin at the sleek, narrow length of brushed metal in front of him.

"It'll be locked."

I say nothing. I stand and wait for him to try the fucking door handle.

Cam places a gloved hand on the handle, huffing as he checks to see if the door's already open. He gives me a smug *I-told-you-so* look when it doesn't budge. "Should I smash it now?"

"No! Fuck. Haven't you heard of the element of surprise? Get out of the way."

Cam glares at me, but he steps to one side, giving me access to the door. I pull a hairpin and a slim, hooked pick from my wallet, sliding both into the door's lock, feeling around for the moment when I hit the catch. Two seconds later, I find the point of resistance inside the barrel of the lock and I work my magic, popping it open with a deft twist of my wrist.

"I should be worried by that," Cam mutters under his breath. "The sad truth is that I'm just impressed."

That's nothing. He'd be seriously fucking impressed if he saw me break into a Tesla in under five seconds flat. I keep that to myself, though.

The door to the pool house swings silently open and I creep inside first, eyes sharp, squinting into the darkness. We've walked straight into the living area. A huge sectional couch monopolizes most of the space, arranged around the biggest flat screen T.V. I've ever fucking seen. It's obscenely big, really. Cam arches a derisive eyebrow in the television's direction as he follows behind me, silent, taking note of his surroundings. It's great that he's on the look-out, but he won't be looking for the same things *I'm* looking for. Cam's looking for people. Jake, to be precise. I'm scanning the bookcases and the shelves. The ceilings at the corners of the room. The Weavings are bound to have a camera system set up inside the main house, but inside the pool house? That's a tricky one. This is Jake's domain. He's unlikely to want Big Brother spying on him in his private sanctuary. The shit he gets up to in here would probably even turn his father's stomach.

My instincts prove to be correct. I see no blinking red lights as I cast my eyes around. I hear no faint electronic whirring that would spell disaster for us and our mission.

There are two rooms leading off from the main living space of the pool house. I head toward the door on the left first since it's closer. The blinds are drawn inside the room, but a faint blue glow from the lit pool outside works its way between the gaps, casting enough light to illuminate our surroundings. Not a bedroom, it would seem. Mirrors line the far wall. In the very center of the room, a bench press takes up most of the space, the bar still loaded with weight. By the window, a treadmill and an exercise bike loom out of the shadows. Obviously, Jake uses this as his private home gym, though God knows why he would ever need to use it. Coach Quentin drills the football team to breaking point every single day after school. Those training sessions are fucking exhausting. Jake's definitely taking steroids if he comes home and hits this place up after taking such a beating for the Roughnecks.

I'm backing out of the room when Cameron turns, catching sight of himself in the mirror next to us. Fuck knows how he didn't notice the mirrored wall before. He jumps when he sees the dark shape moving next to him and immediately thinks he's under attack. The wrench he tried to smash the front door with almost goes flying as he lashes out with it.

I catch him by the wrist in the nick of time. A split second later and he would have sent the tool crashing into the glass. "Jesus *fucking* Christ," I hiss. "Give that to me." I rip the wrench out of his hand, confiscating it in a swift move that should honestly have taken place before we even entered the pool house. "You are a fucking liability, Parisi," I tell him under my breath. "Just be cool man. Take a deep breath. Get your shit together. Chill. Don't you dare get another weapon out of that bag until I tell you to. Stay behind me and don't move a muscle until I tell you to."

Cam's expression says it all: like me, he doesn't appreciate being told what to do, but he's gonna land us in hot fucking water if I don't rein him in once and for all.

My pulse should be racing. My adrenaline's high, pumping urgently around my body, making me hum with energy, but my heart rate is a slow, steady thump in my chest. I've always been like this in dangerous, high-stakes situations that would leave others anxious, bouncing on the balls of their feet, ready to explode into action. I'm galvanized, sharper, focused, my synapses firing so rapidly that I jump from one thought to the next in a flurry of mental activity. Shame Cameron wasn't wired the same way. This would be going a lot smoother if he was.

We cross the living room, heading for the other door, and once we reach it, I open it without hesitation. We've already wasted too much time. Also, we've made enough fucking noise since we walked into the pool house, and the last thing I want to do is give Jake an opportunity to bail out of a window and disappear off into the night before we've had a chance to spend any quality time with him.

This time, we hit pay dirt.

The door swings open, and voila. Definitely a bedroom. There are clothes strewn all over the floor, along with discarded shoes, books, plates, cutlery, and empty fast food wrappers. Unlike the rest of the pool house, this room is a fucking dump. It looks like a bunch of vagrants have been squatting in here for weeks. It's a miracle we didn't *smell* the damn bedroom the moment I picked the lock and we entered the pool house,

Gross doesn't even cover it. The place is a health and safety hazard. I don't know if Cam's up to date on his shots but I, for one, am glad that I had a tetanus booster last year.

In the corner, the king-sized bed shoved up against the wall contains a body. A hand pokes out from underneath the welter of blankets. A foot. Tufts of dark hair are visible against white, fluffy pillows. A loud, juddering sound splinters the silence. The mother-fucker is snoring like a goddamn chainsaw. Doesn't look like Jake knows we've broken into his home and are planning on causing him serious harm. From the sounds of things, the bastard could sleep through an air raid and be none the fucking wiser.

Ahh, Jake. Jake, Jake, Jake. Our individual codes of ethics are diametri-

cally opposed. Our hearts and our consciences pull us in different directions, but we both have strong personalities. We both inspire strong feelings in others, that sometimes result in them contemplating murder. We are both the kind of guy who shouldn't let his guard down, even when he's sleeping. Except you've dropped the motherfucking ball, haven't you, son? You have let your guard down. Here you are, sleeping like you're already fucking dead...

I motion down the duffel bag, giving him the go-ahead to take out another weapon. The moment he and I have both been waiting for has finally arrived. Jake should never have been allowed to go this long unpunished for what he did to Silver, although there is something bittersweet about the fact that so much time has passed since that party at Leon Wickman's house. The first couple of weeks after Jake raped Silver, he was probably on edge. Antsy. Wondering if a pair of handcuffs were going to be slapped on his wrists and he was going to be carted off to jail. He probably held his breath a lot. Every time his father's phone rang, he probably suffered at the hands of his own paranoia, but as the days and weeks continued to roll on without consequence, Jake must have become more and more complacent.

Darhower shut Silver down when she tried to report to him what had happened. She didn't tell her parents. Her friends were actively shunning and bullying her in the corridors of Raleigh High. She had no one by her side. No one was listening to her. No one believed her, which essentially meant that Jacob was in the clear.

Now, after months of rote Raleigh High routine, showing up at school, intimidating Silver in the classrooms and the canteen, making life as miserable as possible for her at every available turn and absolutely nothing happening about it, Jacob must think he's gotten away with his crimes scot-free. Well, tonight, here in his pool house, with none of his dumb, knuckle-dragging Neanderthal football cronies to back him up, Jacob is about to find out just how *wrong* he was.

Cam's nerves have dissipated since we entered Jacob's bedroom. They've gone. Evaporated. The bumbling, panicking guy, tripping over his own feet and shaking with uncertainty is gone, and the Cameron from pizza night has finally made an appearance. His downturned mouth is locked in an unhappy grimace, firm but set. He's made up his mind. He's accepted what he's about to do, and he's made his peace with it. The change in him is miraculous.

When I glance over and see the weapon he's chosen to draw out of the black duffle bag, a cold chill skates up my spine. There are plenty of implements Cameron could have selected to hurt Jacob, plenty of things that could cause him immense pain, and drag out this whole experience for a very long time indeed. Cameron's choice of weapon is endgame, though. It's the most final option he could've chosen. It's the desert eagle.

Aiutami, Passerotto. Aiutami...a premere il...grilletto.

The cool, silver metal in Silver's father's hands gleams.

My heartrate slows.

Time slows.

What the fuck am I supposed to do here? It's one thing terrorizing a vile asshole who hurt someone you love. It's one thing doling out much-needed justice. It's another thing entirely staring down the barrel of a murder charge and preparing to pull the trigger. If I allow Cameron to do this, I'm more than complicit. I'm an accessory. Even if we aren't caught for the crime, this kind of violence leaves a stain on the soul that can't be undone. How far am I willing to go here? How much am I willing to lose? Am I willing to pay the ultimate price? Am I willing to lose Silver? Really lose her, for good?

Cameron raises the gun, determination sparking in eyes that have hardened to flint. There's nothing soft about him now. Nothing comedic or unsure. His finger hovers over the trigger, a millimeter above the steel. If I'm going to stop this, I have to do it now. The moment presses down on me, weighing in from all sides. I am underwater. I'm drowning in the depths. The pressure of a billion tons of water crushing my lungs. Cameron's eyes narrow. His hand's steady, arm outstretched. The moment hangs heavy as poison in the air, and I—

Jacob's loud snoring abruptly cuts off, and the boy in the bed jerks awake. Cam's lips peel back, his teeth bared. He takes a half step forward, ready of fire, but then the covers on the bed move and Jacob is sitting up, suddenly alert and awake, scrambling back against his pillows.

Fuck!

Shock washes through me. This is really happening. This is really happening. I'm about to watch Cameron Parisi put a bullet in the evil piece of shit who raped his daughter. But...

"Whoa, whoa, whoa! The fuck you playing at, Moretti? I know you're still mad but having me murdered in the middle of the night seems a little excessive, don't you think?"

Holy fucking shit!

Now, my heart kicks into overdrive.

Now, I can feel my pulse racing at my temples and thumping in my ears...

...because the guy Cameron Parisi nearly put down in his sleep like a dog isn't Jacob Weaving after all.

It's Zander fucking Hawkins.

25

SILVER

I shower and get ready for bed, taking time to give myself a face mask. My phone dings while I'm rinsing my face, but I'm still covered in gunk, so I don't read the message right away. I'm in no hurry. It's probably Dad. Given how weird he was acting earlier, I'm almost one hundred percent certain he was going to meet a woman. He can deny it until he's blue in the face but that bag he was carrying around with him could only have been an overnight bag. And I know him; if he's planning on sleeping over at someone's house then it has to be fairly serious. He doesn't mess around with people's feelings. He must like whoever he's been seeing for it to have gotten this far, which is confusing.

When has he has time to meet and date someone? And who the hell could it be? He goes to the office for a couple of hours every day, but other than that the man seems to have decided not to leave the house come hell or high water.

It's past midnight now. He knows I'll be heading to sleep soon so he's probably just checking in with me, making sure everything's okay before I pass out for the night. I pat my face dry, wiping remnants of the thick cream from the edges of my face with a towel, and then I head back into my bedroom, picking up my phone from the end of my bed.

+1(564) 987 3491: All alone for the night. How sad. Poor Second Place Silver.

My blood runs colder than Lake Cushman.

Second Place Silver.

I've known exactly who has been sending me all of these hateful texts. It's been obvious, but for some reason I've been unwilling to accept that Jake would be dumb enough to do it. The messages are a very permanent trail. They're evidence, and Jake's always been careful about avoiding that at all costs. They're impossible to deny now. He's the only person who calls me by that name. Jake has been texting me, threatening to kill me, and now he knows that I'm all alone?

Me: Get a life, Asshole. Leave me the hell alone.

I shouldn't antagonize him. It was sheer luck that I managed to unbalance him and take him to the ground outside the locker rooms. He'll never allow me to get the better of him again. The chances of me hurting him like that a second time are a big fat zero. I want him to slip up, though. I want to rile him just enough that he'll confirm his identity in a text.

+1(564) 987 3491: Doesn't look like Moretti and your old man are gonna be around for a while. Feel like playing me a song?

How? How does he know Alex or Dad aren't here? I could be sitting on the couch with both of them right now, for all he knows. There's only one way he can possibly be so sure, and that's if he's seen it with his own two eyes. He'd have to be sitting outside the house, spying through the windows, watching the place…

Oh. Holy. Fuck.

No, he can't be. He wouldn't be so stupid. If someone saw his car here, it'd spell disaster for him. He'd give my story credence and destroy his own credibility at the same time. He would never, *never* do something that stupid. He's fucking with me. Screwing with me. Trying to mess with my head. Still, I should probably—

Bang.

Bang.

BANG.

The sound: a sledgehammer pounding on hollow stone.

It rings down the empty halls and abandoned rooms of the Parisi household like a death knell. It clangs off the rafters and vibrates deep within the bones of the home where I grew up long after the sound fades and dies.

There is someone at the door.

"No. *No, no, no, no, no.*" The word tumbles from my mouth, spilling out of me, rising up and overflowing from a deep well of fear. This isn't real. I'm imagining it. I'm making a big deal out of nothing. This has nothing to do with Jacob Weaving.

It's not him. It's not him. Just ignore them. Whoever They'll go away if you don't make a sound.

My phone, clutched against my chest, buzzes, and panic snaps through me like ten thousand volts. I choke on my own breath as I look down at the screen.

+1(564) 987 3491: Rude, Silver. Come down and let me in. Thought *I* was the coward?

Oh my god.

The time for lying to myself has come and gone. How did I not know this was going to happen? The texts stopped, Jake started ignoring me in the halls for one fucking day, and I thought that was it? The end of it? How fucking stupid have I been. Jake never gave up on his let's-destroy-Silver-Parisi campaign. No, he's been biding his time, waiting for me to be alone so he can come torment and hurt me inside my own damn house.

I can barely see the screen properly as I pull up my conversation with Alex and fumble out a message.

Me: Come to thehouse. He;s here. Q2ucik.

The words are jumbled. Full of typos. Legible enough, though. It's going to have to do. There's no time to fix the message before I hit the blue button and shove the phone into the pocket of my flannel pajama pants.

I need to move.

Dad's room's at the end of the hall. I have to pass the top of the stairs to reach the door to his bedroom, which gives me a perfect view down toward the frosted glass in the front door. Shit. There's some there—a shadowy dark outline, lurking on the doorstep.

It's him.

Jake.

What the fuck are you doing, Silver? Call Dad. Call the fucking cops!

I fly down the hallway toward Dad's room and throw myself through the door, slamming it shut behind me. Heading straight for his closet, I'm shaking like a leaf as I duck down, pulling out shoebox after shoebox, trying to locate the gun I found hidden here a couple of years ago.

Only...the gun isn't here.

A loud crash shatters the silence downstairs—the sound of breaking glass. My hands cover my mouth of their own accord, trapping the scream building in my throat behind my fingers.

Fuck. Fuck, fuck, fuck. I need Alex here right fucking now. Common sense kicks in, though; I can barely hold the phone in my shaking hands as I dial 911.

"SIIIIILVERR..."

Jacob's voice echoes up the stairs. The sound of broken glass hitting the floor tinkles prettily downstairs as I kick the shoe boxes aside and crouch down inside Dad's closet, shutting myself in. I can't...fucking...breathe...

"911, what's your emergency?"

I screw my eyes shut. "Home...home invasion." God, I sound so fucking loud. "Someone's breaking into my house."

On the floor below me, in the hallway, the front door slams.

He's officially inside.

"What's your address?" the 911 operator asks.

...paralyzed...

...can't...

...speak...

"Ma'am? Your address? I'm gonna send a car out to you, but we're going to confirm your location."

"Fif-fifteen twenty-three Barkley Meadows Circle."

"And your name?"

"Si—it's Silver."

Inside the closet, my whispered words are as loud as exploding bombs. I press my forehead against the door jamb, gritting my teeth together, straining to hear what's happening downstairs.

Is he coming up here?

He's going to find me.

There's no way out of here.

I'm going to die in my father's fucking shoe closet.

This is not *how I was supposed to go.*

"SILVER!" My name rips through the tense quiet that's blanketing the house. I jump, nearly dropping the phone.

"Was that the intruder?" the 911 operator asks.

"Y—yes."

"Is the intruder known to you?"

"Yes. His—his name is Jacob Weaving. We go to school together."

"Do you believe Jacob to be armed?"

"Yes. Yes, I do."

"All right, Silver. Sit tight. A cruiser's been dispatched. They should be with you any moment. Stay on the line with me while we wait for them, okay?"

"Okay." It's reassuring that there are cops on the way, but how long are they going to take to get here? Five minutes? Ten? Jacob's already let himself in. He's not the smartest, but it won't take a genius to figure out where I'm hiding. Under the bed; in the closets: these are the first places people always look. I left Dad's bedroom door open. Jake might have seen me flit across the top of the landing before he smashed the window in the front door. Even if he didn't, there are only two floors to the house. Once he's done searching the ground floor, it won't be long before he's stalking up here to find me.

Jesus Christ, this can *not* be happening. This can *not* be happening.

I shouldn't have attacked him so viciously outside those locker rooms. I should have thought it through. I should have known he'd snap and come looking for me. I should have just fucking run.

Beneath me, a series of loud barks emanate from the kitchen. Oh, Christ! Nipper! I haven't been shutting him in the living room like I'm supposed to. Every night for the past week, he's been grumpily nudging my bedroom door open at about two o'clock in the morning and jumping on the edge of my bed, shooting me a belligerent sideways glance before knotting himself into a pretzel and falling asleep next to my feet.

He's down there now...

With Jake...

My eyes begin to burn. *Just let him be okay. Dear God, please, just let him be okay.* I stifle a cry of horror when the barking downstairs is cut of, replaced by a pained squeal, Everything falls threateningly silent again.

Nipper's probably okay. Jake probably just kicked him to shut him up. Dread presses down on me, crouched in the bottom of the closet, though. The seconds tick by and Nipper doesn't make another sound.

"Silver? Silver, are you still there?"

I haven't dared breathe for the past two minutes; the emergency operator's obviously making sure I'm alive. It's a risk to answer her, even in a whisper, but I chance it. "He's downstairs. I think…" A tear streaks down my cheek. "I think he hurt my dog."

Shaking like a leaf, I lower the phone, hiding the keypad so I can pull up my texts while still keeping the operator on the line. I hit Dad's name, opening our conversation stream, and quickly tap out a desperate message.

Me: Jake in th house. Hiding. Police on way. Come home!

Lord only knows what he's gonna think when he reads that Jake's broken into the house. For such a common name, Jacob Weaving is the only Jake at Raleigh. There's no mistaking who I'm talking about. Like everyone else in town, Dad follows high school football it's a certified religion, and just like everyone else in town, he thinks Jacob walks on water. After the rape, I would rush to the bathroom and run both taps full blast to hide the sounds of me violently throwing up every time my father paid the sick fuck a compliment.

Unlike Jake, however, my father is smart. He'll put two and two together. He *will* figure out why I'm scared of this boy breaking into our house, and he will come running. The question is when? I don't know where he went tonight. He was so secretive. He could be in the middle of a late-night movie at the Regency. They have an eleven thirty showing on Friday nights. If my father's on a date and that's where he chose to take her, then his phone will be switched off in his pocket. It'll be—

"Silver! What the fuck? I thought you were some kind of badass now. Why don't you come out and face me? You don't realize how lucky you are. I know plenty of girls who'd kill to spend their Friday night with me."

I bite down on the inside of my cheek, fear scattering my thoughts to the wind. I'm not coming out of this closet by choice. No fucking way. Whatever violence he has planned for me will not be good. The text messages he sent were dark. They grew worse, more graphic and ruthless each time my phone chimed. There are no limits to Jake's frightening imagination, and I have no plans to walk willingly into whatever violence he has in mind for me.

Slow, steady footsteps ascend the stairs. The steady *thum, thum, thum* sounds like nails being hammered into the lid of a coffin.

My mind flashes, dragging me back to that night in the upstairs bathroom of Leon Wickman's house. Jake's crazed, half-mad eyes. The weight of him bearing down on me. His fingers gouging into my flesh, driving my legs apart. Such shame, surging around my body, carried along by the reluctant push and pull of my heart every time it beat in my chest.

"You're nothing. Worse than nothing. You're a piece of meat, put here on this earth for our pleasure. Don't you know how this works, you dumb fucking cunt? Me and my boys? We're from different stock. Purebreds. We do what we want. Say what we want. Take what we want. You should be fucking grateful we even deigned you worthy of our attention."

He'd believed that. He'd believed, forcing me into submission on the cold tile of that nightmare room, that I should have been *grateful* that he'd noticed me. Months later, so much pain later, and here we area again, Jacob Weaving forcing his way into my home, convinced that I should be thankful he's paying me the visit.

The guy's a fucking psychopath.

"Just stay hidden," the operator advises quietly. "Don't make a sound. Not long now."

I keep quiet. Jacob's on the landing now. His boots find every creaky floorboard possible as he slowly makes his way toward me.

"I came here once, remember?" Jake's voice is closer. Softer. He's not shouting anymore. He knows that I'm close and I can hear him just fine. "Your twelfth birthday or something. You had a movie night, and your dad turned the basement into a make-shift theater. Hot dogs. Popcorn machine. Red vines. I told everyone I thought it was dumb, but you wanna know the truth, Silver Parisi? Your movie theater birthday party was the coolest party I'd ever been to."

So...fucking...close...now...

I close my eyes, trapping the breath at the back of my throat, trying to hold back tears.

"Meanwhile, my dad had this assistant, Susannah. It was part of her job to remember when my birthday was. Dad paid her to keep track of what was cool with kids my age and buy an appropriate gift when the time came around. She was also in charge of organizing all of my parties. Figuring out new and interesting ways of celebrating every year. For my tenth birthday, Susannah actually sent my parents *invites* to the party she arranged, like they were distant relatives or so⌐⌐ shit. And..." Bitter laughter floods the upstairs landing. The footsteps, worryingly, have stopped. "D'you know what happened? My mother RSVP'd very courteously. Said she was sorry but unfortunately she had a prior engagement and wouldn't be able to attend. My father came. It was a baseball party, and he showed up wearing an L.A. Lakers shirt, then proceeded to fuck Susannah in my mother's walk-in closet. I found him grunting over her like a sweating, hairy pig and thought he was trying to fucking kill her."

"Hello? Are you still there, sweetheart?" the operator whispers.

I am silent as the grave. I don't make a sound.

I'm gripped by a bottomless terror that knows no end.

"That movie theater party probably didn't cost your folks much. I told everyone your family must be poor if they couldn't afford to even hire a D.J. or book a venue for you. We laughed behind your back about it for weeks. Truth was, I was jealous. You were so happy that night. You were beaming from ear to ear. You were stoked to hang out at home with your mom and dad, and all your friends. You spent most of the night laughing, happy as a pig in shit, and I...I couldn't remember a time when I'd *ever* laughed like that with my parents. I couldn't remember a single time when my dad had put away his work for five minutes, looked me in the face, and saw me."

Jake sighs heavily. Wearily. His boots scuff against the bare floorboards again...as he steps into my father's bedroom.

"Your dad didn't just look at you like he was seeing you, Silver. He looked at you like you were the most important thing in the world, and it made me so fucking *angry*. None of that matters now, I guess. He isn't here to see you tonight, is he?"

When the door to the closet opens, it isn't a theatrical reveal. Jake doesn't rip it off its hinges, trying to surprise me. He opens it slowly, letting the lacquered wood swing open. He stands there with his hands driven deep into the pockets of his Raleigh High sweatpants, disappointment mingling with boredom on his handsome, blood-streaked face.

His shirt is soaked in blood. His bare forearms are coated red.

The bruises I gave him when he attacked me at Raleigh haven't faded all that much. Leaning against the wall beside the closet, the captain of the Roughnecks football team, king of Raleigh High, is a terrifying sight to behold.

"Silver? Silver?" The operator's hushed voice whispering out of my cell phone's speaker sounds worried.

Jacob arches a sardonic eyebrow at me. "Hang up the phone, Silver. You and me, we're going for a little ride."

26

ALEX

"What the *fuck* were you doing in there?"

I slam the driver's side door, abandoning all attempts to be quiet. Cam's already in the passenger seat beside me. Zander's casually sprawled out across the back seat, long legs bent at the knee while he hikes his hips up and zips the fly on his jeans; I barely gave him enough time to stick his legs inside the damn things before I was dragging him out of the pool house and up the long driveway, spitting out curse words in Italian between my bared teeth. These are the first words I've been calm enough to utter in English since I realized it was Zander inside that bed and not Jacob.

"I told you I'd found myself some sweet digs, didn't I? I would have explained everything the other night outside the Rock, but you weren't feeling particularly friendly, were you? This is on you, bro."

"On *me*? Fuck you, man. You've had plenty of opportunities to tell me what the fuck you're up to since then and you haven't breathed a word."

The Impala's engine roars to life, snarling in the dark. I don't even bother to wait and see if a light goes on inside the Weaving's main residence. My blood's up; I don't give a shit about being covert anymore. I only care about dragging Zander Hawkins' carcass somewhere secluded, so I can beat the living shit out of him for fucking up our take-down.

Next to me, Cam hasn't said a word. He's been quiet ever since I forced him to lower the desert eagle he was aiming at Zander's head. His eyes are distant, a deep, miserable frown forming two lines between his brows.

I peel out of the Weaving's driveway, glaring at Silver's father out of the corner of my eye. "What? No sarcastic commentary?" I demand. "No, *'what the fuck's going on?'* No, *'who the fuck is this?'*"

Cameron blinks. "Not worth it," he responds tightly. "I also don't care."

"You don't care."

"No. The kid's annoying as fuck, but he's not Jacob. We need to find Jacob. That's the only thing I care about. I'm going to fucking kill him, Alex."

"You sure are hanging out with some weird types these days," Zander comments. "I mean, I know they told us at Denney that spending time with older, wiser people might help us make better choices, but for real, yo. This guy's talking about murder. I wouldn't call that a *smart* choice if you're looking for some Friday night entertainment. I heard they're having some sort of lucha libre event over in—"

"Shut the fuck up, Hawk."

"Ooookay. Shutting the fuck up."

"Get rid of him," Cam growls.

"Oh, you guys just dragged me out of my only crash pad in Raleigh," Hawk says. "You're not just dumping me on the side of the street in the snow and ditching me like an unwanted child. I've already been through that shit. I'm gonna have to object pretty fucking strongly if you—"

I slam my fist into the steering wheel. "God, can you just please be fucking quiet!" *Breathe,* passarrotto. *That's it,* mi amore. *In...and out. In...and out. See. You control your temper. Your temper does not control you. Va bene.* "Either tell us what you were doing in Jacob Weaving's pool house, or keep your goddamn mouth closed while I try and figure all of this out, Zander." I'm going to fucking kill *him* in a minute.

Zander makes a familiar bored sound. "All right, all right. Jesus. Q sent me here to try and find Caleb Weaving's safe. He wants reparations. We've had to turn down shipments now that we're down three guys. As far as Q's concerned, Caleb was the one who sold him out to the cops, so now he owes him. Big time."

"So Caleb's just letting you stay in the fucking pool house while you snoop around, searching for a fucking *safe*?"

In the rearview, Zander rolls his eyes dramatically. "Stupidity is *not* a good look on you. Caleb has no idea Q knows he snitched on us. He thinks everything's copasetic between the Dreadnaughts and the Weaving operation. We have a huge deal going down at the end of next week. Like, *huge*. Caleb's sitting on a monster delivery at his place until then. He asked Q to provide a little extra protection until the trades are ready to be made. He essentially invited a Dreadnaught into his home. Dumb motherfucker."

This can only be the same deal Monty mentioned to me in his office. The deal that the DEA are going to bust. The one that will lead to Jake subsequently being arrested for raping Zen, and his life finally ending as he knows it.

I grunt as I swing the car through the narrow switchback turns that guides us down the mountainside, toward the town of Raleigh. The Christmas lights in the trees twinkle merrily down in the bottom of the valley, and for a moment I just stare at the little knot of glowing yellow light. Eventually, I say, "What has any that got to do with Raleigh High? Why the fuck have you shown up there, pretending to be something you're not, when the Caleb Weaving'll be behind bars by the end of next weekend."

"I'm on loan."

"What?"

"From the Dreadnaughts. I'm on loan to Monty for the foreseeable. Apparently, I am the glue that'll cement ties between Montgomery and the Dreadnaughts for good." He flashes me a fake-ass grin in the mirror when he catches me glaring at him. "S'nice to be appreciated every once in a while. Monty told me he wanted me enrolled at Raleigh, so off I went and enrolled. The preppy get-up was his choice, too. He wants me to fit in. I'm supposed to make friends and report back on what I learn from them."

I shake my head. "You? Make friends with Raleigh kids? Pssshhh." I can't imagine anything more ridiculous.

"Some chick, Winters, I think her name was…she was dealing coke for Monty on the quiet. Got banished to some stuffy prep school in Seattle. Now her Raleigh High clients have been bringing in their own supplies, trying to distribute them right under Monty's nose. He wants to know exactly who's trying to cut in on h—"

"Kacey Winters?" Cam says incredulously. "Kacey was dealing *cocaine* at *school?*"

I'm equally surprised. I never saw Kacey at the Rock. Not once. The first time I met her was at Raleigh, long after I'd decided I needed to have Silver Parisi as my own. Monty's never mentioned the girl's name, not even when I wound up getting shot because of her. If Zander's telling the truth, then obviously my boss isn't being as up front with me as I've previously assumed.

Cam closes his eyes, shaking his head, as if the action will dislodge the information he just heard. "Look, I don't really give a shit about the why of you being in that pool house. I don't know who Q is, or who the new dealer is at Raleigh High, and I don't particularly fucking care about any of that either. All I care about is Jacob Weaving. If you know where he is, then spit it out so we can finish what we started."

Zander studies Cam blankly. After a long second, he leans forward, arms braced against the backs of our headrests, and whispers loudly to me, "This guy's not important, is he? 'Cause he's got collateral damage written all over him. I'll willingly put money on him not lasting the night."

"Zander, just sit back and button your mouth shut," I snarl. "Cam's Silver's dad, and you're lucky he didn't just shoot you in the fucking head back there. *You're* only making it through tonight because he managed to pull back at the last second."

"Hoo-rah. I'll pin a medal of honor onto the fucker for not accidentally murdering me, then."

Cam turns a bright shade of crimson. If he were a cartoon character, there'd be steam blowing out of his ears. "Pull over, Alex. I've changed my mind. I *am* going to shoot him."

"Just both of you, calm the fuck down. Tonight's already a big enough mess as it is, and none of this is making it—"

DING!

My phone buzzes in my pocket.

DING! DING!

And again.

Another round of chimes fills the car, this time from someone else's cell. Cam pulls his device out of his pocket at the same time I reach for mine. The car lights up as we both check our screens, and a thick, painful silence fills the vehicle. Never one to respect other people's personal space, Zander peers over my shoulder.

"Looks like the infamous Silver Parisi's been blowing you both up. There's no reception up at the Weaving place. I always have to drive halfway to the Rock to find out what's going on in the—"

Zander rambles on about cell phone reception. Cam and I both ignore him, trading a hard look. "Get to the house, Moretti," he says. "Run every red. Mount the fucking curb. I don't care what you have to do. Just get us there right fucking now."

I know as soon as we come screeching into the Parisi's driveway that we're too late. The front door is yawning wide open into the night, the house in darkness. Silver's Nova is sitting in the turning loop underneath the live oak where she always parks it. Icy, cold dread pools in my stomach. My heart, surging and pumping like some kind of manic, careening machine up until now, stutters to a jarring halt.

"Holy Mary, mother of God," Cam hisses under his breath. He primes the gun in his hand, ripping at the door handle, trying to get out of the car, but he can't seem to open the door. I don't have the same problem. I'm out and tearing up the driveway so fast my feet struggle to keep up with the rest of my body.

"SILVER!" The door crashes against the wall as I fly through it. I haven't seen the glass on the hallway floor. Skidding on the broken shards, I go down, landing hard on my side. Sharp diamonds, like teeth, bite into my forearm and my hand, stabbing through the material of my shirt.

The pain is quite something; I only manage to take a breath because I need it to scream Silver's name again. "*ARGENTO!*"

No reply.

I find my feet. The house is silent as the grave as I hurtle through the ground floor, slamming my way through closed doors, through the living room, through the dining room, into the kitchen.

Empty.

The place is fucking empty.

"*ARGENTO!*" The walls and abandoned hallways echo with my roar as I hit the stairs, taking them four at a time. I check her bedroom first, hoping against hope that this is all some sick misunderstanding and the girl I love is sleeping in her bed, unaware of the fear that's bleeding through my veins. Her bed is neatly made, though, the comforter undisturbed. Her clothes are folded neatly on the end of the mattress, ready to be put away...

"*FUCK!*"

Where is she? WHERE THE HELL IS SHE? I barrel down the hallway, checking each room as I go, not finding her, not finding her, not finding her, until...

Cameron's room. His bedroom door's wide open.

Inside: destruction.

There are boxes everywhere. Shoe boxes. Their contents—sneakers, postcards, papers, knick knacks, pens, receipts, even more shoes— are strewn all over the bedroom floor. A small table has been toppled over, and a fern type plant lays on the hardwood in the remains of a ceramic pot, clods of dirt scattered all over the place. By the door, the mirror hanging on the wall is cracked, a spider's web of fractures shooting out from one point in its center, where it looks as if something hit it really, *really* fucking hard.

In the dark, it takes a moment to notice to streaks of blood down the wall.

My body wants me to keep on searching, to keep on charging forward, but there's nowhere else to go now. The house is empty. Silver isn't here. Jacob Weaving broke into the house while I wasn't here, and he took her. That motherfucker *took* her. It looks like she put up a fight...

What the fuck am I supposed to do?

What the fuck...

"Where is she?" Cameron storms the bedroom like a whirlwind, fists raised, ready to fight. His rage almost eclipses my own.

"We're too late." The words are razor blades, slicing their way up my throat. They eviscerate me from the inside out. Hanging my head, I stand, immobile, as Cameron roars and proceeds to pound his fist into the already broken mirror.

"Where?" he snarls. "Where would he have taken her?"

There is only one place Jacob Weaving would take Silver. The one place he feels most powerful. The place where people worship and adore him. I know exactly where he's toying with her right now...but there's no way I'm telling Cameron Parisi that.

"We should split up. I'll take the Rock. You head out to the Wickman place."

"The—*why*? Why the Wickman place?" He rounds on me, eyes narrowed. He doesn't suspect, though. His eyes are vacant, staring off into a void. He's too afraid to see the truth: that I'm sending him off on a wild goose chase.

"That's where he attacked her the first time. The building's empty. It makes sense that he might take her there, where no one will bother him."

"Right. Right..." The poor bastard's in a daze.

"Give me the gun, Cam."

Fire flares in his eyes. "No. Fucking. Way. The moment I set eyes on that piece of shit, he's fucking dead," he growls.

Just as I thought. He's got no hope of reining in his anger right now. I'm angry, too. Angrier than I've ever been in my entire life. But anger and I are well acquainted. We're the very best of friends. I know how to think around it. Breathe around it. Anger can be burning through me, eating me alive, but I can still take action without letting my blind rage get the better of me.

Cameron's Silver's father. He has every right to protect her. More of a right than I do. I'm a selfish son of a bitch, though. May the universe and all of my mother's Catholic saints have mercy on me, because there's no way in fucking hell I'm gonna let him risk her life in his madness.

"The gun, Cam," I demand, holding out my hand.

He looks like he wants to shoot *me* with it as he resentfully slaps the weapon into my palm. "Fine. If I find him, I'll just kill him with my bare fucking hands."

We're both heading down the stairs and rushing for the door when Zander emerges from the shadows, carrying a small, bundled up, bloody towel in his hands. His usual swagger is gone. His eyes are solemn as he looks down at whatever he has swaddled in his arms. "Uh. We need to stop by a vet, guys. Like right now. I think it might already be too late…"

SILVER

Drip.

Drip.

DRIP.

Drip.

My head's pounding.
   So, so cold.
   Something smells…*wrong*.
   Groaning, I try to crack my eyes open, but a jolt of pain lashes

through my head, startling and terrible enough to make me whimper. I sink back down onto the freezing cold floor beneath me.

Where the hell am I?

What…what the hell happened?

It comes back in flashes—brutal snapshots, so violent that I curl myself up into a ball, shrinking from the assault of memories. Jake, in my father's bedroom, standing over me as I cowered in the closet. A cruel, satisfied smirk on Jake's face. His hands on me, ripping and dragging me out from my hiding place.

Pain.

Fear.

Screaming.

Pleading.

Laughter.

Anger.

Hate.

Hatehatehatehatehatehatehatehate….

In my head, Jake picks me up and hurls me into the mirror hanging on my father's wall. I recoil away from the echo that rattles my bones. I almost bit straight through my lip when my shoulder hit the glass. I can still taste the blood.

"Looks like you and the Moretti freak are the real deal, huh?" The voice sends a thrill of terror up my spine. He's here with me—though I don't know where *here* is—and more than that. He's close. The sound of his shallow, even breathing pierces my whirring thoughts, reminding me of the all too real, very present danger at hand.

I don't want to, it hurts to even contemplate, but I need to open my eyes. I have to see…

Explosions of color twist and dance across my vision as I peer into the darkness. My pulse beats against the insides of my ears like a frantic war drum. And then there he is, sitting on a bench in front of a wall of lockers, his face cast into blue highlight and shadow as he stares down at the screen of a phone.

"I thought I knew everything there was to know about Alessandro Moretti, but looks like I was wrong. Turns out the guy's covered in all that ink and puts on a good show when he feels the need, but underneath the bravado and the stone-cold façade,"—Jake

REVENGE AT RALEIGH HIGH | 263

lowers the phone, looking me dead in the eye—"*he's basically just a fucking pussy.*"

I don't respond. I can't. My jaw feels like it will shatter if I try to open my mouth. Jake hums quietly, turning his attention back to the phone in his hands. *My* cell phone. "*You're the most important thing that's ever happened to me. I was a broken shell before I met you. I can't picture my life without you,* Argento. *I could lose everything and still feel like the luckiest bastard alive if I still had—*" He cuts off, rolling his eyes. "I mean, the guy's a fucking dickless punk. What kind of loser says this stuff? I'm struggling to understand what the hell you see in him. He's already had you on your back. That's obvious. So why the fuck is he spouting all of this sappy bullshit?"

I swallow, wincing at the raw pain that burns in my throat. I screamed myself hoarse back at the house; it feels as though I've been eating glass.

"Moretti's got a lot to learn. Girls never respect a guy if they wear their bleeding hearts on their sleeves." Slowly, he gets to his feet, grunting. I force myself to move, shoving myself away from him, even though every bone and muscle in my body protests at the effort. It's all for naught, anyway. My back hits a wall behind me. There's nowhere for me to go. Jake smiles wickedly as he steps toward me. Crouching down, he purrs to himself as he strokes a sticky strand of hair back out of my face. "You...you're not most girls, though, are you, Silver? You're damaged goods. You'll cling to even the weakest man if you think he'll keep you afloat. God," he says, shaking his head. "I mean, look at you. You're a fucking mess. Face all busted up. Blood everywhere. I hate to tell you this, but I doubt even a guy as desperate for affection as Alex Moretti is gonna be interested by the time I'm through with you. I hope you got some rest, Silver. Tonight's gonna be a long night."

The whisper that I push past my lips sounds pathetic. "You can... hurt and...bruise me all...you like, Jake. But you...you won't *break* me."

Jake's smirk sours. He lets his hand fall away from my face. "I already broke you. I broke you in that bathroom, when I shoved my dick inside you. You've tried to fight it, but you knew it was a losing battle, didn't you? I saw you in that basement at the Rock. I watched you. I saw your need to hurt when he fucked you. You looked like you were trying to tear each other apart. The truth is that you see me standing over you whenever he's inside you. You want the pain. You want the humiliation. You want to be degraded, hit and kicked and spit on. It's all you know now. It breeds inside you like a plague."

I shrink from the words. They're not true. At least not all of them. When I'm with Alex, he is all I ever see. But the violence I've tried to instigate, when we should have been trading nothing but a gentle touch... "You're *sick*," I whisper. I don't know if I'm referring to him, or to me.

His eyes shine brightly in the dark, brimming with amusement. "Maybe. That doesn't make me wrong, now, does it?"

"You don't know what the fuck you're talking about."

"Of course I do. I showed you the only real love you've ever known in that bathroom."

"That wasn't love. That was *hate*."

Unfazed, Jake sits back on his heels, shrugging. "Hate. Love. They amount to the same thing. They're built on the same foundations, aren't they? Both are seeds planted in our hearts. You can try to feed only one of them, but it doesn't make any difference. One will flourish right alongside the other. Doesn't matter which you bring to the light and which you keep hidden in the dark."

"You're wrong," I wheeze. "No one's ever loved you. How...could they? It's impossible to love something so twisted and...dysfunctional. Your own mother couldn't even bring herself to give a shit about you."

Talking about his mother isn't going to do me any favors, but... when he was pinning me down and raping me all those months ago, I didn't think he was going to kill me. Hurt and humiliate me, yes. He was going to force himself on me and laugh about it afterwards. I knew I was walking out of that bathroom at some point, though. Tonight, he has something different in mind. He's planning on brutalizing me, and then he's going to take my life. He told me so much in those text messages. It's plain to see in his eyes, here in the shadows of the boy's locker rooms, where he carried me when I was unconscious. I won't be leaving this cold, damp room, reeking of sweat, so fuck it. I'll bait and antagonize him. If these are my final moments on this earth, then I won't waste them cowering like a frightened, injured little bird.

Jake wants to taste my fear. I refused to give it to him when he roughly threw my legs open and thrust himself inside me at that party, and he hasn't been able to swallow the fact that I defied and denied him ever since. He thinks that tonight, that wrong will be righted. He's bigger than me. Stronger. He thinks he'll be able to hold the threat of more pain over me until I crack and supply the fuel that he's been craving for months now. But he's wrong.

If I die tonight, then let the act be naught but ash and death on your tongue. Let my steel cut you to the quick, even as I fade...

Am I afraid of dying? Yes. A thousand times, yes. But more than that, I regret not getting to see what comes next. All the places I haven't explored. All of the life events I won't experience. I'll never know the kind of person Max becomes. I'll never know if my parents find happiness again. And Alex...Alex will go on and live without me. Once all of the hurt and the anger subsides, and the world no longer feels like it's crumbling down around him, there'll come a day when he wakes up and the pain feels just that little bit less. Someday, some girl will come along, who makes him feel the way I make him feel, and that...god, it hurts more than I can bear, but it's a good thing. He deserves to be happy, after all the shit he's been through. So I can do this. I can get through the next few hours with Jacob Weaving, and I can make sure he never gets what he wants from me. He's going to rot in prison for what he's about to do. He's going to spend those long days and even longer nights trapped behind the bars of his cell, having never won his victory over me.

Fuck. Him.

Jake's lips peel back, exposing his perfect, twenty-thousand-dollar teeth. My defiance is getting under his skin. He fists my hair, getting to his feet, and I have no choice but to follow along with him, biting back a cry as I struggle to stand. Before he knocked me unconscious, he hit me. He wound his arm back and he hit me, giving each swing everything he had. He knocked me off my feet, only to lift me back up so he could knock me down again, and when he finally left me on the ground, disoriented and bleeding, he laid into my ribs with his boots. He kicked until the both of us felt my bones splinter, and then he kicked me some more. I've never known pain like this before.

My head swims, my vision warping, darkness pressing down on

me, trying to force back down to the ground. God, I'm going to throw up. My stomach squeezes, nausea rolling over me like a wave, but I clamp my mouth shut, drawing a deep breath in through my nose. Expanding my ribs is agony, but the extra oxygen helps me stop myself from retching. My vision stabilizes, but I'm so damn weak.

"I know what you did to Sam's headstone." Jake leans down, spitting the words viciously into my face. "Shouldn't have done that. He was a fucking moron most of the time, but he was one of my best friends. Now people are whispering behind my back, giving me dirty looks. They're *wondering*, and I can't have that. It's only a matter of time before the busy bodies in this Podunk fucking town start asking questions.

"He told me you did your best to clean yourself up after we were done with you that night. He stood outside the bathroom door and listened to you sobbing like a little bitch in the shower. I was almost sad I didn't hang back to hear it. That kind of abject misery is fascinating to me." He leans even closer—so close that his lips brush against my cheek as he pours his vitriol into my ear. "You were right. My dick really only does get hard when other people are suffering. I know that's messed up. I know that's not normal, but hey. Telling the truth can be cathartic, right? It can be healing."

God, he's such a fucking joke. I give up trying to pull my head free, letting myself fall limp. "Don't play games, Jake. You don't care about healing. You like yourself just the way you are."

His wide grin reminds me of a shark, opening its maw to expose its teeth just before it bites. "Looks like you know me well, Second Place. Come on, now. I figured we'd go and take a shower together. For old times' sake."

∼

I fight. I fight like I've never fought before. I kick and scream, lashing out with as much fury as I can muster as Jake drags me through the boys' locker rooms toward the showers. In the end, all of the thrashing and hollering is futile. Jake knows I'll take an opportunity I get to slip free from him and do him some damage. I taught him that in the hallway, when I climbed on top of him and laid into him with my fists. He's not taking any chances now. He holds me close to his body, pinning me to his side, which makes it impossible to gain any momentum to hit or land a proper kick.

The harder I struggle, the harder he laughs.

"That's it, Parisi. Let it aaaaall out. Scream at the top of those whore lungs. Doesn't make any difference. No one's gonna hear you. No one's gonna find you. This place is gonna be deserted until Monday morning. And then? The janitor's gonna find himself a nasty surprise when he unlocks the place, that's for sure."

The boys' showers are a mirror to the girls' showers, except the smell is much worse—damp and mildew, punctuated with the over-ripe tang of adolescent male sweat. My cries echo off the tiled walls. My numb, bare feet can't make purchase as Jake hauls me toward the bank of showers, still laughing under his breath. Moonlight pours in through the strip of narrow windows at the top of the walls. I can see the night sky through the glass, a scattering of stars burning brightly in the midnight blue.

My pulse is racing out of control. It's freezing inside the shower room, but it gets infinitely colder when Jake fumbles for a shower handle, and a jet of frigid, icy water pelts down on me. The tempera-ture is so shocking that I let out a strangled, frightened gasp.

I'm drenched in seconds. Jake is too, but he doesn't seem to care.

"Darhower insisted we get some hot water in here, but Coach Quentin's a hard ass. He thinks making us shower in cold water will toughen us up. Make us real men. What do you reckon, Parisi? No fun, huh?"

I strain away from the water, but Jake has me by the back of the head. He forces me into the torrent, angling my face so that the cold, stinging beads of water drive into my eyes, nose and mouth. It's hard to breathe. Impossible, almost. I cough and splutter, attempting to drag in a sip of air any way I can, and Jake doesn't let up. He croons like a madman, imparting the most vile, hateful things into my ear. Eventually, just as I'm about to pass out, he jerks me out of the stream of water and shoves me, sending me crashing into the wall.

I land in a heap on the dirty tile. My clothes cling to my broken, stinging skin, the water still pouring down on me. Jake stands back, placing his hands on his hips. He's breathing hard, his shoulders hitching up and down. Using the back of his hand, he wipes his nose, then clears his throat. "All right, Parisi. Get undressed."

I stare up at him dumbly. He wants me to get undressed? Strip for him? Stupefied laughter bubbles up the back of my throat. "You…you can't be serious. No fucking way. I'm not…I'm not getting undressed."

Malice flashes in Jake's eyes. "I'm not asking, you stupid cunt. That was an order. Get on your feet and take off your fucking clothes. You wanted to be a Siren again, so here. I'm making you one." I haven't noticed the clothing hanging from the hook by the door. Jake snatches it up, throwing the fabric down onto the floor, just beyond the gathering pool of water.

It's a Raleigh High cheerleading uniform. How nice of him to try and keep it dry for me.

"*No.*" If he thinks I'm going to help him fulfill some sort of sick fantasy, then he is out of his ever-loving mind.

Jake digs his teeth into his bottom lip, scraping it through his teeth. The front of his t-shirt is plastered to his skin, his jeans so dark with water that they look almost black. "Don't you think I could make you, Silver? Don't you think I'd enjoy stripping you naked? You remember the last time?"

I was wearing a dress at Leon Wickman's party. It was easy for him to relieve me of it. Now I'm wearing my space pajamas, and he's going to have to fucking fight me for them. "Why the hell would you want to watch me change anyway?" I lean to one side, nearly toppling over, and a spasm of pain fires through my ribs. Shiiiiiit. I taste blood again. "You think it matters to me anymore if you see me naked? You've already seen everything there is to see. I haven't grown another pair of tits since the last time."

"I couldn't give a shit about your body. *I. Am. Going. To. Burn. Your. Clothes.*" He says the last part slowly, enunciating every word as if I'm too stupid to comprehend what he's saying. "My blood's all over them, too. Why make forensics' job easier for them."

Another burst of laughter rattles out from deep within my broken-ribbed chest. "Jake, I called 911 back at the house. I gave them your name. I've got half your skin under my finger nails. Your hair's probably all over me. Your hands are gonna match the bruises you've planted all over my skin. Nothing you do will separate you from this. *You're fucked.*"

Jake's nostrils flare. "You think you're so fucking smart. Don't worry about me. I've got this all taken care of. By the time I leave tonight, it'll be like I was never here. My father won't let Sheriff Hainsworth anywhere near me once your body's found. He'll have me relaxing, safe and sound behind so much red tape, it'll take five years to get through all the paperwork required to even fucking interview me. By then, everyone will have forgotten you even fucking existed. It's gonna be fucking beautiful."

I've been skating on the surface of a black mirror, hovering above reality, not really here, trying to think of a way out of this nightmare, waiting, hoping against hope and my better judgement that someone is going to show up and save me, but this brings me crashing back into the moment.

Forget me?

Forget I even fucking existed?

Something about that rings true. People like Mallory Hawkins are still stalking through town, demanding to have Leon Wickman's body exhumed and unceremoniously tossed into a landfill, but the rest of the people in Raleigh? The shops, the elementary school, the bars and restaurants…they're all open and operating like it's business as usual. How easily people have already moved on from such a horrific, monstrous event. Eighteen people died at Raleigh High the day Leon turned his gun on everyone…and that was only six weeks ago. I'm just one more meaningless student at Raleigh High. *One.* How long will people mourn me before it's back to the status quo? A few days? A week at the most.

I don't want to be forgotten.

I don't want to think about what Jake plans on doing with my body after he's silenced me. I don't want Alex to grieve over me, only to recover and move on with someone else down the line. It turns out I'm too selfish, after all. I want what's owed to me. I want my fucking life.

The cold water splashes down, mostly hitting me in the legs. Mercifully, I'm free to breathe. Jake looms over me like a sentinel, arms folded across his chest, his jaw working as his eyes bore twin holes into the top of my head.

"I never got it, y'know. I've never been able to figure out why you hate me so much." I sound resigned to my fate. I'm anything but, though. I'm trying to buy myself some time to figure out what I should do next. There's nothing in the shower room. Like, nothing. No furniture, no benches, no pictures mounted on the walls. There are the shower heads, the taps and the tiles. There's nothing I can use as a weapon in here, which means I have to find a way to get out of here and fast.

I've never seen a sneer as spiteful as the one that flickers briefly across Jake's face. "Do I need a reason?" he says. "Maybe you're just really fucking easy to hate."

I actually think about this. Over all the noise and chatter going on inside my head, I take a moment to assess his statement to see if I can find any truth in it. "I used to be a bitch. Before, when I was hanging with Kacey. I was nothing compared to her, though. And you seemed to like *her* just fine."

"Pssshhhh." Jake shakes his head, the veins standing proud in his forearms. He's tensed up; the muscles in the column of his throat work, his Adam's apple bobbing. "What does it matter, hmm? I fucking hate you and that's all there is to it. I don't need to explain myself to you or anyone else."

"So there *is* a reason."

"Shut up, Silver. Just take your fucking clothes off!"

He's teetering on insanity. He wants me to quake in fear before him. In his mind, he's imagining fear dancing up a storm in my eyes, my shaking hands fumbling to peel my soaked pajamas from my body. I probably look terrified as I stand before him in his mind's eye, naked, goosebumps from my ankles to my neck, arms wrapped around my torso as I try to hide the secret parts of myself away from his venomous eyes.

Unwillingly, my gaze dips, and I find the bulge in his pants that confirms my suspicions. His dick is hard. He *is* getting off on this.

Disgust churns in my stomach. I look away. "You want me in that uniform, you *are* gonna have to come down here and strip me."

"Don't you understand? If you don't do it, *I'm gonna fucking hurt you.*"

I watch him, my gaze to roving over his features—features I once thought made him the hottest guy on the face of the planet—studying his face, trying to find any tell-tale sign that might have been a warning to me back then. There's nothing. I let the silence grow heavier, stewing in it while I think. "It doesn't matter how much you hurt me, Jacob," I tell him. "I won't trade in my dignity to avoid a little pain."

"It won't be a little. It'll be a lot."

I splay my hands out in front of me, palm up, wincing when I realize that the little finger on my right hand looks (and feels) broken. "And yet the fact remain the same..."

Jake grinds his teeth together, eyes narrowing into slits. I trap a frightened yelp behind my teeth, determined not to make a sound as he comes at me, his fingers digging viciously into my upper arm. "You wanna make things harder than they need to be, then so be it. You're not as tough as you think you are, bitch. You're gonna be begging on your knees for me within the next thirty minutes."

I've seen people on morning television who can turn off their pain receptors in their brains. They can 'mind-over-matter' the shit out of their extremely painful medical diagnoses and go about their day. It must take a lot of practice. There's no way I can turn off my pain as Jake punches me in my side. Bone grinds on bone beneath my skin, and a wicked, sharp white flare of light stuns me. I don't know which way is up.

I'm numb, bent slightly forward, trying to pull in a breath that will never come, and I still don't make a sound. Jake chuckles maliciously as he grabs hold of my pajama shirt and yanks it forcefully up my body. I pin my arms to my sides, twisting, determined to get away from him, but he locks a hand around my throat and shoves me back against the tile.

"You think this is some kind of game, don't you? You don't think I'm being fucking serious? You're about to die. You should probably start treating the situation with the gravity it deserves."

Fear me.

Show me that I scare you.

Give me your terror.
Give me your panic.
Let me revel in it all.

I'm so tired all of a sudden that it's an effort to keep my eyes open. With a monumental force of will, I arch an eyebrow at him, pulling one side of my mouth up into a smirk. "Whatever you say, Jake." It was a stroke of luck that I laughed in his face when he raped me. I had no idea how badly it would fuck with his head. I know perfectly well how it affects him now. "Just get on with it, Weaving. You're boring the shit out of me."

"*URRRRAAAAGGHHHH!*"

I don't see his fist until it's too late. I blink, and when I open my eyes, there are his knuckles, an inch away from my face. I broke my leg when I was a kid. Broke my arm at my first ever cheer rally when I was fourteen, too. Never broken my nose, though. The *POP!* comes first. The searing, eye-watering pain doesn't come until a couple of seconds later. Blood gushes down my face, running over my lips, seeping in between my lips; it's also pouring down the back of my throat, effectively cutting off my airway again.

"It's hardly a scream, but I suppose I can be satisfied with a little coughing and spluttering. Hey, Parisi. Parisi, hey, look at me." Grabbing me by the chin, he tilts my face up, but again I don't give him what he wants. I can't look at him. I can't see a thing, because my eyes are watering so badly. Jake turns my face one way, and then another, grunting quietly, taking a moment to appraise his handiwork.

"Jesus fucking Christ, Silver. You are gonna make one *fucked up* looking corpse."

Bile burns like fire as it climbs up my esophagus. Fighting my natural urge to retch, I ride out the pain spreading its fingers across my face, and I wait.

Not yet…

Not yet…

Jake's oblivious until the very last second, when I pitch forward and violently purge the contents of my stomach all down the front of his t-shirt.

"Uhhh, what the ffuu—*you dirty fucking bitch!*" He lets go of me, pulling his shirt away from his chest, and I'm ready.

I take the opportunity, and I bolt.

My body vibrates with adrenalin—*Free. He let go. I'm FREE*—and for one blissful moment, nothing hurts. My ribs are numb. My head is numb. My face is numb. My fight or flight reflexes kick in beautifully. Even my vision clears for a second. Long enough to see the door to the shower room approaching fast. I slam through it, immediately taking a left, gunning for the exit to the locker rooms, but then...

This is the boy's locker rooms. Everything is flipped, not where it's supposed to be. Before me lies a solid brick wall.

Jake charges out of the showers, a storm raging on his face as he comes right at me. I pick up the first thing I lay my hands on, and I swing...

The lacrosse stick makes contact with the side of Jake's skull, cracking him on the side of the head. He roars, his face turning a purple as he presses the heel of his palm to his temple. The blow doesn't stop him coming. It only makes him angrier as he barrels straight at me.

I lurch backwards, half jumping, half falling over a bench. Jake, in his fury, doesn't see the bench either and collides with it, the wood smacking him square in the shins.

Left, left, left, Silver. Run!

The voice of reason in my head, somehow still functioning despite the terror and fear pounding out a frantic tattoo against my ear drums, urges me forward, drives me on, desperate that I should make the most out of every single second Jake falters.

Left I go.

Planting my hand against the wall of locker doors beside me, I use what little strength I have to propel myself forward. My legs are going to give out. My heart's going to explode any second. The burning, needling in my lungs makes it feel like I've inhaled a colony of fire ants. Still I manage to run, and I do not look back.

"*SILVER!*" Jake's shout bounces around the locker rooms, ricocheting off the walls. "Where are you gonna go, Silver? All the exits are locked!"

The door to the locker room slams closed behind me. A hundred feet away, down the long, narrow hallway that yawns out in front of me, lies the main entrance to the school.

My way out.

Freedom.

Blindly, I race toward the doors, fists pumping, hope coming alive with every forward step I take.

Halfway to the doors, I see that Jacob lied. The door isn't chained or locked. It's chocked open with a rock; there's a crack in the door, revealing a couple of inches of empty parking lot beyond.

If I can just get outside…

If I can just make it through those doors…

If I can just—

I'm floating. My feet are off the ground. I'm flying forward, hurtling even faster, arms stretching out…

The impact steals my last, exhausted breath. Jake hits me from behind, tackling me with the force of a Mac truck. When we go down, he lands on top of me and the synapses in my brain short circuit.

Darkness closes in.

Before me, my open hand reaches for the door, now only five feet away.

Those five feet might as well be five miles.

I should have known.

A five-foot six ex-cheerleader was never going to out-run a high school quarterback.

_____

ALEX

What kind of sick fuck takes a knife to a small, defenseless fucking dog?

The hairs on the back of my neck are bristling, sick chills racing down between my shoulder blades as I drift through a right-hand turn. Every time I do this, I'm skating on thin ice. Literally. The night is clear, not a cloud in sight, which means it's bitterly cold, and the black top is as slick as an ice rink. The car's wheels fight for traction as I coast through every turn; it's a miracle that I've been able to judge when to spin the steering wheel and lay off the gas each time I've hit a junction or a bend in the road. By rights, I should probably be dead in a ditch right now.

I did the right thing giving the Impala to Zander so he could rush Nipper to the emergency vet. Cam took the Parisi's van, which left me with only one choice: Silver's Nova. I should have replaced the tires on the Nova; I should have taken a look at the clutch a long fucking time ago, but I was too distracted by all the shit we've been dealing with. Now, the vehicle feels like it's about to rattle apart, and I'm paying the price.

"Salve, Regina, madre di misericordia, vita, dolcezza e speranza nostra, salve. A te ricorriamo, esuli figli di Eva—" I mutter the words under my breath. Sheer desperation forces them up from the annals of buried, childhood memories and sends them tumbling out of my mouth. My mother used to kneel at my bedside every night and fervently whisper the prayer over me, begging the Madonna for mercy and guidance. I've never needed either of those things more than I do right now.

"A te sospiriamo, gementi e piangenti in questa valle di lacrime. Orsù dunque, avvocata nostra, rivolgi a noi gli occhi tuoi misericordiosi. E mostraci, dopo questo esilio—"

The car's engine whines, pushed to its limit as I hit a stretch of straight, open road and gun the gas. If another vehicle turns out on the street, I'm dead. If I hit a patch of ice at the wrong angle, at the wrong fucking moment, I'm dead. Worst of all...if I'm too late, if I don't get to there in time, then *Silver* is dead.

"Il frutto benedetto del tuo seno. O clemente, o pia, o dolce Vergine Maria. Amen. Salve, Regina, madre di misericordia, vita—"

I never thought I'd be *that* person—the kind of person who would suspend their disbelief and embrace superstition or religion in a dire time of need. I wouldn't do it for myself. I'd never cling to a fairytale in order to make facing my own death a little easier. But Silver? I'll believe in Big Foot, the Chupacabra and fucking unicorns that shit rainbows if there's even the slightest chance that believing might help her make it through tonight. Mary of Nazareth did exist. Whoever she was, she gave birth to a son who changed the world. She is worshipped and venerated in every corner of the globe, and that has to count for something. I pray to her, hoping that, through the span of two thousand years, she somehow hears my despair and takes pity on me.

"—Piangenti in questa valle di lacrime. Orsù dunque, avvocata nostra, rivolgi a noi gli occhi tuoi misericordiosi—"

Be okay. Be okay. Please, please, please be fucking okay.

One mile out from Raleigh High, the Nova's engine begins to groan. The shudder that shakes the car does not bode well.

"Don't. Don't you fucking *dare*," I growl. "Not yet. Not fucking yet, you piece of shit."

My threats go unheard. I'm still nowhere near Raleigh when the engine gives one final, last coughing splutter…and cuts out altogether. A shockwave of panic explodes outward from my chest, my arms and legs suddenly very, very cold.

It takes a moment to register that the car's losing speeding, coasting dangerously without any sort of power pushing it forward. And then *I* explode. "*MOTHERFUCKER! NO!*" A jagged bolt of pain chases up my arm as I lay my fist into the car's dashboard. "You piece of fucking…"

Nope. No time. No fucking time for any of that. I hit the brake, gritting my teeth so hard I can feel the bone judder inside my skull. I've opened the door and I'm already out before the car's even stopped moving.

Huge snowbanks line either side of the narrow road, tall spruce trees punching up toward the sky like an ominous, looming guard. Orion, blazingly bright and perfectly framed in the window of sky overhead, seems to be pointing the way toward my destination.

"*Sbrigati, mi amore!*" My dead mother's voice whispers frantically in my ear. I don't need her to tell me twice.

I set my jaw, suck down a deep breath, and I get to it.

I run.

29

***

SILVER

I come to, and my immediate response is to scream.

The pain is excruciating.

I can barely breathe around it. My right arm, pulled awkwardly over my head, is dislocated…and Jacob is dragging me by it down the hall. He's whistling a tuneless, cheery song as he pulls me roughly behind him.

Pain.

Pain.

Pain.

Pain.

Pain.

It's spread to every cell of my body. There's no running from it. No escaping. It's too fucking much…

I try to wrench my arm free from Jacob's grasp, and it's the worst possible thing I can do. A hot, white flash momentarily blinds me, and a fractured scream builds at the back of my throat. I can't keep it in. The cry bounces off the walls, rattling around inside the row of hollow lockers to my right. Jacob pauses briefly, casts a bored look at me over his shoulder, and laughs. His grip tightens around my wrist as he continues on his way. The whistling starts up again, and I realize, sickened, that I know the song after all. It's 'We Didn't Start The Fire,' my favorite Billie Joel song.

Jacob sounds insane as he stumbles through the chorus of the song, trying and failing to hit the correct notes. The rhythm of the song is unmistakable, though.

It's then that I realize what I'm wearing: a red Raleigh tank, and matching red and white pleated skirt. My pajamas are gone, and I'm decked out in the Siren's uniform. He did it. He stripped me while I was out cold and changed my clothes. The gasp I let out is a mixture of horror mingled with bitter, frustrated rage.

"Don't worry. I didn't take advantage," Jake says casually. "Your tits *are* nice, but I'm not into the whole touching-girls-when-they're-unconscious thing. No point touching you at all if you're not awake to hate me for it."

Looking down and seeing the vivid bruises all over my legs, the deep slash on my right thigh, and the blood that's already seeping into the fabric of the Siren's tank I'm now wearing, I realize just how bad this is. I look like I've been beaten half to death. Panic gets the better of me. "Let me fucking go, Jake. Just…just let me go. We can both walk away and pretend like this never happened."

The whistling cuts off. "I think we've come a little too far for that, don't you?" He seems to think for a second. The soles of his boots squeak against the linoleum with every step he takes. "No, there's only one possible outcome here tonight, Silver. You need to die. That's just the way it's gotta be. No hard feelings."

"No hard fe—ARGHHH!" I nearly pass out as a wave of pain fires like a bullet down my arm, burning in my shoulder joint. Jake gives my arm another swift, sharp tug, and a wave of nausea rolls over me.

"Probably best if you just shut the hell up. Bargaining's pointless. I'm not a particularly merciful person. I feel like I shouldn't have to tell *you* that," he chides.

He's right, I should have known better. I *do* know better, but I had to try. I twist, bracing as hard as I can against the pain, trying to use my bare feet to gain some sort of a grip on the floor. Jacob's fingers are closed tighter than a steel vise around my wrist. My efforts get me absolutely nowhere, as he continues to pull me by my arm. We pass a glass cabinet, full of Raleigh's awards, commendations and trophies, and I'm able to pin point where we are just as Jacob rounds a corner, jerking me roughly around the bend and we pitch up in front of the set of double doors that lead into the gym.

Instinctively, I know that I'm dead if he manages to get me through those double doors.

With everything I've got, I strain against Jake's hold, desperation forcing me to pull, pull, pull. Towering above me, Jake pauses in front of the gym doors, casting a condescending smile down at me. "Pathetic. You're so fucking *weak*. I thought with all the big talk recently you'd put up more of a fight than this. Shame there's no one here to see you like this. They began to fall for your bullshit, didn't they? They began to believe that you were better than me. Fucking *better* than me. Hah. They'd change their minds if they were here right now. They'd see just how fucking useless and scared you are. Come on. Guy Lovell's having a party. I need to get there by midnight, before people are too fucked up to remember seeing me."

God, he even has an alibi squared away. I bite back a howl of pain as he shoulders open the gym doors, dragging me along behind him. My panic ramps up to an eleven when I look up ahead and see what awaits us in the middle of the gymnasium; in a beam of silvery moon-light, lancing through the gym's high windows, I see a chair. And above the chair, hanging ominously from a broad, strong support beam…is a noose.

30

ALEX

My body is on fire. The cold needles at my lungs. I'm a machine, feet pounding against the snow, fists pumping as I sprint along the side of the road. With every step, I'm convinced I can't go any further, and yet I manage to lift my feet again and push forward.

I won't stop running until I find her. I have no choice. I'll ignore the exhaustion and the pain, increasing exponentially every time I draw in a frozen, icy breath, until I have Silver safe in my arms. My body can quit on me after that if it needs to. Until then…

Lights skitter and dance across my vision. In my pocket, my phone begins to ring. I hardly hear the sound over the crashing, slamming rhythm of my thundering heart. I burn, I ache, I hurt, and I seethe. And I run.

My phone doesn't stop fucking ringing.

I ignore it until I realize that it might be Silver. I pull the phone out of my pocket as quickly as I can, then, making sure not to drop it in the snow. Hope flares inside my chest for a second as I strain to focus on the name lit up on the screen…but then I make out Cam's name and that hope crashes and burns.

Keep running.

Just keep running.

Don't fucking stop.

I can feel myself hitting a wall. I'm exhausted. Normally, I can run for hours without stopping, but it's different when the ground's covered in ice and snow, and the cold is pulling the heat out of you. You have to use every muscle in your body to stabilize. There's no way to find a steady rhythm and settle into it. Plus, I'm not just running. I'm sprinting. Uphill.

"Come on, you worthless bastard. Put some effort into it." This time it isn't my mother's voice in my ear. It's another voice from my past. A voice I'd rather forget. Gary Quincy's sneering tone has the same effect as a bucket of ice water being dumped over my head. I gasp, gulping down air, not breathing efficiently at all.

"You let your mother down. You were a constant source of disappointment to me. Now you're going to let this girl down, too?" Gary snarls. *"Fucking typical. You're gonna prove me right tonight, aren't you, boy? You're gonna prove just how fucking worthless you really are."*

Fury digs its claws into my back. I hate him. I hate him so fucking much. I wish the monster was still alive so I could fucking kill him all over again. I wait for the surge of energy to hit me, fueled on by Gary's cruel, vindictive words, but that sweeping wave of adrenalin never arrives. I'm still dog-tired. I'm still on the verge of collapsing. Gary's vitriolic words have turned my blood into battery acid, though, and I somehow manage to dig deep and go faster.

Gary used to heckle me when I'd run as a kid. He'd follow me in his Pontiac, drinking a beer, his arm hanging out of the window, flicking a cigarette. The car's engine would rumble at my back as my skinny legs forged forward, feet slapping against the blacktop.

"Forget it. Give up. You're never gonna be fast enough. You're never gonna make the cut."

I hear the same words now and they spur me on, driving me up the frozen, frigid hill toward Raleigh High.

I *will* be fast enough. I *will* make it to Silver in time.

I growl with every exhalation, roaring as I power closer to my goal. I am a rabid wolf, chasing down its prey.

The school building is in sight now, little more than five hundred feet away. The windows are in darkness, the building bathed in moonlight. At first, I think the parking lot is empty, but as I draw closer I spot the black Ford F150 that's tucked out of the way in the back, close to the pathway that leads down to the dell. The same dell where Cillian Dupris learned what it was like to crawl.

Jake drives a Tacoma, but I'm not the only one who can borrow a vehicle. He's smart. Smart enough not to drive his own truck on a night like tonight. I know I should slash the fucker's tires before I head inside the school, prevent him from making a run for it if he manages to give me the slip, but that would take precious seconds and I don't know how many of those I have to spare.

The world is startlingly quiet as I finally reach the last leg of my run, speeding toward the school entrance. I'm surviving on adrenalin, my body shaking wildly as I reach the doorway, preparing to drive my clenched fist straight through the glass. I see I don't need to, though. It isn't even locked. The door's been propped open with a rock.

Flying through the entrance, I haven't planned where I'm going to look for Silver first, but I come to a screeching halt regardless. There, on the floor, a dark mass lays on the linoleum, not five feet away. I'm so hopped up, my nerves jangling, flooded with uncontrolled energy, that I have to fight exploding into a nervous rage. It's clothes. A pile of mangled, torn clothing. The shreds of navy blue fabric are familiar, dotted with star constellations. They're Silver's pajamas, and they're covered in blood. I take a step forward, my blood singing through my veins, and something crunches beneath my right foot. Something fragile. Something breakable. Something glass.

Gingerly, I lift my foot and find myself looking down at the shattered face of Silver's Mickey Mouse watch.

SILVER

The noose creaks, the thick length of rope complaining as Jake takes hold of it, pulling it taut. His eyes are lit with a sick excitement that chills my blood to sub-zero temperatures. "Get up on the chair," he commands.

I've never been more scared than this. I want to sob and cry, but instead I say, "Suicide? You think you're gonna sell this as *suicide?*"

"There's one way to make sure they can't pin this on me," he remarks icily. "I could just burn the entire school down once I'm done with you."

I laugh. The derisive sound echoes around the gym. "Please. Do you know how long it'd take to rebuild this place? You'd get sent to Bellingham to finish out the school year. You'd have graduated by the time Raleigh opened again. That wouldn't work for you, Jake. You're a hero at Raleigh. Everyone worships the ground you walk on inside these walls. You'd never destroy the alter where people kneel to worship you. You'd be no one at Bellingham. *No one.*"

"I DON'T GIVE A FUCK! I'm done with you throwing up roadblocks, you stupid bitch. Get on your fucking feet." He takes hold of my by the arm, pinning me to his chest as I try to thrash and kick, struggling to get free. My heart climbs up into my throat as he tries to dump me on the chair.

Holy fuck. *Fuck*, this is really happening. He's not going to back down. The rope scrapes against my cheek as Jake attempts to loop it over my head.

I lose my fucking mind.

Kick.

Gouge.

Claw.

Bite.

Scream.

I will not go fucking quietly. I will not just fucking die because Jacob Weaving has decreed it so.

I will not.

I will not.

I will not.

I land a knee in his side.

Feel his skin break beneath my nails.

Hear his spit and curse as he wrestles with me, hoisting me up his body, his arm locking around my throat.

I can't...

I can't fucking breathe...

The thick rope scrapes against my skin again as it slips over my head.

"Quit flailing, Silver. It's done. It's fucking *done*."

Jake's voice is harsh. It also carries within it a note of relief. Like he truly is experiencing a moment of catharsis, now that the hard part is done. His arms loosen, releasing me from his vise-like grip, and as I slide down the length of his body, the rope tightens around my neck.

"JACOB!"

The roar fills the gymnasium, loud and furious. I can barely see out of my swollen eyes, but I'd know that voice anywhere. It's Alex. He's finally here...and he's going to be too late.

32

ALEX

A piercing, high-pitched scream cuts through blistering quiet.

The halls of Raleigh High whip past in a blur as I fly toward the sound of the panicking screams that come one after the other.

She's alive.

She's fucking alive.

"Sbrigate, Passerotto! Hurry! Faster!"

The double doors to the gymnasium slam open with a deafening crash as I hurl myself through them. In the middle of the large, open space, right on top of the midcourt line of the basketball court, the captain of the Raleigh Roughnecks football team is trying to fight with a bloody creature in a Siren's cheerleader uniform, threading a fucking noose around her neck.

I don't recognize the girl in his arms.

Her face is a mess of split skin and bruises. Her hands are bleeding, her knees and feet cut open. I only know that it's Silver because of the way she's fighting him like a possessed hellcat, battling for her life.

My vision turns crimson red.

Death red.

"*JACOB!*"

Silver's eyes open, startled, bloodshot but still blue. They meet mine, and I see her abject terror, her fear, and worse—her resignation.

Jacob turns, pivoting at the waist, his face marred by two long, deep scratches down his cheek. He snarls, showing me his teeth…as he lets Silver go.

Her body immediately goes stiff, her back bowing, hands reaching up to claw at the fat rope that's pulling tighter and tighter around her throat. She didn't fall far from his arms, but it's enough. Not enough to snap the vertebrae in her neck, but the tips of her big toes are hovering an inch from the lacquered floorboards. She can't relieve her weight from the rope.

"Well, fuck me," Jacob hisses. He takes a step forward, putting himself between me and Silver's convulsing body. "Looks like you're a little late, Moretti. No way you're gonna fight your way past me before she's out of time."

"Are you fucking out of your mind?"

Silver makes a choking sound, her face turning redder and redder as the seconds slip by. She doesn't have long. If I don't cut her down from there in the next few seconds, she's going to fucking die, and I'm going to have to watch it happen.

I don't have time to fight Jacob. Fuck, there's no time for anything.

The captain of the Raleigh Roughnecks isn't going to let me just slip on by him and rescue her, though.

"Get out of the way, Jake. Right fucking now!"

Jacob pouts, casting a quick glance over his shoulder. "You're kinda spoiling my night, y'know. I wanted to watch this. More than anything, I've been waiting *really* fucking patiently to watch this stupid cunt breathe her last. You're fucking annoying, Moretti. Has anyone ever told you that before?"

I take three steps, then another two. I'm close enough, now. Jacob's head cants to one side, his eyes slitting like a snake's. "What are you gonna do, Moretti? You're big, but I'm bigger. Who knows, maybe you can take me, but I'm not gonna go down easily. She'll be fucking worm meat long before then. You're fucked. And so is *she*." He jerks his thumb over his shoulder at Silver.

Her face is purple.

One of her fingernails has snapped back, and blood is running down her hand, down her forearm, dripping from her elbow as she frantically claws at the rope.

Jake wants me to bicker with him. He's expecting me to beg and plead for him to release her. Releasing Silver isn't an option, though. Not for him. He's leaving me no choice.

"Well? What's it gonna be, motherfucker? You gonna tackle me or wh—"

The sound of the gunshot is deafening. The recoil punches up my arm, slamming into my shoulder, throwing my hand up in the air. Monty said a gun like this would have a mean kick on it, but the shock of the unexpected force almost throws me off balance.

Jacob frowns, confusion marring his smug expression. He looks down at his chest, just as the first ribbon of scarlet blood unfurls down the front of his shirt.

"You—you shot—" He looks up, his skin white as a sheet, and then staggers, holding out a hand to steady himself.

I don't waste another second. I hear the thud and tumble as Jacob collapses to the floor, but I don't stick around to watch. I race to Silver, grabbing her around the waist, not bothering to try and find something sharp enough to cut her down. Lifting her, the rope loosens, but the loop of the noose is still firmly fastened around the column of her throat.

Fuck, fuck, fuck!

I hold her in one arm, using the other hand to yank and pull at the noose, and fraction by fraction it begins to work free.

Then she's breathing, pulling in a wheezing, painful breath that makes me want to drop down onto my knees and fucking cry tears of relief. "Alex?" Silver's eyes meet mine, and for a moment I think everything's going to be all right. Then those beautiful blue eyes of hers roll back into her head, her spine bows, and she begins to seize.

"No. *No, no, no, no, no.*" Using every scrap of strength I possess, I rip the noose free from her neck and pull it over her head, hurling it away. Silver shudders violently in my arms as I carry her past Jacob's prone body where he's lying on the floor. I'm as careful as I can be when I place her down on the boards, making sure not to let her hit her head.

"You shot…me," Jacob gasps. "You fucking *shot* me."

"In the stomach," I remind him, through my teeth. "You'd better hope she doesn't die, otherwise I'm gonna be shooting you right between the eyes next, you fuck."

"My father…"

Come on, Silver. Come on. Please be okay. Let her fucking be okay. Come on!

She's still shaking, her body trembling, the whites of her eyes showing. I lower my face over hers, positioning my cheek in front of her mouth, waiting to feel somet—wait, yes, there it is. Shallow, uneven…but she's breathing. At least she's fucking breathing. Relief courses through me, but it's tempered by fear. The convulsions aren't stopping; they seem to be getting worse.

Silver's head snaps back, her teeth grinding together as she shakes in my arms.

Behind me, Jake's breathing is a wet, unhealthy rasp. "Are you… listening? My father…"

I ignore him. His father isn't going to be able to shield him anymore. Not from behind bars. He's probably going to spend the rest of his life rotting in some prison cell, ruing the day he ever crossed Q and the Dreadnaughts Motorcycle Club. I'm pretty sure Jacob will be the last thing on Caleb's mind by tomorrow.

With an unsteady hand, I reach out and stroke a matted, blood-soaked tangle of Silver's hair out of her face. Her lips are split, her jaw bruised, her temple oozing blood, her nose obviously broken. She looks like she just went ten rounds with a UFC fighter, which says a lot. It says that she's a fighter, herself. She didn't give up. She didn't give in.

"So don't give up now," I whisper, holding her to me. "Don't give up now, Silver. Come on. Fucking *fight*."

I call an ambulance. I barely hear what the guy on the other end of the line says. I tell him where we are, what's happened, and that the girl I love needs help, then I hang up the phone. A long, brutal minute passes. I don't know anything about seizures, but I do know they probably shouldn't go on for this long. Eventually, as quickly and abruptly as it started, the seizure just...stops.

I bite the inside of my lip, watching her face, waiting for some sort of sign that she's going to be okay. "Silver? *Silver?*"

"Is...she dead?" Jacob pants.

The vile...fucked up...sadistic... I close my eyes, breathing around the knot of anger in my chest. I was aiming for his heart when I pulled that trigger. I lifted the desert eagle, steadied it in my hands, and I made the call. It's better that the bullet found its mark in his gut. He'll still be alive when the cops arrive, so he can answer for what he's done without the mercy of death letting him off the hook. But I swear to god, if he asks me if Silver's dead with the same hope in his voice again...

"Doesn't matter," Jake wheezes. "I broke her in the end. She screamed...at the top...of her lungs...for me."

Am.

Going.

To.

Fucking.

DESTROY.

Him.

"*Al...ex?*"

The gears of hate come to a grinding halt. Silver's eyes are open, and she's staring right up at me. For one blissful moment, everything else is forgotten. "Shhh, it's okay. I got you, *Argento.* I have you. You're safe. Everything's going to be okay."

"*It...*" Her eyelids flutter, her face contorting, brow furrowing, and the rage insides me spikes again when I realize that it hurts her to fucking *blink.* "It's okay," she whispers. "I know. You're...here...now."

33

ALEX

The ambulance ride is tense, primarily because I won't let Silver go. I punch one of the EMTs when he tries to tell me I can't ride with them to the hospital, but eventually, to keep the peace, they let me into the back of their rig with her. If Silver hadn't been so royally fucked up, then I doubt I would have gotten my way.

I can't be too mad at them. They listened to Silver's faltering account of what had happened and they decided to leave Jacob writhing in pain on the gymnasium floor, even though they probably should have prioritized him as the more emergent patient and taken him with them, while Silver was forced to wait for a second ambulance.

I would have shot them both, stolen their fucking rig, and driven her to the hospital inside it myself if they'd made that call.

Silver mumbles incoherently the entire way across town toward the hospital, and I hold her hand tightly, chanting the same prayer in Italian over and over again...

"The cops are gonna be waiting there for you," the kid I punched in the face, Dave, informs me as we draw close. "The doctors are gonna rush out first, and they're gonna take her. She's in shock, and she's barely conscience. Looks like she's taken a number of blows to the head. They're gonna wanna do a thorough examination so they can treat her properly. You're not gonna get in their way. Do you hear me?"

"Fuck you, man."

"Do you love this girl?"

I glare at him out of the corner of my eye. "What do you think, asshole?"

"Then you'll do what's best for her, and you'll let them take her. That's when the cops are gonna swoop in and pick you up. They ain't gonna be gentle about it, either. That other kid flat-out accused you of shooting him."

"I *did.*"

Dave rocks back in his seat, blowing out a stiff, unhappy breath. He can't be much older than me. Twenty? Twenty-one? Aside from having slow reflexes, he seems to have his shit together. "I'm gonna pretend I didn't hear that. And don't repeat that until you have a lawyer, either. Things'll get messy if—"

"I'd say things were already kinda messy, wouldn't you, Dave?"

He holds his hands up, mock surrendering, and doesn't say another word until the ambulance brakes jerkily in front of the hospital. From there, everything pans out just as he said it would: numerous doctors arrive in a confusion of shouted orders, needles, back boards and scrubs. They shove me out of the way, tell me I can't go with Silver, and I force myself to listen to them. Dave slaps me on the shoulder as the doctors wheel my girlfriend away, giving me a tight smile.

"Incoming. Twelve o'clock. Remember what I told you, man. Don't say shit until you've spoken to a lawyer. Otherwise..." He shakes his head, pulling the black nitrile gloves from his hands and dumping into the HAZMAT bin as he heads for the hospital exit. "...A kid like you is probably gonna end up serving some *serious* jail time."

CAMERON

Max wrinkles his nose, staring down at his iPad, "What does... *justifiable homicide* mean?" He stumbles over the legal term, frowning heavily.

I grab hold of the iPad, ripping it out of his hands. On the screen: a news piece from the Raleigh Reporter, stating that the prosecution in the case Weaving vs Moretti are filing to have Alex tried for attempted murder. The journalist hazards a guess that Alex's legal team will be pursuing a self-defense verdict. Damn right, they are. I *know* they are. I'm paying them a hell of a lot of money to make sure of it.

"Dad, I'm eleven. I can just google it if you don't tell me," Maxie grouses.

"Justifiable homicide is when someone kills someone to protect themselves or someone else," I sigh, rubbing awkwardly at the back of my neck. I shouldn't have to be talking about stuff like this with him. He just said it himself—he's *eleven*, for Christ's sake. Whatever happened to the age of innocence? Things were hardly peachy when I was a kid, but they're infinitely *so* much worse now.

"They can't say Alex did that, though, because he didn't actually kill anyone, did he? That Jacob guy's still alive."

A hot stab of regret hits me square in the chest. "Yeah. Yeah, he is, Bud." He shouldn't be. He should be rotting in the ground with maggots feasting on his eyeballs. It's better for Alex that Jacob didn't die, though. Better for all of us, really. Better that Jacob and that sack of shit father of his are finally being shown for the monsters that they really are. The DEA swept in and arrested Caleb before he even found out if his son was going to make it through surgery.

I kill the news report on the iPad screen, not wanting Max to read the rest of the information within the article. I sure as fuck don't feel like explaining why certain members of Raleigh are claiming that Silver is making up her story of abuse, rape, assault and attempted murder.

"Mom says you guys shouldn't try and shield me from anything anymore," Max says, as we pull into the hospital parking lot. "She thinks it's hiding things that got us into this mess in the first place."

There are a few things I could say in response to that, but I hold my tongue. It won't help Max if I go off the rails, calling his mother every name under the pitiless fucking sun.

"Let's not focus on any of that now, shall we? Silver's coming home today. We should just be grateful that she's going to be okay, and that we all get to spend Christmas together."

Max grunts, pressing his forehead against the van's window. "I wasn't very nice. To Silver," he says quietly under his breath. "I was pretty horrible to her when she picked me up from Jamie's place before Thanksgiving."

"That's okay, man. She understands. Things have been rough for everybody since...well, since..."

It doesn't need saying. None of it does. The past few months have been like a waking nightmare, and it'll be a while yet before that nightmare is well and truly over.

Inside the hospital, Dr. Killington's waiting for us with Silver's medical charts and a bag of medication big enough to require holding with two hands. "As you know, the bleed on Silver's brain was severe. It's a miracle we were able to get to it before it caused any meaningful damage. There's still a possibility that she could suffer the occasional seizure from time to time. It's vitally important that she's observed over the coming months. If she does have any more seizures, then we may have to start looking at medication for that, too."

We've been over this a thousand times. I'm all too aware of the complications created by the beating Jacob Weaving dealt her when he kidnapped and tried to kill her inside that accursed school.

Max listens quietly, chewing on his thumb nail as Dr. Killington—what kind of person doesn't change a name like that when they become a doctor, for fuck's sake?—goes over the dosages and potentially harmful interactions of all the meds Silver's going to have to take for next few months. He sticks close to my side, owl-eyed and nervous as the doc goes through rehabilitation exercises and physiotherapy appointments.

"She's walking fine on her own now, and that's the main thing." Dr. Killington attempts to end his brief on a positive note. "Her ribs are healing nicely. You can barely tell her jaw was shattered, and the best plastic surgeon in Washington took care of her nose. There's barely even a kink. The rest of it, the scar to her chin and beneath her right eyes—you're gonna be surprised at how well those heal. In six months, she's going to look like her normal self. Outwardly, no one's going to be able to tell that she went through something so terrible. Mentally…"

Since that night at the high school, my daughter's been quiet. *Too* quiet. Reserved. She's tried to hide it, but the trauma of the past year has been weighing on her more than she wants to admit.

"The therapy sessions are going to help. It's going to be one step at a time, Mr. Parisi. One step at a time. Oh, oh, Dr. Romera. Have you got a second? You remember Cameron Parisi, Silver's father? He's here to pick her up and take her home."

A tall brunette wearing blue scrubs stops in the hallway. She's thirty, maybe. Beautiful. A bag's slung over her shoulder, a set of keys in her hand, and she's bouncing a little baby boy on her right hip. We've met before, just once, the night Silver was admitted to the hospital. As one of the leading trauma surgeons in the state, Dr. Sloane Romera was flown in at three o'clock in the morning to save my daughter's life. She managed to stop the internal bleeding inside

Silver's chest that many other doctors wouldn't have been able to. The woman's a fucking hero in my eyes.

"Ah, yeah, Mr. Parisi," she says, smiling warmly. "I'm glad Silver's finally being cut loose. Three weeks in a hospital bed's enough to make anyone crazy."

I shake her hand like my life depends on it. "You came to check on her before she was released?"

"No, unfortunately I was brought out on another emergency. One that didn't pan out as well as Silver's. A mother and her son. Car accident. They were coming home early from vacation and—" Dr. Romera eyes Max and frowns; obviously she thinks the details of the accident are too gruesome for such young ears. "Anyway, it was great to see you again, Mr. Parisi. My ride's here, and it's a long drive back to Seattle. I'd better be going." Her eyes travel to a monster of a guy, covered in tattoos, leaning against the wall of the waiting room, watching us intently. He smiles when he sees Sloane, and the brooding, dark expression on his face instantly lightens. I bid the doctor farewell, unable to tear my eyes away as she approaches the man in the leather jacket who is obviously her husband or her boyfriend. The baby gurgles like a drain when the bruiser takes the little boy out of Dr. Romera's arms and tickles him.

"Shame we can't convince more doctors like Sloane to transfer permanently out to our smaller towns," Dr. Killington mutters. "She's on the fast track to a shining, very illustrious career in the city, though. All the money in the world wouldn't tempt her away from that. Believe me, the hospital board has already made her some pretty staggering offers. Come on, now. We should probably go and find your daughter."

~

SILVER

I haven't looked in a mirror for weeks. Time and time again, I've told myself that there's simply no need. Alex has been locked up, stuck behind bars in a dingy Grays Harbor County prison cell while he awaits trial, so what was the point in making an effort? Reality's a bitch, though. You can try and lie to yourself until you're blue in the face, and maybe you'll succeed in convincing yourself of something on the surface, but deep down you're always going to know the truth.

My truth is this: I haven't looked in a mirror, because I've been too damn afraid of what I'll see in the reflection.

Jake did a real number on my face. The broken nose, the split lip, the shattered jaw, not to mention a fractured cheek bone. For days after I was admitted to hospital, people would walk into my room and I'd have to react quickly, preparing myself for the moment when they took one look at my bruised, swollen, unrecognizable face, and they would flinch. I could handle the pain, that was tolerable, what with all of the extra special meds the doctors kept shooting into my I.V. catheter, but the looks on their faces... They scared me. I've been terrified that I don't look like myself anymore. And if I don't look like regular old Silver, then how the hell can I expect Alex to still be attracted to me?

It's shallow. Stupid. There are plenty of more important things to worry about right now, namely how we're going to be able to get Alex cleared of all his charges without Caleb Weaving's legal team pinning something damaging on him, but I can't help it.

If I've survived all of this, and Alex is freed...but then he doesn't want me anymore? I don't know how the fuck I'm going to handle that.

"Okay, Silver. Stop frowning, baby. Seriously, it's nowhere near as bad as you think. Here, use this." Mom hands me a piece of doubled-over toilet paper, miming the action of blotting her lips as I take it from her. She's been here a lot. Nearly every day. She and dad came to some kind of agreement between themselves which meant they weren't running into each other in the hospital hallways, but occasionally it couldn't be helped. They'd both have to come in for the results of one of the eleventy billion tests that have been run on me over the past three weeks, and I'm giving them credit where credit is due. They haven't made it awkward or weird. They've been polite and considerate around one another. They were even laughing in the hallway together three days ago.

Their behavior might give other people hope that they might attempt to repair their relationship, but I can feel the change in them now. There's something missing, and by the way they look at each other when they think I'm sleeping, they both know they're never going to get it back again.

"I have three different shades of eye shadow if you wanna use it. Eighties make-over?" Mom asks hopefully, holding up the palette so I can see it.

"I don't wanna walk out of here looking like some kind of Halloween sideshow. A little eyeliner and some mascara's fine."

She pretends to be disappointed. I've never worn much in the way of make-up, though, so she can't be all that surprised. "Okay, then. Are you ready? I have a paper bag in my purse just in case. You can put it over your head and make a run for the car—"

"Oh my god. Just give me the stupid mirror." I'm not a vain person, but I feel a little light-headed as I snatch the hand-mirror from my mother, lifting it gingerly until I'm holding it in front of my face.

"Breathe, sweetheart. In and out. Just rip the Bandaid off and look."

I look, and…there I am.

My face.

My completely *normal* face.

There's a tiny, pinkish scar below my bottom lip, and a very faint scar on my left cheekbone where they operated to repair a few fragments of bone, but aside from that…

"I didn't use much foundation," Mom tells me, perching on the edge of the hospital bed beside me. If you use something a tiny bit heavier, then you won't be able to see those marks at all. Dr. Rami said they'll be practically invisible in a couple of months, so…"

Huh. I tilt my head, studying myself from different angles, searching for the hideous disfigurement that I assumed was going to have marred my face for life, but I am almost exactly the same as before. The bruises and the swelling have gone. Aside from the fact that my nose isn't even slightly turned up at the end any more, I am just…*Silver*.

Mom clears her throat. "I was going to wait for your father before I told you this, but I knew you'd want news about Alex as soon as I had it, so—"

I nearly drop the mirror in my haste to spin around. "What! What is it? What's happened? Have they convicted him?" I've been having nightmares every night for weeks. Every time I've closed my eyes to fall asleep, I've been haunted by the fact that Alex was lying some-where, on a hard prison cot, trapped in one of the shittiest, most terrible places on earth, and all because of me. Because he had to come to my aid.

His current predicament is all my fault, and I haven't even been able to speak to him. Tell him how sorry I am. Those text messages were a sign. I decided that being strong and not letting anyone fuck with me was more important than anything else, and I didn't heed those signs. If I'd shown Alex all of the spiteful messages I received, then perhaps things would never have reached the point they did with Jake. With a little outside perspective, I might have seen that the situation was worsening, and it was time to take steps to end the cycle of hatred and abuse. Instead, my stubborn refusal to seek help resulted in my own kidnapping and brush with death, as well as Alex's incarceration.

Mom quickly shakes her head, taking my hand and squeezing it. "No, sweetheart. There was a closed session this morning at the courthouse. They haven't released the news to the local press yet, but Alex was tried as a minor this morning."

"What? A minor?" The lawyers Dad hired to defend Alex told us right out of the gate that there was no chance that was going to happen. They said it has been a miracle that he'd been treated as a minor after the graveyard incident, and because of his previous misdemeanors he was definitely going to face whatever charges were brought up against him as an adult. To find out that they were wrong is kind of shocking.

"I know. I'm as surprised as you," Mom says. "The Mayor shouldn't have even let me sit in. I guess she felt bad for me, knowing you were still stuck in here."

"Wait, you were inside the court? Mom, you've been here for forty minutes. You sat here and applied my make-up like we were having a fucking sleep-over. What happened?"

She gives me a disapproving look. She forgets and curses around me and Max all the time, but it appears I'm not allowed to do the same. "What happened is Alex's social worker is some kind of hotshot ninja, that's what. Marion, or Mary or something. I can't remember her name, but she was on fire in that court room, Silver. I've never seen anything like it."

Maeve? I've only seen her from a distance, and I can't remember a single thing about the woman. That was the day I saw Alex for the very first time, in the hallway outside Darhower's office, and I was far busy persuading myself that I needed to stay the hell away from the sexy motherfucker with all the black ink to notice some woman in a pantsuit. Alex has told me plenty about her, though, and from what he's said he didn't think she was anything less than ill-equipped to do her job.

"It was quite something to watch. There was this DEA agent there. Detective Lowell? She made some sort of closed deal with the prosecution team. The Mayor told me once the court had cleared that Caleb Weaving agreed not to peruse Jacob's shooting as attempted murder if they knocked some time off of his sentence. I mean, what kind of parent does that? I'd never throw my kid under the bus for my own personal gain, and that's essentially what he did. By agreeing that Alex acted in self-defense, Caleb's agreed that Jake is guilty."

Mom's having difficulty wrapping her head around the fact that Caleb would be so mercenary, but I'm not. He's a Weaving, after all. It's in their DNA to be selfish, evil, cold-hearted pricks. "I don't care about any of that right now. I'm going out of my mind, Mom. For crying out loud, just tell me what happened! Was Alex remanded, or—"

"Wow, I'm an idiot. I'm sorry, I should have lead with that part, shouldn't I? My head's all over the place. No, Alex was not remanded," she says. "The charges against him were dropped, baby girl. He was released a couple of hours ago."

Released?

A couple of hours ago?

What the…

"What's wrong, Sweetheart? I thought you'd be thrilled?"

"Oh, I am. It's just…it's nothing." My mind is racing. Alex was released from prison hours ago, and he didn't come to the hospital. He didn't come to see me. If that doesn't speak volumes, then I don't know what does. Alex is angry with me. He hates me, and I don't blame him either. He's been trying so hard to stay out of trouble since he came to Raleigh, and yet *I* managed to fuck things up for him. The past three weeks must have been hell for him, stuck behind bars. I don't blame him for avoiding me like the plague.

How am I going to get through the rest of the school year if I have to see him every day...

Fuck, how am I going to live with myself if my inaction and stupidity leads to the family court deciding that Alex is an unfit guardian for Ben? He's been vindicated of any blame in Jake's shooting, but the fact that he was caught up in such a messy situation in the first place is definitely going to destroy any hopes he had of bringing Ben home with him soon.

"Shhh, oh—oh my god, sweetheart, are you *crying*? It's okay." Mom pulls me into her, letting me fall against her as I softly sob into her silk blouse. This is the very best outcome we could have hoped for. It's a miracle that Alex isn't going to suffer any devastating consequences because of the fact that he protected me. This is wonderful news...but at the same time it feels like the world is fucking ending.

"I ruined it," I whisper. "I ruined everything, Mom."

"No! No, I'm not gonna let you sit here and come out with dumb shit like that. None of this is your fault, Silver. You hear me? None of it. Jacob Weaving's a certified psycho, and he deserves everything he's got coming to him. Alex has probably just gone home to shower or something. Get a change of clothes. If I were him, I'd need a moment to decompress, too. Just give him a little time, okay, sweetheart."

There's a light rap at the door. Dad's standing there with a frown on his face, holding a bright pink, *"It's a Girl!"* balloon in his hand. Next to him, Max is strangling a bouquet of flowers, radiating anxiety as he meets my gaze. "Everything okay?" Dad asks wearily.

"Yeah. Yeah, everything's fine." I sniff, wiping at my nose with the back of my hand. "Ready to go home, that's all." Jerking my chin at the balloon, I arch an eyebrow at my father. "Seriously? *It's a girl?*"

"Sorry. They didn't have, '*Hey! You survived a near death experience, and you're finally getting the fuck out of here!*'"

"I suppose it'll have to do then." I smile, but it doesn't reach my eyes. I put on a valiant show as Mom and Dad chat amicably, packing up the rest of my things, but the entire time I'm pretending to be okay, pretending not to hurt, there three words echoing on repeat inside my head, over and over again.

Alex didn't come.
Alex didn't come.
Alex didn't come.
Alex didn't come.

EPILOGUE

SILVER

The *click, click, click* and *snuffle* outside my bedroom door lets me know that I have a visitor. I've been hiding in my room, feeling desolate and lost, for the past ten hours, and the time has stretched out, each second a minute, each minute an hour, each hour a lifetime.

I can't believe it.

I can't believe it's ending like this.

Alex—

Dum dum dum dum dum!

My visitor scratches at the door, rattling the wood in the frame, requesting to be let in. Groaning, I drag myself up off the bed and shuffle zombie-like over to the door. I don't really hurt anymore. I get twinges in my ribs, since it's harder for those bones to knit and heal, but apart from the occasional shitty headache when I watch too much T.V., I feel almost back to normal. My lethargy today is purely because of my mood.

When I open the door, Nipper is sitting neatly on the rug in the hall, ears pricked, gazing up at me expectantly. His black, wiry coat is tinged with grey on the ends, and his dark, soulful eyes seem to hold a lot of questions: *Are you okay? Where did you go? What's wrong with you now? Can I come in? When are we going to play?* And most, important of all: *Got any food?*

I sigh, shaking my head, stepping to one side to let the small dog past me as he gets to his feet and hobbles into my bedroom.

The night Jake broke into the house and kidnapped me, he'd come across Nipper in the kitchen. From the mess, Dad thinks Nipper had been going through the trash at the time; he couldn't conceive why Jake would have dumped out the trash can onto the kitchen floor, so Nipper had seemed like the likely culprit.

I'd heard Nipper barking ferociously from my hiding spot. I'd heard him growl, and then I'd heard him yelp and go quiet. While I was trembling, afraid and alone in that closet, Nipper had faced-off with Jake, and the evil monster had taken a steak knife to him. Three times: that's how many times Jake stabbed Nipper with the knife. It's also how many times the vet at the emergency animal clinic told Dad to put Nipper down in the days after I was admitted to hospital. Thankfully, Dad refused.

It was a close call. The scrappy little dude is always going to walk with a limp, but he seems to be getting better every day. He also seems to have decided we're best friends. Dad says it's because Nipper knows I'm a fighter, just like him, and fighters need to stick together.

The dog growls at the end of the bed, biting the corner of the duvet. He can't jump up yet. He'll probably never be able to, what with the damage that was done to his hind legs, so this is how he tells me that he wants me to pick him up.

I oblige him, allowing myself a small smile when the cheeky bastard scurries up the length of the bed and proceeds to make a nest for himself amongst my pillows. I curl up into a ball beside him, letting him nestle into the hollow created by my body, and after a while, he falls asleep.

I never knew a dog could snore so loud.

I stare at the new clock beside my bed, not thinking. Trying desperately and failing not to *feel* anything...

"Silver?"

Max hovers in the open doorway to my bedroom, looking down at his socks. Over the past three weeks, Max has come to visit me nearly every day, but he's been quiet and withdrawn. I've wanted to spend time with him, hang out and talk to him about school, and Jamie, and whatever video game he's been playing, but the opportunities have been thin on the ground. At the hospital, there were always doctors and nurses coming in and out like my room had a revolving door on it, checking on me, asking questions, recording my stats, running more tests. My parents were there without fail, one of them always sitting by my bedside, trying to make me laugh or feel better, when all I wanted to do was shrink into a fetal position beneath my sheets and cry.

This is the first time we've been alone since the night I nearly died.

Propping myself up on my elbow, I close one eye, squinting at him. "Hey, buddy. What's up?"

Max swallows hard, gradually lifting his gaze to look at me. "Are you mad at me?" he whispers.

This has me sitting upright in no time. "God, no. Why would I be mad at you, bud? Come on. Come here and sit down."

My brother comes and perches on the edge of the bed, halfheartedly petting Nipper when he nudges his nose into his hands, looking for a treat. "Well, I was mean to you," Max whispers. "I called you a bad name."

Bitch. He'd called me a bitch at Jamie's. With everything going on, I completely forgot that even happened. "Dude. It doesn't matter. We all get frustrated and lash out sometimes. It's not a big deal."

He sniffs. "I felt bad about it. Afterwards. At the new house. And then you got hurt, and I thought you were gonna die, and—"

"Hey, hey, hey, it's okay. I'm okay now. And I love you, Maxie. It doesn't matter. It's tough being eleven. Sometimes, it feels like the world's against you and you react badly. I know you didn't mean it."

"You do?"

"Of course." He looks so miserable, but when I tell him this, a spark of life seems to return to his dark eyes. Eyes like Dad.

"Okay. Well. I'm sorry. I won't ever call you a bad name again. And, um, I know you don't ruin everything. I was just mad, because Mom moved out and took me to the new house, and I didn't like it, and—"

"Shhh, it's fine. I know." I pull him further onto the bed, into a tight hug. He sniffles, hiding his face into my hair. "I know everything's different now that Mom and Dad aren't together anymore, but it doesn't really change that much. They both still love you. And so do I. You just get to have two bedrooms now. And double the cool stuff. Dad got you a new PlayStation to keep here, didn't he?"

"No. He got an *Xbox*."

"Ahh, you know Dad. He has no idea. We can take it back and exchange it if you like."

"No." Max leans back, smiling a little. "I like having both. I just need to get some new games."

"See. Twice the cool stuff. Maybe next week, I can come get you and we can go to the store or something."

Max nods. He seems much happier now that he knows I don't despise him for being difficult. "Mom can't stop sneezing. She says she's allergic to the dog. We have to go home in a minute. Are you gonna be okay?"

"Yeah, bud. I am, I promise. Everything's A-Okay now." Lies, lies, and more lies. For Max's sake, I'll tell them.

"Are you gonna go and see Alex tonight?" he asks. "I like him. I didn't mean to call him stupid."

"Uhhhh, I don't think so. I don't think Alex and I are gonna be spending much time together from now on." Man, it's a miracle that I managed to get that statement out without bursting into tears. I'm quite proud of myself; my voice barely even wobbled.

Max's frown takes up half of his face. "But why? Don't you love him anymore?"

Oh, god. Come *on*. This is excruciating. "Yeah. I love him more than anything."

"So…he doesn't love you?"

My chest pinches, a sharp pain stabbing into my heart. It's just my ribs, I tell myself. But it's not. My broken ribs never hurt as much as the idea that Alex doesn't love me anymore. "I—I guess I don't know. But he doesn't seem to want to be around me right now, so…"

"You should go see him," Max says firmly. "I think you should find out. And if he says he doesn't love you anymore, then you'll know. And you can burn down his trailer."

"Shit, Max." I laugh. "I'm not going to burn down his trailer. That's crazy." I've thought about it, though. I've already struck the match and flicked it into the gasoline doused double-wide more times than I can count over the past ten hours. I shouldn't have. None of this was his fault. This is all on me.

I haven't texted Alex. It felt wrong to make contact somehow, knowing that he was out there, free as a bird within the Raleigh city limits, and he hasn't made any attempt to come and find me. It's been three weeks, for crying out loud. We haven't seen or spoken to each other in three long, horrific, painful weeks, and Alex has just gone about his life, probably heading on home when he knows I've been in the hospital? Reaching out to him...it's just felt like the wrong thing to do.

"Still. If you don't go and see him, you'll never know what's going on, will you?" Max says. "And Mrs. Jensen at school says talking is important. She says talking can solve anything, if you put your mind to it."

I sit very still, mulling the words over. My eleven-year-old brother is smarter than his years. I should go talk to Alex before this drags out any further. School doesn't start up again until after the new year. Am I going to just let this eat away at me for all that time? To ruin the holidays, not knowing what's going to happen when I walk back through the entrance of Raleigh High and I see him there for the first time since he came careening into the gym with that giant silver gun in his hand? It's going to hurt if he confirms my worst fears but slumping into a depression over the Christmas break isn't fair to my family. It *will* be better to face the inevitable now, rather than put it off.

I've learned my lesson. Finally. From here on out, I am going to face my problems openly, head on. No more hiding, pretending or ignoring. If I'd handled my business like that in the first place, then we likely wouldn't be in this mess.

Ruffling Max's hair, I plant a kiss on his cheek. He tries to squirm away from me, groaning loudly about girl germs, but I get him good. "Thanks, little dude. I needed those words of wisdom. Now quit being smarter than me. I'm supposed to be the clever child. You're supposed to be the cute one."

≈

Dad's hidden the keys to the van. It's like he *knows* me. Clearly, he suspected I'd try and pull some kind of stunt in an attempt to make my way over to Salton Ash, and he prepared accordingly. He finds me rummaging in the drawers of the mail stand in the hallway, once Mom and Max have left. "Don't bother. They're not there," he tells me. "The doc said you're not allowed to drive while you're on all these meds. You're not operating a vehicle any time soon, kiddo."

I scowl, shoving the drawer closed. "They only say that in case you fall asleep at the wheel or something. I feel fine. Those rules don't apply."

"They definitely do. It's not just the meds, smart ass. They're worried about you having another seizure and driving off a fucking cliff."

"I haven't had a seizure in two weeks."

Dad leans against the wall, folding his arms across his chest. He's got that look on his face—the 'I-ain't-budging-on-this-one' face. "Six months. You have your check up, and you get the all-clear. Until then, I'll happily chauffeur you wherever you wanna go. Within reason," he adds quickly. "I'm not driving to Bellingham at two in the morning, no matter how many tacos you buy me."

"Dad. You are not driving me anywhere. I'll get Ubers if I need to. You're being crazy, though. I am *fine*."

The smug bastard smirks. "Sorry, *dolcezza*. When you run out of funds for Uber, give me a shout. You know where I'll be."

All of the blood drains from my face. "Dad. Do *not* call me that."

"*Dolcezza*? Why not? I checked up on Moretti and looks like he was telling the truth. It does mean sweetness."

"I don't care what it me—" I let out a very frustrated, very horrified breath. "Just...don't, Dad. Seriously. It's not appropriate."

"I *knew* it." Dad flares his nostrils, throwing his hands up in the air. "I *knew* that punk was using the Italian language to seduce you."

I cringe, hiding behind the curtain of my hair. Well, this is fucking awkward.

"Don't worry, Sil. I don't mind driving you over to Salton Ash. I'm gonna be having a few choice words of my own with Alessandro Moretti."

"No, Dad. God, no. Just…just stay here, all right. I'll order a car. I swear I won't try and hot wire the van. I need to see him on my own, okay?"

The fake annoyance on my father's face slides away, replaced by something else. Something unreadable. Secret. Mercifully, it isn't pity. I don't think I could handle him feeling sorry for me right now. "Okay, sweetheart. But…give him a chance to speak before you lay into him. There's no point tearing him a new one before you've even heard what he's got to say."

I don't think my father's ever been more unlike himself than he is in this moment. There's no name-calling. No yelling, and no threats to dismember the boy who's broken my heart. He gives me a casual wink and pushes away from the wall, about-facing and heading into the kitchen.

"Oh, and text me every fifteen minutes to let me know you're okay," he calls over his shoulder. "Miss one message, and I will come out and find you. I don't care how embarrassing it is. You've just gotten out of hospital, Silver Parisi."

Ah. *There's* my old man.

~

SILVER

The Uber driver chats incessantly on the way over to the trailer park. He doesn't seem to remember that one night, nearly nine months ago, in the middle of the night, he picked me up from a beautiful house hidden amongst the trees and drove me to a pharmacy, covered in blood. I remember him, though. I remember the worried look on his face when he told me that he had a daughter my age, and he wouldn't be able to forgive himself if he didn't make sure I got home okay.

Raleigh has plenty of Uber drivers, and yet I manage to get the same one twice? Fucking small towns. I stay quiet in the back of the car, watching the snow come down in thick flurries that obscure the view out of the window from time to time. I make the appropriate noises whenever he asks me a question, but mostly I'm trapped inside my own thoughts, worrying about what's going to happen when I finally arrive at my destination and I come face-to-face with Alex.

The driver gets as close as he can to Alex's trailer before the snow banks and the iced-up blacktop make it impossible for him to go any further. I get out, mumbling a quiet thank you, and I walk the remaining hundred feet or so down the road, the freezing air prickling at my face and my hands.

My heart's pounding as I climb the steps to Alex's door, sorrow pooling in my chest at the sight of the lights blazing inside the trailer. A part of me had hoped there would be no one here. That maybe something had happened, and Alex was held up in custody longer than Mom thought, filling out paperwork, or…or…I don't know. It gave me hope, thinking that something might be physically preventing Alex from coming to find me, but it's pretty damn obvious that he's just been chilling at home, kicking his feet up with a couple of beers or something.

I knock, then immediately wish that I hadn't. I haven't thought about what I'm going to say. I need more time to think. To figure out what I'm go—

The door rips open, throwing a pillar of golden light out into the dark and the snow, and my mind goes blank. The guy standing in the doorway isn't Alex. Not even close. Zander Hawkins grins, arching an eyebrow down at me from inside the trailer. The black ACDC shirt he's wearing has a small hole in the right sleeve, confirming that it's one of Alex's.

"Well, well. If it isn't Helen of Troy. The face that launched a thousand ships," he remarks.

"Don't start," I mutter. "Where's Alex?"

"Y'know? Helen of Troy? 'Cause Paris sacrificed everything for her, 'cause she was so beautiful, and everyone went to war because of her. And—"

"Yeah, yeah, I get it. I'm *Helen*. Alex is *Paris*." I clench my jaw, trying to breathe deep. "I didn't mean to cause so much trouble. Now, please…tell me where he is."

Zander shrugs, shoving a sandwich into his mouth and taking a bite. I didn't even see that he was holding a sandwich to begin with. "How should I know?" he says, the words muffled around the contents of his mouth.

"Because you're in his trailer. And you're wearing his clothes?"

He swallows. "Ah, right. But it's not his trailer anymore, is it. He packed up all his shit and moved out. It's my trailer now. He gave it to me. And if he didn't want the box of clothes he left sitting on the counter, then he should have taken them with him. S'all I have to say on the matter."

"*What?*" A loud, high-pitched humming sound fills my head. It's taking way longer than it should to process what he's just told me. The only conclusion I can come to is that my ears couldn't have heard correctly. "I'm sorry. Did you just say…Alex left?"

"Yeah. He said he wasn't gonna need this place anymore, and since all of Caleb Weaving's assets have been frozen and I can't crash in his pool house anymore, I thought fuck it? Why not? I could use some more permanent digs. So here I am."

I'd say Zander is a very unobservant person, but there's something conniving about him. He's being purposefully obtuse, and I can't figure out why. He must be able to see that I am flat-out stunned right now. Maybe he's trying to protect his friend. He was the one who rushed Nipper to the vet for Alex, when he and Dad came looking for me. He obviously cares a little about Alex. Or, perhaps he just doesn't want to deal with a crying, wailing girl on his brand-new doorstep, ruining his one-man house warming party. Either way, it doesn't seem like he's going to address the fact that, as far as I'm aware, I am still Alex's girlfriend, and I know nothing about the fact that he's apparently upped and left town.

"I'd invite you in for a cup of tea, but I only have whiskey. And I'm not really into sharing whiskey, y'know. On account of it being so delicious," Zander says airily. He maintains his entertained expression until I take a step backward down the stairs, my throat closing up, my eyes burning, and I cover my mouth with my hands.

"Oh, Jesus Christ. Look. All I know is that Alex was planning on heading over to see some guy in town called Henry about selling some mechanic's tools before he took off. He only left an hour ago. If you hurry, you might catch him."

Henry? Henry owns the hardware store on the high street. Dad's rented tools from him before, when he's only needed to use something once. I had no idea Henry bought used tools, though. Fuck, if Alex is selling all the stuff he uses to work on his bike and the Camaro, then he isn't just leaving town temporarily. He's leaving town for good.

I nearly puke into the snow as I stagger away from the trailer. Zander calls something behind me, but I don't hear a word he says. Numb from the cold, numb from shock, I stand at the exit of the Salton Ash trailer park, waiting on my second Uber of the night, incapable of forming a thought that doesn't make me want to burst into tears.

I get in the car when it arrives, grateful that it's not the same guy as before. I stare at the back of the headrest, trying to come to terms with what's happening; it feels like no time at all has passed when the driver stops in front of Harrison's Home Hardware and Electrical Supplies.

I'm not in my right mind. It doesn't even register that the place is in darkness until I'm standing in front of the doors to the store, and I see the 'closed' sign in front of me.

"*Fuck.*"

It's nearly nine o'clock at night. Of course the place is closed. Amidst all of my panic and upset, I didn't even consider the time. I just came over here, blindly acting without thought.

He's gone. I'm too late. Alex has already left Raleigh.

Blinking back tears, I move to the corner of the street, shivering against the cold, my fingers so stiff that they barely work as I type out a message to Dad.

Me: Everything's fine. I'm okay. Coming home now.

Defeat washes over me as I step to the curb, readying to call one final last ride for the night. The corner of High Street and Paulson is deserted, which isn't unusual. The fresh snow is keeping people indoors, wrapped up warm in front of their fires. My finger's hovering over the 'Request Ride' button on my phone's screen, when I hear the sound behind me.

The hair on the back of my neck stands to immediate attention.

Jake...

It isn't Jake.

It isn't him.

It can't be.

Jake's on a prison ward, recovering from his gunshot wound.

Breathe, Silver.

Breathe...

Easier said than done, though. I can't even turn around to see who's waiting in the shadows behind me; my body is tensed, my shoulders rigid. I'm rooted to the spot, paralyzed by fear. And then...

"Ti stavo aspettando, Argento."

Oh...my...god...

I close my eyes at the sound of that voice. Like rough silk, soft and rough in equal parts, murmuring over the muffled silence of the snowfall.

"Sembra che stia aspettando da una vita."

Slowly, I turn around and see him. He's leaning against the brick wall around the side of the hardware store, in the exact same spot he waited for me weeks ago, when we kissed and devoured each other under a star-studded night sky, much like tonight's.

His sable hair is longer than it was back in the Raleigh High gymnasium. His face is marked with stubble. His eyes, so dark they almost seem black, bore into me with the same intense fascination that they always have.

I am suddenly unable to breathe for an entirely different reason. Alex pushes away from the wall, approaching me slowly with his hands shoved deep in his pockets.

"I take it you didn't use your free time in hospital to learn any Italian," he muses softly.

Dumbfounded, I shake my head from side to side. "I thought...I thought you'd left," I whisper.

Alex moves an inch closer, looking me up and down, his eyes sharp, as if he's looking for something. He's tense, too. The muscles in his jaw jump, his nostrils flaring. He's close, only six-feet away, but it feels like an uncrossable divide separates us.

"And yet here I am." He takes another step toward me, breaking the illusion.

"You moved out of your trailer."

"I know." Another step.

"You didn't call me."

"I know." Another.

"You didn't message me."

"I know."

My voice cracks on my last accusation. "You—*you didn't come find me."*

There's only one foot left between us now. Alex's expression softens at the pain in my voice. He takes his hands out of his pockets, blowing hard down his nose, and then he whispers quietly under his breath. "I know, *Argento*. And it fucking killed me not to."

I'm moving before I can stop myself. I hurl myself at him, raising my fists, slamming them into the front of his leather jacket. I hit him. I hit him as hard as I can, screaming through my teeth.

"How could you do that? How could you stay away? After everything!"

Alex allows me to seethe for a second, but then he takes hold of my wrists, gently restraining me, pulling me in toward his chest. "Shhh, stop, *Argento*. Stop, stop, stop. I'm sorry, I'm sorry, okay. Shhh."

My anger turns to tears. I fall against him, hiding my face in his jacket, my emotions twisting and turning like a hurricane as he wraps his arms around me and squeezes me tight against him.

"I was gonna come and get you. I was coming for you, baby, I swear. I wanted it to be a surprise," he says into my hair. "God, I wanted to fucking surprise you. And then I just got a message from Zander, and I realized how fucking stupid I've been. I should have come to you right away, but there was so much to do here, and I wanted everything to be perfect, and...Silver, please, shh, please don't cry. It's okay. Everything's all right. I'm here. I'm here. I'm here."

He leans back, stooping down, cupping my face in his hands. He wants me to look at him, but my tears aren't even close to ceasing. "Silver. Don't you know that I love you?" he says softly. "Don't you know that I'd do anything for you? I'd never leave you, *Tesoro*. Never, ever, ever. I made a fucking mistake. A big one, and I'm hoping you'll forgive me for it, but…look. Just come with me, okay? Please. There's something I have to show you."

What the fuck is happening? I have no clue what he's talking about. He's not making any sense. I only heard him say that he wasn't leaving Raleigh. Beyond that, my thoughts are so out of control that I don't know which way is fucking up.

I let him take my hand and I follow after him, fighting to regain my senses as he leads me behind the hardware store, toward a steep, narrow staircase.

"What—where are you taking me?"

"Just wait and see. Everything'll be clear in a second. Just…give me a second." Up the stairs he goes. I climb the steps behind him, confusion clouding every corner of my mind. Before us is a blue door, the paint on the woodwork chipped and peeling, with brass numbers screwed into the wall beside it that say 'Apt. 23a.' Alex takes a key out of his jacket pocket, sliding it into the lock, and then pushes the blue, peeling door open.

Two seconds later, I'm standing in an apartment that…that's full of Alex's stuff?

"I know it's a mess right now. I was trying to get everything set up before I came and got you, but…it won't take long. It'll be tidy and perfect in a couple of days. I have a new couch coming on Thursday. And new kitchen stuff, too. I just…I don't know. Um. I guess…this is where I'm gonna be living from now on."

I look around, completely silent and bewildered. Alex's record player is sitting in the corner. His book shelves have all be placed in the main living space, his books already lined up in neat rows. The place smells of new carpet and fresh paint. I reach out, extending my fingers, attempting to touch the wall, but Alex quickly grabs my hand.

"Whoa, whoa, whoa, that's, yeah…I wouldn't do that. That's still wet." He looks anxious. He bites down on his bottom lip, his eyebrows slowly climbing up his forehead. "I had this big, grand plan in my head, *Argento*. I knew you were home, but I told myself you'd be tired and probably sleep. I wanted to come over and blindfold you. Drive you over here, like it was some big secret...but, fuck. I see how moronic that was now. I am so, so sorry. I shouldn't have waited. I was just excited, and—"

I hold up a hand. "Stop."

He winces. "Stop?"

"Yes. Stop. I need a moment." I skirt the perimeter of the apartment, running my hands over his things, picking up his books, stroking my hand over the new dining table that smells of fresh wood, and Alex remains quiet. I walk into the kitchen, into first one bedroom, and then another, smaller one, already set up with a small, single bed. I inspect the bathroom, digging my fingers into the stack of fluffy towels balanced on the edge of the bath that still have their tags on them. He's still closed-mouthed and tense when I walk back into the living room, his eyes following me as I return to stand in front of him.

"You weren't angry with me," I say flatly.

"Angry at you? Why would I..." he shakes his head.

"Because I put you in a dangerous situation. Because I didn't tell you about the text messages Jake was sending me."

"I mean, I wasn't stoked that you didn't tell me about that, but...no. I'd never be mad at *you* because Jacob Weaving is fucked in the head. You did nothing wrong, Silver."

"Okay." I fidget, finding it difficult to stand still. "And...you aren't dumping me for risking your chances of winning custody of Ben?"

Alex's eyes widen. "Dumping you? No! *Fuck.* Haven't you listened to anything I've been telling you since we met? I am gonna ask you to marry me one of these days, Silver Parisi. Don't fucking look at me like that. You know you want to marry me. I'm not asking you now, but one day I'm gonna ask, because I want you. I want all of you. I want our life together, whatever that looks like, no matter where we end up. There is no me leaving you. Not now. Not ever. You're stuck with me for life. Now if you'd only stop going around, trying to get that life cut short, then I would be really fucking grateful."

The look on my face must say everything I can't. Alex places his hands on my hip, stepping into me. He rests his forehead against mine, breathing shakily. "Say something, Silver. Tell me you forgive me for being stupid. Tell me you're okay. Tell me you fucking love me. I can't take the silence anymore."

I will never be more relieved than the moment when he cut through the rope that was strangling me to death three weeks. But the relief I feel right now comes pretty damn close.

The worry that's been crippling me since I learned the charges against him had been dropped disintegrates into vapor. Turns out Maxie was right: any problem can be resolved or overcome if you just take a second to talk…

So I give him the answers that he needs.

"I forgive you. I'm okay. I love you, Alessandro Moretti. Now please…just shut the hell up and kiss me."

$\sim$

Need to know what's next for Alex and Silver? Want to know what Zander's up to? Want to know if Jake gets what he deserves?

Book Three in the Raleigh Rebels series will be coming out end of September/early October 2019.

In the meantime, keep on reading if you'd like to know more about the owner of Monty's mysterious black bag of tricks…

KEEP ON READING TO MEET THE
OWNER OF MONTY'S BLACK BAG...

SLOANE

WHEN I SAY I'M A GHOST, I'M NOT BEING LITERAL. I'm very much alive. Or at least some days I hurt just enough to know I'm still clinging onto a heartbeat. No, when I say I'm a ghost, I'm referring to the fact that people rarely see me. I'm the girl in the background. The average height, average weight, average hair color, non-event that eyes skip over instead of lingering on. I slip silently through this yawning city I live in without smiling. Without having to greet anyone for days at a time. It's been that way for the last six months. It's rare that I have to speak to strangers, and when I do it's perfunctory; people know instinctively that I'm not primed for small talk. Today is no exception.

"Here's your room key, Ms. Fredrich." The receptionist in downtown Seattle's Marriot hotel slides the plastic key card across the marble countertop. Once she's withdrawn her hand a safe distance, I reach out and palm it.

"Thank you."

Eyes down, she's stapling the paperwork created by my payment. "So...business or pleasure?" The warmth in her eyes dies when she finally looks up at me and registers the blank look I'm wearing. The smile slides from her face like butter from a hot knife.

"Business," I tell her, because nothing has ever been truer.

"Okay, well...I hope you enjoy your stay." She looks away as soon as she's done with the appropriate front desk script. She doesn't ask why I've turned up at her hotel with no bags, or why I'm only booking in for one night. Or why I've left a spare key card at the front desk for a Mr. Hanson. She doesn't ask any of that; she's not supposed to. Eli's given me a rundown of how this thing will play out, and so far it's almost to the letter. I lift my purse from the desk and head to the elevator, straightening my coat.

Twenty-two, twenty-one, twenty, nineteen, eighteen....

I watch the numbers light up one by one. Each disc, the size of a dollar coin, lights up and darkens in turn, and the elevator descends while I wait, patient and unblinking. There are other people waiting for the car to arrive. If this were an office building or a shopping center, I'd take the stairs; closed spaces and I aren't exactly the best of friends, but since this hotel is forty-seven floors high and I've booked a room on the forty-second floor, I'll just have to tolerate the inconvenience of their presence.

The doors slide back and I walk in first. The other hotel residents —four businessmen—are staying somewhere mid-level, and I don't want them brushing past me as they exit. It's easy to label them as mid-level guys. They're wearing mid-level-guy suits, and all four of them have mid-level-guy hair-cuts. Their accommodation is being paid for by a cost center funded by an accounting department, and accounting departments don't spring for penthouses. They spring for double rooms with en-suites that have access to the gym and not much else. No mini bar for you, Mr. Corporate.

The lift doors roll closed and I retreat within myself, pressing my back against the rear wall of the elevator car. I close my eyes, exhale down my nose. This will all be over soon, but my heart still dances in my chest all the same. The fear of being trapped, of what I am about to do, is like a coiled snake, ready and waiting to wreak havoc on my insides.

"Hey. Hey, are you okay? You're looking a little freaked out."

One of them talks to me. He thinks my panic is tied to the elevator ride, which it is, but only partially. He has brown eyes, a soft, warm color that reminds me of melted chocolate. He has dimples, too, probably twenty-three or so, around my age. He looks nice. The kind of nice I might have dated once upon a time, before…before any of that became impossible.

"I'm fine, thank you," I tell him.

"Good." The guy with chocolate eyes smiles at me. "Deep breathing sometimes helps my sister. She's not fond of elevators either."

He's so sweet. Way sweeter than I deserve, considering my purpose here today. I reward him with a watery smile—he grins back—and then the doors open, and the four of them leave. I jam my hands into my pockets to stop them from shaking. I'm alone for eighteen floors, which is better than being trapped with four strangers but still not great, and then, finally, it's my turn to alight. This hotel is much like any other I've stayed in. The only difference about it, the thing that will define it from all others in my memory for as long as I live, is that I'm here for a very specific reason: to have sex with a total stranger. And I'm doing it to find my baby sister.

∾

SLOANE

BY THE TIME I'm inside and my coat is hung neatly on the hook behind the door, I'm pretty much ready. I'm wearing what I've been told to wear—black lace. Eli, the private investigator I hired to help me find my sister, wasn't any more specific than that. He's the one who set this whole thing up.

"Sometimes money just isn't enough to buy what you're looking for, sweetheart. Sometimes it takes a little more... persuasion to buy information like this. I tell you what...I'll share what I know in return for a little favor."

"What kind of favor?"

"You spread your legs for a paying customer and I'll tell you everything you need to know." The disgusting pig has the audacity to smile. "Oh come now, Ms. Romera. Don't look at me like that. You want to find your sister, don't you?"

And in the end, I'd agreed. He was right; I do want to find Lex, and I'll clearly do anything to make that happen. Even if I'll never be able to live with myself afterward.

Aside from the lingerie, Eli told me to bring something else with me today, something hidden in the pocket of my jacket. I take it out and put it on. The mask is a black lace number with blood-red lace edging and makes me a feel a little more disguised at least. I hit the light switch in the bathroom and rummage in my purse for the only thing that's going to keep me sane during this experience: a bottle of Valium. One of the perks of being a fifth-year resident is that there's always someone available to prescribe medication when you need it, no questions asked. The sedative's not even in my name, will never appear on my medical record. I pop one, just enough to keep me calm but not enough to make me drowsy, and then I peer into the mirror, fixing the band of my mask underneath my hair.

You look like shit, Sloane.

I tell myself this every time I look into a mirror these days. It may be the truth, but then again it may not. I've been staring at myself in mirrors for so long now that the reflection just doesn't make any sense anymore. Lex was always the beautiful one. I know I have a nice body. Eli said that was the only reason he was willing to do business with me, because my tits were real and I had a nice ass. *Your height might make some guys uncomfortable, but hey...not a lot you can do about that.* I focus on the dark rings under my eyes, trying to remember that this is all temporary. It's not forever. I'm a medical student after all. The body is just a machine, full of cogs and intricate parts all ticking away, working in harmony to keep you moving. Having sex is just making use of that machine, nothing more.

You can do this, Sloane. You can do this.

And then, not even two seconds later...

Lex wouldn't want this for you. She wouldn't want you used and abused, selling yourself for so little. I hate that voice inside my head. It makes it so hard to justify going through with this, but it's not as though I'm auctioning off my most valuable possession for drugs or money, or even fame and fortune like some girls do. No, I am doing it out of love. Love for Lex. Any sister would do the same.

It's been six months and I'm still no closer to finding Alexis, and this really does feel like my last resort. Eli's smart—he's given me just enough information to keep my hope alive, but nowhere near enough to risk me backing out of our little arrangement.

Thud, thud, thud.

"Holy shhhh—" The door. I suck my bottom lip into my mouth, trapping the curse word behind my teeth. It's go time.

Mr. Hanson will have collected his key from the chirpy concierge downstairs. I was told to expect the knock. Let's me know the guy I'm going to be sleeping with is here, and I have to wait in the bathroom until he comes to get me. I pull the door closed and for a brief second a rush of fear grapples hold of me. If I lock myself in here and refuse to come out, how long would he wait until he gets pissed off and leaves? I can't do that, though. Eli would never hold up his end of the bargain, and besides…none of this matters anymore. None of it. It's just something I have to get through.

I hear the electronic beep of the key card being accepted into the door, and the rough catch of the lock sliding back. Silence follows after that. The edge of the sink digs into the back of my legs as I remain frozen, leaning heavily against it, before I remember I shouldn't do that. It'll mark my body, and that's against the rules, even temporary marks like that.

Thankfully the drugs begin to kick in, washing over me with a muted sense of peace. A good thing, too, because whoever is out there takes their sweet time in making themselves at home. Without it, I'd have been on the verge of making a run for it by the time a knuckle raps against the door. "Come on out. Turn the light off first," a voice commands. It's gruff and full of gravel, maybe the voice of a smoker? Fucking great. I'm going to have to spend the next two hours with my tongue down a smoker's throat, and then I'm gonna have to bleach my mouth out. I turn the light off and open the door, and I'm perplexed by what I see beyond.

Nothing.

Absolutely nothing. The room is pitch black.

"Couldn't find the light switch?"

"Don't touch it. Just come here," the voice tells me. He sounds young enough, and he's alone. Not that I was expecting more than one guy, of course. Eli swore it would only be the one guy. And only this one time. I step gingerly into the room, wishing I'd paid more attention to where the furniture was positioned before I'd locked myself away. I immediately stub my toe on god only knows what and hiss with pain.

"You okay?" There's an amused lilt to his voice, which is kind of irritating. What kind of a guy gets off on a girl breaking her toes?

"Well...I can't see a thing," I mutter.

"That's the point, I'm afraid. Come here."

If I knew where *here* was, I'd probably be a little less turned around. I try again, and this time I manage to stumble to the bed without colliding with anything else. The mattress dips as I climb onto it, wondering where the hell *he* is. I'm not half as scared as I should be. In fact, I feel almost a little giddy.

"Sit in the middle of the bed with your hands behind your back," he whispers. I wonder if he's going to tie me up. That should bother me. Would bother me any other time.

"Do you need a name?" I ask him; Eli said I should ask.

A low rumble, deep and throaty, breaks the silence of the room and I realize he's laughing. "Are you offering to tell me your *real* name?"

"Eli said that's against the rules."

"Then no." The mattress dips again. He's moving, coming closer. His hot breath grazes across the skin of my neck when he speaks. "I don't need to call you Melody or Candy or some other fake-ass name. We'll just be strangers for a while. That square with you?"

"Yeah, I—I guess."

In the darkness my skin is alive. So are my other senses. My nose keeps on whispering to me, hints of mint and the ocean. Whoever he is, this guy smells incredible. Not a whiff of cigarettes on him at all, which means that voice...that voice is one hundred percent natural. I'm curious about him in the most detached way.

"You done this before? Like this?" he asks me.

"Never." My breath actually catches in my throat. I'm so spaced out that I can barely think straight, but the lack of lighting in the room is making my heart race. Maybe it's because this guy could be a serial killer. He could still be a serial killer with the lights *on*, but at least I'd have the chance to see it in his eyes and run for my life.

Mystery Guy exhales, sending another warm breath across my chest. My nipples harden even though I'm not cold. I've never experienced that before. Never. Probably because I've never been this close to a guy before. "Place your hands in your lap," he tells me.

I do it. I jump a little when I feel his hand reach out and touch my leg. "Scared?"

"No."

He laughs, and it's a cruel and wicked thing. His hands gently trail up my leg until he finds my hand, where his fingers curl around my wrist. "You're braver than most girls."

"You do this with a lot of girls?"

"Yes."

Well at least he's honest. He lifts up my hand and brings it toward himself, and stubble prickles against the sensitive skin on the inside of my wrist.

"You smell like flowers. What perfume do you wear?"

"Afresia," I tell him.

"It's clean. Not too heavy. I like it."

So glad you approve. I feel like giggling. His nose brushes against my wrist and then the soft touch of his lips follows soon after. The kiss is barely even there, soft and gentle, but I can read a lot from it. His lips are full and he's gentle with his mouth. That's unexpected. I fidget on the bed, wondering where this is going. Where his mouth will be going next.

"Have you ever thought about what it would be like to be blind?" he rumbles.

"Why? Are you blind?"

"No. Answer the question."

"I suppose so. Sometimes."

He guides my hand upwards and takes it in both of his, un-curling my fingers so that my palm is open. He does it slowly, running calloused fingers down the length of my own, and I can't help but shiver. It's a fairly simple thing, but the way he does it feels intimate and considered, not just grabbing and touching for the hell of it. I hold my breath as he guides my hand again, until my fingertips meet his hair, and then down to his face.

"Tell me what you think I look like," he says, his voice a resonating growl. He lets go of my hand, and I have to lean forward to reach him properly. I shimmy closer, tucking my legs under my butt so I can balance properly, and then I raise my other hand to his face, too.

His hair is short, a little stiff from the styling product he's got in there; his facial features are strong, pronounced. Jaw's

a little square, nose mostly straight apart from a slightly flattened part near the ridge of his brow. His eyelashes are surprisingly long, and his lips...I was right. His lips are full and way softer than any guy's lips have a right to be. Especially a guy with a voice like his. From the tingling pads of my fingers, I can sense this guy has the face of an angel. A barbaric one—maybe like one of those guys who did a lot of smiting back in Babylon.

"What do you think?" he asks.

"I think you're probably very attractive," I admit.

He grunts. "And what about the rest of me?"

He applies a little pressure to my forearms so that they travel down to his chest, where my fingers meet with smooth skin and hard-packed, rippling muscle. His pecs twitch as my hands brush lightly over them, and then downward. I come across three horizontal ridges in his skin that shouldn't be there, to the right of his abs spaced a couple of inches apart, and my fingers draw circles over them, trying to tease their story from them, trying to figure out where they came from. There's an untold history of violence here, written in the planes of his formidable body. He shakes a little as I explore him, probing with a feather-light touch until I've traced my way across his wash-board stomach and up over his obliques. He sucks in a sharp breath and tenses when I do that, and I smile a little. I actually *smile*. This guy's ticklish. He doesn't laugh or tell me not to touch him there, but his body tightens further still when I go over the area one more time to test the theory.

I move up to his shoulders, which are powerful and strong, and I lace my arms around the back of his neck, feeling over his shoulder blades. He's huge, but I'm not really afraid of him. Of course I should be, yes, but I'm not. The valium has flattened out my fear, and besides, the way I'd imagined this, the guy was going to come in here and want to lay his hands on me; he'd poke and prod and examine every inch of me, and he'd most definitely want to see what he was paying for. So far, this guy has touched me sparingly and that was on the hand.

"Well?" he asks.

"Where did the scars come from?"

"I was stabbed." He doesn't ponder on whether he's going to answer me; he just comes right out and says it.

"Did you nearly die?"

"Yes."

"Did it hurt?"

"Yes."

I let my hands fall from his shoulders and find the scars again, one, two, three of them. They feel jagged and terrible under my fingers. "What happened to the person who did this to you?" I almost don't want to ask. Mystery Man's been unnervingly candid since we began this bizarre interaction five minutes ago, and I'm afraid his answer will finally put the fear of God into me.

"He got what was coming to him," he says softly. The bed sheets rustle when he moves, his stomach muscles contracting under my hands; when he touches my hair, tangling his fingers into it, I'm still trying to decide whether he means he killed whoever did that to him.

"I'm very particular about what I want. You need to do what I ask you without question and this will go nicely for both of us, okay?" he breathes.

A shot of adrenaline finally lights up my nerve endings—the appropriate reaction to my situation. What the hell have I gotten myself into here? Valium or no Valium, I know that sounded like a threat. I'm in way over my head, but there's little I can do about it. Besides, Alexis. *Always* Alexis. "I can do that," I whisper.

"Good. Lie on your back."

I let go of him and suddenly I feel like I'm afloat in the middle of an ocean, drowning, with no way of saving myself. The sensible, smart part of my brain that still clings onto a vague sense of self-preservation is screaming that I should probably get the hell out of here, and for the first time the wrath of Eli almost isn't enough to keep me pinned to the bed. But the thought of finding Alexis is. My muscles are jumping, ready to explode into action, when the guy gently takes hold of my right ankle.

"Did you touch yourself today?"

What the?! "Do...do you mean—"

"Have you made yourself come today? Have you played with your pussy?"

My cheeks heat up to an uncomfortable temperature. No one has ever asked me that before. "No. No, I—I haven't," I stammer.

"Good. Then you'll taste so much sweeter." Instead of hook-ing his fingers under the waistband of my panties and pulling them down, he draws them to one side. My legs lock up when I feel his hot breath skimming over my exposed flesh. I'm not sure what I'm supposed to be doing with my hands. This is untrodden ground for me in a very big way. When a guy gives you head, it's usually because he's done something very, very bad and needs to make up for it, or at least that's what Pippa, my only friend in the world, says. I've never had a boyfriend to treat me badly in the first place, so I've never experi-enced it myself.

"Do you want me to lick you?" His voice is even deeper now, laden with the promise of sex.

"I want whatever you want," I gasp. That's what he's paying for, after all. That's what's going to help me get Lex back. He grips me hard around the top of my leg, squeezing until I cry out.

"That's not the game we're playing, here. Own me, or I'll own you. And trust me...you don't want that."

Shit. "Y—yes, I want you to lick me."

He makes a satisfied grunt and immediately moves, pushing his way between my legs. When his tongue darts out and laps at me, my leg muscles tense up. It feels hot and...and *good*. What the holy hell? I shouldn't be reacting like this. Embarrassment prickles at my cheeks. What sort of person am I, enjoying a complete stranger giving me head? And under these circumstances? I can't help it, though. My whole body feels like it's being caressed.

His tongue moves expertly, applying a subtle pressure to my clit, stroking up and down in a rhythmic pattern that sends wave after wave of heat crashing through me. I'm just letting go, letting the tension in my arms and legs relax, when he stops lapping and sucks.

"*Fuck!*"

He doesn't stop. He growls when I push back against him, rocking into his mouth shamelessly. I've never felt anything like this before. It feels…incredible. I'm panting and moaning like an animal when he pulls away, running his hands from the very tops of my knees, down the insides of my thighs to my panties. He rips them off in one swift motion.

"How badly do you want me to fuck you?"

I'm not here because I *want* to fuck him, but it is my job to make him *think* I do; yet the lines between acting and the truth are so blurred when I murmur, "Really bad. I want you really bad."

"Spread your legs," he commands. I spread them, wonder-ing what's coming next. The room is like a black void, so dark I can't even make out the shadow of him as he moves quickly around the bed. I hear a zip being undone and then the rattle of metal, like a buckle being undone. Sucking my bottom lip into my mouth, I wait for him to do whatever he's about to do, worryingly piqued with curiosity. He restrains my left leg first, strapping something wide and tight around it and then affix-ing it to the bed. My right leg is next, and then he carefully does the same to my wrists. I'm starfished on the bed and completely vulnerable. His restraints aren't the kind for show; they're the kind made to stop people from getting away, and I'm sure as hell not going anywhere. Six months ago, I might have said a prayer. Now I just whimper, half out of fear and half out of anticipation.

He climbs up onto the bed, kneeling at my side, his breath still playing across me. I tense when I feel something cold and hard press against the skin of my stomach. "Are you still a brave girl?"

"Yes," I exhale.

He doesn't reply or tell me what he's going to do. The cool, sharp object he's leaning into my skin travels slowly upwards until it's poised directly under my breasts. I gasp lungful after lungful of air into my lungs, trying to keep still, because I know what it is he's got in his hand: it's a knife. A really fucking sharp knife.

His fingertip lifts the underwire of my bra in the middle, and then in a single, clean sweep, it springs apart, freeing my breasts. He cut through my bra! This is the most exposed, terrified, exhilarated I've ever felt. My Mystery Man straddles me, and the material of his pants, rough, slides up against my sides. He lays the flat, cool edge of his knife against my right nipple, sending a bolt of panic through me.

"Don't move," he whispers. I don't move. I am the stillest still thing ever. He leans down and touches me, his hand finally finding my breast. "You're so fucking perfect," he breathes. "So well behaved." And then his mouth is on my nipple, licking and sucking, hotter than anything I've ever felt before. My back arches up off the bed, and he chuckles. "You want me inside you?"

"Yes."

"You sure? Be careful what you wish for."

I wish for death on a daily basis. I wish for pain and suffering and blood and misery upon the heads of those who took my sister. Wishing for this feels just as dangerous but somehow safer than all that at the same time. He wanted me to own him, and despite the fact that he's tied me up now, I still think that's what he wants. I brace, hoping this is the right thing, and I demand, "Do it. Fuck me now. Don't make me wait any longer."

The knife vanishes from my skin. He shifts off the bed, and I hear him undoing his pants; slipping them off; the swish of him drawing something hard over something soft. Panic sings through me again when I hear another buckle.

"Ready?"

There's no backing out of it now. "I'm ready."

And he does something I hadn't even considered. Not even for a second. He threads a loop of leather over my head—his belt—and cinches it tight. I'm in trouble now.

"Open your mouth."

"I—"

"Do it." The tone of his voice is firm yet gentle at the same time. He brushes a hand down the side of my face, a reassuring gesture —*this is scary right now, but trust me.* Trust him? I'd be fucking mad to trust him. And yet I do what he tells me to. He pushes forward and guides his cock into my mouth. I've never done this before, so I'm basically wondering what the hell I'm supposed to do now. He's rock hard and tastes clean and slightly musky…and he's massive. I can barely fit him inside my mouth. I can tell he only fits half the length of him inside before he hits the back of my throat.

"Shit!" He hisses as I suck, forming a vacuum around him. I think I got that part right. His hips rock back and he slides out of my mouth causing a wet popping noise. "Still think you want me inside you?" He knows just how big he is; he's fucking smug about it. This is going to hurt like nothing else, but I don't want him to realize I'm a virgin. Even Eli doesn't know that part. I'm sure he would have charged this guy a whole lot more if he did, and that thought just turns my stomach.

"Yes," I tell him. "Yes, I want you."

"Good. But let's do this first." He fists a handful of my hair and lifts my head closer to him, and then he pushes back inside my mouth, thrusting in and out while applying a gentle pressure to the back of my head. I writhe on the bed, surpris-ing myself with how much this turns me on. I'm floored when he tugs on the belt strap, though.

Floored.

My eyes, even in the dark, see stars. I can barely breathe with my windpipe cut off and his cock pulsing in and out of my mouth. "Stay with me, okay?" he grunts.

Fear and excitement pool in my stomach. It's the same sort of sensation I used to get when I was a kid waiting to ride a roller-coaster, only amplified a thousand times. And a whole lot scarier. Between my legs, my pussy tightens as he works his hips back and forth, keeping just enough tension on the belt strap so that I can drag the tiniest amount of oxygen into my lungs.

He shivers as his erection turns granite-hard. If he doesn't stop now, I think I know what will happen. But he does stop. Breathing heavily, he withdraws and crouches down beside the bed, easing his fingers beneath the belt and loosening it. His face is so close to mine, I can feel the intense power of his gaze as he stares at me in the dark. I still can't see a thing, but maybe he has better night vision than I do.

"Your mouth is perfect," he whispers. And then he does two things that surprise me. Firstly, in the most reverent of ways, he brushes his hand against my sweat-soaked skin, sweeping my hair out of my face. And then secondly, he places the softest kiss against my forehead.

"For being such a good girl, I'm going to make you come now," he breathes. A tremor of anticipation shimmers across my skin, and he chuckles. "You're being a *very* good girl."

He climbs up onto the bed and positions himself, hooking his arms underneath my hips, hoisting me up to meet him. The position is awkward with my ankles still bound to the bed, but all thoughts of my discomfort are forgotten when he buries his face between my legs and starts sucking on my clit again.

"Ahhh!"

The sensation is too much. I can feel myself climbing, ascending higher and higher as an unfamiliar, unfathomable feeling builds between my legs. It unfurls in gentle pins and needles throughout my body, growing more and more intense ...and then...

I'm screaming. Unintelligible screaming. I'd scream for God but I doubt He would approve of this situation right now, and I have no idea who this guy is so I can't scream for him, either. I just scream for myself and the fireworks going off inside my head, the inferno licking over my skin, burning me out, leaving me hollow and spent. I fall slack, trembling as he continues to sweep his tongue over and over my clit.

"Stop, stop, please," I rasp.

"Mmm, so selfish," he hums into my pussy, making me clench. "Don't forget. It's my turn." He fiddles around for a moment—*condom? Fuck, I hope that's a condom.* And then he drops my hips and thrusts into me in one fluid motion, his hands tight on my pelvis, trapping me.

Oh...my...

The pain is almost crippling. An uncomfortable feeling, a buildup of pressure and then a stinging release, let's me know that it's done. He stops.

"What...?" He inhales deeply. Exhales. "You probably shouldn't have kept that from me," he says softly. He sighs, as though he's disappointed in me, which is the most messed up thing ever. "Are you ready?" he asks.

My voice is a faint whisper when I reply, "Yes."

"Try to relax." He fills me up, stretches me, makes me whole. He starts off slow, gentler than I think he would have done if he hadn't just deflowered me. After a while the pain subsides, gradually transforms until I'm no longer tensing with every thrust, but leaning into it. By the end, he's fucking me like a freight train—unstoppable and raw with need. He comes so hard, he practically roars.

I don't, of course. It's my first time, and the pain just about outweighed the pleasure. My mind is too fogged to understand what's going on as he climbs off me and slides down my body. His lips caress the inside of my thigh, and I shiver as his fingers carefully stroke over my core. The touch isn't designed to excite me—it's more of an apology. He moves around in the dark, undoing my wrists, my ankles.

"You enjoy that?" he rumbles, and the depths of his voice make my legs press together.

"Yeah, I—I did." The most startling thing, the thing that makes me most sick, is that I'm telling the truth. What the hell is wrong with me?

He grunts, unthreading his belt from around my neck. The release of pressure makes me feel like I'm floating two feet off the bed.

I'm immobile as he packs up his things. I can sense him next to me pulling on his clothes. Then, when he's dressed, he stands beside the bed looking down on me. He brushes his fingertips against my cheek again, so soft it's almost not a touch at all.

"Be seeing you." He heads for the door, and the light from the hallway nearly splits my skull apart when he opens it. And there my mystery man pauses, and I catch the one and only glimpse of him I ever get. Wearing a worn leather jacket, his back to me, a black duffel bag in his right hand, he tips his head down to his shoulder. He's doesn't look back at me. He hovers there long enough for me to make out the silhouette of his profile, his dark, mussed hair, the bruised pout to his full lips.

And then he goes.

I never find out his name.

Want to know if Sloane ever meets her mystery man in the light of day? Click here to keep on reading! You can also read the entire story for FREE on KU!

FOLLOW ME ON INSTAGRAM!

The best way to keep up to date with all of my upcoming releases and some other VERY exciting secret projects I'm currently working on is to follow me on Instagram! Instagram is fast becoming my favorite way to communicate with the outside world, and I'd love to hear from you over there. I do answer my direct messages (though it might take me some time) plus I frequently post pics of my mini Dachshund, Cooper, so it's basically a win/win.

You can find me right here!

Alternatively, you can find me via me handle @calliehartauthor within the app.

I look forward to hanging out with you!

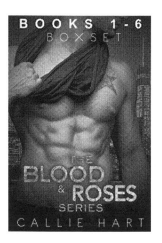

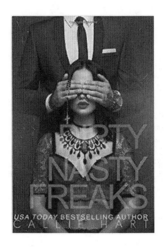

WANT TO DISAPPEAR INTO THE DARK, SEDUCTIVE WORLD
OF AN EX-PRIEST TURNED HITMAN?
Read the Dirty Nasty Freaks Series
FREE on Kindle Unlimited!

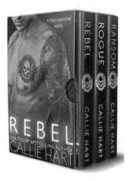

LOVE A DARK AND DANGEROUS MC STORY? NEED TO KNOW
WHAT HAPPENED TO SLOANE'S SISTER?
Read the Dead Man's Ink Boxset
FREE on Kindle Unlimited!

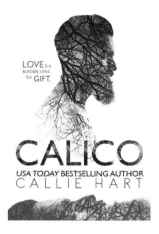

WANT AN EMOTIONAL, DARK, TWISTED STANDALONE?
Read Calico!
FREE on Kindle Unlimited

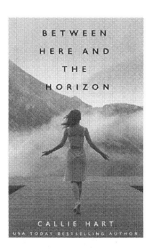

WANT A PLOT THAT WILL TAKE
YOUR BREATH AWAY?
Read Between Here and the Horizon
FREE on Kindle Unlimited!

WANT A NYC TALE OF HEARTBREAK, NEW LOVE, AND A HEALTHY DASH OF VIOLENCE?
Read Rooke
FREE on Kindle Unlimited!

THE DEVIANT DIVAS

If you'd like to discuss my books (or any books, for that matter!), share pictures and quotes of your favorite characters, play games, and enter giveaways, then I would love to have you over in my private group on Facebook!

We're called the Deviant Divas, and we would love to have you come join in the fun!

ABOUT THE AUTHOR

USA Today Bestselling Author, Callie Hart, was born in England, but has lived all over the world. As such, she has a weird accent that generally confuses people. She currently resides in Los Angeles, California, where she can usually be found hiking, practicing yoga, kicking ass at Cards Against Humanity, or watching re-runs of Game of Thrones.

To sign up for her newsletter, click here.

Made in the USA
San Bernardino, CA
28 January 2020